THE HANGMAN'S CRUSADE

By James Barwick

SHADOW OF THE WOLF

THE HANGMAN'S CRUSADE

The Hangman's Crusade

James Barwick

Coward, McCann & Geoghegan   New York

First American Edition 1981

Library of Congress Cataloging in Publication Data

James, Donald, 1931-
   The Hangman's crusade.

  1. World War, 1939-1945—Fiction.
2. Heydrich, Reinhard, 1904-1942—Fiction.
I. Barwick, Tony, 1934- joint author.
II. Title.
PZ4.J283Han 1981 [PR6060.A453]   823'.914
ISBN 0-698-11037-4   80-18536

Printed in the United States of America

Author's Note

The Hangman's Crusade is a work of historical speculation. The object in writing it has been to attempt a plausible answer to one of the greatest mysteries of the twentieth century—the silence of Pius XII in the face of the Nazi persecution of the Jews.

No satisfactory explanation has yet emerged from the volumes of documents published by the Vatican. *The Hangman's Crusade* offers a speculative solution.

At the same time we have examined the lesser but still intriguing mystery of Reinhard Heydrich's death. No official British or American explanation has been offered for this, the single Allied attempt in World War II to assassinate a senior member of the Nazi leadership. The consequences were predictable and are today known to the world—thousands of Czechs were executed, the village of Lidice was razed to the ground, its menfolk shot, its women and children sent to concentration camps. How did Churchill persuade President Beneš, the head of the Czech government-in-exile, to risk the vengeance of the Gestapo? Again we have speculated on the basis of known facts.

The Hangman's Crusade is a work of fiction—but many of the characters, major and minor, existed in fact. The Nazi Bishop Alois Hudal lived out the war to smuggle prominent Nazis, including at least one concentration camp commandant, Höss, to South America. Father Dorsch, the strongly anti-Nazi adviser to Pope Pius, is based on Father Leiber; Hardenberg is based on an amalgam of RSHA intellectuals like Walter Schellenberg, Otto Ohlendorf and Dr. Six. United States correspondents like Franklyn *did* become involved in undercover peace moves, most notably Louis P. Lochner of The Associated Press in Berlin during this time.

Equally, though the events described in *The Hangman's Crusade* are fictional or speculative, perhaps some of the apparently least plausible are based on historical fact. Thus Molotov and Ribbentrop *did* meet in the middle of the slaughter on the Russian front, although the distinguished military historian Captain Basil H. Liddel Hart puts the meeting a year later than ourselves. Again it is from the Catholic biographer with the most ready access to Pope Pius XII, Prince Constantine of Bavaria, that we derive the startling story of the pope's visits, as nuncio, to early Nazi party meetings in Munich.

Revelations like these are the bare bones of our approach. The speculative structures built around them are there to provoke and to entertain, but remain, of course, fiction.

PEACE

Bavaria, June 14, 1931

The young couple trudged toward the cluster of gabled houses in the valley below. Behind them the hills rose steeply to the white snow slopes on the Austrian border. Both tall, blond Northerners, neither of them had been in southern Germany before.

In the village the old women taking the spring sunshine watched the strangers with unaffected curiosity. They made a commanding pair, he in a pale gray suit, she perhaps four or five months pregnant, in a flowered dress and fashionable shoes. Gentry, the old women whispered to each other, but why should gentry be walking from the station on a warm day like this?

Reinhard Heydrich and his wife crossed the cobbled square and entered the hotel-café on the corner. Avoiding the *Stammtisch*, the table reserved for village regulars, they sat in the window seat and ordered beer from the fat, long-skirted serving girl.

"From here," Lina Heydrich said, "it can't cost more than a few marks by taxi."

Her husband stared at her with his strange, flinching, wolf-eyed look. "A few marks! And what do we live on for the rest of the week?"

"For God's sake," she said, "this is an opportunity, the first you've had in a long time. What sort of impression would it make to come tramping on foot up the drive? They'd send you around to the delivery entrance!" She leaned forward, taking a cloth from her basket, and lashed at the dust on his shoes. "A two-kilometer walk from the station and you're already looking like a peasant."

The eyes narrowed angrily.

"It's a joke," she said quickly. "We may be poor as church mice but nobody looks less like a peasant than you. You look what you are, an ex-naval officer."

"Cashiered."

"Cashiered by the old guard," she said. "In the new Germany that only stands in your favor."

"The new Germany?" He looked contemptuously across the bare board floor. "When?"

The girl waddled forward, two glasses of dark beer in her hands. "Would the good lady and the gentleman wish to eat?"

Heydrich shook his head.

"My husband needs a taxi," Lina Heydrich said peremptorily. "Is there one in the village?"

"Taxi?" The girl looked blank.

"An automobile to take him to Waltrudering," Lina announced proudly.

The girl shook her head. "No taxis here, *gnädige Frau*," she said. "They have them in the city, of course."

"In the city! You mean in Munich?"

"Herr Lehman has a cart. I will send to ask if he will carry the gentleman to Waltrudering if you wish."

"Lehman, is he a Jew?"

The girl shrugged.

"Better to walk," Heydrich said nonchalantly, "than to turn up in a Jew's cart."

"No, we'll take the cart," Lina said decisively. "Not even

10

Herr Himmler could expect a pregnant woman to walk on a day like this."

The spring sun shone hot on their shoulders. Twenty kilometers distant the mountaintops sparkled white. Along the narrow lanes cowslips brushed the cartwheels and finches flitted and swooped around them. His legs dangling over the side, Lehman the carter muttered incomprehensibly to the straw-bonneted nag between the shafts. After the best part of an hour they turned suddenly off the lane onto a dust track that ran between lines of trees toward a low-roofed farmhouse.

Heydrich looked at his wife, frowning, then leaned forward and prodded the old carter. "Waltrudering we want; Herr Himmler's residence."

The carter pointed with his whip. "This is as far as I go," he said. "The dogs frighten the horse."

They climbed down and started up the track toward the farm buildings. In front of them the dogs barked and chickens cackled and squawked. To their left lay a long, low coop surrounded by a chicken-wire fence. Among the squawks and clucks of the hens came a man's voice, coaxing and minatory in turns.

Lina Heydrich approached the fence as a small, shirt-sleeved figure in massive leather gauntlets emerged from the coop. Only from the glittering pince-nez did she recognize Heinrich Himmler. She stopped dead as chickens fluttered out into the wired yard. "Herr Himmler, Frau Heydrich, formerly Fräulein Lina van Osten . . . "

Behind the pince-nez Himmler blinked in the sunlight. "Of course . . ."

He came forward among a storm of chicken feathers as perhaps thirty or forty hens fluttered past him into the yard. Opening the wire gate he eased through, shooing the chickens back behind him.

"Herr Heydrich." He shook hands amiably. "Very good of you to make this long journey. This"—he turned toward the chicken coop—"this is my proving ground."

"Proving ground . . . ?" Heydrich frowned down at him.

11

"Twelve weeks," Himmler said, "it takes to bring a chicken from the egg to laying. Just twelve weeks."

"Amazing," Lina said.

"Amazing, Frau Heydrich, because in human terms that process takes an average of 21.4 years. Not biologically, of course, but socially, in terms of sociological realism."

In Heydrich's quick mind it clicked. "Thus," he said, "a whole generation can be studied in twelve short weeks."

Himmler beamed. "In a year," he said, "I can breed out every sign of white or brown feathers; I can change the whole physiognomy *for good or ill*. In a single year!"

"Which is almost a hundred human years, five whole generations!" Heydrich said, his tone admiring.

Lina flashed a quick look of incomprehension at her husband, converting it to a solemn nod of understanding as she saw Himmler react.

"Exactly the point, Herr Heydrich." Himmler peeled off his gauntlets. "In one short year, by means of my chickens, I can confirm a whole century of the malign influence of *Jewish blood!*"

While Lina and Frau Himmler took coffee and Black Forest cherry cake together, the men closeted themselves in Himmler's study.

"The truth," Himmler said, "is simple. My chickens prove it."

Heydrich, sitting opposite him, nodded agreement.

"Jews, Gypsies, homosexuals, saboteurs, Communists, all reproduce, all contaminate the purity of Nordic blood. This problem was first analyzed by the Führer. He showed in brilliant theoretical terms the consequences of a dilution of the blood."

Heydrich nodded silently.

"If our National Socialist revolution is to succeed, it can only be by removing the gypsy chickens from the coop. Let us pray to God that we are in time."

12

"I can see no alternative but to move fast and ruthlessly," Heydrich said.

Himmler rummaged in the drawers of his desk. "I don't smoke myself; I abhor smoking. But you young men, I know, can enjoy a cigar." He offered the box.

Heydrich considered rapidly. "Thank you," he said, taking one, "unless you'd really prefer . . ."

"No, no. You hunters"—his eyes twinkled—"must hunt. Now, let's get down to cases. I need an intelligence organization, one that in the shortest possible time will be able to record every Jew in Germany, every Gypsy, every homosexual, Communist or liberal saboteur. I am a man of perception—you, a man of vision. Prove me right. I give you twenty minutes to sketch for me an organizational scheme for a secret state police network." He stood up. "Pen and paper there." He was walking toward the door. "I'll leave you to smoke your abominable cigar alone." Chuckling he closed the door behind him.

Reinhard Heydrich looked with amazement at the closed door. If the new Germany was to be run by men with the mentality of chicken farmers, he saw no obstacle to his own rise. He took the pen and writing pad and in fifteen minutes had outlined the same organization of naval intelligence that every Kriegsmarine Staff College officer, ex-officer in his case, knew by heart. At the top of the page he wrote Reich Security Head Office—Reichssicherheithauptamt—the first time that dread title had ever appeared. On the last page he signed his name—Reinhard Heydrich.

New York, September 1, 1939

The woman standing next to the rear door of the Yellow Cab turned her head away and pretended to find some point of interest in the long white sweep of the ocean liner's hull, which rose above her from the quayside. Her eye settled on the huge swastika floating lazily from the stern. She forced herself to register each staccato shout of the New York longshoremen. She was anxious that the man paying off the cabdriver should not see her angry tears.

A melancholy exchange of ships' horns far out across the Hudson River caused her a sharp intake of breath. Jim Franklyn, taking change from his five-dollar bill, decided to ignore her misery. There was little else he could do, little else they could go over, that hadn't been gone over fifty times already.

He watched her walk away from the cab and stand looking up at the German liner.

"Lois . . ."

She continued to stare up at the S.S *Bremen*, as if counting each small figure leaning over the rail above their heads.

"Lois, for Christ's sake . . ."

She turned, tall, redheaded, no longer young. Looking past Franklyn she signaled the cabdriver. "I've changed my mind," she said to him. "You can take me uptown."

Franklyn walked across to her. "You're not coming on board?"

"No."

"Customs is still searching the ship. It could be hours yet before she sails."

"What difference will a couple of hours make? You've made up your mind."

"For Christ's sake, Lois, every assignment's different. For this one I need time."

"Alone."

"Yes."

She nodded bitterly. "Are you surprised I wonder just exactly what you have in mind?"

He knew all this should have been done a week ago instead of acting it out now on the quayside.

"You won't take me with you?"

"No, Lois."

She looked at him, her lipstick smudging as her mouth worked in an effort at control. "You know, Jim, you're an uncommonly good-looking guy. A bit dissipated under the eyes maybe. . . ."

"What are you saying, Lois?"

"I'm saying you're an uncommonly good-looking guy. . . ."

"But a hell of a son of a bitch?"

"Son of a bitch?" She shook her head slowly. "No, Jim, what I had in mind was more of a horse's ass."

"Thanks."

"What the hell are you up to?" she flared.

He was silent.

"Are you trying to tell me this is it?"

He forced himself not to answer.

"You could have chosen a nicer way, Jim."

"I'm sorry, Lois."

16

"Don't tell me it's the best thing for both of us," she said harshly.

"I was going to say it couldn't have worked."

"Different words, same tune."

"You've got too much money . . . I drink too much. . . ."

She shook her head. "No, you lousy bastard," she said, "there's just something in this German assignment that you want more than me."

Did she guess?

She signaled the cabdriver, who got out from behind the wheel and opened the back door.

Franklyn made a move toward her, then checked himself. The last he saw of her was the angry twitch of the copper-colored curls blazing in the setting sun as she ducked into the backseat of the cab and the driver slammed the door.

He watched the cab speed away along the quayside then lit a cigarette and crossed to where a group of newspapermen and photographers were waiting at the foot of the *Bremen*'s gangway. Most of them he knew well.

"Anything yet on the new sailing time?" he asked Corrie Knox, the *Daily News* man.

"They're just coming down now."

Unsmiling, the German consul and the senior U.S. Customs official made their way down the gangplank and took up positions behind the standing microphones that the press had set up.

Among the photographers jostling for the right angle and the reporters calling for quiet, Logan, the U.S. Customs man, stepped forward. Taking a sheet of paper from his pocket, he read in a slow, clear drawl:

"Today on the instructions of the president, the U.S. Customs Service examined and inspected the German liner *Bremen*. The object of the inspection was to ensure that no armament or war matériel was on board at the time of sailing from the neutral port of New York. The U.S. Customs Service apologizes to passengers for the inevitable delay."

He folded the paper carefully and stepped away from the microphones. The consul came forward, his expression set, his hands deep in the pockets of his black overcoat. As the flashbulbs popped around him he lifted a hand for silence. That picture was destined for front pages as the consul's Hitler salute.

"What will be the reaction of your government to this search, Mr. Consul?" Corrie Knox called from the back.

"The German Foreign Ministry is at this moment considering the form our inevitable protest will take."

"Are there any plans in existence to convert the *Bremen* into an armed ocean cruiser?" Franklyn couldn't see the questioner in the middle of the group.

"The *Bremen*, as you know, held the blue ribbon for the Atlantic crossing as recently as 1933. She is a fast passenger liner and will remain a fast passenger liner. The outbreak of war this morning between Germany and Poland is irrelevant to the issue. Poland is not a naval power."

"But Great Britain is, Mr. Consul."

"Germany is not at war with Great Britain."

Franklyn turned away. He'd made a mess of the whole thing with Lois, he knew that. But then he'd made a mess of a hell of a lot of things lately. He finished his cigarette and flipped it into the oily water between the quay and the rising white side of the *Bremen*. Maybe a new job and new life in Germany would straighten him out. He walked toward the gangway.

Afterward he found he could not be sure how long he had been aware of the man standing there. He seemed to remember him, tall, balding, dressed in tweeds, leaning on a stick in the lee of the great liner, moments after Lois threw herself into the cab and rode away. And again as the German consul snapped out his answers to press questions. Then as Franklyn found his cabin and struck up a ten-dollar friendship with his steward, he had seen the man again, at the end of the companionway, his stick hooked over his wrist as he lit his pipe, his eyes on Franklyn across the pungently smoking pipe bowl.

When he regained the deck, where eleven hundred passengers waved to friends and relatives as the tugs hauled the liner out into the middle of the Hudson River, Franklyn had other things to think about. The *Bremen* slid past the Statue of Liberty. On the liner's upper deck a twenty-piece dance band played "Anything Goes" under a brightly lit swastika awning. On the boat deck, Jim Franklyn looked back at the broken teeth of New York's skyline and wondered not whether he had done the right thing about Lois, but whether in fact, as so often in his life, he had done the right thing for the wrong reasons.

Greg Sefton, AAP's head of bureau in Berlin, had, after all, made it very plain. Two months ago they had sat together in Searcey's Bar on West Eighty-sixth Street drinking their third Chivases and talking horses, wire service gossip and the chances of FDR running in the 1940 election, when Sefton had sprung his surprise.

"This Munich job," he had said casually; "I've got to find someone pretty quick. I'll break my ass if I go on trying to run the whole of Germany from Berlin."

"I thought that's what you're back over here for."

"Right."

"You going to give it to Collins?"

"Nope."

"I thought he did pretty well in Madrid."

"Sure." Sefton shrugged. "But Nazi Germany's different, Jim. To begin with a guy's best off if he's an unknown as far as the Propaganda Ministry's concerned. A guy like Collins got himself a big anti-Franco reputation in Madrid. Great. But who the hell's ever going to talk to him in Berlin? Nobody."

"You need a guy who knows how to take Goebbels' handouts and keep his mouth shut, is that it?"

"There's a lot of good work to be done over there, Jim. A lot of discreet digging." He shook his heavy jowls. "Needs a reporter, I sometimes think, more than a straight foreign correspondent."

Franklyn felt a warm flush rising that had nothing to do with the whisky.

"You want the job, Jim?" Sefton said.

"You're kidding. I've never done a damn thing outside the United States. You know that."

"That's good. I told you, in Germany a new man doesn't need a reputation. Especially an anti-Nazi reputation."

"You're serious?"

"Serious and sober."

"That's a hell of an offer, Greg."

"You're not a young guy. You've had a fairly uneven time these last few years. You're too fond of the booze. But I think you're the man I want over there. Yes or no?"

"Hell, yes!"

"You've got some German; I checked."

"College. In those days I planned to go foreign."

"Here's your chance." Franklyn would always remember Sefton's sad eyes as he said it.

They'd celebrated with a couple more Scotches in Searcey's, and another round Greg Sefton had set up as what he called a stirrup cup. For a few moments they had talked about the dollar–Reichsmark exchange rate and the plumbing in Munich, but Sefton's answers, Franklyn suddenly realized, were those of a man with something else on his mind. Then finishing his drink, Sefton had swiveled on his stool.

"How're things with Lois?" he had asked casually.

"Okay. She's got too much money. She's always had too much money." Franklyn raised his eyebrows. "Who would have thought I'd ever see that as anything but an asset in a wife?"

Sefton had turned away on his barstool, his face suddenly grim. "A wife? Somehow I never saw you two going that far along the line."

"Jesus, who knows?" Franklyn said. "We've talked about it. Mostly *she*'s talked about it. That's as far as it goes."

Sefton nodded without speaking.

"What is it, Greg? What's on your mind?"

Sefton took a pack of Chesterfields, deliberately slowing the action of selecting a cigarette, putting it in his mouth and lighting it.

"I guess I never saw you as a married man, that's all."

"Lots of the guys in Europe have their wives with them. What's the problem?"

"Lois Goldwyn," Sefton said. "In Nazi Germany a wife whose name is Lois *Goldwyn* is the problem."

"Are you telling me it's either Lois or the assignment?"

"That's your decision, Jim, not mine."

"Jesus Christ."

"It's a tough world over there in Europe." Sefton had eased himself off the barstool and waved casually to Searcey. "Let me know if you still want to take it on."

The last of the sun had disappeared behind New York now and banks of bright lights flickered on along the deck levels and aerial rigging of the *Bremen*. Franklyn was surprised and faintly uneasy to find that the man who had politely pressed his way to the rail beside him was the stranger with the pungent-smelling pipe.

The pipe was knocked out, the cinders watched as they fell glowing toward the black water below. The New York skyline was examined with something approaching approval. The pipe was refilled and lit with difficulty in the wind. Smoke and cinder plumed horizontally from the bowl.

"You know, Franklyn"—the stranger beside him pointed his pipe reflectively—"this could be your last glimpse of a world at peace." He smiled crookedly. "At least for many, many years."

Jim Franklyn recoiled at the use of his name, then guessed the man had got it from the cabin door.

"I don't plan to be in Europe that long," he said brusquely.

"I'm not talking about Europe," the man said easily. "Or not just about Europe. You wouldn't think, watching all these people"—he stabbed his pipe at the passengers lining the ship's rail—"that a world war had broken out today."

Franklyn pushed himself off the rail. "This morning Hitler invaded Poland. So what? Did the British and French do anything when he invaded Czechoslovakia?"

"Did *we*?" His accent was soft New England. He straightened up. "We've got plenty of time to see who's right. Six days before

21

we reach Hamburg. By that time I think we shall be threading our way through the ships of the British navy. As a newspaperman, Mr. Franklyn, it could be your first good war story," he said, drifting away with an enigmatic smile.

A newspaperman! How did he know that?

In the second-class lounge that evening the tension was palpable. Every hour the ship's loudspeaker system made an announcement in German and English on the progress of the battles in Poland. In response, it was said, to yet another border infringement by the Polish army, German Panzer armies, supported by the Luftwaffe, had retaliated with a full-scale invasion. You didn't have to be a newspaperman, Franklyn reflected, to read between the lines. The frequent mention of the word "blitzkrieg" in the German-language version was a tip-off in itself.

Yet the reaction of most of the German passengers was puzzling. They seemed to take no obvious chauvinistic delight in the news of the victories of Guderian's armored columns, nodding soberly when this or that Polish town was mentioned; but they listened with tense concentration for news of the expected reaction of London and Paris. As Poland's allies in the recently concluded treaty, it seemed incredible that Britain and France would not delcare war. And yet over thirty-six hours had already passed and, at least according to the ship's news service, London and Paris remained cravenly silent.

On the second day out, Franklyn saw the tall New Englander again. But this time he passed purposefully along the companionway, his stick briskly stabbing the wooden decking, his strange, secret smile on his lips.

On that second day there were few of the normal shipboard activities. The swimming pool was empty; nobody seemed to want to play tennis or deck quoits. The passengers crowded the bars and lounge and looked fearfully toward the loudspeakers as the news hour approached.

It was during the three o'clock broadcast that the blow fell. The speaker, who till then had been the radio officer, announced that the captain would address the passengers. Franklyn's German was just sufficient to get the drift of the announcement: the ship would be altering course; arrival in Hamburg might be delayed for anything between a day or so and a week. Beginning at dusk the ship would steam with all deck and navigation lights extinguished. Curtains would be pulled in all public rooms. Passengers were required to ensure that no lights were visible from staterooms and cabins. British or French passengers were ordered to report to the purser immediately.

Nobody needed to be told the meaning of the new arrangements. The darkened ship was now clearly about to change course. Lloyd's of London charted every major vessel on the high seas. If it were to be war, Royal Navy warships would be waiting for the *Bremen* in the Western Approaches. By tomorrow, avoiding action would be too late.

"A wise precaution, but nothing to get alarmed about," a voice with a faint German accent said. Franklyn turned. Leaning against the bar was a German of about his own age. "Excuse me for approaching you like this unintroduced, but perhaps we are entering less formal times. Learned from you Americans, perhaps." He clicked his heels and extended his hand. "Hardenberg," he said. "Klaus von Hardenberg."

Franklyn shook his hand. "Jim Franklyn. So this is just a wise precaution? You don't think Britain and France are going to war over Poland?"

"Do you?"

"I guess not."

"I think the war in Poland will be over in a matter of weeks. You will be able to have your holiday in Germany in peace."

"No holiday," Franklyn said. "I'm going to be working in Germany. I'm a newspaperman."

"In Berlin?"

"No, that's the senior assignment. New boys start in Munich."

"Then perhaps we shall see something of each other. You will be registering with my office when you arrive."

23

Franklyn frowned. "Your office? Are you in the newspaper business too?"

"No, Mr. Franklyn," Hardenberg smiled, "I'm a policeman. Reich Security Head Office. Gestapo."

The next morning, September 3, brought brilliant late summer weather over the Atlantic. At breakfast the passengers seemed to Franklyn notably more relaxed. The Polish war was entering its third day. The German army had advanced fifty miles in thirty-six hours; Warsaw, Kraków and Łódź had all been bombed by the Luftwaffe, and still there was no declaration from London and Paris.

And then, just before lunch, the loudspeakers crackled all over the ship. "Ladies and gentlemen"—the radio officer's voice was subdued—"Captain Beckmann will speak to you."

Klaus von Hardenberg crossed the lounge with his aperitif in his hand and sat down next to Franklyn. "May I join you?"

"Sure."

Hardenberg leaned toward Franklyn. "I was in the radio room last night," he whispered. "It appears that the British have completed evacuation of schoolchildren from London and other cities. Are they bluffing?"

"What sort of country evacuates schoolkids for a bluff?"

"We shall know perhaps in a very few seconds' time," Hardenberg said.

Franklyn nodded and both turned their attention to the silent loudspeaker. All across the lounge, passengers were watching the small walnut box with its green, baize-backed grille fretworked in the shape of a swastika. There was a rattling of papers, then the sound of the captain clearing his throat. Then again silence.

Franklyn sipped his whisky and glanced across the lounge. An old woman crossed herself, her husband straightened his back, stretching his neck within his wing collar, his eyes never leaving the loudspeaker grille. A small boy turned toward his young mother and was silenced with a brisk movement of the hand. Standing just inside the doorway the tall New Englander smiled briefly across the tables at Franklyn. The loudspeaker crackled.

"*Damen und Herren.*" The captain's voice was little more than a whisper. "I have just received the following radio signal from Berlin. 'At eleven A.M. this morning, Berlin time, the British government declared a state of war to exist between Great Britain and the German Reich.' That is all."

The stark brevity of the announcement left the passengers stunned. Then the old man in the wing collar rose to his feet and lifted his right arm. "Heil Hitler," he said in a ringing voice. Uncomfortably a few passengers got to their feet. "Heil Hitler," they responded tonelessly.

Hardenberg had remained seated. His face was grim. He turned to Franklyn. "Who would have thought Chamberlain had it in him?" he said quietly. He lifted his glass. "Well, Mr. Franklyn, you couldn't have chosen a better time to come to Germany. Given your profession, that is," he added wryly.

The evening of the first day of war was humidly warm over the Atlantic. Returning from the radio room, where he had been firmly refused permission to send a cable to New York, Franklyn was surprised to notice that the sun was sinking on their port bow. It meant that the *Bremen* had turned north and was planning to run across the top of the Scottish Islands before doubling back to slip between Jutland and the Swedish coast into the safety of the Baltic.

Standing at the rail, watching the sky darken, Jim Franklyn tried to imagine the Europe still two thousand miles away beyond the horizon. The bombs were already falling, the armies mobilizing or already on the march, and at the very moment that he had been assigned to one of the principal belligerents. He thought of what Hardenberg had said—and could hardly believe his luck.

The loudspeaker clicked. The radio officer's voice said softly, "*Achtung, Achtung!* Captain Beckmann will speak to you."

Looking toward A Deck, Franklyn saw the silhouetted figure of the New Englander descending the accommodation ladder.

The heavy odor of pipe smoke drifted along the boat deck. "Good evening, Mr. Franklyn." The man stopped, leaning his back against the rail.

The captain's voice said: *"Damen und Herren . . .* I have decided that during the night we shall hold one, possibly two, full boat drills. This will obviously cause inconvenience, most evidently to our elderly passengers. There will, however, be no exemptions. I will use my powers as captain to place under arrest any passenger, including American and other neutrals, who fails to assemble at his boat station when the alarm is sounded."

The captain paused. "In order to underline the seriousness of our position, I have decided to pass on to you the contents of a radio signal picked up at nine o'clock this evening. It was from the British passenger liner *Athenia* some two hundred miles west of the Hebrides. The signal was repeated many times. It was a distress call. The *Athenia* had been the subject of a U-boat torpedo attack. It was sinking fast. On board were one thousand four hundred passengers." The captain paused. "Between our present position and our home port of Hamburg the oceans are patrolled not only by U-boats of the German Kriegsmarine but by British submarines as well. For this reason, whatever the inconvenience involved, nobody will be excused from boat drill. That is all."

"Well, Mr. Franklyn," the New England voice said in the gathering darkness, "your war has really begun."

"It's not my war," Franklyn said. "I'm just reporting it."

The man moved forward from the shadow so that the faint light from the night sky outlined his angular features. "Munich'll be an interesting place to do it from," he said.

"You never told me your name," Franklyn said slowly, "or why you make a point of dropping these little items of information about me."

"Stanhope," the man said. "Dr. Robert Stanhope. I administer a small family trust, the Stanhope Foundation. Nothing like the Ford or Rockefeller, of course. Small beer by comparison.

But we offer scholarships and fund certain offbeat educational projects."

That's only half the answer to my question, Dr. Stanhope."

"Yes."

"And the other half?"

"Yes, there is another half." Stanhope drew on his pipe and let the smoke flow thickly from the corner of his mouth. "I wonder if you are aware, Mr. Franklyn, that the United States is the only major world power without an intelligence service of its own."

"No, I wasn't."

"Can you imagine what that means?"

"It means Congress is unwilling to underwrite, sight unseen, the activities of a bunch of spies. I can't say I disagree."

"That's because you're still in blinkers, Mr. Franklyn. A few months in Nazi Germany will soon change all that."

"You're not answering my question, Stanhope. How come you seem to know so much about me?"

"Greg Sefton did give me the details."

"You know Greg?"

"He works for me."

"Dr. Stanhope, I think I'm out of my depth. The Greg Sefton I know is German head of bureau for AAP wire services, New York."

"Correct. But he also works for me."

"For the Stanhope Foundation?"

"For the United States government, Mr. Franklyn."

"Greg's on the government payroll?" Franklyn said incredulously.

"Greg Sefton is an officer in the United States Army."

Franklyn shook his head at the image of his fat, balding, sad-eyed friend in uniform. "Greg Sefton is the most unmilitary man I've ever met, Doctor. Now I'm not sure what your pitch is, but why don't you just come right out and say your piece?"

"No pitch," Stanhope said. "Three months ago the president decided to construct a skeleton intelligence organization under

27

a Colonel William Donovan. Greg Sefton was one of the first volunteers."

"If it's true, why the hell didn't he tell me?"

"You can answer that for yourself, Franklyn."

"Okay. So why are *you* telling me?"

"I am empowered to offer you a similar presidential commission."

"In the army? You're crazy."

Stanhope took a folded paper from his pocket. "No, Mr. Franklyn, not crazy. Nor am I, if the thought has crossed your mind, some sort of con man who works the transatlantic liners."

He handed Franklyn the paper. "Read this in your cabin. Return it to my stateroom as soon as you are satisfied it's genuine. The number is 7B. Make absolutely certain you're not seen, especially by your friend Hardenberg."

Stanhope turned away abruptly, and Franklyn listened to his footsteps receding along the boat deck. Then he pushed the document into his inside pocket and hurried to his own cabin on the deck below.

Locking the door behind him, Franklyn made sure the porthole was curtained and switched on the light. Then he took the document from his pocket and opened it. He didn't know quite what he had expected, but the thick gray paper looked forbiddingly authentic. A presidential crest was embossed on each page, at the foot of which was printed: "From the Office of the Secretary of the Army."

The three pages were set out with the oath, his rank and regimental assignment to something called the Office of Strategic Services and his serial number. Some of the pages were countersigned by an officer named Colonel William Donovan.

Franklyn folded the document and pushed it back in his pocket. What completely stunned him was the realization that he believed the document was genuine. Up to the moment he had opened it he had been convinced that it would prove an obvious counterfeit, for what purpose he had no idea, but a readily recognizable counterfeit all the same.

This document had not merely the physical appearance of the genuine article, but the content. His New York address, his correct date of birth, his father's name and address as next of kin. None of this information was difficult to discover. But why do it?

Franklyn switched off the light and unlocked the cabin door. He obeyed Stanhope's instructions and made certain nobody saw him as he reached stateroom 7B. He knocked and Stanhope opened the door almost immediately. Stepping across the sill Franklyn let Stanhope close the door behind him.

"You read it?"

"Yes."

Stanhope stretched out his hand for it, waiting for Franklyn to take it from his pocket and pass it to him.

"I think," he said, putting the document on the desk, "that this calls for a drink."

"I think it calls for an explanation," Franklyn said evenly.

"What the United States needs above all, Franklyn," Stanhope said slowly, "is good, reliable information. We can no longer depend on the British and French intelligence services because the one interest of their governments will be to bring us into the war."

"So?"

"We must have our own men."

"In Germany?"

"Among other places, yes."

"Count me out, Dr. Stanhope. I'm a reporter, not a goddamn spy."

"You mean of course that you're a foreign correspondent, not a goddamn spy."

"That's right."

"And how do you think you came to get the job?"

"Through *you*?"

"I ordered Greg Sefton to select someone suitable, yes."

Franklyn looked at him slowly. "I'm still not sure I believe you one hundred percent, Stanhope. But let's play the game. Suitable, you said."

"Those were my orders to Greg, yes."

"And if I prove not to be suitable?"

Stanhope poured two glasses of Scotch and handed one to Franklyn.

"We would not be asking you to stick your neck out merely to keep your eyes open. You were chosen for this assignment because in the opinion of Greg Sefton you were the man I needed. Was he wrong?"

"I was under the impression I was chosen for the assignment because I was the man Greg Sefton needed."

"The two are not incompatible. I want your answer Franklyn and I'm afraid I want it now."

He knew that he was being manipulated. He was even dimly aware that he was being led deeper into the snare, first by being persuaded to break with Lois Goldwyn and now to cooperate with Stanhope. He could refuse now and go back to reporting ghetto slayings or City Hall corruption. But he had to accept that Greg Sefton had made no mistake, whatever mix of frustration and dormant ambition the head of bureau had seen in him.

"It seems to me," he said to Stanhope, "that I don't really have a choice."

Stanhope smiled. "Sefton will be pleased. He was sure of you all along."

"Sure about this too?"

Franklyn picked up the gray document from the desk.

"No," Stanhope said, "that was my idea. A mistake."

"Yes. Because about this I do have a choice."

Stanhope watched while Franklyn ripped the thick gray paper in half.

"If there are any duplicates in Washington," Franklyn said, "I'd be grateful if you make sure they go the same way." He pulled aside the curtain and opened the porthole, hurling the papers into the blackness beyond. "I'd hate to get paid for a captain's job I wasn't really doing."

Jim Franklyn left stateroom 7B and climbed to the boat deck. The fine evening had turned to an impenetrably black night. Only the faintest line marked the horizon. Leaning on the rail Franklyn seemed to hear a change in the low throb of the liner's engines. Then seconds later they cut completely and the great ship wallowed silently in the black swell.

Minutes passed as he stood tensely at the rail, scanning the waters for a periscope breaking the surface or the rippling silver wake of a torpedo. Then suddenly he understood. Far out on the horizon the line dividing sea and sky was beginning to lighten and, what seemed like no more than moments later, a ship sparkling with lights from four layered passenger decks appeared on a course across the *Bremen*'s bow.

Across the miles of ocean Franklyn fancied he could hear the faintest strain of dance music as the brilliant neutral steamed on and the silent *Bremen* slunk back in the dark seas waiting for her to pass.

To Jim Franklyn his presence on the wrong ship seemed to him to be a metaphor for his new life.

WAR

Chapter One

Venice, November 1941

The fall of moonlight divided the great square in two, on one side reaching deep into the pillared arcade to gleam on footworn marble flagstones, on the dark side leaving the line of a colonnade in dense shadow. The bells of midnight struck in the campanile and duller chimes carried across the rooftops of the city, sluggishly in the damp heavy air.

The two figures skirted the silent facade of St. Mark's and stopped in the archway beside the Trattoria Falciani.

The tall man in the long dark topcoat held out his hand to the priest with him. "Thank you for coming this far, Father," he said as they shook hands. He spoke Italian with a marked German accent.

"I would willingly accompany you to the hotel, Colonel. The carabinieri would never stop a priest to ask his business."

The tall German smiled. "It's not the Italian police I worry about, Father. My passport is in order, my military papers are duly stamped. To the Italian police I'm a simple tourist."

"You mean the Gestapo operates in Italy?" The priest looked perplexed. "In a fellow Axis country?"

The German shrugged. "The Gestapo is not concerned with diplomatic niceties." He paused. "A report of our discussion will reach the Holy Father?"

"I can guarantee it will reach the Vatican," the priest said carefully.

"That's not quite the same thing."

"No." The priest shook his head. "You must understand, Colonel, that the Church is deeply divided. I regret to tell you that some churchmen, some bishops even, see the pursuit of peace as less important than the destruction of Soviet Russia. And now that Adolf Hitler has attacked in the east . . ." The priest lifted his hands, turning the palms upward. "In the Church what was called 'the white war' has now become 'the red war.' This is a cause for great satisfaction to some."

"And the pope himself?"

"The Holy Father has vast responsibilities. If your proposals reach him, and I believe they will, he will decide."

"The question is when. I can only stay in Venice a limited time waiting for the Holy Father's call to Rome."

"When he hears that you have photographic and documentary evidence of this appalling thing, then I believe the Holy Father will act quickly."

"You'll describe in detail what I have shown you?"

"In every detail, so there can be no doubt left."

"I am told the pope has a deep feeling for Germany," the German said.

The priest nodded. "As Eugenio Pacelli before his election to the Holy See, he was nuncio in Munich and Berlin for many years. And, of course, Germany remains the pivotal Catholic country of Europe. Many of us in the Church pray nightly for the downfall of Adolf Hitler."

"And many others . . . pray differently?"

"No, not many others. Some."

The German inclined his head.

"Good night, Father."

"God be with you."

Colonel Manfred Erikson turned into the shadowed archway. His hotel, on a narrow canal behind the Teatro Fenice, was less than five minutes walk from St. Mark's. He lit a cigar as he threaded his way through alleys lit only by small, low-powered blackout lamps. It was a chilly, damp night. He buttoned his dark overcoat around him. Puffing the cigar, striding through moonlit Venice across stone bridges, between crumbling palaces and warehouses of equal magnificence, he had no sense of being a traitor. A German officer who had long ago decided that the ideas of Adolf Hitler and the values of civilized Europe were aeons apart, the colonel was not troubled, like some of his fellow conspirators, with the memory of the *Fahneneid*, the oath of allegiance to the Führer. In Erikson's mind the position was clear: for what he had already done, Adolf Hitler deserved a public trial and the gallows. What he might yet do more than justified an assassin's bullet or a bomb in his Mercedes limousine.

Erikson had reached the church of San Moise and, turning back toward the canal, came to the landing place in front of the small hotel.

In the moonlight a thin mist rose like steam over the waters of the canal. The hotel door was closed and no chink of light showed behind the warped shutters. He unbuttoned his coat and took his key from his trouser pocket. Letting himself into the dark hallway, he closed the door behind him.

The sense of another human presence was overwhelming. Of perhaps more than one. The hair stood on the back of his neck.

"The light, Franz," a voice said in German, and a pair of dim, brocaded wall lights glowed as a switch clicked.

Three men stood in the small hallway, another, the speaker, on the stairs.

"You're sure he was alone?" the man on the stairs said. They seemed almost to ignore Erikson's presence in the middle of the flagstoned hall.

"He crossed the bridge alone." A short figure in a creased,

37

long, black leather coat came out of the shadow. He gestured to a window hooked open, the outside shutter an inch ajar. "I could see him all the way."

The first moments of terror had left Erikson. Still the four SD men ignored him.

"We'll wait two or three minutes—just in case there were two of them."

Phrases rolled through Erikson's head: "The optimum escape opportunity"—the words were from the Wehrmacht manual, *Escape Obligations of German Officers*—"is in the first minutes, even seconds, after capture."

Hurling himself across the room, Erikson dived through the window opening, his shoulder and the side of his head bursting open the unlocked shutter. His legs scraped the stone sill before his body tumbled once, the topcoat flapping like the wings of a great raven, and then hit the still surface of the canal below, pluming fountains of water.

He was a powerful swimmer. Using the weight of the overcoat to keep his body well below the surface, he kicked out, propelling himself across the muddy bottom of the canal. Before him he could make out the submerged base of a line of stone pillars on the far side of the canal, shimmering below the green, moonlit water. He had barely passed between them when he was forced up gasping for air.

His head broke the surface and almost immediately touched the underside of a stone platform perhaps six inches above the water level. With his mouth and nostrils barely clear, he gulped deep drafts of dank, fetid air. He was, he realized, below a stone loading platform of a sort not uncommon along the Venetian quaysides. Looking back toward the canal, four supporting arches rose from the water hardly a foot above the surface. From the hotel he could hear voices shouting in German.

Using both hands against the slime-covered stone above his head, he turned his body. Squinting through the darkness he could make out the shape of a rusting iron grille behind him. He reached out for it and drew himself and the dragging weight of the overcoat across to the wall in which the grille was set. But the centuries-old ironwork was still firmly set in the stone. At both ends of the platform the water slapped against stone arches. If they knew he was there below the quay, there could be no escape.

Unable to see higher than the very surface of the canal, the sounds of voices and footsteps swallowed intermittently by the slap of water rising to the level of his face, Erikson clung grimly to the iron grille.

It seemed to him that almost an hour had passed. But he was sufficiently experienced as a soldier to know that that probably meant no more than twenty minutes. Nevertheless, he had heard nothing in that time. He had even begun to nurture the faintest hope that the SD men had been misled, thinking he had either drowned by the weight of his overcoat or successfully escaped along the canal. He listened intently. Then breasting the water in one silent stroke, he reached the nearest of the stone pillars and peered out from under the arch. On the bridge not twenty yards away, a man stood in the moonlight. In the open window of the Hotel San Moise, another figure scanned the length of the canal.

Then somewhere along the line of overhanging tenements where the canal curved away into the darkness, a strange, throbbing echo boomed off the surface of the water and the balustrade of the stone bridge was silhouetted by a powerful light.

His hands, slipping on the submerged moss and canal weed that covered the pillar, found an iron tie-ring. Pushing against it, he moved his body silently through the water until he floated vertically in the deep shadow of the overhanging stone.

From his angle he watched the police launch approach the bridge, its searchlight in the prow slowly sweeping the crumbling quaysides. Then the engine cut. The launch glided forward under the bridge, sinister in its silence and in the bright eye of the cyclops searching the water.

Opposite the Hotel San Moise it stopped, riding on the still water. Ten feet away a German voice on the launch said, "When I was a boy in Bremerhaven we used to hunt rats like this."

Two peak-capped men in gray uniforms, a flaming grenade as their cap badge, fitted a metal derrick on the side of the launch, the arm curving out over the water. A long chain was attached to its pulley with great, blunt, iron hooks shaped to catch the body of a drowned man.

"Five people drown in Venice every week," the Italian said in halting German. "If your man is down there we will find him."

"This is where he went under," the German voice said. "If he's not there, he's still under that quayside. I tell you it's just like a rat hunt in Bremerhaven."

The bitter wind had come at the end of November chasing snowflakes across the Englischer Garten and reminding Munichers of the approach of their third Christmas at war. To Jim Franklyn, turning onto the long empty avenue of the Leopoldstrasse, the difference between last winter and this was marked. The flood of French luxury goods, which had reached the shops via blackmarket deals by Wehrmacht soldiers on leave from Paris, had completely dried up. Only the highly privileged now knew the taste of French champagne, or the sheen of silk stockings on their girlfriends' legs. Gasoline, never plentiful, was no longer available for the ordinary citizen, and the few taxis now ran with clumsy woodburning contraptions, or a methane gas balloon on the roof rack. Soldiers were as ubiquitous as war rumors, and, although most Munichers knew which of the janitors on their streets doubled as low-paid Gestapo blockwarts, they continued to pass on scraps of information about increasing aid to Britain from neutral America or grisly tales of terror bombing in the north.

As yet Munich had suffered little from the RAF, but relatives and evacuated women and children from Hamburg or Essen, which had already experienced its first thousand-bomber raid, vividly described the nights when the terror fliers arrived and whole blocks of the city collapsed in the thunder of explosions and pluming, fire-reddened dust.

On the Russian front after a summer and autumn of fanfared victories on the radio, most Munichers were well aware that the great advance had been halted before Moscow, and the Goebbels campaign for fur coats and woolens for the men at the front evoked images of a desperate, ragtag army fighting for survival rather than the sleek, all-conquering Panzer divisions of a few months before.

Then, perhaps in some ways most menacing because it was a complete unknown, was the possibility of the United States entering the war. Even the radio said that Roosevelt and Churchill were so friendly as to be partners in crime. And yet it was true that this would be the third Christmas of the war and still America was neutral. . . .

Jim Franklyn turned up the collar of his topcoat as the wind whistled down the darkened Leopoldstrasse. At the great victory monument, the Siegs Tor, he hesitated. There were two foreign press clubs in Munich, as indeed there were in Berlin: one was run by Dr. Goebbels' Propaganda Ministry and the other by Herr von Ribbentrop's Foreign Service, both departments of state having equal and overlapping responsibility for the international press. For the Swiss, American and Swedish journalists themselves, the rivalry simply meant a competition to provide better booze, better steaks and better-looking girls.

The closer of the two clubs to Franklyn's Giselastrasse apartment was Ribbentrop's Deutscher Presseklub, opposite the university in Schwabing. In the last two years the American journalists had more or less taken it over, and bar staff, girls, everybody, spoke English the moment they passed through its rather grand-portaled entrance. In this birthplace of the Nazi movement, the club was a small enclave of American skepticism and anti-Nazi jokes. Yet in just this homely atmosphere Jim Franklyn no longer felt entirely at home.

That first year of the war had been so good, thundering through France with the press corps attached to the German army, in Paris in the first month of the occupation, dispensing women and food and wine, filing stories on the new, up-and-coming Panzer general, the young Erwin Rommel of the 27th Panzer Division. And still Dr. Stanhope had not called in his debt.

That happened, Franklyn saw easily now in retrospect, when he returned to Munich in the New Year after spending Christmas of 1940 in occupied Paris. He had written a piece for Greg Sefton in Berlin on the hardening of Parisian attitudes and the arrival in the French capital of Heydrich's SD, the special security police. To his surprise Sefton had exercised his undoubted right to spike the piece, setting it aside for some future use. The following week a second article he had written, on SD orders that all French Jews should wear, on pain of death, the yellow star sewn to their coats, had received the same treatment. But before he had time to protest, Franklyn had stumbled across the real pointer, an article in the New York isolationist journal, the *German American Review*, using his name, proposing a U.S.–German exchange of military advisers. He had phoned Greg Sefton immediately and had been told peremptorily to catch the first train up to Berlin. There he had found Dr. Stanhope waiting for him.

It had been a tough interview. When Franklyn launched into his protests, the mild Dr. Stanhope had dropped the mask. Sitting behind Greg Sefton's desk while the head of bureau stood diffidently by the window, Stanhope had taken a folded document from his briefcase.

"Two days ago, as you are aware," Stanhope said, "President Roosevelt introduced the Selective Service Act, calling a limited number of men, mostly specialists, for military training." He paused. "Last time we met, you remember, I offered and you refused a commission in the U.S. Army."

"I remember."

Stanhope pushed the papers across the desk. "You no longer have the constitutional right of refusal. These are your induction papers into the American army. Study them and return them to me before you leave this building. You will see that you have been granted the substantive rank of captain."

Perhaps even at that late hour he could have refused. But

Sefton and Stanhope had both made it more than clear what refusal would have entailed. He would remain in the army as an enlisted man and could expect long months in some boot camp in Kentucky. On the other hand he could return to Munich, where the neutral press corps was treated like visiting lordlings, and continue his assignment as a bureau correspondent.

Standing in the snow flurries that swept up the Leopold-strasse, below the great monument commemorating the last-century German victories, Jim Franklyn was bitterly aware that he had made the wrong decision. Too gregarious, too sybaritic, to give up the life of a correspondent in Munich, he had nevertheless lost all he had hoped to retain within a matter of months. Through the summer of 1941, as a member now of Wild Bill Donovan's new Office of Strategic Services, he had extended his contacts with those German officials he had got to know through his work. And inevitably he was believed by his fellow Americans in Munich to have just too close a connection with the Propaganda Ministry. His apparent friendship with Klaus von Hardenberg at the Marienplatz Gestapo office was looked on with open disapproval. It was true that there was perhaps a touch of envy involved. Franklyn often got big news a vital few hours before the other correspondents, but the price he paid was the slant he wrote into many of his stories—sometimes so goddamn pro-Nazi that the other correspondents wondered why his head of bureau, Greg Sefton, kept him on.

Alone in the great dark avenue, Jim Franklyn decided against the American familiarity of the Ribbentrop club. The Goebbels establishment was a large, converted cellar in the old red-light district, on the far side of the Marienplatz; there German was the language of the Swiss and Swedish journalists; there, there were always enough girls to go around and the Scotch was twenty pfennigs a shot.

Continuing to the end of the Leopoldstrasse, Franklyn crossed the dark empty space of the Marienplatz, glancing up instinctively at the windows of the Gestapo offices in the Gothic Rathaus. Faint chinks of light showed through the blackout curtains at five or six windows. They claimed the Gestapo never slept. From what he had seen of Klaus von Hardenberg's life-style, lashed by the mania for efficiency of his chief, Reinhard Heydrich, in Berlin, Franklyn was prepared to believe it was probably true.

Descending the stone steps of the Goebbels club, Franklyn guessed from the noise level that tonight it was not particularly full. It was almost eight o'clock, and by now on a normal Sunday night the dancing would have started; Rudi Gerstheimer, the big *Züricher Zeitung* correspondent, would be lurching around, lining up a girl for the night, and the Swedes would be yelling from the phone tables for enough quiet to get their copy taken down in Stockholm.

The cellar was flagstoned and wooden-beamed, the bar, in chromium and pale wood, something out of a transatlantic liner, and portrait-sized pictures of Adolf Hitler and Dr. Goebbels dominated one wall. Old Joe Conway was buying a girl a drink in one of the alcoves. He waved amiably enough to Franklyn as he came in, but two years ago they had been close friends despite the difference in their ages. Today a not unfriendly wave and a few words exchanged were all that remained of their friendship. Among the girls at the bar, Franklyn spotted Helge Rademacher in her blue German Women's Guild uniform. He took the empty seat beside her.

"Time you had a little more in that." He'd met her briefly two or three times before; girls weren't allowed to buy their own drinks at Dr. Goebbels'.

"Whisky," the small, neat blonde said.

"And again," Franklyn told the barman.

He turned to the girl. "You know the radio gave a preliminary air alert for Bavaria half an hour ago."

"It's nothing."

"Don't you be too sure," he said, for the sake of something to say while his drink was poured. "One of these nights they'll forget to dogleg for the Ruhr and come straight on down to good old Munich."

The whiskeys were put in front of them. "You seem to like the idea," the girl said.

Franklyn shook his head. "Not me," he said, "I don't like hit-and-miss bombing of women and kids whether it's done by the Royal Air Force or the Luftwaffe."

"I work in Luftwaffe Bomber Control," she said. "We raid military targets only. Airfields, docks, factories."

"You think the RAF believes any different?"

"I don't like this talk." She took her drink and slid off the barstool. Franklyn followed her, glass in hand, to the alcove seat by the door.

"No offense," he said.

She shrugged, half turning away.

He leaned over her, one hand flat on the wall above her head. He lifted Dr. Goebbels' whisky to his mouth, barely controlling the churning in his stomach. He knew he had to do something about his drinking, but equally he knew he couldn't support his way of life without the bottle.

"Listen," he said to the girl, "I'll get a couple of steaks from the kitchen here and a bottle of ten-year-old Scotch and we'll go back to my apartment. What d'you say?"

He felt the prospect of spending the night alone suddenly unbearable. His anger and resentment against Stanhope boiled up. Without that goddamn meeting on the boat, he would now be at the Ribbentrop, maybe inviting a couple of the guys back to Giselastrasse for a drink, doing the job he was hired to do. Now even a night with this hard-faced peasant girl was better than nothing.

The corner of the girl's mouth had turned down. "You Americans are all the same," she said. "What makes you think you can buy a German woman for the price of a kilo of steak?"

"Honey," Franklyn said abrasively, "don't you be too sure the time won't come."

She frowned angrily.

"When Germany loses this war," Franklyn continued recklessly, "and believe me it will, this poor benighted country will be in such a way that a kilo of steak will buy me Miss Luftwaffe Bomber Control of 1941 and all half-dozen runners-up!"

She looked at him with contempt.

45

"Just go away," she said. "Thanks for the drink."

He knew he'd been a fool to push that fast. Another drink or two and a few maudlin questions about her family in Westphalia or wherever, and she would have been happy enough to go back with him. He downed his whisky and in the mirror saw Joe Conway had abandoned his girl and was ambling toward him.

"What can I get you, Joe?"

"I'm buying," Conway said. He nodded to the barman. "One Scotch, one bourbon." He took the stool next to Franklyn.

"How're things, Joe?" Franklyn turned on his barstool. "Long time since we split a bottle together."

"That's because I drink bourbon and you drink Scotch."

Franklyn knew exactly what he meant.

"It's not a bottle I want to split tonight, Jim," Conway went on, "it's a story."

"You're giving me a story?" Franklyn was incredulous. When it came to work, nobody played his cards as close to his chest as Joe Conway.

"No, I'm not giving you a story." Conway took his bourbon from the barman. "I'm asking you to work with me on one."

"Why me?"

"You'll see why. Tonight, about an hour ago, my landlord's daughter came rushing home, very excited. She's a young kid, sixteen maybe. She said the Führer was in Munich."

"What?"

"She was wrong, but she had seen something. A leadership Mercedes; you know, a big supercharged job, with an escort on motorcycles."

"Coming in to Munich."

"Right into the Marienplatz. To Gestapo headquarters. Something big, Jim. I think it could be Himmler maybe."

"And how do I get in on this act?" Franklyn said slowly. He already knew the answer.

"You get in because you're the only foreign correspondent who can ever get in when there's anything going at Gestapo headquarters. You get in, Jim, because of your friend Hardenberg. Okay?"

"Let's have another drink."

"Goddamnit," Conway exploded, "something's going on at the Marienplatz and you want another drink!"

"I can't just walk in there, Joe."

"You've done it a hundred times and come out with a story the rest of us get twenty-four hours later. Now d'you want to split on this one or not?"

"Sure I want to, Joe." The last thing he really wanted to do was to barge his way into the Gestapo office if Himmler was there. But this was the first time in a year he had been invited to work with someone on a story. He slid off the stool. "I'll go down now," he said. "I'll see what I can get."

Leaving the club, Franklyn walked quickly through the back streets past the Peterkirche toward the Marienplatz. He wished desperately that he had insisted on just one more whisky before he left. But the dim light of a café showing through a crack in the blackout curtain gave him another idea. He pulled open the door, pushed aside the curtain and entered the smoke-filled room. The schnapps in places like this was raw and tasteless but at least it was strong in alcohol. At the bar he ordered two.

Himmler, Conway had said. Well, maybe. But plenty of the other SS or Gestapo bigwigs rated a Mercedes and an escort. The truth was that not many of the foreign correspondents knew a lot about the Reich Security Office setup. With Klaus von Hardenberg as a friend, Franklyn had had more opportunity than most to find out.

By the summer of 1941 the police organization which the world called the Gestapo controlled the political activities of over two hundred million Europeans from the French Atlantic port of Brest to the Russian cities of Minsk and Kharkov, from the fjords of Norway to the bays and islands of the Aegean. In truth the Gestapo itself numbered only forty-thousand men, a handful of senior administrators, the rest plainclothes executive agents, all of whom were at the same time commissioned or noncommissioned officers of the SS. Technically the Gestapo was Section IV of the Reich Security Head Office, the RSHA,

47

the organization controlled by Reinhard Heydrich, which since 1939 had incorporated besides the Gestapo, the Criminal Police (Section V) and the SS Security Police, the SD (Sections III and VI).

To Jim Franklyn, as to millions of others, the organizational differences between Gestapo agent and SD man were unimportant. Though they wore SS uniforms only occasionally, they were still immediately recognizable in cafés or in parked cars by the menacing arrogance of their manner and more often than not by the long black or brown leather coats they favored.

Their headquarters in every major German city and in the occupied countries rapidly acquired that sinister aura of which Reinhard Heydrich was so proud, which he had commended the executive agents for developing in a speech on Police Day in February of this year. A reputation for "brutality, an almost sadistic inhumanity" he regarded as a major asset for the men of the Gestapo and the SD.

Thus it was that even as a protected neutral and citizen of the United States, Jim Franklyn knew he had to be pretty drunk to approach the Munich Rathaus without at least a slight tremor of nervousness. The Gothic facade overlooking the Marienplatz, with its carved stone figures and the lazy fall of a swastika banner from the flagpole, combined to produce in him that same sense of guilty unease that the simple articulation of the word "Gestapo" produced in many ordinary German citizens. The fact that he was on drinking terms with the man who occupied the biggest and by far the most important office behind that Gothic facade didn't really help. That Klaus von Hardenberg was Brigadeführer meant that Jim Franklyn passed into the flagstoned courtyard more often than he would have chosen. But then most of his best news tips came through Hardenberg, and Franklyn knew that he would not last long in the fierce competition for stories without easy access to the top.

Steeled by the two large schnapps Franklyn walked past the long black Mercedes parked in the courtyard and turned into the arched doorway that led to Hardenberg's office. He knew the young plainclothes clerk in the outer office. Usually he received a polite, "*Grüss Gott*, Herr Franklyn," and an immediate phone call was made to Hardenberg. It was a long time since he had shown his identification.

Stopping at the window, iron-grilled like a ticket office, Franklyn noticed for the first time two armed SS troopers beside the door leading up the stairs to Hardenberg's office.

"*Grüss Gott*," he said to the young clerk and in his fluent but still strongly American accented German. "Your chief free to see me?"

The clerk stretched his hand below the iron grille. "*Papieren bitte*," he said formally.

Franklyn shrugged and reached for his papers. "Something on tonight, Forster? I noticed you got yourself an honor guard." He gestured to the SS troopers.

"The Herr Brigadeführer is in conference."

Franklyn nodded toward the courtyard. "Who gets a supercharged Mercedes in these times of gas rationing?"

The clerk ignored the question. "Brigadeführer is in conference," he repeated.

"With the owner of the Mercedes?"

"Please, Herr Franklyn, if you could come back tomorrow . . ."

"Can I hell," Franklyn said. "Now either you give me a decent explanation of what's going on, or I report you to Hardenberg for a lack of cooperation with a neutral journalist. Which is it to be, Forster?"

The clerk hesitated. "Perhaps if you could wait, Herr Franklyn," he said, chewing his lip. "Perhaps the conference will not go on much longer."

Franklyn shrugged; the schnapps had emboldened him. It was a long time since he had sniffed a scoop. Given Hardenberg's friendly cooperation over the last two years, it was a long time since he had even raised his nose to the wind. "Yuh, I'll wait," he said.

"Please be so kind as to wait upstairs in the main office," Forster said.

The clerk let himself out of the small office and relocked the door behind him. Franklyn watched him in silence, his confidence growing as the clerkly figure pocketed the keys and turned. Franklyn gave him an ingratiating smile.

"Come on now, Forster," He nudged the clerk's elbow. "Who owns the big automobile in the courtyard?"

An SS trooper stepped forward, the rim of his helmet nodding above his apparently immobile face.

"Herr Franklyn is an American," Forster said hurriedly. "He is well known to the Herr Brigadeführer."

The helmet rim nodded. The face below remained hard and still.

"This way, Herr Franklyn." The clerk stepped around the trooper and passed through the door.

Franklyn followed. The wide stone staircase with the nineteenth-century stained-glass windows on the first floor was comfortably familiar to him. Yet he always glanced quickly at the arched doorway on his left. Down there, they said, the long staircase led to a set of iron-grille doorways entered by men, and left, if at all, by the shadows of men. Throughout Munich, these medieval cellars of the Rathaus were known as the Stone Room. Nobody in the city spoke of it without a shudder, an assistant Kriminalkommissar had confided to Franklyn at the Police Day dinner last year. And if they really knew what went on down there, he'd boasted, they'd be most of them too paralyzed with fear to raise even a shudder.

"In America," Franklyn was saying, "the only people who get to drive big official limousines like that are the president and a few very top people."

Forster dodged in front of him and led the way to the foot of the staircase. Perhaps ten feet separated them as Franklyn passed the door to the Stone Room.

Like Forster he had heard nothing, but he stepped back against the far wall, rigid with disgust, as a tall, bloodied figure stumbled through the arch, propelled by the push of a warder in the dark passage behind him.

"Manfred Erikson," the man muttered through torn lips. "My wife at Hochlingen. Hochlingen . . ."

A stick fell across the stooped shoulders, driving the prisoner toward the staircase. He reeled forward, shuffling in his ankle-chains. Jim Franklyn watched in horror the trail of blood and slime dribbling from the shapeless trouser legs onto the floor.

In Klaus von Hardenberg's office, Reinhard Heydrich pushed the last photograph aside. "Your prisoner had these on him when he was arrested in Venice?" he asked Hardenberg.

"Those and a series of forged travel permits."

"Forged?"

"No officer of the name on his papers exists in the German army."

Heydrich again shuffled through the photographs. "Where were they taken? Dachau?"

"All of them."

"So we have an army officer with contacts in Dachau preparing to hand over this material to someone in the Catholic Church."

"That's all we have, General," Hardenberg said. "It's not that much more than we started with. Except, of course, we have the man himself downstairs."

"But you've got nothing out of him? Not even his real name?"

"So far no, but it's a matter of time, nothing more."

Heydrich scowled. "I'm not sure how much time we have, Hardenberg. Look, we're almost certain he's an army officer."

"From his age probably fairly senior," Hardenberg agreed. "A colonel, perhaps."

"Good, so why not print a thousand copies of his photograph and send them to every military district headquarters? Someone's bound to recognize him."

"Not the way he looks now, General," Hardenberg said uneasily. "It's not just the work done on him downstairs. He was fished out of a canal in Venice with what they call a dredge hook. Nasty implement, it tore open his mouth. I don't think his own mother would recognize him at the moment."

"Then get the doctors to work," Heydrich said. "Fly a plastic surgeon down from Berlin. Patch him up and get him photographed."

"I'll get to work on it tonight. In the meantime you'd like to see him?"

Heydrich sat down, sliding low in the chair. "I don't have to tell you how damaging this information could be if it got out." He lit a cigarette and drew on it until the ash fell on his silver-gray uniform. "It's one of the few things that could bring the United States into the war."

He crushed out his cigarette and stood up. "All right. Let's see him, this man without a name."

Hardenberg crossed to the door. Opening it he stood aside. "I've had him put in the secretaries' room," he said. "It's the only place on this floor with secure windows."

"Perhaps your secretaries will get more out of him than your weasels have managed to extract so far."

Hardenberg knew how to treat his chief. He smiled. "I took the precaution of evacuating the girls, sir. But perhaps you're right. Perhaps I should have left them all in there together. One or two of them are strapping wenches."

The two officers passed the entrance to the waiting room where Franklyn sat with Forster. The clerk leaped to his feet.

"Can't see you now, Franklyn," Hardenberg said in English. Heydrich stopped, looking down curiously at the American.

"James Franklyn, sir," Hardenberg said, "an American journalist."

Franklyn got to his feet. He immediately recognized Heydrich from photographs. Since his elevation to Reichsprotektor of Bohemia his face had become widely known. His reputation had in any case always preceded him.

"A friend?" Heydrich nodded toward Franklyn.

"I'd say a fair journalist—neither for nor against us," Hardenberg said.

"Unusual in an American," Heydrich nodded. "I must read some of your articles."

"Call in tomorrow," Hardenberg said to Franklyn. "I might have something for you."

He turned away. Forster was at Franklyn's elbow. "The Herr Brigadeführer will see you tomorrow, Herr Franklyn."

"I heard. So the automobile and the SS guards belong to General Heydrich?" He was looking down the corridor to where Heydrich and Hardenberg had stopped while the guard opened the door to the secretaries' room.

"God in heaven!" Heydrich pushed past Hardenberg and ran into the room. "You idiot!" Franklyn heard the angry voice from where he stood in the waiting room. Before Forster could stop him he had taken half a dozen steps along the corridor. From where he stopped he could see the shapeless body of Erikson hanging by the neck from a cord wrapped around a heavy light fixture.

Chapter Two

In his apartment in Giselastrasse, Franklyn found he was unable to forget the image of that broken, slowly spiraling figure in the secretaries' room.

Erikson, the man had muttered through his broken teeth. Manfred Erikson. With a wife waiting for news at a place called Hochlingen.

He looked it up on the map. A small village off the autobahn just south of Berlin. But if he'd heard the man so clearly, Franklyn wondered just how much the clerk, Forster, had heard. True, he had been some few yards ahead; it was possible, he supposed, that he'd missed it.

Franklyn poured himself a glass of whisky, not by any means his first that evening. Evidently, the man Erickson had the kind of information that made them beat him half to death, and on account of which he'd been prepared to hang himself, to stop Hardenberg getting it. Franklyn took his whisky to the window. A dull, leaden sky hung low over Munich. What's more, he was important enough to claim Heydrich's time.

In the street below a woodcutter was unloading logs from his handcart. A wall poster bleached almost colorless by sun and rain solicited funds for Winterhilfe, the Nazi relief organization. Somebody switched on a radio in the next apartment. The muffled voice formed a German background to his thoughts.

He was, he recognized, homesick for hamburgers, baseball scores, American voices on the radio, the color and excitement and anarchy of New York. One big story, his first really big one since he had arrived in Munich, and he would be able to go back home with flags flying. Even at secondhand he had had enough of the brutal realities of this war.

But if Forster had heard Erikson's words and had passed them on to Hardenberg, the last thing Franklyn wanted to do was to involve himself.

He finished his whisky and poured another. He found it impossible to tackle decisions without drink. The woodcutter had finished across the road. Soon he would be at Franklyn's door trying to sell his unburnable laurel logs for the price that oak should fetch. Franklyn emptied his glass. It was a risk—a hell of a risk—but for once he would go for broke.

Ten hours later, after a night on the troop-packed Munich–Berlin express, Franklyn stumbled out into the wet, misty dawn at the small town of Krevenden. It was an unscheduled stop, thanks, it was rumored, to RAF bombs on the line between Krevenden and Berlin's Anhalter Station. In any event his map showed the little market town to be only ten kilometers from the even smaller village of Hochlingen.

It was still barely eight o'clock. The old, red-capped stationmaster punched his ticket and, cheerfully abandoning his responsibilities, conducted Franklyn across the gabled square to the Bahnhof Hotel. Over acorn coffee and a schnapps, Franklyn asked the stationmaster, one Herr Frettner, about the village of Hochlingen.

"Just women there now," Frettner said. "All the men have gone off to the army." He chuckled. "Women and a French prisoner-of-war camp. The Frenchmen work the women's farms for them. And that's not all they work, I've heard."

"All farms"—Franklyn offered him an American cigarette—
"no big houses?"

The old man took the cigarette and ran it below his nose as if
he were appreciating a fine cigar.

"Big houses? Just the one. Colonel Erikson's estate lies on
the edge of the village. You see the house as you come in from
the Krevenden road."

"I'd like to shave and clean up here," Franklyn said. "Any
chance of finding me a taxi?"

The stationmaster shrugged. "Bauer Sepp might just let me
take you down there in his truck. It's the town ambulance," he
explained. "He gets a special gasoline ration for air-raid
duty."

The late autumn sun had barely triumphed in its struggle
with the mist as the converted farm truck turned off the road at
the entrance to Hochlingen village and followed a winding,
well-made road through the pine forest. When he had just
begun to catch glimpses of a low, half-timbered building
through the trees, the truck rumbled around a sharp bend and
stopped. Blocking the narrow way, a woman in riding clothes
sat at the reins of a pony and trap.

"I'll back up," Frettner said. "There's the Countess Erikson
now."

Franklyn quickly slipped a pack of Chesterfields to the old
man. "Can you pick me up in an hour?"

"If it's all right with Bauer Sepp," the stationmaster said
doubtfully.

"It will be," Franklyn said, dropping another pack of Chesterfields into his lap.

"You're probably right," the old man smiled. "And I don't
have another train through till midday."

Franklyn climbed out of the truck. "He's backing up," he said
to the woman in the pony trap.

She frowned slightly at the accent.

She was in her early thirties, a tall woman with rich chestnut
hair which, pulled back from her forehead, gave her a slightly
severe, disapproving look. Then she smiled and a sudden soft-

ness changed her features. He had the immediate impression of a woman in which two elements challenged each other for expression. "Are you American?" she asked, laughing.

"Yes," he said.

"I'm sorry but there's something incongruous about an American arriving in Hochlingen village in Bauer Sepp's old ambulance."

He stood beside the trap, looking up at her. There was something equally incongruous, he thought, about such an attractive woman being a countess. He had imagined that you'd have to be horsefaced and in your seventies to qualify for a title.

"Come and sit up here, and if you'll risk it, I'll drive you back to the house."

He clambered awkwardly up to sit beside her.

"I was at school in England once. But"—she smiled her open smile again—"that was a very long time ago."

With a splutter of its old engine the truck began to retreat in front of them, while she concentrated on edging the pony forward to a wider point in the road where they could make a turn.

"Well, Mr. . . . ?"

"Franklyn. I'm Jim Franklyn. I work for a U. S. wire service."

"Wire service?"

"I'm a journalist. We supply stories for any newspaper that cares to buy."

"I see. And why have you come to see me?" She frowned again.

Franklyn realized for the first time that whatever his intention was in terms of following up a story, what he was immediately about to do was to tell this woman beside him that her husband was dead.

He could delay it no longer. "I've some bad news for you, I'm afraid."

He saw her grip tighten on the reins. They were opposite the drive to the house now and she disguised her alarm by executing the turning movement.

"Bad news about my husband, Mr. Franklyn?"

"About Colonel Erikson, yes." He paused, swallowing. "Your husband is dead, Countess Erikson."

She pulled the pony to a halt and turned toward him on the bench seat. Her free hand went very slowly to her mouth. "You know this for certain?" she asked behind her hand.

"Yes. Yes, I'm afraid I do."

She slapped the reins on the pony's back and the trap moved forward into the cobbled courtyard of the old farmhouse. Then reining the pony back again, she applied the brake and climbed down.

"Where did this happen?" she asked softly as Franklyn climbed down beside her.

"In Gestapo headquarters, Munich."

"You were there?"

"I was visiting an officer there. As a journalist."

"And this is a story for your wire service? That's why you are here?"

"Partly," he said. "And partly because your husband, before he died, asked me to come."

"I don't understand."

"I'm not sure I do, either," Franklyn said as they walked toward the house. "Maybe he heard my American accent. Took a long shot, I guess."

"A long shot. That's all he had left to take, you mean ?"

Franklyn nodded. "I'm afraid so."

They walked into a warm, timbered hall.

"Tell Franz to look after the trap, Maria," she said to the old woman who appeared through a curtained doorway.

The woman half-curtsied and ducked back through the curtains.

"This way." Countess Erikson led him into a long room with heavy sofas arranged around a fireplace where logs burned in an iron grate.

"When did this happen?" She had crossed to a cupboard. Opening it she took out two glasses and a bottle of schnapps.

"Two nights ago."

She nodded, pouring two glasses of schnapps. Franklyn was aware that she was timing her questions, pacing herself for all she could take from minute to minute. Yet her control seemed absolute.

"You haven't told me how he died."

"He died," Franklyn said slowly, "because he chose to."

"He killed himself," she said with a sharp intake of breath.

"Yes."

"And I don't imagine the Gestapo are the sort of people who would provide a revolver for an officer's death."

"No."

She drank her schanpps in a single gulp. "Yesterday. Why haven't the Gestapo been here? It's against their principles to allow a wife of a traitor to go free."

"A traitor. Is that what he was?"

"In the eyes of the Gestapo, yes."

"Perhaps at Munich they didn't know your husband's name."

"Perhaps." She sat on one of the deep sofas, holding the empty glass. "Was he tortured?" she asked at length.

"Yes," Franklyn said. And because he found to his surprise that he meant it, added, "But I don't think it would get them very far with a man like that."

She smiled sadly. "I can't see how you can possibly know, but you're right."

He bent over and took her glass. Carrying it to the cupboard he filled it. His own he saw with surprise was barely touched.

"Why are you really here, Mr. Franklyn? You would need a permit to travel from Munich to Berlin. And that permit would be issued by the Gestapo."

He handed her the glass. "Yes, it was. I have a head office in Berlin. I have no problem with a travel permit to this part of Germany."

60

"So you claim to be simply a journalist?"

"I don't claim to be, that's what I am."

"And as a journalist you came here looking for a story?"

"I came here"—he hesitated in the half-truth—"because your husband asked me to. If there's a story to tell . . ."

"Oh, there's a story to tell, Mr. Franklyn."

"Will you tell it?" he asked.

She thought for a long time. "Yes," she said finally, "I think I will. If you guarantee to publish it in the outside world."

"If it's important it'll be published in the United States."

"It's unbelievably important, I warn you. Perhaps even something you would prefer not to hear."

"Go on."

She stood up. "Some months ago," she said walking to the window, "my husband, among others, became aware that the regime was about to take a radically different attitude to what they call the 'Jewish Problem.' "

"The way things have been for German Jews since 1938 that could only be an improvement."

"Not so," she said sharply.

"Sequestrations, arrests, concentration camps where even doctors and scientists work as laborers . . ."

She was watching her man unharness the pony out in the courtyard, her back turned to Franklyn. "Even so . . ." She turned toward him. "I speak, you understand, with shame as a German. The Hitler government has decided on what it chooses to call the Final Solution. The final solution for ten million Jews under their control in Europe. They are to be exterminated."

Franklyn shook his head in total disbelief. "Ten *million* people? I don't believe it. I don't believe it could be done."

"It can be done, Mr. Franklyn, if they are given the time. Certain large concentration camps, mostly in the Government-General in Poland, but some here in Germany too, are to be fitted with gas chambers. Vast crematoria are being built. It is happening now. In charge of the whole disgusting operation is a

61

man without pity, the man they already call the Hangman, Reinhard Heydrich. If he is given time he will destroy every Jewish man, woman and child in Europe."

Franklyn sat numbed. "Is this the story you want me to tell?"

"Part of it."

"Part of it!"

"Yes, there's more."

He felt his hair standing on the back of his neck.

"The Final Solution is part of something called Plan East, 'Fall-Ost,' " she said in slow, deliberate tones. "Fall-Ost envisages the clearance through extermination of vast areas in Eastern Europe. My husband had reason to believe that Himmler and Heydrich are talking, in their appalling terms, of the annihilation of approximately thirty-two million people."

He sat openmouthed in sheer disbelief.

"You think I am quite mad. I can see it on your face."

He took a deep breath. "I think," he said, "if I hadn't seen your husband in Munich, if I hadn't seen that Heydrich considered it important enough to come from Prague on his account, I'd get out now and walk back to Krevenden."

"You believe me then?"

"Of course, I don't," he said, white-faced. "I'm too damn scared to believe you."

"That's honest, at least," she said. "And I must admit that I felt the same when Manfred first told me. At that time it was just drunken talk from an SS transportation officer."

"At that time . . ." He swallowed hard. "You mean now you've got evidence?"

"Perhaps not what you'd call evidence; I don't know. The National Socialist leadership knows this evil must be shrouded in fog, the camps hidden in the Polish marshes or disguised as work camps."

"So you've got nothing?"

"For whatever reason, there is one exception to the rule that these death camps are to be in remote areas. That is Dachau."

"Dachau? Outside Munich?"

"Yes. Perhaps it will not prove a successful site in the end but my husband had evidence that Dachau is being prepared for exterminations at this very moment."

She crossed to the cupboard and took the schnapps bottle across to where he was sitting. She filled his glass.

"If you could prove that," he said, "you'd be well on the way to persuading the world that Fall Ost exists." He tossed back the schnapps. "Do you mind if we get some air?" he said.

"You're looking pale, Mr. Franklyn."

"I'm feeling sicker than I've felt for a long time," he said.

"Because you believe me?"

"Because I can't imagine anybody taking the crazy risk of telling all this to a stranger unless she believed it herself."

"I must telephone my brother Karl," she said. "Then we'll take a walk."

"Your brother, was he involved in this?"

She silenced him with a cold glance.

He shook his head. "I'm sorry, Countess Erikson. I'm new to this. I haven't yet learned the questions not to ask."

She returned a few minutes later wearing a heavy coat. She had let down her hair so that it now flowed around her face. He could see she had been crying.

She led the way out of the house and across the cobbled courtyard. "Let's walk up to the cross." She pointed to where a bald hill rose from the surrounding pine forest. A small cross stood at its summit.

They took a narrow path through the wood. The dark pines closed in around them. For some time they trudged on in silence while Franklyn tried to absorb the enormity of what he'd heard. In Munich everybody knew of the nearby Kz Lager (camp) at Dachau village. But nobody, correspondents or local Munichers, ever dreamed it was other than one of Germany's dozens of concentration camps.

Fall-Ost. The words had already acquired for him a chilling ring. He trudged on, almost forgetting the woman at his side. He had seen the beginnings of the transportation horror while

63

he was in France—the yellow Star of David on the sleeves, the death penalty for failure to wear it. The young Jewish girls in Paris giggling self-consciously on the first day, the old men striving to wear it proudly. Twice he had seen long trains of cattle cars, the open doors crisscrossed with barbed wire, the silent figures inside. In this context Fall-Ost was possible.

He had been a journalist all his adult life. His values were news values. Happiness and grief were colorful elements that gave roundness and dimension to bare facts. But before this story, before the unspeakable horrors of Fall-Ost, he felt an unaccumstomed awe. The woman beside him had been widowed in an attempt to expose this enormity. Her own life was certainly in danger. And Jim Franklyn was left with the ghoulish sense of being the robber at the grave.

"I haven't thanked you," she said.

"Thanked me?" He frowned.

"For coming here. There must be a risk for you too."

He stopped, turning to face her.

"Risk!" he said. "You make me feel pretty small."

"I don't understand you, Mr. Franklyn."

He shook his head. "Don't ask me to explain."

"Very well," her wide gray eyes never left his face.

He turned in the direction of the hill and slipped his arm through hers. "Let's walk."

She smiled slowly. "You're a strange man, Mr. Franklyn."

They walked on until they arrived at the simple stone cross.

"What is it?" Franklyn asked. "There's no inscription."

"No," she said. "I'm not even really sure what it's meant to be. My husband was a Catholic, not particularly devout. He had the cross erected the day the Nazis came to power."

They stood for a few minutes in the biting wind.

"The evidence your husband had is now presumably in the hands of the Gestapo."

"Back in their hands, yes."

"Do you have copies?"

She shook her head.

"Does anybody?"

"I don't think it's likely. But we'll know more when my brother arrives from Berlin."

He glanced at her quickly.

"Yes," she said, nodding, "I'm beginning to trust you."

They began to walk slowly back to the manor house. As they reached the final slope they saw a Wehrmacht staff car pull into the drive below them. A tall, hatless officer got out of the driver's seat.

"Your brother?"

"Yes."

"One more thing, Countess Erikson." He had removed his arm from hers and the formality again seemed natural. "You haven't told me how your husband planned to let the world know about Fall-Ost. Through a neutral journalist like me?"

"No. His object was to get the evidence to the Vatican. You remember I told you he was a Catholic. His hope was that Pope Pius would use the moral power of the Catholic Church to condemn this barbarity."

"But the evidence never reached the Vatican?"

They were entering the drive. "I think, from what you tell me, we have to believe that it did not." She paused. "Let me talk to my brother alone for a few moments. We'll join you in the house."

Before he could reply she ran forward and threw her arms around her brother. He held her, and as Franklyn moved away he could see, in the convulsive movement of her body that she was sobbing.

"There are a number of problems that I don't think my sister has yet had time to consider." Karl von Brombach stood with his polished boot on the fender. Looking into the fire, he said, "Things won't end with my brother-in-law's death."

He turned from the fire to face Franklyn and Countess Erikson.

"You mean the Gestapo will continue its investigation?" Franklyn said.

"More than that. I think they're bound, in the end, to establish the identity of the man they arrested. That means Christina will be in immediate danger. Manfred, my brother-in-law, was on leave from his unit in Prague. In a few days when he has not returned, his adjutant, who is a loyal officer, loyal to Colonel Erikson, that is, will nevertheless be forced to report to division that his battalion commander is missing. It will be just such a report that the Gestapo will be on the lookout for."

"What can we do, Karl? Is there anything to be done?" asked the countess.

"Perhaps," her brother said. "Manfred was traveling to Italy, with false papers. His uniform and his military record are here. The first step is to get them to Prague."

"How will that help?" Franklyn asked.

Brombach looked at his sister. "Forgive me," he said, "but this is the only way."

"Go on," she said tensely.

"Captain Lindemann, the colonel's adjutant, will be prepared to do whatever is necessary. The documentation can be arranged to report Manfred dead in Prague. An accident, or a terrorist attack, perhaps."

"But . . ." Franklyn sensed a qualification to the idea.

"But we will need a body."

Franklyn stood in the corridor as the long gray train drew through the marshaling yards of Berlin's Anhalter Station. Heavy-rescue engineers were still bringing out bodies from the bombed railway workers' tenements on either side of the tracks. Lines of ambulances stood in rubble-strewn side streets, and women served soup from iron field-kitchens to huddles of still-dazed local people, their faces blackened where the blast had driven soot and dust deep into the pores of the skin.

Over everything hung the burned-wet stench of newly extinguished fires, and the December sun filtered through rising palls of dust as the engineers demolished dangerously swaying walls. The young soldiers standing at the train windows, fresh from four months' training camp in the quiet forests of south-east Germany, fell silent. For most it was their first sight of war.

Shouldering his way through the heavily laden troops on the platform, Franklyn saw that Anhalter itself had lost its glass canopy in the raid. Shards of green glass had been swept into huge, glittering mounds through which snaked the long lines of hopeful travelers. Outside the station, harsh, gray Berlin looked as it always did to Franklyn, the people just that much more drab, the buildings that much more pockmarked with shrapnel than on his last visit.

His eye caught the black and white check markings of a taxi. Stepping into the road he flagged it down and, emphasizing his American accent, gave the Unter den Linden address of the AAP office, and jumped into the back before the couple at the head of the taxi line came stumbling up with their bulging cardboard suitcases. The driver, apprised by the accent of the possibility of a big tip, put the cab into gear and swept past the protesting Berliners.

Berlin's cabdrivers fell into one of two categories these days, either full-time Gestapo informants or fiercely independent men from the working-class Wedding district of Berlin with a long tradition of bucking authority behind them. It wasn't really difficult to tell which.

"How's the bombing?" Franklyn asked the stocky figure beside him.

"We're giving it to London, the Tommies are giving it to us. Stands to reason. Cockneys or Berliners, we're the ones that get it. I bet Winston Churchill's not sitting in his London palace when the Luftwaffe comes visiting."

"And what about the Führer?" Franklyn said. "I've heard he's quite fond of his place down in the Bavarian mountains."

"Ah." The cabby allowed just the faintest smile to touch his lips. "That's different, Mein Herr. The Führer's down there for the clear air. All these years of speaking on behalf of the German people has strained the chest. Or so they tell me," he added flatly.

No Gestapo tout, this one, Franklyn decided, and when they pulled into the courtyard at the Unter den Linden, he added a pack of Chesterfields to the tip.

Greg Sefton, jacketless, his waistcoat hanging open, his shirtsleeves rolled to the elbows, was coming out of his secretary's office as he saw the ancient grille elevator rising in the well and recognized the occupant as Jim Franklyn.

Coming forward across the landing at a fast waddle, he arrived in time to pull open the elevator gate.

"Jim," he said, and the pleasure showed on his face, "nobody told me you were coming in."

They shook hands.

"Nobody knew," Franklyn said.

"You drink the Munich Goebbels club dry of cheap Scotch, or what?"

Franklyn shook his head.

Sefton's eyebrows moved slightly upward. "Business, huh? Let's go into my office."

He led the way into a large room which looked across the Unter den Linden to the Adlon Hotel. Piles of cables and books covered the enormous mahogany desk. Dark-wood bookcases lined the walls and a plum-red Turkish carpet covered the center of the floor. Apart from the surface chaos of a newspaperman's office, the room was unchanged since a firm of lawyers had had it in the days of Bismarck.

"Sit down. I'll get you a drink."

Franklyn took off his topcoat and threw it across the back of an upright chair. A worn black leather club chair stood in front of the desk. He sat, watching Sefton pour the Scotch.

"How's Munich, Jim? Much bombing?" Sefton asked, his back still toward Franklyn. It was becoming more and more the first question everybody asked.

"Some. Not like here. I think the RAF finds it a long drive down south."

Greg Sefton turned. "Wait till they get their new four-engine bombers into service. It's no secret to anyone it must be any day now. Then Munich, Mannheim, Berlin, they're all going to catch it—every goddamn night."

"The idea seems to give you a charge."

"Why not? As long as I'm not underneath a stick of thousand-pounders."

"A lot of civilians get killed," Franklyn said. "Women, kids . . ."

"That's the way war goes, Jim. You've seen enough to know that."

"So it's that easy, huh? That's the way war goes—and the bombers can come over every night they like. . . ."

"Jesus, what did the Luftwaffe do to London?" He handed Franklyn a Scotch and water.

"Greg, I thought we were Americans. I thought we were supposed to be neutral."

"Neutral, my ass! The sooner FDR leads us into this war, the quicker it'll be over." Sefton pushed a pile of papers across his desk and sat in the empty space. "Business, you said?"

"Yep, business."

"You got a story?"

"I may have the most fantastic story ever."

"Go on."

"I mean *fantastic*. Unbelievable, incredible, inconceivable. . . ."

"Okay, you've grabbed me."

"Listen, Greg, I'm using all these words in their original, pristine meaning."

"Okay."

"If we did this story I'd have to leave Germany—*before* it was published."

"That big?"

Franklyn nodded, "Does the term '*Endlösung*' —Final Solution—mean anything to you? Does 'Fall-Ost' mean anything to you?"

Sefton remained silent.

"Does it?"

Greg Sefton's small eyes were half closed. "What does it mean to you, Jim?"

"For Christ's sake," Franklyn said, "let's not play games. You already got someone else on this story? Or are you working on it yourself? I thought I had something new."

Sefton shook his head. "No, I'm not working on it, Jim." He slid off the desk. "And I don't see it just as a story, either."

"Nor do I. It's a hell of a lot more than that. What do you know about it?"

"A few rumors. I can't check them; I've no way of knowing how true they are."

"Greg, they've slated ten million people," Franklyn said urgently. "More than twice that number for the whole Fall-Ost madness."

"That's the rumor. And that Reinhard Heydrich is in charge of the operation."

"I believe it's true, Greg."

"You've got evidence?"

"I've got a contact—the wife of a German officer arrested while trying to let the world know just what's being planned."

Sefton was silent. "What do you want out of this, Jim, a Pulitzer prize?"

"You don't have to be a bastard with me, Greg. If I get a Pulitzer for this, great. But first and foremost the United States must know what's going on."

Sefton pointed. "There's a typewriter. Give me all you've got. One copy only. Then we'll both go around and find a quiet little place for a drink with a friend of mine."

Dr. Stanhope sat in the back room of the Moabit S-bahn station *Bierstube*, slowly turning the sheets of Franklyn's typescript. To Jim Franklyn his face seemed expressionless as he finished the last page. "Good," he said. He inclined his head and slipped the papers into his inside pocket. "Good," he repeated thoughtfully, "good. . . ."

Franklyn looked at Sefton. "So what's the next step, Greg?"

"The next step," Stanhope answered the question, "is to get some real confirmation of what we have here." He tapped his pocket.

"I explained in the typescript," Franklyn said. "Erikson's adjutant in Prague, Captain Albert Lindemann, is the only man who knew Erikson's source."

"Then you must follow up in Prague," Stanhope said easily.

"Stanhope," Franklyn said, "I still consider I work for AAP wire service, and Greg here as head of bureau in Germany."

"Okay, Jim," Sefton said, "let's play it your way. In two days' time Heydrich and the puppet president of Czechoslovakia take part in a symbolic handing over of the Prague city keys. The press is invited. I'm instructing you to go."

Franklyn shrugged.

"You're not going to get your Pulitzer by sitting on your butt in Munich," Sefton said.

"Listen to me, will you?" Franklyn said angrily. "There are people involved in this thing—Erikson's wife, his brother-in-law, this guy Lindemann. They could all go the way Erikson went."

"I'm instructing you to go to Prague, Jim. That's all. What you do there is your business."

Stanhope looked on without speaking.

"Okay, I'll go to Prague. But the only way to buy this information from Lindemann is to produce a body." He turned to Stanhope. "What sort of cloak-and-dagger contracts does the United States government have with the Prague Central Mortuary?"

Stanhope thought for a few moments. "The British have some good connections with resistance groups there. I'll see if I can get them to help out."

He got to his feet. "Keep at it, Franklyn," he said. "This one will fly you all the way back home."

After Stanhope left, Franklyn ordered another stein of beer for himself and Sefton. "It won't come as any great surprise, Greg, if I tell you I don't like Dr. Stanhope one bit."

71

"I'm not sure I do myself," Sefton said.

"But you're caught up in this war stuff, huh?"

"Aren't you? After what you heard this morning?"

"I'll tell you the truth, Greg—I don't know where I stand. I've seen what the Gestapo can do to people. If going to Prague can keep Erikson's widow out of the Gestapo's hands, I'll do it. Maybe it's part bravado, I don't know. But I'm not planning to stick my neck out too far on this. I want to go back to the States, I've no doubts about that now. And I don't mind that much if I go back because you've just fired me—or I go back with the Pulitzer-sized story we both know this is."

Sefton looked at him for a few moments. "Okay, Jim," he said. "Now let's see if there's somewhere in this capital city where we can lay our hands on a big bottle of Chivas Regal."

Chapter Three

Even from the bottom of the stone steps Jim Franklyn could see
that the vast station hall of the Munich Hauptbahnof was
packed with young soldiers in field-gray uniforms. The one-
armed porter carrying his cases on a leather strap over his
shoulder grunted irritably at the prospect of again pushing his
way through the dark mass of men, banging against the steel
helmets strapped to their hips or tripping over their piles of
equipment, the rolled blankets and black-ribbed gas-mask con-
tainers.

"Where are they going?"

"I'm not supposed to say, am I?" the porter said acidly, then
added in a throwaway tone, "two hundred and twenty-first
Regiment. Boy soldiers. Part of a replacement division for
Prague."

"Just my luck," Franklyn said.

The porter began to shoulder his way through the young
Feldgrau who thronged the great hall chewing *Wurst* and
drinking bottled beer. Since 1940 the lights inside the station
had been progressively reduced and were by now hardly more

than softly glowing stencils above each platform giving the time and destination of the trains.

"When does the Prague express leave?" Franklyn asked the porter.

"Express!" the old man snarled. "There hasn't been a real express from this station since the bombing began. With any luck you'll be in Prague by morning. Which morning," he said, "is another question."

The young soldiers laughed and jostled the porter with their steel helmets as he tried to push his way through.

"You're laughing now," he spat angrily at one cheerful group of eighteen-year-olds, "but by the time this war's over, half of you'll be like me, missing an arm or a leg for the Fatherland."

The boys stopped laughing. The red-capped stationmaster at the Prague platform pushed his way across to the porter. "Hold your tongue, Hans, you old fool!"

Taking the travel permit that Franklyn held out to him, he glanced quickly at it and tore off the top sheet. He had certainly not missed the red overstamp of a Gestapo issuing office.

He looked up quickly at Franklyn. "This way, sir. . . ." He gestured to the porter bringing up the rear. "He's a bit quick-tempered, that's all. Lost his arm on the Somme in 1917"—he spoke as if the porter were not there—"decorated twice before that. A Feldwebel in the Führer's own regiment, Sixteenth Bavarian Infantry." He shot the porter a warning glance over his shoulder.

The old man sniffed and grumbled behind them.

"First class, of course, sir," the stationmaster said unctuously. "I think I can find you an empty compartment at the front of the train. You may get one or two officers in when the troops get on, but I'll do my best to see it doesn't get too crowded."

Jim Franklyn settled in the corner of his compartment and listened and watched for the next two hours while companies were formed on the platform and marched into numbered compartments.

His two cases had been placed in the wooden rack above his

head, but he could see them both reflected in the mirror set in the woodwork above the empty seats opposite. He had been assured that the chances of a frontier inspection between Germany and the Czechoslovak Protectorate were minimal. But he also knew that if he were ordered to open the flat brown case with Colonel Erikson's documents and uniform neatly folded inside, then the only part of Prague's beautiful Hradčany Castle he was likely to see would be the Gestapo dungeons.

For the hundredth time he asked himself what had made him do it. It was true that as a journalist he was on the most fantastic story of his life. But to be a real investigative journalist a man needs first to be something of a megalomaniac hero and Jim Franklyn knew he was not that. The fear of playing the coward in the face of Countess Erikson's extraordinary quiet courage had been a factor too. But whatever the mixed motives that had brought him into this compartment with the Wehrmacht uniform and papers of a traitor to the Reich in that flat brown case, he now desperately regretted it. Just before midnight, when two SS captains entered his compartment politely asking if they might join him, he had already decided to hurl the brown suitcase from the train as soon as it got started.

The two officers took corner seats, and removing caps and belts and loosening their collars settled down with cigars. Ten or fifteen minutes later the train jerked forward gently and began its journey to Nuremberg and the Bohemian frontier at Waldhaus, the brown suitcase still in the rack above Franklyn's head.

In Prague it was a public holiday. From early morning the convoys of trucks had brought into the city regiments of helmeted soldiers, their uniforms parade-pressed, their rifle butts polished. In Malostranské Square, under the green dome of the church of St. Nicholas, military police, with silver gorgets glittering at their throats, shouted orders and blew whistles, struggling to form the field-gray masses into columns of march. In the cobbled center of the great square, a hundred and thirty men of the 16th Panzer Grenadier band, in white gauntlets and braided epaulets, like some leftover from a Napoleonic past, unpacked instruments and unfurled their banners.

The winter sun rose toward midday. The parade marshal, Colonel Anton Ritter, stood beneath the stone arch of the Plague Tower while breathless, red-faced adjutants reported on the arrival of units and their position in the order of march.

The colonel checked his watch. The flyby Messerschmitts would be leaving their Augsburg base in nine minutes. In just twenty-one minutes this milling horde of men should be formed in columns of eight abreast. He could see from the frantic air of his adjutants that they doubted such order could be imposed in time, but Anton Ritter was an old hand. Before the war he had handled party marches in Nuremberg and commemoration parades in Berlin and Munich. And afterward the great victory marches in Warsaw, Oslo, Brussels and Paris. Indeed he knew that OKW had already nominated him for Moscow and London. When Anton Ritter organized a march-past it never went wrong.

A mile from the Plague Tower by way of the traditional route of the kings of Bohemia, or a few minutes' hard climb by the two hundred medieval steps above Zamecka Street, the pale outline of Hradčany Castle rises above the city. In the former royal apartments in the inner court, SS Sergeant Klein finished laying out his master's uniform, his ear attuned to the hissing of the shower in the bathroom next door. A tall, powerfully built Saxon, he nevertheless moved rapidly about the room, first opening a bottle of champagne and resealing it with a silver stopper before replacing it in the ice bucket, then filling a box from packs of English cigarettes.

The sound of the shower stopped. Klein looked quickly around the room once more and withdrew. His master preferred to dress alone.

A moment later Reinhard Heydrich walked naked from the shower into his dressing room. The pale gray uniform of an SS general hung from the mahogany stand. The high boots stood beside the dressing table; an almost liquid black sheen reflected the silver buckles on the crossbelt draped across the back of a chair. He glanced right at his naked figure in the long mirror, his satisfaction at his tall, lean body only tinged by the knowledge that if he turned full face, the strangely rounded width of his hips would become apparent. Nothing he had been able to do, since he was seventeen, no amount of fencing, swimming or riding, had had any effect on those near-feminine curves.

He could hear the children being dressed along the corridor, the voice of Klaus, his son, raised peremptorily. Heydrich smiled. At seven years old, Klaus would slip easily into the role of eldest son of the Reichsprotektor.

He began to dress. Standing in front of the window he buttoned his shirt and looked down at the courtyard below. In the light autumn breeze the swastika banners on the saluting base billowed and tugged at their moorings. Across the cobbled courtyard three bent, green-aproned figures were rolling out a red carpet. From a side door the SS honor guard, in black dress uniforms, white lanyards and gloves, their steel helmets boot-polished to a deep black glow, filed out and stood, incongruously smoking, awaiting the order to form.

Reinhard Tristan Heydrich had every reason to be pleased with the way fate had dealt the tarot pack. Just ten years ago he had been a junior naval officer, recently dismissed from the service for refusing to marry a girl he had made pregnant. Unemployed in a Germany beset by unemployment, his only assets were his own intelligence and his new Danish-born wife, Lina van Osten. Passionately devoted to Adolf Hitler's National Socialist German Workers' Party, she had persuaded her nonpolitical husband to seek a job as a clerk in the seedy, top-floor offices of the Hamburg party.

Years afterward Heydrich liked to remember, or hear one of his subordinates tell the story of Himmler giving Heydrich twenty minutes to draft a state organization for a secret security police force.

Reinhard Heydrich never added, and no subordinate would

dare to add, that he had simply written out the command structure of naval intelligence, memorized by all junior naval officers at the Kriegsmarine officer training establishments.

When the great day came two years later and Himmler asked for, and received, the relatively modest position of police chief of Munich, Heydrich had already made plans for the take-over of all police functions in the Reich. Thus it was that in ten years he had risen from a virtually unpaid clerk in the strong-arm office of one of Germany's many political parties, to first the commander of the whole secret police network in the German state and, from last month, the Reichsprotektor of twelve million Central Europeans in the ancient kingdoms and principalities of Czechoslovakia. His wife Lina had been right to insist there was a future for anyone with real ambition in Herr Hitler's National Socialist German Workers' Party.

A future for a man with real ambition. Heydrich poured himself a glass of champagne and lit an English cigarette from the silver box on the table. This day's ceremonies would finally remove him from the shadow of Himmler, would publicly announce to the world his standing in the eyes of Adolf Hitler, and would confirm him in absolute power of life and death over twelve million people. Even so, for the future he had been promised so much more.

He leaned against the stone-mullion window and looked down across the Vltava River and the jumbled rooftops beyond. He had no politics, no ideology, beyond his own authoritarian drive, no religion beyond a complete belief in himself. He knew that he was not a man to make revolutions—but he believed fervently that he was the man to capture them. Just a few weeks ago, at Hitler's mountain retreat at Berchtesgaden, he had been singled out by the Führer who had presented him with an opportunity so monstrous that even now his hand shook at the thought of it.

It happened without exception every day the Führer held court at the Berghof. An hour or two after lunch had finished, the ritual would begin with the guests assembling in the main hall.

Eva Braun would join them, usually seeking her friend Albert Speer, if he were present. The SS adjutants, the immensely tall Schultz and Gunsche, would move discreetly through the milling guests, bending to murmur that the Führer would like a word in private with Luftwaffe General Kesselring, or perhaps with a young tank battalion commander newly decorated for an action outside Leningrad or Moscow. But in the daily ritual, the object of envy, and often of suspicion too, was always the man Gunsche approached last, the guest chosen to accompany the Führer, the man accorded precious moments alone with Adolf Hitler on the short walk from the Berghof main building to the small teahouse he had had built in the woods.

That day the Führer's adjutant had moved through the groups of officers and party officials, and stopped before Reinhard Heydrich.

When Gunsche spoke to Heydrich, he nodded. All eyes were now covertly on Himmler, but Schultz, the other adjutant, had moved away to take up a position at the foot of the staircase. A suppressed shock wave ran through the hall: Himmler was not to be asked to accompany the Führer and his own SS deputy on the walk. Already the guests were speculating.

When Hitler appeared in a light raincoat and slouch hat with a Tyrolean walking stick, the procession began. His German shepherd dog, Blondi, bounced ahead. The senior Nazis present, on this day Himmler and Wahl, the Gauleiter of Berlin, naturally took the places directly behind the Führer and his chosen companion. The walk itself took as long as Adolf Hitler decided. On some days he would stride out, waving his alpenstock toward the towering peak of the Untersberg on his right. On others he would stop and talk in a serious or joking vein with his companion for minutes at a time. Then, like the tense courtiers they were, the whole entourage would stop and generals would pretend an admiration for the mountains, city Gauleiters would nod appreciation of the blue Alpine flowers along the way, and all would watch, and if possible listen, for some sign that the procession was moving on. It had been known for the short walk to have taken up to two hours. But that had been in the early summer when the invasion of Russia was being worked out on the teahouse walks.

"I count myself lucky," Hitler said to Heydrich, "to have been able to give German youth the opportunity to go to war. As an old frontline soldier myself I know what war means in terms of inculcating the hard decency which is expressly German. Of course," he added, "it can only come from comradeship with other German soldiers. Other armies are different—the British are class-ridden, the French think only of the quality of the wine issue and our Italian allies think soldiering is the same as being in the village brass band, that soldiering like charity should begin and *end* at home."

Heydrich, slowing his long stride to the Führer's short paces, laughed his high laugh. "My war experience so far, Führer, has been confined to the war in the air. But the spirit on Luftwaffe airfields in Holland is much as you describe."

Hitler stopped abruptly, forcing Heydrich to swing around to face him, and the long, trailing entourage to seek its own amusements in woodland flora and the antics of the Führer's dog.

"I am told your last exploit was a bombing raid on London."

"Yes, Führer."

"Have you considered what would happen if a senior Reich officer like yourself were to be shot down, especially after the whole Hess farce?"

"I carry cyanide on every mission, Führer. If I were to be shot down I would use it."

Hitler snorted derisively. "These missions must cease, Heydrich. I have plans for you. I could not afford for you to fall into enemy hands. They must cease immediately."

"Of course, Führer." Heydrich stood rigidly at attention. He was happy enough for the watching Himmler to believe he was receiving a reprimand.

"I am fifty-two years of age," Hitler said suddenly. "I need five more years to achieve all I set out to achieve. Not just the creation of a Reich paramount in Western Europe, but the destruction of Bolshevism, of the Jews and the reduction of Catholicism to the irrelevance it is. I shall then be ready to withdraw."

"Withdraw, Führer?"

"First and foremost, Heydrich, I am an artist, a creator, a builder."

"I know your plans for the opera house at Linz, Führer," Heydrich said warily.

Hitler waved his arm dismissively. Behind them Himmler and Gauleiter Wahl exchanged a glance.

"I plan to rebuild Europe, Heydrich. As I have reshaped it politically, I will now reshape it physically. My last years will be devoted to this immense artistic task."

Not for the first time Heydrich looked at the Austrian and wondered where the line was drawn between fanaticism and madness. He had no doubt that Europe would be reshaped within five years—and it was not impossible to imagine the razing and rebuilding of all Europe's principal cities in the decade after that. But then Heydrich was an artist himself, a concert standard violinist, and he knew a philistine when he saw one.

"While I re-create, Heydrich, I must be free of political care. The Reich will need a new Führer. . . ."

Heydrich stiffened. For the first time he realized that these were not the usual self-glorifying ramblings of a teahouse walk.

"Hess—yes, for many years I thought he might measure up to the part." Hitler shook his head. "And then Goering too—"

Heydrich stood without speaking. He knew too much of the mystery surrounding the Hess flight to Scotland to intrude on the Austrian's private grief.

"Of all the younger leaders"—Hitler fixed him with his remarkable eyes—"I see you as my only possible successor."

To Heydrich the words had the force of a physical blow. He had dreamed already, woven fantasy in many a drunken reverie. But this was no fantasy.

"Could you be ready within five years to be Führer of the German Reich?" Adolf Hitler had demanded.

He was halfway down the bottle of champagne and had just finished dressing when Lina Heydrich came in to present herself and the children for inspection. Heydrich always insisted his family be present, even though in the background, on these march-past shows of force, which he staged on every possible occasion.

He glanced at the two boys and then turned his attention to Lina. She was losing her looks fast now. Her broad hips may well have seemed a celebration of Nazi ideals of childbearing womanhood, but Heydrich's own preference ran to something considerably slimmer and younger.

"You wore that coat at the Veterans' Parade in September," he accused her.

"Once, two months ago. What do you expect me to do, throw it away?"

"You wore it once. All Prague saw it. Today they will be asking if the wife of the Reichsprotektor is too cheap to buy herself a new coat."

Lina shrugged angrily. She had read the police reports. All over Prague the meanness of the Reichsprotektor's wife was a standard joke.

"It's too late now." Heydrich poured himself another glass of champagne without offering her one. "We have to be on the rostrum in twenty minutes, Reinhard Heydrich and his fashion-plate wife."

With a clash of cymbals the parade moved off. Among his sweating adjutants, Colonel Ritter calmly watched the gray columns wheel into position, mark time and move on again. It was exactly midday as the band passed the Plague Tower and started down the Royal Mile to Hradčany.

Colonel Ritter could organize a parade but there was a limited amount he could do to command spectators. Along the length of the route only a few hundred Prague citizens stood desultorily behind the lines of Czech police. Thousands more watched silently from behind tavern windows or from the deep shadow of their own doorways.

Only around the saluting base at Hradčany Castle were there recognizable crowds, thickened by factory workers and school-children on compulsory attendance. Here Colonel Ritter had made an effort to create a festive air. The banners were thick on the surrounding buildings. Pipe bands played to entertain the waiting crowd, timber and tarpaulin stands dispensed *Wurst* and beer at giveaway prices.

Across the Vltava River in the Old Town, Jan Hopner had left his lodgings in Pork Lane as he heard the Wehrmacht band start from the Plague Tower along the Royal Mile. The pale sun gleamed on the slow-moving Vltava and the last copper leaves floated from the towpath trees to land lazily on the gray surface of the water. Jan Hopner, forty-three years old, was particularly pleased with the events of the last two years. As a Czech policeman he had spent his life cycling from village to village in the Tatra region, investigating innkeepers' complaints and registering the arrival of strangers in the area. Despite the wild talk in the taverns he had seen no one who might even remotely be a parachutist on a mission from the Czech government in London. He had once arrested an old drunk and got laughed at by his colleagues, and reprimanded by his police captain, for imagining that a sixty-four year old with an arthritic hip was likely to have made a parachute jump into the rugged Tatra foothills. But Jan Hopner was an ambitious man, and in Czechoslovakia at the beginning of 1939 there were ways for a tall, fair-haired Nordic to better himself.

He had been born and brought up in one of the many bilingual frontier villages. By applying for Germanization (his new forenames were Heinz Jakob) he now became eligible for an interpreter's post with the German administration in Prague. Eight months ago his zeal as a police interrogations interpreter had led to an appointment with Fleischner's Gestapo office at Hradčany. When General Heydrich became Reichsprotektor in September, it was natural that he should look to his own Gestapo for his personal interpreter, and Jan Hopner, now Heinz Jakob Hopner, had become an officer in the SS, entitled to the black dress uniform he now wore.

He walked confidently along the wide gravel path beside the river, although many would have said that it was rash to walk alone in an SS uniform in Prague even in daylight.

Today was different, however. He knew the Czechs. Today those who weren't compulsorily attending the parade would be off the streets, locking themselves in their own houses, or morosely drinking in the taverns. Tonight, for the return to his lodgings, he would of course change into the suit of civilian clothes he kept in his office at Hradčany.

He looked at the handsome Swiss watch Heydrich had given him on his SS appointment. It showed 12:05. By the time he had crossed the river and reached Hradčany by Zamecka Street and the two hundred steps it would be perhaps 12:40. He would not be required at the lunch reception until 1:30 at the earliest.

He trod the gravel path, careful to avoid the occasional puddle so as not to splash his shining black boots. There was, as he had predicted, not a soul about despite the declaration of a public holiday. Across the river the parade route ran parallel with his own and he could hear clearly the clash of cymbals and the blaring trumpets.

It was with a distinct *frisson* that he saw the girl sitting on the riverside bench fifty or sixty yards ahead. He stopped and took out a cigarette, although it was forbidden to smoke in a public thoroughfare in SS uniform. Lighting his cigarette, his eyes on the girl, he began to think that even at this distance she looked familiar. He walked forward quickly, his boots crunching on the gravel, but still the girl's head did not turn.

He was certain now: it was Dana Hassner from the interpreters' pool. He reached the bench and saluted. "Fräulein Hassner . . ."

She turned her head slowly toward him.

He pointed across the river to where the sounds of drums and trumpets were approaching Hradčany. "Aren't you on duty this afternoon?"

"Yes," she said flatly.

"Then should you not be . . . ?"

"On my way? Yes, Jan."

He recoiled not just at the familiar use of his Christian name, but more so of his Czech Christian name.

"Fräulein, my name is no longer Jan Hopner."

"No. More's the pity."

He was suddenly aware of movement first behind him, and then almost simultaneously from the bushes ahead. A small man stood before him with a flat length of plank. Hopner turned quickly, his hand fumbling for the pistol in his hip holster. A second man, bigger, with a thick stave of wood, took a quick step toward him. Hopner lifted his arm. It reached shoulder level as the heavy timber came down on it, snapping the bone. He screamed, and stumbled back. The other man stood with the length of board raised like an ax above his head. As Hopner stumbled helplessly toward him, the man brought the edge of the plank down on Hopner's shoulder with an executioner's force, shattering his collarbone. In his mortal terror Hopner realized, from the callous efficiency of the beating, that they intended to kill him.

He reeled backward toward the bigger man, mouthing animal grunts of fear. The thick stave clubbed him across the head and he went down on all fours, vomiting, squealing with the pain singing in his skull.

Even above his own screams he heard a man's voice say, "You'd better go, Dana. Any creature takes a long time to kill. Even one like this."

And the girl's voice responding, "I'd sooner stay. And watch."

Then the blows came thudding hollowly down across his back.

Jim Franklyn mounted the wide Pacassi Staircase in the midst of the foreign press group and was shown to a position at the far end of Hradčany's Great Hall. Behind him the long windows overlooked the stone statuary of the Matthias Gateway and the courtyard buildings decorated with the heraldry and emblems of Bohemia's past. In front of him, over the dark-suited shoulders of his press colleagues, he could see long tables laid with enormous carp and Czech hams. Along one wall dozens of bottles of French champagne stood in silver ice buckets, each elegant wrought-iron stand draped with white cloth. Young SS adjutants in black uniforms and white gloves politely instructed each category of guest to assemble in the order protocol demanded. Uniformed officers and civilians flowed from the wide staircase, hesitated, were brushed by others coming up the stairs, apologized, smiled and were directed to their positions by the SS adjutants. Today Czech and Slovak puppet government ministers were to be given pride of place with senior Wehrmacht officers near the head of the Pacassi Staircase at which the Reichsprotektor and his party would appear.

To Jim Franklyn the whole proceeding had a contrived, semi-regal air. When the fanfare of trumpets sounded, and Heydrich and his carefully spaced entourage began to climb the long staircase toward the Great Hall, Franklyn, with more bravado than he felt, whispered to a Swedish journalist beside him that all that was lacking now was for the whole assembly to drop to one knee.

At the top of the staircase the Protektor's party arranged itself in a semicircle, facing the most illustrious guests, and Heydrich delivered a brief speech of welcome, concluding with a Hitler salute rapidly executed to save anyone the embarrassment of response. Stepping quickly forward he began to shake hands with the Czech and Slovak ministers.

After several minutes at the head of the line of guests, Heydrich moved rapidly down past the police contingent and local government officers towards the foreign press and munitions factory managers, stopping occasionally to shake a hand or ask a question. His interpreters, the last an exceptionally pretty girl of about twenty, moved nimbly forward whenever they were needed, then faded as the Reichsprotektor moved on.

He was taller than Franklyn remembered, his long blond head fronted by a sharp beak nose. The narrow-set eyes did nothing for his good looks, but as he approached the foreign press group Franklyn saw how the chilling quality of his fixed stare could be dissipated by an easy laugh, or a joke that brought a nervous smile to his listener.

He stopped before Franklyn. His head rode back, his hand came up snapping his fingers. "Franklyn," said. "Herr Franklyn, the friendly American."

"I'm with the AAP wire service, sir," Franklyn said, trying to keep out of his voice the unctuousness he found he almost automatically felt.

"I'm surprised to see you in Prague. For most American correspondents the Protectorate seems to be considered something of a backwater."

"If it's true, I can't imagine why, sir."

"Why? Because the American press is not on the whole interested in positive reporting. A minor setback for the Reich or for National Socialism will command more column inches than the positive achievements of the Czech war industry. True? But your friend Hardenberg tells me you're something of an exception."

"I try and report what I see. Of course I'm not always shown everything."

"In wartime what else would you expect?" He seemed about to move away down the line, then he stopped and turned back to Franklyn. "Stay on for a few days in Prague, Mr. Franklyn. Then tell the American public what's really going on here."

The narrow eyes set close on either side of the beaked nose stared hard at him. Franklyn knew he had no choice but to accept.

"Thank you, General," he said. "I'd welcome the opportunity."

Heydrich nodded briefly and passed on toward the factory managers. From the body of the Protektor's party the Czech interpreter detached herself, her eyes resting on Franklyn for a moment as she moved up to Heydrich's shoulder, ready to relay his greeting to a Skoda works engineer or a Slovak production manager.

When the reception was over, lunch was served and bottles of champagne opened. Within an hour most of the guests were gorged and already a little drunk. By five o'clock the winter dusk was settling outside in the castle courtyard and in the Great Hall, and down the Pacassi Staircase huge chandeliers glittered over the guests. Jim Franklyn had already drunk the best part of a bottle of champagne, but the alcohol for once failed to relax him, and his anxiety about the case with Erikson's uniform and papers in it at the hotel only increased. The case was locked and the Gestapo would not willingly offend any neutral journalist by breaking open his suitcases, but a simple skeleton key would presumably do the trick. Franklyn shuddered at the thought. He looked at his watch for perhaps the tenth time in the last half hour. Just past five—another three hours before he would be able to get rid of the bag.

From behind him a hand grabbed his arm. He turned to see the Swedish journalist who had stood next to him at the reception, swaying dangerously before him, his face flushed below the smooth yellow hair.

"I don't feel well," the Swede said.

"I can believe that," Franklyn said. "You've had a snootful."

"You couldn't get a car to take me back to the hotel?"

Franklyn saw his opportunity. "Sure," he said to the Swede, "you're looking really bad. I'll find a car and take you back myself."

In late 1941 the city of Prague, yet to suffer from its first air attack, still imposed no more than a partial blackout on its citizens. On both sides of the river, the streetlights, at reduced gas pressure, threw an uncertain yellow light. Only Hradčany itself seemed to sparkle with the brilliance of the short-lived Czechoslovak Republic.

Across the greatest medieval bridge in Europe, the gas lanterns flickered on the walls of the watchtowers and gleamed through the narrow slits of the stone bastions overlooking the river. Constructed as a defensive approach to Hradčany Castle, the Charles Bridge was built by the architect Peter Parler six hundred years ago in the form of a double dogleg across the river to prevent the shot or arrows of attackers being fired across its whole length.

Before annexation and war came to Czechoslovakia, this arrangement was found ideal for couples seeking some privacy in the deep shadow of its bastions. But the German curfew had put an end to assignations, at least to the innocent assignations of prewar Prague. By 1941 the bridge at night saw only pairs of policemen as its sole legitimate traffic, or Wehrmacht military Police *Kübelwagen* rolling slowly across.

Jim Franklyn stood in the shadow of a statue of the King Charles who had commanded the bridge to be built, and drew on a cigarette cupped carefully in his hand. From where he stood he could see the lights in the castle on the other side of the Vltava. He moved the brown suitcase from hand to hand. If he were caught in the curfew he had decided to say he was out looking for a girl. But he would only be able to do that once he had handed over the case. He drew on his cigarette again and knelt to place the end carefully under his heel.

A man coughed in the shadow close by and his heart leaped and raced. He stood still, pressing a moist palm against the cold stone wall behind him.

"Mr. Franklyn," the man said, and a figure stepped forward under a gas lamp.

"František." Franklyn gave the name Stanhope had provided.

"František," the man said, to Franklyn's immense relief.

The man stepped forward. He was young, bareheaded and wearing an old Czech army coat from which the buttons had been cut. "I suggest we don't hang about here," he said.

"You bet," Franklyn agreed. "Here." He proffered the case.

The young man frowned. "My instructions are to take you to the meeting place."

"What?"

"Those are my instructions. The German officer Lindemann will be waiting for you."

"My God," Franklyn said. "There's a curfew on!"

The young Czech nodded grimly. "And if we are caught I'm the one who gets shot."

"Listen. If I'm caught with the goddamn case, the Gestapo isn't just going to drive me back to my hotel! How far is this meeting place?"

"Krasny in the Old Town, just across the river."

"You've got a car?"

The young Czech gave him a pitying look. "With a car we would be stopped and arrested in five minutes. Here." He wheeled a bicycle out of the shadows and turned to get another for himself. "If you hear a car approach, turn into the first courtyard or alley or whatever you can find. Only Germans drive in Prague at night."

Without speaking, they rode across the bridge and on through the ill-lit streets, sometimes carrying the bicycles down steep flights of stone steps, once lifting them over a closed railroad crossing.

To Franklyn it was a nightmare of apprehension.

The sound of car engines carried clearly through the silent, gaslit lanes of the Old Town. Twice he stopped in panic, ready to abandon the bicycle and throw himself into a dark doorway as a car approached. But each time the young Czech gestured him on, assuring him that the German curfew patrol was several streets away.

At Krasny they rode into a cobbled courtyard. Two brass gas lanterns revealed in their yellow light an outside wooden staircase rising to a platform above double stable doors.

They propped the bicycles against the wall and silently climbed the blackened wooden steps. On the timber platform above they paused outside a half-glazed door. First tapping out a pattern of knocks on the glass, the Czech took a key from his pocket and let them in.

A heavy curtain hung just inside. Closing the door behind Franklyn, the Czech swept the curtain aside and gestured him

forward. They were standing, Franklyn saw, on wooden plank-
ing above a line of stables. On the floor of the coach house
below, a man and a girl were looking up at them.

The young Czech led the way to a wall ladder and climbed
down, followed by Franklyn awkwardly clutching the brown
case.

As he turned from the ladder a tall, strongly built man in his
sixties, his blond hair balding, extended his hand. "My name is
František," he said. "Stefan you know already."

As Franklyn shook hands he looked past František to where
the woman came forward. In the light of the oil lamps he
recognized the blond Czech interpreter who had been at Hradčany.

"Did you enjoy the royal performance this afternoon, Mr.
Franklyn?"

"I enjoyed the champagne."

"This is my daughter Dana," František said. "I think she too
enjoyed the champagne this afternoon. Rather too much of
it."

The girl grimaced, sticking her tongue out at her father who
grinned back at her. Franklyn watched her, realizing with
astonishment that she was hardly more than eighteen years
old.

"No word from the German officer?" Stefan asked tensely,
the edge in his voice reminding Franklyn where he was.

František shook his head. "He's not due for another ten
minutes. You made good time from the Charles Bridge."

Stefan nodded. "All the patrols were over on the Malostranské side."

He looked at Franklyn with his thin-lipped smile of contempt, then turned to Dana, his manner changing. "What happened this afternoon?"

She shrugged. "When Jan Hopner didn't turn up they called
in someone from the interpreters' pool." She smiled. "It happened to be me."

"You worked for the Hangman himself?"

"All afternoon. Afterward the staff administrator, Captain

Hartmann, said Heydrich had commented on how well I'd stepped into the breech."

"What happened when they went looking for Hopner?"

"Uproar," she laughed delightedly. "They went to his lodgings and found the Sten gun and grenades. Captain Hartmann told me that he believed an attempt on the Reichsprotektor's life had been narrowly averted."

"They fell for it," František said. "They've already started a big search for Hopner."

Franklyn looked from one to another, trying to follow the conversation. "This Hopner," he asked, "where is he?"

Stefan picked up an oil lamp from the table and took Franklyn by the sleeve, turning him. "Jan Hopner's right here," he said, leading him forward.

Jim Franklyn stopped, recoiling in horror. In the light of the oil lamp held high, he could see the white naked body lying beside the wall in one of the shallow sluice channels in the cobbled floor, the left arm broken grotesquely, the blue-black bruises discoloring the chest and neck.

Franklyn dragged his sleeve from Stefan's grip. "You killed him! You killed a man to put Erikson's uniform on him!"

"He was a collaborator," Dana said from behind him. Her voice was as hard as stone. "A Czech who was proud to wear the uniform of the SS."

"Jesus." Franklyn turned, looking in the girl's beautiful, unrepentant face. "Jesus . . ." He was trembling. He felt almost as if he wanted to laugh. He quickly fumbled for a cigarette.

"It's war," František said. "Our instructions were to make the body look genuine. There was nothing we could get from the public morgue that looked like that."

He leaned forward and lit Franklyn's cigarette with a brass lighter. "Come and sit, Mr. Franklyn. We have some beer."

They moved away from the wall where the body lay, and the lamp was replaced on the table in the corner. František opened three bottles of Pilsner and handed one each to Stefan and Franklyn. The last one he kept for himself.

Dana raised her eyebrows.

"You've had enough for one day, my girl," František smiled.

"At least I can have one of Mr. Franklyn's American cigarettes." She reached out and took the pack from Franklyn's hand.

"Who will get Jan Hopner's job?" Stefan asked, perching on the edge of the table.

"As personal interpreter to Heydrich?" Dana blew inexpert smoke rings. "It will be a man, I expect. But"—she glanced at her father—"Captain Hartmann asked if I would do it temporarily."

"Even temporarily could be useful to us. An interpreter hears all sorts of juicy tidbits," Stefan said.

František nodded. "Yes, even temporarily it's a great opportunity."

Jim Franklyn saw the girl glance at her father again.

"There is, however," František said slowly, "a condition."

"What sort of condition?" Stefan slid from the edge of the table. He was facing Dana.

"I will be expected at the same time to share the Reichsprotektor's bed," she said without flinching.

"No!" Stefan's voice was a shout.

Her father remained silent.

"You must refuse," Stefan said furiously. "A Czech girl—you must refuse. Tell her, František."

"The choice must be Dana's," František said quietly. "Dana's alone."

She nodded. "I've already made my decision."

"I won't let you do it." Stefan grabbed her shoulders. "It's too horrible to think about."

Franklyn's head turned toward the dark corner where the body lay in the sluice.

"Mr. Franklyn's right," the girl said, following his glance. "This morning you beat a man to death. If that was justified—this must be."

Outside, a truck engine coughed and whined.

"That's him," František said, "the German." He took the Sten gun hanging over the back of his chair and slung it by its strap over his shoulder.

"Let him wait, the swine," Stefan snarled, shaking the girl. "You're not going to do it, you hear me?"

"Enough!" František pulled Stefan away from the girl. "You presume, Stefan. There is no betrothal between you. Let the German in."

For a moment the boy stood his ground. Then he turned and walked quickly to the coach-house door.

From where he stood, Franklyn could just see the shadowed figure of Stefan, his head bent toward the crack in the carriage doors as he talked in a low voice to someone on the other side. Then he heard the screech of metal as the heavy bolts were pulled back and an officer in German uniform stepped through the narrow gap opened by Stefan.

The officer stood motionless while Stefan reclosed and bolted the door, then the two men, one in his long, shabby, Czech army greatcoat, the other in the impeccable gray-green of a Wehrmacht officer, walked toward Franklyn and the other two standing in the lamplight.

The German halted. Grim-faced, he clicked his heels to Dana. "I was told to ask for František," he said.

The big man nodded. "I am František." He turned to Franklyn. "This is the American, Mr. Franklyn."

The German again clicked his heels, his manner infinitesimally more relaxed as he turned to Franklyn. "Captain Albert Lindemann," he said. "We are grateful to you, Mr. Franklyn."

"The uniform and papers are in the case." Franklyn took the brown leather valise from the table and handed it to Lindemann.

"And the body?"

"In the gutter," Stefan said harshly.

František picked up one of the lamps. "This way, Captain."

There was almost tangible hostility between them, between this officer of the occupying army and the leader of the resistance cell, even though they were obliged, momentarily, to be working together. With František leading, the small group crossed to the corner of the coach house.

"There he is." František held up the lamp. "Age about forty. Height one meter eighty-five. Blond hair."

Lindemann looked down at the corpse in the water sluice. "Who is he?" he asked coldly.

"Not one of yours," Stefan said. "One of ours, working for you."

"I see." Lindemann turned to Franklyn. "Perhaps you will help me?" he said in English. And kneeling beside the case on the cobbles he opened it and took out the uniform.

Franklyn eyed the corpse queasily. "Help you?"

"Get him dressed." Lindemann ripped buttons from the uniform jacket and rubbed the cloth across the cobbles.

František put the lamp on the floor beside the corpse. "You have no further need of us." He straightened up. "Good-bye, Mr. Franklyn."

Franklyn looked toward Dana. She inclined her head briefly, her eyes held his for a moment, and she turned to follow Stefan and her father.

Franklyn looked after them with a hollow sense of having been abandoned. Then as the door opened and closed again in the darkness, he turned back to where Lindemann was standing, a uniform shirt in his hand.

With sick revulsion Franklyn knelt beside the body and lifted the dead hand while the German pulled the shirt sleeve over it. Neither spoke as they worked, rolling the stiff, heavy body to get the jacket on, lifting and heaving the cold white flesh.

When they had finished almost half an hour later, they stood, breathing heavily, looking down at the fully dressed corpse.

"Thank you," Lindemann said. "Not a pleasant task." He took a silver flask from his pocket and handed it to Franklyn.

"What happens now?" the American said, unscrewing the cap and lifting the flask to his mouth.

"We drop the body in a side street somewhere. It will be found in the morning. There will be no close examination. I have already arranged that with the duty medical officer. Murdered by Czech terrorists; that will go down on the certificate."

Franklyn took a second mouthful of the brandy and handed the flask back to Lindemann. "You have some information for me," he said. "The information Colonel Erikson was trying to get to Rome."

The German screwed the cap slowly on the silver flask. "We don't know yet how far the colonel succeeded."

"What route did he take?"

"In Venice there is a certain Father Wenzler, an ex-German officer who became a priest after the last war. Colonel Erikson planned to hand the evidence to him. Father Wenzler had already agreed to make every possible effort to place the material before the pope himself."

"What was the material?"

Lindemann hesitated. Franklyn was aware of the officer's vast effort to overcome his reluctance to speak the words.

"Photographs, some documents; all from a concentration camp just outside Munich, a village called Dachau."

"How were the photographs obtained?"

"An SS girl, one of the camp guards. She wanted some sort of favor done in return. I don't know the details."

"But you do know who she is, or how Erikson contacted her?"

"She contacted the colonel. She came from Hochlingen apparently. At one time she had worked as a house servant for the Eriksons."

"You have her name?"

Lindemann shrugged.

"Jesus . . ."

"Countess Erikson will know immediately."

"Every time I go to Hochlingen increases the risk for her, for me, for all of you."

Lindemann nodded. "How long will you be in Prague?"

"Two or three days at the most."

"It will be enough. I will arrange that the colonel's so-called body will be buried the day after tomorrow. Czechoslovakia is technically a Wehrmacht home assignment. That means Countess Erikson has the right to attend the funeral."

Lindemann crossed the room and pulled open one of the carriage doors. Shivering in the blast of cold air, Franklyn could see the outline of a German army truck backed up with its tail flap down.

"A last service, Mr. Franklyn," the German said, indicating the body.

Almost inured to the horror of the corpse's bruised face and the staring eyes, Franklyn took the shoulders while Lindemann took the legs. Together, clumsily, the body half slipping from their grasp, they heaved it up over the tailgate into the back of the truck, and pulling the carriage door to, climbed up to stand over it.

On a signal from Lindemann the engine was started and the truck eased forward through the narrow courtyard archway into the street. Standing in the back, hanging onto metal struts for support, neither man spoke. Then after perhaps five minutes of jolting over cobbled streets and turning through twisting narrow lanes, Lindemann reached forward and with the heel of his boot rolled the body off the back of the truck.

It hit the road awkwardly, bounced half upright along behind the truck as it if were alive again and pursuing them, then subsided in the gutter.

After what he had done that evening Jim Franklyn knew he could claim to be a neutral no longer.

Chapter Four

He sat on the sofa with one hand around her waist, cupping her naked breast. In his other hand he held a glass of champagne.

Rigid in her humiliation, she tried not to look at the mirror in front of her, at the reflection of a fully dressed, uniformed man, one polished, booted leg thrown casually across his knee, and the tense, upright girl, herself, stripped to the waist.

"Hartmann told you I like pretty women?" Heydrich said.

"Yes, General."

He sighed. "My dear girl, I am not inviting you to call me by name. But I do not want to hear 'Yes, General' when we're in bed."

"No. I understand."

"And for Christ's sake, smile," he shouted, standing up abruptly. "Or get out."

She felt spilled champagne soak through her skirt. "I'm sorry," she said.

He stood looking down at her. "Or is this your first time?"

"I'm not very experienced," she said softly.

He walked across to the ice bucket and took the champagne

bottle by the neck. "I wouldn't hold that against you," he said.

He poured the champagne. "Stand up," he ordered, not looking at her. "Take your skirt off; it's wet."

She stood slowly and unhooked her skirt. He turned, watching her. As she stepped out of the skirt, he nodded. "Not very experienced, you say."

"No, sir—no."

"Good. And that was an attempt at least at a smile, unless I am mistaken."

"Yes."

"Walk about a bit," he said. "Relax."

She walked across the room and at the bed turned and stopped.

"To please a man, Dana," he said, "takes very little. We are all brutes at heart. Get into bed."

Franklyn saw Dana twice in the next two days, once briefly crossing the inner courtyard of Hrodčany and the second time while he waited in one of the castle anterooms for an interpreter to be assigned to him from the pool.

She had stopped, glancing along the corridor to make sure they were alone. "My father sends his greetings," she said. "He was sorry he had to leave you with the German swine."

"That German swine seems to me a brave and honorable man," he said.

She looked at him gravely. "I think you will learn soon enough that in this war there's no neutrality. There is black and there is white."

"And nobody has to ask you twice which is which?"

"No," she said, "nobody. But perhaps that's because we come from the Chodenland."

"That's part of Czechoslovakia?"

She smiled grimly. "It was."

"Near the German border?"

"Domadzlidze," she said. "But I suppose to you it means nothing, that name."

"I wish I could say it did."

"You've never been there—not even as a German-sponsored tourist?"

"No."

"Nine hundred years ago," she said, "Prince Bratislav settled a village of peasant farmers there. They were to be the guardians of the Bohemian hills, exempt from all taxes, freemen with the right to bear arms. Over the centuries the settlement grew to be a town, Domadzlidze. Then other villages were added, fourteen in all, to make up the Chodenland."

"Guardians of the hills you said. Against whom?"

"Against the Germans. Even then."

She had looked at him once more with that grave, penetrating look which had nothing to do with her smooth, unlined, eighteen-year-old's face. He liked her better, he decided, when she had laughed, sticking out her tongue at her father, until he remembered that even at that moment they had been standing not five yards from a naked corpse.

He found, above all, as they shook hands that he wanted to ask her if she had yet slept in Heydrich's bed, but he lacked the courage.

"After the war, Mr. Franklyn," she said, laughing suddenly, "you can take me to dinner in Paris. What's the best restaurant there? Maxim's?"

"The last time I was there," he said, "Göring dropped in for lunch."

"I would expect you to arrange that that didn't happen while we were dining together. Is it a date?"

"It's a date that might take some time to fix," he said. "Especially if there's to be absolutely no chance of Marshal Göring or any other of the party bigwigs being at the next table."

"We must all do our best to make it as soon as possible," Dana said, and turning away, she walked quickly down the corridor.

Tall cypresses lined the gravel paths between the mausoleums of the defunct Austro-Hungarian Empire. As the fusillade cracked out, reverberating off toward the city of Prague twenty kilometers distant, the crows rose from the trees, cawing in feigned alarm.

The coffin was lowered, the prayers for the dead were spoken by the Wehrmacht chaplain and the bugler sounded "The Last Post." The small group of officers surrounding the woman in the black veil drew back to allow her to the edge of the grave. After a few moments she turned away and, accompanied by Albert Lindemann, began to walk toward the parked staff cars that the army had provided for the mourners.

Countess Erikson stopped beside Jim Franklyn sheltering from the wind-driven snow flurries between a grim marble family tomb and a creaking cypress. To his astonishment he saw, as she lifted the veil, that she had been crying.

She smiled briefly. "Yes, what could be more stupid than to cry at a stranger's funeral? But the stranger had my husband's name. He was mourned by my husband's friends."

Franklyn was silent.

"What you did," she said slowly, "deserves all our thanks. Many officers would have died with Manfred if the Gestapo had discovered who he was. Many officers and friends—and myself too, no doubt."

"The gray sky released more snow, larger flakes chasing through the cypresses and settling among the tombs.

"The girl who worked for me, Lise Ruhl, is a young country girl. Not at all clever, and, as I remember her, not particularly pretty. Her father runs a small photographer's shop in Hochlingen, a minor Nazi official. He had Lise, and four sons; two of them are already dead and one reported missing in action on the Russian front. The remaining son, Karl-Heinz, is just eighteen. He is training with an SS replacement division somewhere in Germany. His mother is mortally afraid that he too will die or be lost on the Eastern front."

"Why are you telling me this?"

"Because we believe that the favor my husband was to do for Lise in return for the photographs of the Dachau concentration camp was the transfer of young Karl-Heinz to a quiet assignment in France."

Captain Lindemann nodded. "I found the transfer papers

when I went through Colonel Erikson's files. I removed them."

"So the favor was never done?"

Lindemann shook his head.

"It means," Countess Erikson said, "that we are in a position to get a new set of photographs from Lise."

"Blackmail?" Franklyn said.

"Blackmail—or complete the transfer, what does it matter?" she said urgently.

Suddenly Franklyn was reminded forcibly of Dana's commitment to her own cause. "This girl, Lise Ruhl," he asked, "is she still at Dachau?"

"Who knows? But if she is we must find her."

"We?"

She nodded sharply. "Yes, Mr. Franklyn."

Franklyn looked uncomfortably at Lindemann, then back at her. "Even as a neutral correspondent," he said, "I could get five years for inciting a German citizen to reveal restricted information. That's small stuff. With something like this I'd end up in the Englischer Garten with a piano wire around my neck."

"Too many lives have already been lost—too many more are in the balance. We desperately need you to get this information out of Germany. You can't desert us now," she said with finality.

Lindemann turned and walked a few paces away along the gravel path. The wind, soughing through the trees, cut into Franklyn's face.

She took off her veiled hat and shook her hair into the wind. "Well?" she said.

"For God's sake," he said, "we've all done enough."

She shook her head slowly, her eyes never leaving his face. "Believe me, you're wrong. There's so much more to do."

"My friends in Berlin who arranged this"—he gestured toward the grave—"they know about Fall-Ost."

"Then why aren't they doing anything about it—why doesn't the BBC talk about it?"

He realized he had trapped himself.

"You know why," she went on relentlessly. "Because they have no solid evidence. The sort of evidence this SS girl can give us."

He found he could no longer pretend, even to himself, that he was simply working on a story. He wanted to tell her that it was her struggle, not his—just as he had wanted to tell Dana. But the intensity of the two women's commitment seemed to block off that avenue of escape. "You want me to see this girl in Dachau?" he said.

"Yes."

"When?"

"As soon as we return to Germany."

"She's not going to give me anything."

"She will if I'm there too," she said. "I'll make sure of that."

Five years before Adolf Hitler became chancellor and Führer, the village of Dachau was a cluster of gabled houses, and a hotel or two, around the low-roofed railway station on the Hackenbrücke line from Munich's Hauptbahnhof. Then it was celebrated only for a monastery that had once existed there and for a short period in the nineteenth century when a number of Bavarian painters made it their home. Within two years of the Nazi seizure of power, however, the village of Dachau became celebrated, if that is the word for the grim notoriety it acquired, for another building and the works of other men. The Kz Lager, the first concentration camp in Germany, was the brainchild of "Papa" Eich whom Reinhard Heydrich had had released from an asylum, destroying the medical record describing him as a criminal psychotic, to put him in charge of the Kz Lager building program, of which the new Germany would soon find itself in desperate need. Heydrich knew how to choose a man for a job.

Thus the wall came to Dachau, running along the tiny main road just a kilometer or two outside the village, then cutting back into the flat fields to form an enormous, rectangular enclosed area. In 1934 the administration blocks were begun, and with them the long, single-story accommodation buildings.

Not long after that, the first groups of prisoners arrived, shuffling off the special trains at Dachau station to be marched under a guard of the Allgemeine SS to the grim, fortresslike structure outside the village.

From the early days the camp was heavily staffed and a small proportion of the guards were women, responsible for the minority contingent of female prisoners in transit or permanent detention at the camp.

Lise Ruhl had joined the SS, as her elder brothers had, on her eighteenth birthday, and had been assigned as an administrative assistant to the small, well-run concentration camp at Sachsenhausen, just outside Berlin. But her shorthand and typing had proved weak and her secretarial talents few. When volunteers for guard duties were invited for the growing Kz Lager in Bavaria, she submitted her name.

Over four years she had come to look upon the prisoners as something less than human. The political lecturers called them *Untermenschen*, subhumans; some, the Jews, even repulsive subhumans. To her they were all the same, the very old, stumbling and unctuous, the younger ones only respectful because it had been beaten into them. But her ration levels were high, even after war broke out, and since female guards were required to live off the camp, she had found herself a two-room apartment in Munich from which she conducted a quite satisfactory love life. Indeed the only sadness that the war had brought was the loss of her three elder brothers in Russia, a tragedy that had so reduced her mother in health that every leave now was spent quelling her compulsive tears, assuring her that somehow she would make sure the youngest, Karl-Heinz, would not go to the front.

Now walking through the camp barrier among the group of laughing, gray-uniformed girls, off duty until six the next morning, she consciously put aside the terrible risk she had taken to gain Karl-Heinz a home assignment. Instead she concentrated on her arrangement to meet a Scharführer from the camp in the Black Cat *Bierstube* in Schwabing at 8:30 that night—and on Scharführer Kelb's big reputation among the SS girls.

She walked through the arch of the cottagelike guardhouse,

oblivious to the irony of its painted slogan *Arbeit macht frei—* work makes us free. A woman was standing perhaps twenty yards away, at the corner of a small clutch of farm laborers' houses. But there was nothing unusual in that. Wives, sisters, mothers, constantly waited at the camp gates in the hope of a glimpse of their pajamed loved ones across the great square where *Appel*, the twice-daily ritual of roll call was performed. Mostly the unwanted visitors were chased away by the guard commander at the gate.

Lise began to cross the road to where the station truck picked up the girls. The woman was walking forward, quickening her pace now.

"Lise!" The sound of her own name stopped her dead. She forced herself to take a step forward. The other girls were a few yards ahead, some already climbing onto the back of the truck.

"Lise!" The familiar voice was at her shoulder.

She swung around. "My God, Countess, are you mad?"

"I've got to talk to you. My husband's dead. You yourself are in grave danger."

The girl's teeth bared like a frightened animal's.

"Where do you live? Munich?" Countess Erikson's sheer relentlessness drew a nod from her.

"Then meet me at the Konditorei at the Hauptbahnof as soon as you can get there. You might just be able to save yourself."

The laughter had stopped as the girl was hauled up into the truck by her friends.

"Lise," they chorused like eager schoolgirls, "hurry, we'll miss the train."

"I must go," she said.

"The Konditorei, in about half an hour."

The girl nodded and turned away.

"For your sake," Countess Erikson said as the girl ran forward to the truck.

The Konditorei was a section of the bigger station café, its prewar coffee-and-cakes status reflected in the high-back leatherette seats discreetly arranged around polished oak tables. From the main café, where lines of soldiers lined up for beer and *Wurst*, Franklyn could see the corner seat where Countess Erikson waited. Few people used the Konditorei at this time of the evening, although a few more prosperous civilians and officers preferred to drink their acorn coffee there to avoid the din and clatter of the main café.

When the heavy chromium bar of the glass door was pushed open by a girl in a gray uniform, Franklyn knew it had to be Lise. He waited a moment as she glanced along the line of tables, then, as she joined the countess in the corner seat, he left the café. Cowardice or prudence made him careful. He scanned the waiting businessmen as they stood reading newspapers waiting for their train. None of them seemed particularly interested in the door to the Konditorei.

He bought a *Münchener Abend* from the newsstand. From his visits to Hardenberg at Gestapo headquarters, he knew most of the agents by sight. But then again that meant they knew him. He opened the newspaper casually and across the top of the page took one last look. Then folding it quickly he entered the Konditorei.

A waitress was serving the countess and the girl coffee. He sat down with them, sliding into the farthest corner, and shook his head when the waitress asked to take his order.

When she had left, the countess turned to Lise. "This man is an American journalist. He has a great deal of influence, naturally, with the authorities in Munich. In particular he is closely acquainted with the Gestapo officer Hardenberg. You will have heard of him?"

The girl nodded sullenly.

"Good." She turned to Franklyn. "I have explained the position to Lise. She now knows my husband died before he was able to arrange her brother's transfer to a unit safely removed from the fighting. She also knows that you are anxious to acquire the sort of material that she gave my husband."

"I can't do it," the girl said. She drank her coffee, sniffling into the cup. "You don't know the risk."

"Is it a greater risk than young Karl-Heinz would be taking on the Eastern front?"

"I can't do it again." The girl wiped tears with the back of her hand.

"Our American friend needs your help." Countess Erikson's voice had a steely, threatening quality. "At the same time you'll be helping yourself, saving yourself."

The girl's head came up. "They don't know I gave the Herr Oberst those pictures," she said defiantly.

"Who else did my husband know who worked in Dachau camp? Unless we intervene"—she included Franklyn—"the Gestapo will be on to you in no time."

She was a country girl, but she was no fool. "You mean you'll tell them?" she snarled at the other woman.

Countess Erikson was silent.

"That's right, Lise," Franklyn said, "we'll tell them." He paused as the girl's head turned toward him, her eyes screwed up with hate. "We'll tell them," he went on, "unless you give me what you gave the colonel. Do that and you'll get away with it. And young Karl-Heinz will get his home assignment."

The girl turned slowly to Countess Erikson. "And I thought you were gentry," she spat.

They ate together that evening in a small workman's *Bierstube* near the Hauptbahnof.

"You're afraid," she said, sitting opposite him across the scarred wooden table.

He looked at the calm face framed by the chestnut hair. "You know I don't think I even know your name?"

"Christina," she said.

"Christina, yes," he repeated. "Well, you're goddamn right I'm afraid. I think anyone with half an ounce of sense, anyone who's seen that Gestapo Stone Room . . ." He stopped. "I'm sorry. I forgot."

The pain clouded her features, then cleared. "You're afraid that Lise will talk? That she hates us both enough to tell the police?"

"Maybe."

Christina shook her head. "She's trapped. I think she's got to meet you as she promised. I think you'll get your story."

"I think I'm crazy," he said. "You know, I chose to stay on in Germany because it was a good life. As a foreign correspondent, especially one who's willing to toe the line, you get the very best. The best drink, food, girls. You don't even have to work very hard. The news gets handed to you on a platter. It may be lukewarm when you get it, but all you have to do is hand it on to New York."

"You don't sound as if you like your job."

"Here in Germany, or in New York?"

She shrugged. "Either."

"Look," he said, "back home, just before I was offered this job in Munich, I reached a point—I don't know, I was nearly forty years old, I was still visiting morgues or drumming up stories from the local cops at the precinct house. You say I didn't like my job. Maybe. Or maybe I realized I wasn't really that good at it."

"What are you good at?"

"I was pretty good at boozing. I was even pretty good with the girls. But when this job in Munich came along, for a brief moment I thought I was on to something I could get more out of then wine, women and song."

"So what happened when you got here?"

"It happened before I got here. It happened on the boat coming over. A man introduced himself. He had a few home truths to tell me."

She frowned. "Home truths?"

"Oh, like that I'd been chosen for the job because only an overeager, near-washed-up, last-chance half-drunk like me would be willing to make all the compromises I was going to have to to keep this job."

"I still don't understand."

"Who did you think organized a body in Prague at the drop of a hat? Journalists?" he asked bitterly. "No!"

The large gray eyes looked at him evenly. "In the world we

inhabit, Mr. Franklyn," she said, "the kindest thing to tell one's friends is nothing. It's also the safest thing for you."

"The world *we* inhabit?" he said with alarm.

"Yes. This distortion of the German world I used to love. You too inhabit it now. By saving my life and the lives of my husband's brother-conspirators you've stepped clear out of limbo. For the part your friends in Berlin played in the arrangements, I'm far too grateful to want to know anything at all about them."

He nodded slowly. "What about tonight?" he said. "You can't risk a hotel."

"No. Guest lists are sent to the Gestapo every morning. My name would mean nothing to them, but they still might want to know why I had chosen to return from Prague to Berlin via Munich."

"You can stay at my place."

"Thank you," she said.

For a long time afterward Jim Franklyn wondered just what it was in Christina Erikson that brought out these extraordinary gentlemanly qualities in him. To answer that it was her own obviously aristocratic manner was, he felt, too simple. To answer even that it was her mature attractiveness wasn't it either. Perhaps the answer lay in some subtle flattery that emanated from her, not in words, but in her insistence on rejecting his view of himself, somehow recasting him into an arbitrarily different, more heroic mold.

They left the streetcar at Münchener Freiheit and walked beneath the blue-slit blackout lighting down Trautenwolfstrasse to his apartment.

The iron stove in the big hexagonal corner room glowed red. She took off her coat and looked around the lined walls. "You keep a lot of poetry," she said, running her fingers across the spines of the volumes. "And I thought you were a tough American extrovert."

"You're a poor judge of character," he said, "if that's how you saw me."

She pulled out a volume of French poetry. "You read French?"

"Not well enough," he said.

"Read me a poem." She gave him the book.

He took it and flipped through the pages, "Do you like Nerval?"

"I don't know."

"*Je suis le ténébreux,*" he read, "*le veuf, l'inconsolé. Le Prince D'Aquitaine à la tour abolie . . .*"

"What does that mean?"

He closed the book and slotted it back in its place. "I am the evening shadow, inconsolably womanless. The Prince of Aquitaine in the crumbling tower."

"Have you ever been married?" she asked after a moment.

"Twice," he said. "The first time I was eighteen. It lasted two months." He smiled at the recollection. "One morning I woke up and she was packing a suitcase. She said she'd met someone on the El, the elevated railway, and they were going to raise mushrooms together in French Lick, Indiana."

"Were you jealous?"

"Of French Lick, Indiana. Not very."

"Of the mushroom grower?"

"No. The way it worked out, six months later she sent me a box of mushrooms and a set of carbons, you know, copies of the divorce proceeding. I signed them 'The Prince d'Aquitaine,' as it happened. But nobody looked at signatures in Reno or wherever she'd done the deed."

"That was marriage number one. What happened to number two?"

"Out of that one I didn't even get a complimentary box of mushrooms. She was a model. Very beautiful, she kept telling me. But you can't polish a piece of Sèvres pottery for sixteen hours a day; in the end you hope it's going to speak to you. When it does, you find you prefer the silent, perfect glaze. Nothing, Countess," he said, "can come of nothing. We parted

111

as good friends. We even outlasted the first marriage by a month or two."

"You must call me Christina," she said. "When Americans are too formal they sound foolish. It has something to do with the rhythms of their otherwise very attractive way of speaking English."

He opened a bottle of brandy. "Very attractive way of speaking English hell!" he grinned. "It's the only way."

He poured two tumblers of brandy and they sat around the huge glowing stove.

"There are so many appalling things about a war," she said, sipping the brandy, "that it's worth remembering the few good things."

"What are they?"

She moved her long legs from the direct heat of the stove. "One is certainly that only in wartime would two people like us have reached the intimacy of sitting around a stove in your apartment, drinking brandy, after no more than two or three meetings."

He smiled. "That's just the Junker life you've led," he said. "In America you can get a hell of a lot more intimate than this after one meeting on the El. . . ."

"Only," she raised her glass, "if you're a very forward mushroom grower from French Lick, Indiana."

"I like you," he said, "very much."

"I like you."

"But I'm still not sure you've told me the whole story."

She got up and took the brandy bottle from the cupboard. Coming back to the stove she refilled his glass and then her own. "If I haven't told you the whole story it's because other people have to be protected."

"Friends of your husband?"

"Yes."

"Whatever they were planning to do with the Fall-Ost evidence, it was a hell of a lot more than what I could do with it as a journalist."

"Yes."

He drank a mouthful of brandy. "Things have changed some for James Franklyn in the last ten days."

"For the better?" she asked.

"For the better! Listen," he said, "I'm here sitting by a hot stove, drinking good brandy with a beautiful woman . . ."

"So . . . ?"

"All great. Except to get here I've deliberately withheld vital information from the Gestapo, I've become an accessory in the murder of a Czech collaborator, and I'm inciting an SS woman to provide state secrets."

"I suppose I should really do my best to make it all worthwhile."

He shook his head. "This is the first time I've ever turned down an offer from a woman."

She leaned over and kissed him gently on the lips. "Thank you," she said, "although if we ever do meet again I hope you won't find me quite so resistible."

The short, stocky figure in the workman's overalls dropped the brick into place and tamped it into position in its bed of cement. The wall was almost chest height now, the last course of bricks perfectly aligned along the guide string. Tomorrow, Winston Churchill decided, he would tackle the pointing, one of the most satisfying aspects, he found, of his wall-building hobby.

He bent down and washed the trowel in a bucket of cement-gray water.

"Prime Minister," the young man standing beside him said, trying to keep the impatience from his voice, "the American ambassador is due here now."

Churchill looked up. "I've not been wasting my time you know," he said. "That's a fine wall."

"Yes, sir."

"I can see you're unimpressed, young man. All right what does John Winant want to see me about so urgently?"

"The embassy gave no indication, sir. The message was simply a request to see you immediately."

Churchill looked across the top of the wall to where the late summer sun was falling across the lawns. At the main gates of the British prime minister's country house, a black car was drawing up.

"There's the ambassador now," Churchill said. "Run across and stop him. Tell Mr. Winant that the prime minister is anxious to show him his new wall."

The gleaming Packard with the U.S. fender flags drew away from the guardroom beside the iron gates and moved slowly down the drive. The young man cutting across the lawn waved it to a stop and bent down to speak to the passengers in the back.

Churchill wiped the wet trowel on a piece of cloth and, still carrying it, walked the length of the new wall as the tall figure of the American ambassador and his companion got out of the car and began to cross the lawn toward him.

John Winant had taken up his post at the Court of St. James's officially in February of that year when Joseph Kennedy had resigned. A Roosevelt man to his fingertips, Winant had done much to forge the new Anglo-American friendship which both Churchill and Roosevelt saw as the cornerstone of the Free World.

"You're just in time, Mr. Ambassador, to admire my new wall." He gestured proudly with the trowel.

"Very fine, Prime Minister," Winant said dismissively. He turned toward his companion. "This is Dr. Stanhope. He's in charge of our new intelligence service in Europe."

Churchill bobbed his head up and down. "Always enjoy talking to intelligence people," he said. "Chamberlain, y'know, thought they were ungentlemanly. Wouldn't talk to them. What's all this about, then, John?" he said, turning to the ambassador.

"It's about the Fall-Ost program, sir."

Churchill grunted. "Bad news? Let's go up to the house for tea."

They walked together, an Abbott and Costello pair, with Stanhope a pace behind.

"Dr. Stanhope has just returned from Germany."

The prime minister tossed the trowel into a wheelbarrow. "Go on."

Winant nodded to Stanhope.

"Our information suggests the Fall-Ost program is a fact. Starting with the Jews it envisages clearances in the East which could cost the lives of over thirty million people."

Churchill wiped his hands on the cloth he had used to clean the trowel and thrust it back into his overall pocket. "We're fighting the right war, John," he said to the ambassador. "It doesn't happen often to any nation."

"Our agent," Stanhope said, "believes confirmation of Fall-Ost will be in our hands within a matter of days."

"The president has been informed?"

"Yes, sir."

"Where does this information come from?"

"A dissident German officer. His object appears to have been to get the information to the Vatican," Stanhope said. "In fact he was intercepted by the Gestapo."

"So the Vatican never received the information?"

They reached the terrace and climbed the stone steps toward the French windows.

"The German officer was arrested somewhere on his way to Rome. We don't know whether or not his information was forwarded."

Churchill led the way into the library and rang the bell for tea. "Our propaganda did us a great disservice in the First War," he said somberly. "Everybody believed our lies. This time we must not make the mistake of denouncing the very real atrocities ourselves. Today there is only one independent moral force in Europe: the pope must denounce this evil."

He walked to an armchair and collapsed in it, puffing his cheeks.

"Signal your president, Mr. Ambassador. Let's form an Anglo-American front. I will send a signal to our ambassador to the Vatican today. He will be instructed to request the pope to condemn publicly this *res terribilis*, this awesome and appalling plan."

Chapter Five

At seven in the morning of December 7, His Holiness Pope Pius
XII began the day where he had ended the previous one, in his
private chapel, at prayer. His prayers this morning were for
special guidance. He had reason to believe that the decision he
most feared for the papacy was about to be forced upon him:
the choice between Nazi Germany and the ill-paired allies,
Great Britain and Soviet Russia.

Eugenio Pacelli, before his election to the papacy in the early
spring of 1939, had spent his life in Vatican diplomacy. He had
been deeply involved in peace movements as early as 1937. He
had struggled to avert the war which broke out in 1939. He had
offered mediation in 1940, before the German breakthrough in
France. These efforts were inspired not only by his deep love of
peace. Pius XII knew the fate of the Catholic Church was in his
hands in a more immediate sense than it had been in the hands
of any pope for several centuries.

In his prayers the pope reviewed his attitude to National
Socialism, and asked forgiveness for earlier errors. He knew
now that his youthful flirtation with the Nazi movement had

been misguided. He had been nuncio in Munich in those first days when the name of Adolf Hitler seemed to be more and more on anti-Communist lips. Seeking even then a right-wing bulwark to the spread of atheism from the East, Eugenio Pacelli had attended three Nazi party meetings in the year 1922. And his presence at least at one meeting, he had reason to believe, was recorded in the Munich police records.

If this youthful indiscretion came to light today it would totally shatter the papacy's carefully nourished reputation for ideological impartiality.

He had early recognized the hypnotically repetitive Austrian beer-hall orator for the force he was. But equally he had recognized that the new National Socialist German Workers' party was essentially anti-Catholic. Throughout the decade or more he had spent in Germany, Eugenio Cardinal Pacelli had watched the rise of Hitler with deep misgiving. Yet there was always, as there was with many genuinely conservative thinkers throughout Europe, that fatal ambivalence toward the Nazi Führer. Gross, crude and anti-Semitic as he was, he still offered the seductive compensation that he was anti-Bolshevik, that his state formed the one massive barrier to the spread of Russian atheism.

But all this was in the period of what was known in the Vatican diplomacy as the "white war." If the Vatican supported one side more than another, it was the Western Allies, Britain and France. But in June 1941 the nature of the conflict changed totally for the Holy See with Germany's attack on Russia. If the papacy was now forced to choose sides, an anti-Nazi view meant supporting atheist Communism, while a pro-Nazi view meant support for the brutal and essentially anti-Catholic policies of Adolf Hitler.

Yet even an Olympian impartiality was not without massive problems. In 1941 the Nazi government had demanded that the pope condemn the RAF's growing air war on German cities; Britain equally demanded a condemnation of the inhumanities of Nazism.

So far the pope's answer had been a diplomatic silence, or at best a muted response. As a Vatican diplomatist he had specialized, and still did, in political tightrope walking.

Essentially humane, the pope nevertheless lacked the imagination to be deeply and immediately fired by inhumanity. If his outlook appeared to lack fervor, it was because he looked on the world and its vile activities in the longest possible terms. Thus he saw the barbarism of Nazi Germany as a passing phase and the atheism of Soviet Russia as the real threat to the Church.

But now, with this report from Venice, it seemed impossible not to make a choice. It was true that the German officer, Colonel Erikson, had not reached Rome with actual evidence of this appalling Fall-Ost program. But the Venetian priest's report had been detailed enough. The evidence existed. Adolf Hitler, that mad and common dog, planned the annihilation of millions of people, first of Jews from Western Europe, then of Slavs to achieve his racial clearances in the East.

Pope Pius was in no doubt that this infamy cried out for public condemnation. But if Nazism were denounced by the Holy See would that not invite reprisal against the Catholic Church in Germany—and at the same time give succor to the Soviet atheists in the Kremlin?

At 8:20 the pope left the chapel and crossed his private apartments to the breakfast room. A fresh roll, butter, a large bowl of café au lait, was his invariable beginning to the day. Normally he would take breakfast alone, or at most with Stefanori, his valet, anxiously watching from his place beside the window. Stefanori was convinced that any man, even a pope, would fade away on so meager a diet.

But today a tall priest in a shabby soutane stood in Stefanori's usual place. Father Julius Dorsch's role in Vatican councils was envied by many more elevated Vatican figures than himself. He was firstly, of course, a German, and to many Italians in the Holy City the German influence, imported and encouraged by Pius XII, simply reflected the political predominance of Hitler's Germany over Mussolini's Italy in the world outside the Vatican boundaries.

Yet Father Dorsch was no Hitlerian. There were sympathiz-

119

ers enough among the priests of the Collegio dell'Anima, the German college; the faction was solidly united behind the Nazi Bishop Alois Hudal. But Father Dorsch was not one of them. Indeed Pope Pius used Father Dorsch's simple direct rejection of all National Socialism as a balance in the Vatican scales, a necessary balance when the anti-Bolsheviks pressed for the positive endorsement of Hitlerism.

Detaching himself from the shadow of the window hangings, Father Dorsch dropped to his knee and kissed the pope's ring.

"Have you taken breakfast?" the pope asked, raising him up.

"I have, Your Holiness."

"Then you will excuse me." The pope crossed to the birdcage at the window and opened the gilded gate. He stood back, watching with a smile as first one, then the second, canary hopped from the cage and flew across the room.

Together they settled on one of the heavy pieces of Germanic furniture which Pius had brought with him from Munich.

The pope sat at the breakfast table, immobile. Immediately the two canaries swooped down, hovering for a few minutes above the table, then landed on the white cloth, chirping as the long sallow hands began to break the bread roll.

He rolled a pellet of warm dough in his fingers, then gently leaning forward, dropped it in front of the birds. "Will the Soviets fall this year?" he asked Dorsch as the two birds pecked at the bread.

"Those military authorities I have spoken to, German as well as Italian, believe not, Your Holiness. They feel the Wehrmacht offensive was undertaken too late in the year. The snows are now upon them. If the German armies are to be victorious, most believe it will be as a result of next year's summer campaign, at the earliest."

So there was no escape that way. If Dorsch was right, and it seemed likely he was, no massive German victory was about to absolve him of the problem of choice between Nazi and Bolshevik.

He compressed another pellet of dough and sent it rolling across the table. The canaries hopped forward to where it had stopped short. The pope lifted his eyes from the two birds. "You have read the communication from Venice?"

"Yes, Your Holiness."

"The British ambassador and Mr. Myron Taylor, President Roosevelt's special representative, have asked for an audience this morning. They stressed the urgency of the matter." With a small, rounded fingernail he flicked crumbs across the white tablecloth to the two canaries. "They have asked to discuss the Erikson material. We therefore wish to explore with you what our attitude should be."

"Your Holiness knows my view," the old priest said. "The Church in Poland has begged the Holy See for a lead. Like the French bishops they need the word of the pope to act upon."

"I know your view," Pius said, "of the gross brutalities of the Third Reich. But the report from Venice stresses that Colonel Erikson's evidence, had it reached us, would show not just negligent ill-treatment, not even state-endorsed brutality; it speaks of a plan conceived to murder over thirty million people."

"Then all the more reason for the pope to denounce the evil," Father Dorsch said urgently.

"And at the same time the Royal Air Force terror bombing of German cities?"

"That, with a denunciation of the Luftwaffe bombing of Britain, I believe should be left to a later statement. This issue, this Fall-Ost program, is unique. I would go so far as to say that if the Church is to retain its moral position, my country's treatment of European Jewry must be publicly condemned. I speak frankly, Your Holiness."

Pius nodded. "I asked you to. Condemned, you say?"

"Yes."

"At whatever cost?"

"There could be no greater cost to the Church than to abandon its responsibility to act with moral courage."

The pope rose and the two canaries fluttered into the air.

Father Dorsch came forward and knelt, kissing the papal ring. Pius brought him to his feet. "The cost," the pope said slowly, "of antagonizing Nazi Germany might be the Catholic Church as we know it in Europe today."

"Then so be it," Dorsch said quietly. "In that case the Church will rise again, stronger, if anything, than before."

"Perhaps, but other false gods are afoot. They might well fill any vacuum Adolf Hitler creates for them."

When Father Dorsch retired, Pius waited for his next visitor. The canaries fluttered back to their cage, content with their brief hour's freedom.

The bells across Vatican City were tolling nine o'clock when Bishop Alois Hudal was shown in. Small, dark-browed, the bishop of Alea was known throughout the Church and the diplomatic corps for his outspokenly Nazi views. His commitment to the struggle against Bolshevism commended him to Pius, as did Hudal's admiration for Germany. His Nazi sympathies and belief in a rapprochement between God and Führer were not shared by Pius, but the pope saw him as a useful sounding board at this end of the political spectrum, as he did Father Dorsch at the other extreme.

Even while still a cardinal, it had been noted how carefully Eugenio Pacelli had chosen his advisers and how subtly he fed them with just that piece of information to which he required their reaction. By this means the whole equation remained in his hands only. Now, when the bishop had risen to his feet, the pope put the second, more alarming part of the equation the Venice report had presented him with.

"You have the report from Venice?" he said.

"And I am bound to say I consider it no more than a crude piece of Bolshevik propaganda."

"Suspend judgment, my son," the pope said. "Without that your counsel will be valueless."

The bishop inclined his head under the rebuke. He owed his bishopric to Pius; indeed, the ceremony of consecration had been at the then Cardinal Pacelli's own hands. He admired and loved this formidable figure, believing that the time must come when he would see National Socialism in its true historical light. He was still not by any means aware that Pius XII had long ago abandoned such illusions.

"The Anglo-American request for our denunciation of Fall-Ost," Pius said, revealing the other half of the equation, "is aimed at preparing the ground for a change of government in Berlin."

"Treachery?"

"I enjoin you to keep this as a supreme confidence," the pope said.

"Then I commit myself to do so."

"The new German government would plan to make an immediate request for the mediation of the Holy See."

"Peace? Between Britain and Germany."

"Between Britain and the Soviets on the one hand, and Germany on the other," Pius said weightily.

"Then the Church would be instrumental in perpetrating Soviet atheism," Hudal said excitedly. "How could that be?"

"How can it be avoided," Pius said, "if the belligerents ask for our mediation?"

"This change of government must be prevented, Holy Father. The Reich must be warned of this infamy planned against the Führer."

"And what if this infamy which the Führer plans—if Fall-Ost be true?"

Hudal was silent. "I am, as the Holy Father instructed," he said after a moment, "suspending judgment. But if Fall-Ost be partly true, if some must die as martyrs to the recovery of Russia for the Christian faith, then I believe—so be it."

So be it. The words of Father Dorsch.

When Hudal had withdrawn, Pius took the small padded elevator to the library which he used as a study. In his gold heelless slippers he paced the floor, his silk-faced soutane brushing softly across the deep-pile carpet. He knew he lacked the simple faith of a priest like Father Dorsch, a faith convinced that good could come only from good. Pius himself was not a subtle theologian. He was, however, an experienced diplomat.

His soutane brushing the carpet made the only sound in the library. He stopped. He had made at least the first decision. His counselors had presented two ways to engage the problems posed by Fall-Ost—they could be tackled by a saint or by a diplomat. On that fateful December morning, Pius XII decided to resist Father Dorsch's urgings and instead to resolve the moral and practical problems of the embattled Vatican in the way he knew best—by diplomacy, by negotiating skill.

At exactly five minutes to ten o'clock a British embassy Rolls-Royce and a Cadillac flying the pennant of the United States drew up at the Loggia di Rafaelo, the entrance for all, diplomats and private visitors alike, who had been granted an audience by the pope.

Officers of the Swiss Guard, in their brilliant parti-colored uniforms, opened the car doors and saluted as two black-coated men climbed out, each carrying in one hand a briefcase and in the other a silk hat.

Sir D'Arcy Osborne, the British ambassador, joined the U.S. president's special representative, Myron Taylor, and together they entered the Sala Clementina preceded by an officer of the guard. Reaching the far end of the long room they were approached by two red-coated Sedarie for their hats and coats and were conducted through further connecting rooms by the Palantine Guards. From the Bussolanti, the Janitors' Room, an apartment hung with Gobelin tapestries, they were escorted into the apartment of the Guardia Nobile. Across yards of flower-patterned carpet the duty officer, in white breeches and short jacket with gold facings, approached them. Myron Taylor took a quick look at his watch. It was one minute to ten.

A further door was opened and they were conducted into a room hung with rich red damask. Two ornate upright chairs faced a gold-leafed throne. As they entered, a door opposite opened, and Pius moved silently across the carpeted floor toward them.

The two diplomats sank in turn onto one knee and kissed the Apostle Peter's ring, the bloodred stone set in gold.

For some minutes the pope talked to Myron Taylor, asking him to convey his gratitude to President Roosevelt for the material aid, the food and the clothing the United States was providing for the distressed of Europe and for his more intangible but equally important interest in the cause of peace with justice.

The American special representative was not a career diplomat. His inclination was to make it clear that President Roosevelt's interest was not peace with justice so much as victory with justice. And the only just victory would involve the total defeat of Nazi Germany.

"I'm sure Your Holiness knows well the president's concern," Taylor contented himself with saying.

The dark eyes set in the gaunt, pale face moved toward the British ambassador. "Sir D'Arcy, you spoke of a matter of the most extreme urgency."

"I did, Your Holiness. It was in no way an exaggeration of His Majesty's government's concern. And indeed of the equal concern of the United States government." He looked toward Taylor who gave a crisp nod of confirmation.

"In these tragic days," Pius said, "there is so much of concern."

"No, sir," Taylor said sharply, "this is unique."

The pope inclined his head and indicated the chairs set before the sedia which he now took.

"Your Holiness," Sir D'Arcy Osborne said in deliberate tones, "Mr. Myron Taylor's government and my own have received a number of strong indications that the Nazi government is about to institute a complete change in its racial policies." Osborne paused. "A change of such enormity that only the term genocide could describe it."

The pope's eyes rested unblinkingly on Osborne. "This is a grave accusation," he said after a moment. "Does your government or the government of the United States have evidence of this new racial policy?"

Myron Taylor could contain himself no longer. "Strong indications. And we believe that you have too, Your Holiness," he said bluntly.

125

"The Vatican has recently received a certain report. It is being studied now."

"Does this mean the Holy See doubts the authenticity of the report?" Osborne asked.

"Not necessarily," Pius said. "It means it is still being evaluated."

Myron Taylor had a strong sense that the thin, astonishingly ascetic-looking figure opposite him was, in American terms, giving them the runaround.

"Our purpose this morning is to discover what will be the reaction of the Vatican if this report is found to be authentic," Taylor said firmly.

"That question must of course wait until we have established beyond doubt a situation to which the Holy See would need to react."

Taylor felt the frustration rise in him. "A condemnation by the Holy See of this barbaric plan would, President Roosevelt believes, make its full execution impossible."

The pope remained silent. Taylor was aware that he had overstepped some delicate diplomatic limit but he frankly did not care. More important to him was to return to Washington with some indication of the likely Vatican reaction.

"His Majesty's government are acutely aware of the unique position of influence the Holy See and Your Holiness in particular holds among many millions of Germans." Osborne struggled to repair the breach opening between Pius and Taylor.

"It is a position of immense responsibility," Pius conceded. "Our responsibility for the Church in Germany is always with us. As indeed is our responsibility to the Church as a whole."

The American representative was determined to bring the conversation back to the matter at hand. "On the subject of this report—let's call it frankly the Erikson report—does Your Holiness have an estimate of how long it will take to authenticate it? In other words, how long before we can expect a condemnatory statement?"

The pope studied him. He knew he had to avoid a commitment at this time. Diplomacy demanded it. "Mr. Taylor," he said at length, "perhaps your government is unaware that

Colonel Erikson was not acting alone. He was, in fact, the representative of a group of highly placed German officers who are, as Christians, rightly disturbed by this new departure."

"All the more reason to believe what Erikson had to say."

"These officers"—he spoke directly to Sir D'Arcy Osborne now—"were presenting the evidence for a special purpose. Their belief is that if the Holy See denounces Nazism, the Christian people of Germany will more readily appreciate the need to remove Adolf Hitler from power and then open the way to an immediate armistice between Germany on the one hand and Great Britain and Soviet Russia on the other. They ask that the Holy See should speak publicly only when their preparations for a change of government are complete."

Sir D'Arcy Osborne felt a quick tremor down his back. The Foreign Office had mentioned nothing and clearly knew nothing of a German request to the Vatican for mediation. "I have no specific instructions on the subject of His Majesty's government's attitude toward mediation," he said cautiously. "Although, of course, my government's general attitude is well known—that is that peace with a Hitler government is unacceptable."

Pius inclined his head. "But if the question of mediation arose, my understanding is that it would be between Great Britain and Russia and a post-Hitler government. In this question too, Mr. Ambassador, I am taking counsel."

"An armistice," Taylor said slowly, "would leave Germany as the strongest military power in the world."

"Yes."

"There would also be no guarantee that Nazism would not rise again—on another stab-in-the-back platform, perhaps," Sir D'Arcy said.

"Indeed," the pope agreed.

"But the Holy See would nevertheless offer mediation?"

"If all belligerent nations favored mediation, yes." It was the narrowest tightrope Pope Pius had ever trodden.

How far, Taylor asked himself, did this accord with Roosevelt's view of victory with justice?

"Gentlemen," Pius said, "I will ask you to communicate these

127

facts to your governments. An immediate public condemnation by the Holy See is possible. Its consequence could be the planned removal of Adolf Hitler from the German leadership. The new leaders of the German nation will ask for the mediation of the Holy See. We shall not refuse." He paused. "If that train of events is desirable to your governments, re-present to us your request for a public condemnation of Nazism."

"I have to remind Your Holiness that the government in Berlin is still a Hitler government," Taylor said firmly, "and that we have no idea how long it would take for these officers to engineer a successful coup. We have no idea, furthermore, whether they are capable of doing so. Surely what's needed is a public condemnation *now*. Within days these gas chambers may well be at work. As things stand, my government's view is that only you can delay or prevent this obscene operation."

The pope stood, brusquely signaling the end of the audience. "Take this message to President Roosevelt, Mr. Taylor. The responsibilities of the Holy See are to the Church and the world. We believe that an ill-considered denunciation of this most certainly gross and cruel project would nevertheless, *at this time*, completely fail to serve the cause of peace. The Holy See will mediate—but it is most reluctant to intervene."

Chapter Six

She arrived, as they had agreed, exactly at eight o'clock. He heard the footsteps descending the stone stairs and had swung around on the barstool when the curtain was pulled across. She stood there sullenly surveying the smoky, red-lit atmosphere.

He crossed quickly toward the door. "Look pleased to see me," he said wryly. "We're supposed to be on a date."

Without answering she began to unbutton her uniform greatcoat. He took it from her and hung it up.

"Let's sit in one of the alcoves. They're designed to be . . . more intimate."

She walked with him across the room, half a pace behind him.

"Are German women allowed in here?" she asked, sitting down.

"Sure. It's something to do with maintaining the journalists' morale."

"Prostitutes, you mean."

"No," he said, signaling to the waiter, "just girls who like to eat steak and drink good Scotch whisky from time to time."

"You have all that here?"

"Real coffee, French wine. What will you have?" he asked her as the waiter arrived.

"Coffee," she said.

"And a Scotch," he said to the waiter.

The music blared from the phonograph in the corner. Four or five couples, some of the girls in uniform, were already dancing.

"I didn't know such places existed," she said with distaste.

He nodded. "Yep—after the high moral tone of the Dachau camp all this must come as quite a shock."

"Why did you make me meet you here?"

"Because this is where I bring all my dates."

"SS women?"

"You're the first. And last."

Until the waiter returned she sat stonily watching the dancers and the correspondents crouched in the glass booths trying to make phone calls to their offices in Stockholm or Madrid.

"Well," he said when the waiter had gone, "what have you got for me?"

She sipped her coffee, pretending not to like it. "More or less what I got for the other one."

"The colonel?"

She nodded.

"Okay, let's have it."

"Come to my house."

Franklyn looked into her small dark eyes. Was it possible that she was setting him up? Was it possible that she had already made her own deal with the Gestapo?

They were about to stand when suddenly the blackout curtain at the entrance to the cellar was wrenched aside and a big, red-faced man stood swaying drunkenly, trying to focus through the haze of cigarette smoke.

Seeing Franklyn, Rudi Gerstheimer lurched at the table and steadied himself with one hand flat against the stone alcove wall. "I've just been to the briefing at the Ribbentrop," Gerstheimer slurred.

"Anything good, apart from the champagne?" Franklyn asked.

The girl stared up icily at Gerstheimer.

"Something's happened"—the Swiss wagged his finger— "something really big. I don't know what it is but big, big, big."

"You sure?"

"Sure. There were two people from Berlin. Flown down this morning and rushed from the airport straight to the briefing. Foreign Ministry. Very senior. Very, very senior."

"What did they say?"

By now the dancing had stopped and two or three other correspondents had drifted across to listen. Somebody turned off the music.

"What did they say? Nothing," Gerstheimer said triumphantly, glad of an audience. "Nothing at all. They got up there at the briefing table and shuffled all their papers. Old Blaskowitz, who was running the briefing, stood too and called for silence for an important development in the war situation. . . ."

The listeners, even the girl now, were hanging on every word.

"So go on," somebody urged in Swedish-accented German. "What happened?"

"What happened was that the door flew open and young Hardenberg from the Gestapo shot into the room like a bolt from a crossbow. When he discovered the briefing hadn't started, he pushed some piece of paper under the nose of the diplomats. And that was it."

"Gestapo orders not to make the announcement?" Joe Conway said. "The only goddamn briefing I haven't attended in eighteen months and something breaks."

"Or almost breaks," the Swede added.

"Did you get any sort of idea from Blaskowitz?" Franklyn asked.

Rudi Gerstheimer was sobering fast. "Naturally we all

grabbed him when the diplos left, but he hadn't been given any details. He thought maybe it was peace."

"You're kidding," Conway said.

"Well, maybe the opening of peace negotiations. Blaskowitz said whatever it is, America's involved. Maybe Roosevelt is mediating between Britain and Germany."

"I'll wire my office." Conway was already shouldering his way through the press of correspondents and girls.

"Don't waste your time trying," Gerstheimer called. "I just tried mine. There's a twelve-hour closedown on all *Ausland* communications."

Even the waiters had now joined the group around Franklyn, Gerstheimer and the girl. Unfamiliar with the significance of a communication closedown, they could still see from the somber faces of the correspondents that something important was happening.

"What made Blaskowitz so sure the U.S. was somehow involved?" Franklyn asked Gerstheimer.

"The old boy had been asked in advance to prepare a press kit on Roosevelt for distribution during the briefing."

Franklyn looked up at Conway. "What do you think, Joe?"

"I think Gerstheimer is half right."

"About the peace negotiations?"

Conway nodded. The journalists were concentrating on him alone now. "Peace"—he mumbled the wet butt of his cigar from one side of his mouth to the other—"could be. Either that or war."

The correspondents drifted across to the bar, ordering champagne and large whiskies to further their speculations.

The girl watched them go, then turned back to Franklyn. "If it's peace," she said, "you won't need anything from me."

"If it's peace," Franklyn said, "it'll be peace with Britain. Brother Karl-Heinz will still end up with his battalion on the Eastern front." He stood up. "Let's get the pictures."

Without looking back he walked across the room to the blackout curtain. Pulling it aside, he waited for her. Together they climbed the spiraling wooden steps to street level.

Passing the porter's cubicle they reached the blacked-out street. As they walked toward the Marienplatz a first air-raid siren began to wail somewhere near Münchener Freiheit and quickly spread across the city.

Before they had reached the Sieges Tor, the flak batteries in the Englischer Garten had opened up with the first ranging shots, and the hollow echoes of gunfire rolled terrifyingly through the narrow streets of Schwabing. Shrapnel clattered across rooftops and ricocheted off walls, the hot shards of metal hissing in the snow. They ran across the deserted Leopoldstrasse, heading for her apartment.

A viciously close rattle of shrapnel forced them to shelter under the stone gateway of the University Zoological Building. Peering up at the sky, Franklyn saw a huge white marker flare—a Christmas tree, the German flak gunners called them—floating down somewhere south of the Hauptbahnhof. In immediate response the rapid-firing flak units in the marshaling yards hurled cannon shells at the flare, scattering burning phosphorus across the sky. In the sinister dying white light they hurried through the side streets to Amalienstrasse and ducked under a stone arch into a dark courtyard. A faintly illuminated sign glowed beside an open doorway, with the single word Shelter. A dark figure stood just inside the doorway, smoking a pipe. As Franklyn and Lise entered, he greeted them with the Bavarian *"Grüss Gott"* and looked nervously toward the moonless sky. In a lull in the gunfire the engines of the main bomber force could be heard throbbing menacingly closer.

The man took his pipe from his mouth and placed it on a wooden shelf. "If you're using the shelter, Fräulein Ruhl, I shall have to have your friend's name." He picked up a clipboard with a pencil hanging from it on a string. "I have to have it for the TENO records," he explained apologetically to Franklyn.

TENO, Technische Nothilfe, were rescue engineers whose teams dug air-raid victims from their blitzed shelters, their trucks distinguishable by the broad white bands along their sides, their men, with an air of resigned callousness, neither kindly nor unkind. On his trips to the north, during raids on

Essen or Berlin, Franklyn had come to admire the tough devotion of these men. But equally, Franklyn knew, a copy of each night's list went straight to Gestapo headquarters to be fed into their enormous filing system. It was difficult to move anywhere in the Third Reich without the Gestapo knowing, or at least able to know, if it chose.

"We're going upstairs," Lise said shortly. "We won't be using the shelter."

"Ah . . ." The man again looked up at the sky. "If you really think so. . . . Of course it's against the law in a raid."

Lise led the way up the bare wooden staircase and stopped before an apartment door on the top floor. Handing Franklyn her flashlight, she fumbled for her keys in her leather shoulder bag while he directed the masked red light at the lock. The guns began again, shaking the old house with their hollow reverberations.

She opened the door and led the way into the apartment, checking the blackout curtains before she switched on the lights.

They were in a small attic room, furnished in a heavy Bavarian style. A massive oak hanging cupboard and a brass bed with a stained white linen cover occupied most of the room. Lise gestured bitterly. "Not like you have in New York," she said. "I have seen American films."

He shrugged. "Let's get out of here before the raid really starts."

She nodded and opened the oak cupboard. Like clothes on a washing line, four photographs were clipped to a string.

"You develop them yourself?" he said as she began to unclip the pictures.

"You think it better I took them to the corner shop?" she asked acidly. "In Hochlingen my father was a photographer. My brothers and I, when they were all alive, often printed his work."

The first photograph was a document. Without enlarging, it was impossible to read.

"What is it?" he said.

She looked at him sullenly. "It's what the colonel asked for," she snarled.

"So—what is it?"

"It's a general instruction sheet."

"What's that?"

"You have a GIS for every operation in a camp. So that the guards and staff know what is the work norm. It's a guidance sheet, for God's sake."

"What sort of work norm? What sort of guidance?"

"It sets out the capacities of the crematoria. Like any machinery you have to know what it's capable of. You have that in America, surely?"

"Not for crematoria."

He took the next photograph, another document. "And this?"

"It's another one the colonel asked for."

"What is it?"

"It gives reception targets. The number of prisoners the camp can take each month."

"Without getting full."

She glared at him. "Why waste your time on these people?" she said. "If you've seen them as I have . . ."

"No," he said, "I've only seen them in ordinary clothes, with a full head of hair, *outside* your filthy camps."

"Look at the other photographs," she said.

The third photograph showed construction work. Large concrete rooms, but too low for men to live in. A truck marked AB GROELTZ GH, MUNICH, occupied part of the foreground.

"Groeltz is the biggest oven manufacturer in Bavaria," she said.

"Ovens?"

"*Industrial* ovens," she said angrily.

"And this?" He had turned to the last picture. It showed prisoners bent over an open metal door.

"They're feeding the crematorium fires."

"The prisoners?" he asked incredulously.

"Of course," she said, puzzled at his lack of understanding.

Then his eye caught a detail in the corner of the grainy photograph. "Jesus Christ," he said. What he had at first taken for the rear wall of the building he now saw was a vast stack of bodies, the bare feet facing the working prisoners.

"How many people die a day in this place?"

She smiled, then jumped nervously as a stick of bombs seemed to scream across overhead to explode somewhere on the far side of the city.

"Any more?" he asked.

She hesitated, then reached under the oak cupboard. "You get nothing more until Karl-Heinz is transferred." She handed him a sheet of paper. It was a pale green swastika-headed page. It was headed, PRIORITY ONE SECRET.

GEHEIME REISACHE

To the Camp Commandant,
Kz Lager 1A, Dachau,
Wehrkreis V11, Munich

1. Until the current construction program is completed KZ Lager 1A, Dachau, will operate as a staging camp (for all but the aged and infirm) between West European collection points and Kz Lager at Auschwitz, Sobibor and Mauthausen. No ration indent will be made by Commisariat, Dachau, for in-transit prisoners since none is considered necessary. Equally, of course, none will be necessary for the aged and infirm.

2. A further reassessment of all camp guard personnel must now be carried out. Their record of National Socialist loyalty and absolute discretion must be stringently examined. The success of Fall-Ost stage one, the Final Solution of the Jewish problem, is now in the hands of the most junior member of the Allgemeine SS guard personnel.

Signed: R. Heydrich,
Obergruppenführer SS
RSHA, Albrechtstrasse,
Berlin

"Okay." Franklyn slipped the photographs into his pocket. "I'll do what I can. Who knows," he said grimly, "I may even be able to get him transferred to the Allgemeine SS at Dachau."

"You think you could?" she said eagerly.

Downstairs he heard men's voices and heavy footsteps coming up the wooden stairs.

She was staring at the door.

The heavy steps reached the top landing and almost immediately boots and shoulders split the woodwork of the door. The two men bursting into the attic room were big, dark-jowled, dressed in long brown leather coats. They had that confident, ruffianly air that Franklyn recognized in Gestapo lower ranks.

He knew he had been set up. "You lousy bitch." He struck out at the girl. A huge hand grabbed his shoulder and jerked him forward. "*Ausweis!*" The dark jaw jutted toward him.

The second man had almost simultaneously grabbed his other shoulder and was hauling him in the opposite direction. . . . Eight or ten times they pulled him this way and that, his arms jerking uncontrollably, like a rag doll. "*Papiere! Ausweis!*"

Franklyn had seen the technique before, with a French worker prisoner of war, caught without papers at an off limits *Bierstube*. And once with a Polish industrial forced laborer who had been getting too friendly with the patron's daughter. It aimed to dissuade its victims of the notion that reason, justice, common sense or decency had anything to do with the prisoner's relationship to his captors. It struck at the very roots of ten centuries of European social intercourse, and it was immensely effective.

Rolling on the board floor now, Franklyn dragged his papers from his inside pockets and hurled them fluttering toward one of the men. "I'm an American citizen," he gasped.

The German caught the papers in one hand and barely glancing at them, looked down at Franklyn, "On your feet!" he bawled.

The girl, white-faced, was standing near the bed, her eyes

fixed on him. But he was unable to interpret her expression. Certainly not one of triumph.

"Take him down," one of the men said to the other. "I'll take the statement from the Scharführer." He used the girl's SS rank scornfully.

It crossed Franklyn's mind as he was pushed out onto the landing that it wasn't a setup after all. That Lise Ruhl, pale and very definitely scared, was not part of whatever was happening. It had just occurred to him what her expression really was when she had looked down at him. It was imploring.

As he was bundled into the back of the car waiting in the courtyard below, the bombs were screaming down in long sticks across the city. Searchlights probed and crossed. Rapid-firing mobile guns thumped out cannon shells, and the heavy flak units threw eighty-eight-millimeter shells into preset box areas across the sky. At Gestapo headquarters he would be searched. The four photographs would be found and the beatings and kickings would begin. He knew Klaus von Hardenberg would have no power, even no wish, to intervene in this issue.

Yet there was some hope of getting rid of the photographs before the car reached the Marienplatz. A shower of incendiaries bouncing and leaping like fireflies across the rooftops fell spluttering and spitting phosphorus into the street ahead.

The driver yelled a warning as he swung the car into a screeching, half-turn halt.

"Holy Mother of God." The Gestapo agent beside Franklyn threw open the back door and began kicking away an incendiary rolling toward the open door. The driver was transfixed as the magnesium fell back on the road, creating innumerable small pools of blazing Tarmac around the car. This was his chance. Dragging the envelope from his back pocket Franklyn frantically turned the window handle on his side. It spun loosely in his hand.

"Take the Karl Wilhelmstrasse," the Gestapo man yelled to the driver. His eye caught the envelope in Franklyn's hand, then traveled quickly to the window handle. He snatched the envelope and shoved it into the side pocket of his leather coat.

As the car sped into a narrow alley he tapped the window on his side. "None of the rear window handles work in any of our cars"—he patted his coat pocket—"for just that reason."

The driver swung the car through the narrow streets, hurling Franklyn against the shoulder of the Gestapo man beside him in the backseat. After a few minutes they emerged in the Marienplatz and to Franklyn's surprise the car came to an immediate halt, still on the side of the square opposite the Gestapo headquarters.

Bundled from the car, Franklyn was pushed across the pavement into the lobby of what he had always believed was an unused cinema. The thought of the photographs in the Gestapo man's pocket brought him near to panic. He would never forget that image of Erikson as he stumbled up from the Stone Room and was pushed toward the staircase. He had heard that the star torturer was a tall, thin, lugubrious bachelor named Bodel, whose weekly wage supported a widowed sister and three unmarried nieces. Franklyn knew he would never have the courage to stand a beating from Bodel.

A heavy hand thrust him forward into the folds of a dusty velour curtain. Pushing it aside he stopped dead. His first impression was of a cinema audience awaiting the beginning of the feature. Row upon row of people sat silently in the dimly lit cinema, staring to the front. But the aisles were patrolled not by usherettes with flashlights but plainclothes SD men who, pointing their batons, commanded silence.

Franklyn was pushed toward an aisle seat and saw to his astonishment that Joe Conway was sitting just in front of him. He leaned forward. "What the hell's going on, Joe?"

He saw the faces of several other American correspondents he knew in the same row. Another, Carl Sanders, stood in front of a desk set up on the stage, behind which two plainclothes SD men shuffled papers.

Conway leaned backward without turning his head. "They've rounded up all the Americans," he said through the side of his mouth. "Japan attacked a U.S. Navy base in the Pacific this morning."

An SD man swung around menacingly and pointed his baton at Conway. Waiting until the SD man had passed out of earshot, Franklyn leaned forward. "Joe, is the U.S. at war with Germany then?"

Conway half turned and Franklyn saw for the first time that the side of his face was caked with dried blood. "There's no state of war yet," Conway said grimly, "but someone way up told the Gestapo there soon will be!"

Franklyn sat back stunned. So he had been arrested simply in a roundup of Americans, not because the Gestapo had somehow discovered his deal with Lise. And now they had the photographs.

Not for the first time he told himself he was not cut out for this business, that he was too easily scared, panicked into the wrong move. If he had kept hold of the photographs he could easily have slipped them under the tattered carpet at his feet where they'd be safe for the next fifty years.

Carl Sanders was leaving the table on the stage. Another name was called and a middle-aged American woman nervously got up from the front row, smiling ingratiatingly at the SD man who jabbed her shoulder with his baton.

Franklyn watched her mount the steps. From the back of the cinema the Gestapo man who had arrested him followed her up onto the stage. "Franklyn," he said to the man behind the desk. "F-R-A-N-K-L-Y-N. James—J-A-M-E-S."

The other man looked up a list, nodded, and without looking up extended his hand. The Gestapo man drew from his inside pocket a set of green papers which were taken and dropped into a box file. Then, almost as an afterthought, the Gestapo man thrust his hand into the side pocket of his leather coat and pulled out the envelope. He said something to the second agent behind the desk that Franklyn failed to catch. The man nodded, took the envelope and dropped it into the box file with Franklyn's ID papers and residence permit. It seemed safe, so far at least, to assume that the Gestapo man had not yet examined the contents of the envelope.

Two hours passed as names were called and American citizens, journalists, engineers, businessmen and a few vacationing families, nervously climbed the stage and were questioned, some briefly, some at length.

Franklyn's name was called after that of a Minneapolis professor, a senior member of the German-American Bund, as he kept trying to remind the two officers in his fluent German.

"Purpose of visit to Munich?" one of the officers snapped, indifferent to the claims of kith the professor was pleading now.

"I am here in Germany with my family on vacation," the American said. "My wife has aunts in Munich. . . ."

"Address?"

"But the real purpose of my visit is as a senior member of the . . ."

"Addresses of relatives in Munich?" The second officer was on his feet, bawling into the frightened face of the professor.

Meekly this time, he complied, was documented, pushed aside and Franklyn's name was called.

"James Franklyn, American journalist?"

"Yes."

"Franklyn—is that a Jewish name?"

"Not as far as I'm aware."

"The American press is controlled by Jews. It follows that most of its employees are Jews."

This was the sort of simplistic rubbish he never got from Hardenberg. "I'm not Jewish," he said flatly.

"A moment ago you were not sure."

"It was an American turn of phrase; I translated it clumsily into German."

"You were arrested at the apartment of a girl you had met at the Propaganda Ministry club this evening?"

"Yes. Lise Ruhl."

"Scharführer SS."

"Possibly. I'm not familiar with SS ranks."

"Did you tell her you were a Jew?"

"Of course not."

"Ah," the German said triumphantly.

141

The two Gestapo exchanged looks. But still neither of them had examined the photographs in the envelope.

"Scharführer Ruhl has made an interesting report on your conversation." The second officer was leafing through the papers on the desk. "She reports that you were using an acquaintance you claimed was a Gestapo officer to force her to spend the night with you," he said with disgust.

Franklyn stood before the desk without answering. His mind raced to cover the possibilities. Obviously the girl had said nothing about the photographs.

He was aware of the Americans in the front rows of seats watching intently. Even those who spoke little German realized he was in trouble. Whatever the effect on them he knew he had to play his ace. He could leave it no longer.

"The Gestapo officer referred to in the report is Brigadeführer von Hardenberg. If you two don't want to jump into a whole bag of trouble," he said colloquially, "you'll do a little checking before you utter one more word." He took a pack of cigarettes from his pocket and lit one. "You wouldn't be the first Gestapo bungler to end up in the Stone Room."

Perhaps it was the casually lit cigarette, more likely the reference to the interrogation cellar under the Gestapo's Rathaus headquarters. But neither officer was willing to take the risk.

After a moment's silence, one of them looked up from the papers before him. "Please go back to your seat, Mr. Franklyn," he said slowly. "We will make further inquiries."

As Jim Franklyn passed down the aisle only Joe Conway looked up at him. His face was still caked with blood. He shook his head in silent contempt.

Franklyn took an empty seat next to a woman with a four-year-old child sleeping on her lap. "We're Americans. They can't do anything to us, can they?"

One of the men patrolling the aisle turned at the sound of her voice. He had watched Franklyn's interrogation on the stage. No more anxious than his superiors to fall foul of a possible friend of the Brigadeführer, he turned away.

"You'll be okay," Franklyn said. "You've got nothing to worry about; there's been no declaration of war. You'll be home before the shooting starts."

"My husband is right at the back there. They won't let him be with us."

"He can have my seat in a few minutes," Franklyn assured her. "Don't worry, I'll fix it."

"You think you can?" she asked doubtfully.

He nodded, smiling, as the child woke briefly and looked up at him. He couldn't tell her that an internment camp looked the most likely possibility for all of them.

Hardenberg's aide arrived ten minutes later, a young man named Benning whom Jim Franklyn had met half a dozen times before. He was in the Hardenberg mold, intellectual, ambitious, a mile apart from the monosyllabic sadists who carried out the orders.

"My apologies, Herr Franklyn." He looked up at the two officers who had left their desk and were standing uneasily in the aisle.

Franklyn stood up. "This lady's husband is sitting at the back there." He gestured with his cigarette to the two officers. "Have them sit together."

"*Jawohl.*"

"And get my papers," Franklyn said. "I'm not leaving here without my personal property."

The two officers shifted uneasily, eyeing Benning.

Franklyn turned. "Do I get my property back or not?" he asked Hardenberg's aide.

"Of course." Benning gestured and the two officers, relieved of responsibility for the decision, turned quickly and mounted the stage.

Franklyn watched while his file was brought down to him. Taking the green papers and the envelope, he shoved them casually into his pocket.

Chapter Seven

It had been Munich's heaviest raid so far. The casualty lists would show a hundred ninety-seven dead and six hundred twenty-one seriously injured. They would also show what Churchill and the air staffs in Whitehall meant by total war. When in early 1943 the U.S. Eighth Air Force was to join in the air onslaught on Germany, even their commander was to recoil at the ruthlessness of the British civilian bombing strategy.

The raid was over by the time Jim Franklyn reached Klaus von Hardenberg's office. A silver tray with a bottle of schnapps and two glasses stood on the broad mahogany desk. Hardenberg smiled wryly as Benning showed Franklyn in and silently withdrew.

"My apologies," he said, pouring the schnapps. "I sent two men around to your apartment in Giselastrasse and by the time they caught up with your movements the gorillas had picked you up, I gather."

Franklyn took the schnapps, knocked it back and extended his glass for a refill.

"Help yourself, for God's sake." Hardenberg sat back in his chair. "You want to know the story?"

"If I'm allowed to."

"Why not? You know about the Japanese attack on a U.S. Pacific naval base."

"That's all I know."

"It was devastating. Two or three battleships sunk, cruisers, aircraft carriers . . ."

"And Berlin?"

"Berlin has ordered that all American citizens shall be detained and registered."

"That means they'll be declaring war."

Hardenberg nodded, taking up his schnapps for the first time. "Within a day or two, I'd guess."

"And what happens to the U.S. citizens here?" Franklyn asked.

"Frankly, I don't know yet. Internment probably, as far as the correspondents are concerned. Undersecretary Woermann in Berlin informs me that the orders are being made out. In Berlin only Mr. Guido Enderis of *The New York Times* will be exempted. Like yourself, Mr. Enderis has always tried to take a friendly view of National Socialism."

"I see."

The man behind the desk smiled. "As far as your own case is concerned, I have just spoken to my chief."

"Heydrich?"

"Obergruppenführer Heydrich to me," Hardenberg said easily. "He's here in Munich on other business. I asked for permission to treat you as a special case."

"For services rendered?"

"If you like. He was particularly pleased with the stories you did on your Prague visit. Anyway, he's agreed that I can offer an immediate flight to Berlin."

"To me?"

"From there you can catch the army mail plane to Paris. From Paris I can get you on a flight to Lisbon within twelve hours. By tomorrow evening you could be on the Pan Am Clipper somewhere over the Atlantic."

Franklyn lifted his glass. "When most people talk about the long arm of the Gestapo, they've never had it working *for* them. I appreciate it, thanks."

Hardenberg stood up. "If I were you I'd get back home and packed as soon as you can—before the Obergruppenführer changes his mind. He's in a very strange mood tonight—that much I understood on the phone."

He extended his hand.

"See you after the war," Franklyn said, shaking his hand.

"I doubt it, my friend," Hardenberg said. "This is going to be a war to the end. Both of us can't survive."

"You're talking poetically," Franklyn said.

Hardenberg shook his head. "No, I don't think so."

"So if only one of us is to survive—who will it be?"

Hardenberg rocked backward and forward on the heels of his polished boots. "After what happened at Pearl Harbor this morning," he said thoughtfully, "I'm no longer quite sure."

Reinhard Heydrich lifted the champagne bottle, saw it was empty and let it drop back into the bucket, crunching on its bed of ice.

"Get us some schnapps, Hardenberg." He spun in the office chair to face away from the other man.

Hardenberg lifted the telephone and ordered a bottle of schnapps to be sent up.

"How long have you been with me, Hardenberg?" Heydrich asked, his back still to his subordinate.

"Since thirty-five, sir. Since I left Brunswick SS School."

"Six Christmases," Heydrich mused. "The seventh just weeks away."

"Yes."

In the silence between them a discreet tap on the door brought Forster carrying a bottle of schnapps and two glasses. Hardenberg waved to him to leave them on the table. When the clerk had gone, Hardenberg leaned forward and took the bottle, examining the label before unscrewing the cap. "Real Russian vodka," he said.

Heydrich nodded without looking up.

Hardenberg filled two glasses and placed one in front of his chief. By now he was worried. He knew Heydrich's moods, the roué's promiscuous gaiety, the administrator's briskness, the sportsman's heartiness. This silent, ruminative Heydrich was the one who worried him most. In moods like this he would talk drunkenly about music for hours on end, or about friends, or loyalty, or the wretched meanness of his wife. And every single time it would end badly, with Heydrich drunkenly criticizing Hardenberg's Munich operation.

Even worse, tonight Hardenberg was well aware that the criticism was justified. The officer whom the SD had picked up in Venice had been allowed to kill himself. In Gestapo headquarters, with Heydrich present, a helpless prisoner had cheated them both.

Heydrich swung in the chair and reached for his vodka, drank it in one gulp and extended his glass for more. "Six Christmases," he said. "And if I were to ask you Hardenberg, about the seventh or eighth, what would you say?"

"I'm not sure I understand, General."

"Drink up, Hardenberg." He watched while Hardenberg emptied his glass and continued to watch until it was refilled. He was sober enough not to want to get drunk alone.

"Do you know where I was the day before yesterday, Hardenberg?"

"In Poland, you said, sir."

"Yes. At a camp called Maidanek and another called Sobibor. A few days before that I had inspected the complex at Auschwitz-Birkenau. By Christmas 1942, Hardenberg, these institutions will have arranged the disappearance of two, perhaps three million Jews. The disappearance—but not without trace."

Hardenberg remained silent. He had been at all the early

148

briefings during the summer. The Final Solution had lost its power to shock.

"Not without trace," Heydrich said, "because however effectively we disguise the camps, or burn the bodies and spread the ash across half a continent, we shall still be left. The perpetrators!"

Hardenberg sat up straight. He had made a mistake about Heydrich's mood. This new tack was far more menacing.

"But the orders for the Final Solution program come from the Reichsführer SS, and above him from the Führer himself," he said carefully.

Heydrich slopped vodka into his glass. "Only a fool would now think in terms of total victory," he said harshly.

The man opposite him was trembling with fear, at a loss to know whether he was being probed for treasonable complicity, or trapped into a traitor's corner. He had seen Heydrich at work too many times. There was no approach, childish, subtle, theatrical, even treasonable, he would not use to draw a victim.

"Three days ago the Russians, the *beaten* Russians, launched their winter offensive—a hundred infantry divisions and over a thousand tanks. For the first time in this war we are retreating. And tomorrow, or the day after perhaps, the Führer will declare war on the greatest industrial power in the world." Heydrich stood up and began to pace the room. "We won't lose this war by next Christmas, Hardenberg. Perhaps not even by the Christmas after. But what is now certain is that we *will* lose. Who but a *lunatic* could have massed against Germany the world's greatest navy, the world's greatest army and the world's greatest war factory?"

He sat down again, slowly spinning in his chair. "And when the dust settles over the ruins of Berlin, Munich, Hamburg and every other German city, the overseas Jews will come seeking their relatives. And we will be left, you and me, the organizers of the program, with no place on earth to escape to. For you and me, Hardenberg, the only choice will be between the Western bullet or the Russian piano wire."

Tears of self-pity filled his eyes.

"You're frightened, Hardenberg." He reached for the schnapps and drank from the bottle. "You're frightened because this talk is treason. But if you stop to think, treason could be our only chance."

Hardenberg poured schnapps for himself. He was going to have to get drunk enough to pretend tomorrow morning that he could remember nothing of this.

"The officer that hanged himself here, who was he, Hardenberg?"

"We still don't know, sir."

"Find out!" Heydrich hurled the bottle of schnapps across the room. It bounced off a chair back without breaking and rolled back across the carpet. Heydrich retrieved it and drank the last few drops, tipping the bottle to his lips.

"They planned to sell us, *me*, the whole Fall-Ost program for the honor of talking peace with the enemy."

"The information the officer carried on him seemed to suggest that, sir."

"Seemed to suggest that, sir," Heydrich said contemptuously. "Yes, it seemed to suggest that. And his passport and papers, false as we know they were, what did they seem to suggest?"

"Officially a visit to Venice and a few days' leave in Rome."

Heydrich nodded. "The British navy, the Russian army, the American war machine—and the moral authority of the pope in Rome. As a combination of forces, Hardenberg, it's unbeatable."

Hardenberg watched him, white-faced from drink and tension.

"This officer whom you allowed to hang himself—not for a moment do I imagine he was acting alone. We've had too many indications of disaffection in the general staff to believe that." He paused. "The rats are leaving the sinking ship, Hardenberg. The question is, are we going to allow ourselves to be left on board?"

* * *

It was almost dawn as Franklyn climbed the worn stone stairs spiraling up to his small, second-floor apartment. As always, whatever time of the day or night, old Herr Kohler's dachshund barked. As ever, old Herr Kohler himself appeared at the door in an ancient corded dressing gown, his worried face lined with insomnia. As ever his first words were spoken with relief. "Ah, it's you Herr Franklyn . . ." although as often as not it was Herr Franklyn and some girl he had picked up at the Goebbels. But Herr Kohler had a passion for news, real news, bred of long wakeful nights listening to the world's radio stations, illegally, of course. If Franklyn were alone Herr Kohler would always gesture him closer and with what was already known as the *Deutscher blick*, a nervous glance to be sure no one else was listening, would impart some piece of news picked up on Radio Moscow, or Radio Madrid, or best of all on the BBC. Perhaps in Munich, Herr Kohler was the only man who knew Franklyn for what he really was.

"The Japanese have attacked America," he whispered. "It means war with Germany too, almost certainly."

"I know."

"Poor Germany. . . ." Herr Kohler shook his head. "Poor Germany. . . ."

Franklyn felt, not for the first time, an overwhelming sense of sympathy for the old man, and more remotely perhaps, for all those Germans like him who risked their liberty and even their lives to maintain some sort of objectivity in the face of Dr. Goebbels' onslaught on their minds.

"Herr Franklyn"—Herr Kohler pulled him closer, one hand grasping his lapel—"you have a visitor." A faint lasciviousness touched his smile. "Obviously you gave her a key."

He misinterpreted Franklyn's quick glance up the curving stairwell. "I will not detain you." He released Franklyn's lapel and patted his arm. "Later, when you are free, you must tell me about tonight's air raid. The BBC will report the bombing of factories and railway lines in Munich. No mention of houses and schools. Only in this they are not to be trusted."

He disappeared behind the big gray door as quickly as he had come. For a moment Franklyn stood alone on the stone landing, a hand resting on the cast-iron banister. If Lise Ruhl had a key, it could only have been given to her by the Gestapo.

And in his pocket was the envelope with the Dachau photographs.

He let himself quietly into the apartment and moved cautiously down the long, narrow corridor to the turreted room. The door was ajar and he was aware of a fresh, clean fragrance, somewhere between soap and a very light eau de cologne. He pushed the door wide open.

A girl was sitting at his desk, her face in shadow. She got up quickly as he appeared at the door. Very tall, slender, blond, she faced him.

"Dana! What the hell are you going in Munich?"

"It wasn't difficult," she said grimly. "I asked him to bring me with him."

"Heydrich."

"He likes me." A shudder of revulsion passed through her.

"How did you get in?"

"If you work with the Gestapo long enough you soon learn the value of a piece of bent wire. I have a message for you from Mr. Sefton."

"He's still in Germany?"

"I don't know. Perhaps he got out in time. The message is three days old. This is the first opportunity I've had to get to Munich."

"If it's three days old," Franklyn said warily, "it won't take into account tonight's developments."

She shrugged. "Nevertheless . . ."

"Okay, what is it?"

"He wants you to go to Berlin."

"I'm going there anyway. On my way home."

"He wants you to see the Erikson widow."

"No chance," he said. "I've got a couple of hours in Berlin before I catch the Wehrmacht mail plane for Paris. Not enough time to get to her village."

"Those are your orders," she said. "You are to make contact with Colonel Erikson's officer colleagues. According to information received in London they wish to open negotiations for an armistice."

"I can't do it," he said. "It could take days—one day at least—and by that time the U.S. could be in this war."

"Mr. Sefton's message said it was absolutely vital."

"Screw Mr. Sefton's message." He hurried into the bedroom and dragged a case from the wall cupboard. Flinging it on the bed he banged the catches and the clip sprung open.

She came forward and stood in the doorway.

"You know what happened to me tonight," he said, hurling clothes into the case. "Tonight I was arrested, with photographs on me that would have sent me straight down to the Stone Room." He stopped and turned toward her. "I'm not like you, perhaps, Dana," he said. "I couldn't take forty-eight hours in that place with that sadist Bodel. I just couldn't take it."

She shrugged. "Nobody thinks so until they have to. My father, František, was arrested once. Before he escaped he was a week with them. He gave nothing away."

"I believe that," Franklyn said. He pushed a few last things into the case. "I'm not going to Hochlingen, Dana," he said, snapping the case shut. "I've got a Gestapo *laisser-aller*—that will get me through Berlin without any sort of search. So I'm going to take these photographs back to the States—and that's going to be the sum total of my irregular war effort. After that I become a straight war correspondent in uniform."

She shook her head. "No, Mr. Franklyn," she said.

"What do you mean, no?"

"Mr. Sefton also gave me a message from Dr. Stanhope."

"Stanhope—what did he have to say?"

"Dr. Stanhope said that without this final meeting with Countess Erikson, any work you had done so far would be of little use to him. You see, he anticipated your reluctance."

"Stanhope anticipated my reluctance, did he? Well, that takes him to the threshold of goddamn genius!"

"Perhaps I didn't make Dr. Stanhope's message clear," she

said gravely. "The doctor said that unless you went to Hoch-lingen you would be of no use to him."

"Sure, I got it." He grabbed the case by the handle and set it on the floor. "No use to him?" he said.

Suddenly he realized he was leaning over the case, one hand still grasping the handle, looking up at her. "He didn't mean that," he said. "I don't believe he meant that."

"Yes."

"The bastard will turn me over to the Gestapo if I don't do what he wants?"

"Yes."

"Jesus God." He sat down on the bed. "Jesus God!" He covered his face in his hands.

Chapter Eight

It was dawn. The bitter smell of sodden wood ash hung over Schwabing as Jim Franklyn left the Giselastrasse apartment and told the driver of the Gestapo car to take him to the airport. As they passed through Münchener Freiheit the teams of TENO men rode their white-banded trucks through the streets, too tired to do anything but stare grimly ahead. One or two small *Bierstuben* were already open; lines had begun to form for the early streetcars. A city was shaking itself awake still unaware that last night's raid was just a minor presage of the horrors to come.

At the airport Franklyn left the car. Carrying his cases through the checkpoint, he passed out onto the apron where three or four Junkers 52s stood in concrete bunkers next to the runways. A Luftwaffe clerk pointed him in the direction of a small group of officers, their luggage on the ground beside them, sheltering from the wind in the lee of the nearest bunker.

As he walked toward them the big radial engines of the

155

Junkers began to turn over, the chocks were pulled clear and the aircraft rolled forward onto the runway.

Franklyn joined the straggle of officers as they fought to hold their military caps on against the violence of the slipstream. An ancient reserve brigadier general with white mustaches complained bitterly about the absence of orderlies to carry the luggage. The others struggled doggedly on to where the Junkers had half wheeled to bring itself into takeoff position.

In the camouflage-brown corrugated side of the aircraft, a door swung open and a Luftwaffe lieutenant in black flying overalls let down a set of aluminum steps. The slipstream reinforced the wind driving the snow from the runway around the plane.

The officers struggled cursing up the steps, the old reserve general grumbled; behind them Jim Franklyn, the only civilian on the flight, thankfully ducked into the doorway and took one of the dozen wickerwork seats on either side of a narrow aisle. The lieutenant pulled up the steps and slammed the door. Inside the plane the noise of the engines dropped to something slightly more tolerable.

"Gentlemen," the lieutenant said, pulling on his fur-lined bomber jacket, "I'm afraid we're in for a very cold journey. We'll keep as low as we can, but cloud cover will probably force us up four or five thousand meters higher than is comfortable. Flying time about three hours thirty minutes. We should be in Berlin in time for lunch."

Ducking through the low door to the cockpit, he took up his position as copilot. The three engines roared, the plane bumped slowly forward, then awkwardly gathered speed.

Lifting above its own swirling snowstorm the Junkers wobbled into the air. From his position beside one of the small square windows, Jim Franklyn could see the Isar River and the Englischer Garten pass below. Then the plane banked, climbing strongly, and the city of Munich was obscured by thick gray clouds.

* * *

Christina Erikson sat in the high-vaulted anteroom of the War Ministry's Wilhelmstrasse offices, her fur coat wrapped around her against the cold blast of air from the swinging doors.

From where she sat she could see officers and secretaries passing up and down the marble balustraded staircase. But then she knew the building better than any casual visitor. She had first met her husband there eleven years ago when her brother had come down that same marble staircase and, under the portrait of Frederick the Great, stopped beside the tall captain. After they were introduced, Captain Manfred Erikson asked her to join him for lunch, and a car had been ordered to take them to the Adlon Hotel on the Unter den Linden.

That lunch had been the most excruciatingly painful two hours in her life. By the end of it she had completed a bizarre marriage contract with the sardonic captain, and when they had left the Adlon he had shaken hands, still addressing her as Fräulein von Brombach, and assured her that it was an honor to be of service.

In the taxi back to her aunt's Berlin home she had cried bitterly at the thought of all she was about to lose. But as the cab stopped outside the iron gates, she had pulled herself together and vowed that Captain Manfred Erikson would never regret his extraordinary act of friendship for her brother.

For six hundred years the Brombach family had played a leading part in the tempestuous politics of Germany's eastern marches. Estate owners and soldiers, the Brombachs had since the eighteen century produced three field marshals and almost a dozen generals. Not all had achieved great distinction, but such Junker families, with their rigid codes of honor and devotion to the military calling, had provided the backbone of the most consistently successful armies in Europe.

Count Helmut von Brombach, Christina's father, had had a typical Junker career, receiving his promotion to colonel in 1907, the year his son Karl was born. Later that year he had been assigned as an exchange instructor in the Vienna Staff College, and it was while he was absent from Germany that the

157

first rumors reached him of his wife's scandalous behavior in Berlin with the English Lord Connel. When she had announced that she was pregnant, Brombach believed he had no choice but to begin divorce proceedings. His wife had confessed her liaison with Connel but had sworn on the Bible she was not pregnant by him. The child was born and Helmut von Brombach dismissed his wife and child from his life.

Educated partly in southern Germany, and partly in England where her mother had made her home, Christina never knew her father. When he was killed on a military maneuver in 1930, she was twenty-one years old.

That year she met her brother for the first time.

She had stood before him at the Richtefelde officers ball while their aunt had presented them with frosty formality. "Lieutenant Count Karl von Brombach—Countess Christina von Brombach."

He was two years older than she, blond, lightly freckled and with no trace of the Brombach severity. He had asked her to dance with him and had led her onto the floor, while their aunt glowered angrily. For the rest of the evening they had exchanged stories of the twenty years they had not spent together.

They found it impossible to behave as brother and sister. They had no idea how a brother and sister should behave. When they met, secretly, the next day, they had kissed each other on the cheek. But to neither of them had it seemed like a kiss between brother and sister.

That summer the sheer weight of disapproval from the Brombach family forced their friendship on at an unnatural pace. One night walking back from a theater through the Tiergarten, Karl had turned her toward him and kissed her. Fully, on the lips.

It was a question her responsiveness answered. They told each other they were in love.

The idyll could not last. Within a month they talked of going away together, perhaps to make a home in England or America, where they would claim to be married and solemnly agree to have no children. Yet they both knew it was impossible, not only because he was heir to the Brombach estates and responsibilities, but because neither of them could live the lie for the rest of their lives.

They had decided to part after spending a weekend together in the Thüringer Wald. The hotel had been chosen because it was miles from any fashionable spa, indeed miles from anywhere where they might meet someone who would recognize them. As an additional precaution they had decided to register as an English couple touring in the area and to speak only English to each other in the lobby and dining room.

In all the fantasies of discovery they had both indulged, neither had included the autumn rains which had turned the Erfurt–Coburg road to dangerous slush. Neither had included the possibility of their aunt's best friend, the equally malicious Countess Agathe von dem Bach-Zelewski, insisting on interrupting her journey to friends in Bayreuth until the rains stopped.

She had seen Christina pass through the hotel lobby just as she was about to go in to dinner and had required her companion to ask the desk clerk to send a message up to Countess von Brombach's room, inviting Christina to join her.

The nervous figure of her companion had scuttled back minutes later saying that the Countess von Brombach appeared not to be staying in the hotel.

Agathe von dem Bach-Zelewski knew nonsense when she heard it. She marched up to the desk and pointed out that Countess von Brombach had just passed through the lobby.

The desk clerk had asked leave of the countess to suggest that she was mistaken. The lady who had just passed through the lobby was Mrs. Phillips, an English lady staying here with her husband.

Countess von dem Bach-Zelewski found she was trembling with excitement. "And the Englishman, Mr. Phillips," she inquired. "Was he tall, with fair hair?"

159

He was.

"His manner perhaps more like a German officer than an Englishman?"

He certainly spoke faultless German, the receptionist had agreed.

She stood there, her lips pressed firmly together. Should she stay and confront them with their infamy? But the truth was that she was slightly nervous of Christina, with her English-bred lack of respect for the older generation. Even cornered, the young girl might prove embarrassingly formidable.

She snapped her fingers and her companion hurried across the hall. Tell my chauffeur to get the car out again. We're leaving. We're returning to Berlin tonight."

Christina and Karl had also left the hotel that night. When the clerk had told them that Countess von dem Bach-Zelewski had been asking about Mrs. Phillips, they had both flushed red, looking at each other in appalled horror.

It was Christina who, biting back her tears, had given the clerk ten marks and asked him to tell them precisely what had happened. When they heard, they too had left for Berlin.

Their aunt the countess had summoned them the next evening. She sat, upright in a high-backed chair, her friend Agathe von dem Bach-Zelewski in a similar chair to her left.

Karl and Christina had been shown in and took the places their aunt coldly motioned them to.

They said nothing as they sat opposite the two old ladies and listened to their expressions of horror and disgust. They said nothing when they heard that Karl was no longer worthy to bear the responsibilities of the Brombach estates.

Her demand was simple. The price of her silence was that they should leave Germany and that her son Baldur should assume all responsibilities and privileges of the village and castle of Brombach and the lands and tenants of the estate. She saw it as the only possible solution to a situation which Berlin society and the army would find unspeakably revolting.

It was Karl who had answered first. He had said that if the problem was as his aunt was clearly suggesting, the fault would

lie more with the older generation of Brombachs, her generation, who had unnaturally and brutally separated him from his
sister since birth. But, that, in fact, was not the situation at all.
He spoke as the head of the family when he said he could not
condone Christina's visit to the hotel. But moral values had
changed since his aunt was young and neither Berlin society nor
the army would do more than go through the motions of con-
demning a young girl and her fiancé who, impetuously, sought
to anticipate the intimacies of marriage.

"Fiancé!" The old lady spat out in contempt.

"The Mr. Phillips," Christina said firmly, "quite obscenely
believed to be my brother by Countess von dem Bach-Zelewski
in her rumormongering account to you—was in fact my fiancé,
Hauptmann Manfred Erikson. Invitations to our marriage will
go out this week. Neither you nor your friend"—she glowered at
Agathe von dem Bach-Zelewski—"will be in the least surprised
not to be included on the list."

They had laughed and cried on leaving the house. Walking
through the Tiergarten she could think only of the incredible
gesture Karl's friend Erikson had made.

They had sat down on a bench and she had asked shyly about
him.

"He's an idealist, of course," Karl said. "He believes in the
bond between friends. You can see the extent he's prepared to
go. But he's also a political idealist. His hatred of Adolf Hitler
and the Nazi party goes so deep that he says that if they do gain
power it will be the duty of the army to restore the state."

"What does that mean?"

"For Manfred it means doing whatever's necessary. Assassination, a coup, the arrest of the Nazi leadership even if it means
civil war with the SA."

"But personally what sort of man?"

"To look at? Not unlike me, I suppose. In character, he's a
sardonic sort of fellow. He has promised you grounds for
divorce in six months."

They sat together on the bench and watched the snow sifting
under the lamps around the lake. Neither spoke the words but

they both knew their childhood was over. In the shock and shame and fear of the last twenty-four hours, they seemed to have become brother and sister again.

All this she had told Jim Franklyn sitting beside him that night in front of the stove in his apartment in Munich. It was the first time she had told anyone.

After six months she had declined his offer of grounds for divorce. It was not because she now loved him, but she found herself bound to him by respect. And as the grim prospect of a Nazi Germany increased throughout 1932 and became a reality the next year, she began to feel certain that people like herself were no longer entitled to a personal life. It had been savagely ripped from their Jewish friends. Writers and painters they knew were equally deprived of the right to work and as often followed the Jews into exile or imprisonment.

In this new world she had had two or three casual lovers but by choice she had remained married to Manfred Erikson.

And now that he was dead it was up to people like her and Karl to press forward with what he had started.

The British government was prepared to talk. It was obviously exploratory and she had learned enough from her husband to know that the road to peace was not an easy one. But she was certain that Karl would now agree to lead the officer group. And that she would be able to tell Franklyn at Tegel airport that a rendezvous with the British could be arranged.

Franklyn. She let her thoughts play on images of the American. He was as different from Manfred as any man could be. He swore and got drunk. Sometimes he openly admitted he was afraid. In a way she found that the most extraordinary difference between Franklyn and her husband and his friends. What sort of freedom is it that allows you to admit your fear?

She looked up and saw her brother coming down the great staircase. She stood up as he entered the anteroom.

"I was just thinking," she said, "of that first day when you and Manfred came down that staircase . . ."

"Don't think of the past," he said gently.

"I'm not," she said. "I'm thinking of the future."

Clambering down the Junkers' aluminum ladder, Franklyn stepped into deep snow. The wind blasted at his face. He followed the group of officers through the driving sleet toward the yellow twinkle of lights on the other side of the airfield. The old general complained bitterly that his boots were already soaked. The younger officers lifted the deep collars of their greatcoats to protect their faces and trudged silently on.

After a few minutes the lights took shape as windows in a low wooden hut. Somewhere to the left engines roared and spluttered into life and a Junkers 52, its three engines blasting snow behind it, appeared out of the gloom and gathered speed along a runway.

The leading officers reached the door of the hut and let themselves in. Franklyn and the old general arrived a few seconds later, thankfully pushing the door closed behind them, shutting out the growl of the wind and the driving flurries of snow.

In the administration hut, six or seven Luftwaffe clerks, fresh-faced boys in pale blue uniforms, sat behind typewriters at trestle table desks. The reception officer answered questions about flights to Brussels, Oslo and Omsk, dispensing vodka from a liter bottle and apologies for late arrivals, bad weather and uncertain hours of takeoff. When Franklyn reached the head of the line, the Luftwaffe officer barely glanced at his papers.

"The Paris mail flights." He consulted the wallboard with its colored chalk markings. "An hour's delay, Herr Franklyn. In this weather not bad."

"I have to go into the city," Franklyn said. "How long have I got?"

"If you want to be certain, you should be back here at say 0300 hours. No later."

"I want to be certain," Franklyn said. "May I leave my bag?"

The Luftwaffe officer indicated a pile of cases. "Your risk."

He thought of the photographs slipped into the lining. "My risk," Franklyn agreed.

Leaving the warmth of the hut by the far door, Franklyn was momentarily blinded by the swirling snow. He thrust his hands deep into the pockets of his topcoat and started toward the outline of a guard post set in the barbed-wire fence.

He could see her, hunched in a fur coat, long before he reached the post. She wore high boots and a Russian fur hat under which she had tucked her thick chestnut hair. He walked past the window of the post, where the guard waved him casually on from the stove-heated warmth, and stopped in front of her.

Neither spoke. Her face, pinched with cold, looked smaller and more vulnerable than he had imagined she could be. She slipped an arm through his.

"Over on the corner there's a café," she said with something between a shiver and a shrug.

"About up to Munich standards?"

She laughed. "We seem fated to dine in the very best places."

They crossed the road between the gray concrete apartment blocks and stopped before the steamy windows of a workmen's café.

"How much time do you have?" She paused with her hand on the door push.

"A couple of hours."

She nodded and pushed the door. "Not long," she said.

Not long. As if they were lovers with a world to explore before returning to husband or wife.

He followed her into the café. A few blue-jacketed workmen were hunched over their plates. A young sailor with a girl drank schnapps in a corner. Behind the bar a big man with one arm greeted them.

She sat down and peeled off her fur hat, letting the hair cascade from underneath. He took off his topcoat and dropped it across a chair. The big man was standing beside him.

164

"This is the weather for cognac," Franklyn said.

"Or plum brandy," the big man said with a smile.

Franklyn looked down at her. She nodded.

"Two," Franklyn said. "And some coffee."

He sat down opposite her, watching the melting snowflakes glistening on the dark fur of her coat.

"I didn't think I'd ever see you again," he said.

"The roads of war," she said, "are heavily traveled."

"It occurred to me a moment or two ago, when you took off your hat and your hair fell over your shoulders, that I might well be in love with you."

She laughed.

"That apart," he said, "are you hungry?"

"Only for *Wurst* and *Sauerkraut*."

"That's one hell of a piece of luck. I think that's the only thing they have on the menu here."

The one-armed *Viert* came from behind the bar, carrying the two glasses of plum brandy on a pewter tray. Franklyn took them and ordered sausage and *Sauerkraut*.

"I talked to Karl this morning," she said.

"Your brother."

She nodded. "I went to the Wilhelmstrasse. There were three officers there, one a colonel, the others, like Karl, are majors. They would be prepared to go to Switzerland any time representatives of the British and American governments specified." She paused. "They would be prepared to discuss a settlement based on the assassination of Adolf Hitler."

Franklyn felt his whole body twitch. He looked quickly across the room. The German workmen were eating happily. The young sailor was comforting his girl. The one-armed *Viert* was busy at the bar.

"They want to discuss terms based on . . . *that*."

"A provisional military government. After the assassination all leading Nazi party members will be imprisoned until they can be brought to trial by a representative government of the German people."

He looked at her for a long time.

165

"The British and Americans would not accept the proposal?"

He shook his head. "No, I wasn't thinking that. I was thinking I'm probably not in love with you after all."

She smiled her broad, almost Slavic smile. "Are you afraid again, Mr. Franklyn?"

"No," he smiled back at her, "this time I'm not just afraid. I'm scared out of my wits. Listen, I'm a journalist not a diplomat. A journalist, and not even a very good one."

"Take the message back to London. Tell them that before Christmas the negotiating committee could be in the Eden-Züricher Hotel in Berne. A BBC German-language broadcast can confirm or reject: the first thaw will come on the . . . and give the date. The message will be understood in the Wilhelmstrasse."

"And if London and Washington reject the negotiating terms?"

"Then have the BBC broadcast the message: there will be no thaw this year. That message too will be understood."

He nodded slowly. "If it were possible, would you come with me?"

The gray eyes looked into his. The broad mouth smiled gently. "You're so different from my husband I find I feel not the faintest tinge of guilt."

"Guilt? About what?"

"When we last met I wanted to go to bed with you."

He looked down and doodled with the tip of his forefinger in the steam condensing on the oilcloth covering on the table. "You loved your husband."

"Yes."

"And still do."

"Of course. But it's possible, you know, that it was a love for another time."

"What does that mean?"

"Each drumbeat sounded for ideas like honor, courage, faith. For a different world. His death proved that."

"But you could still think of going to bed with me?"

166

"Yes," she said slowly, "but this is a lesser time, and you won't be offended if I say perhaps you are a lesser man."

He shook his head. "You'd be some woman to live up to."

"Easy," she said, smiling. "Really easy."

The Paris mail plane was not designed for passenger comfort. Sitting opposite a pair of civilian engineers and between two Wehrmacht press officers, all on small, hard seats and among piled canvas bags of letters for the occupation army, Franklyn watched the winter sun go down. The darkness seemed to bring a further drop in temperature. Somewhere over Belgium even the dim blue interior lights were extinguished as they entered an area of British night fighter operations. They had been in the air nearly three hours now. At some point between Berlin and Paris, war might easily have been declared between Germany and the United States.

The landing at Le Bourget was a businesslike, single-approach performance with the runway lights flicked on for one minute and the Junkers again plunged in darkness as it taxied past the concrete control tower.

In Movement Control Center the officer glanced curiously at his papers and at the special Gestapo *Ausweis*. "There are some American diplomats in the waiting room," he said. "They're hoping for a Lisbon plane too." He paused, fingering the Gestapo *Ausweis*. "We could find another room for you to wait in."

"Just tell me when the next plane's due," Franklyn said angrily.

The officer smiled. "We have a diplomatic flight for Lisbon in a couple of hours."

"Fine. Now where's the waiting room."

The officer pointed. As Franklyn bent to pick up his bag, the German said, "Unless this ice gets worse."

"Ice?"

"On the runway. If it gets any worse I'll have to delay the aircraft until tomorrow morning."

Franklyn took his bag across to the waiting room and pushed open the door. Half a dozen weary faces turned expectantly

167

toward him. He chose an empty armchair between an unshaven young man in a crumpled suit and a woman of about fifty-five.

"Did they tell you when we might be taking off?" the woman asked anxiously.

"A couple of hours if the ice doesn't get worse," Franklyn said.

A middle-aged man took his pipe from his mouth. "They've been saying that all day."

"You're all diplomats?" Franklyn looked from one gray face to another.

"Consular staff," the pipe smoker said.

"The chargé d'affaires is staying on in Berlin," the woman said, "but he's advised all consular staff to leave."

"You mean he doesn't believe in Nazi fair play?"

The woman laughed with a touch of hysteria in her voice. "Does anybody?"

"After all," said the pipe smoker, "once the United States is in the war, who else do they have to worry about offending?"

They were called at five that morning. Clambering into the inevitable Junkers 52 they took off and headed south. Three hours later they refueled at Bordeaux, and as the late sun rose over the eastern horizon, they crossed the Pyrenees and flew steadily on toward neutral Lisbon.

"Well, sir," the pipe smoker in the cane-backed seat next to Franklyn said, "I guess that puts us over neutral territory."

He leaned across Franklyn toward the window and pointed with the stem of his pipe. "I'd say that was Saint-Jean-Pied-de-Port back there. And this coming up is Roncesvalles on the Spanish side. We'll be refueling in Madrid."

He leaned back in his seat but his position had changed. He had closed the gap between himself and Franklyn.

"You know the route," Franklyn said. "What chance of the Pan Am Clipper to New York today?"

"None at all for you, Mr. Franklyn," the pipe smoker said. His head was now a matter of inches from Franklyn's. The gray mustache was stained just above the lip with pipe smoke. The acrid tang of the heavy tobacco filled Franklyn's nostrils.

"Why not for me?" he asked frowning. "Have you all got seats reserved?"

"No"—the pipe smoker leaned even closer—"but I'm here to instruct you not to take the New York Clipper. Crossfield—his voice dropped to a whisper—"Norman C. Crossfield . . ."

Franklyn could hardly hear the words above the roaring engines.

". . . instructions to wait at Le Bourget to see if you caught the Lisbon flight. . . ."

"On whose instructions?"

"I understand a certain Dr. Robert P. Stanhope. But my orders come direct from the chargé d'affaires."

"Listen, Mr. Norman C. Crossfield. I am catching the first New York Clipper out of Lisbon today. Got it?"

As the aircraft lost height after the Pyrenees, the engine tone lowered.

"Mr. Franklyn, the United States is at war—with Japan if not yet with Germany. If you were to succeed in evading me, the only thing awaiting you in New York would be a long and uncomfortable prison sentence."

"Stanhope said that?"

The pipe smoker's face lost its amiability. "To hell with what Stanhope said or didn't say. Your duty is to obey my instructions. My duty is to make sure nobody gets to you while you're under my care."

"And how long will that be?" Franklyn asked savagely.

"Just as long as it takes to get you safely to London."

To old Karel Moravec the cemetery was a friendly place even on a winter evening; he had worked there for almost fifty years and knew the name and date on every crumbling headstone or marble monument. No fantasies of ghosts or open coffins disturbed him on his nightly walk from the toolshed across the cemetery to the main gate. Normally he would light a pipe at about the Vassny family monument and make it last all the way across to the main gates.

Tonight, stopping as usual in the planted glade of sycamores with the white marble statues of the young Zelenka-Hajskys staring sternly down at him, Karel lit his pipe. Then, about to resume his walk, he hesitated, almost certain he had heard a disconcertingly close sound from the direction of the old stone registry.

He listened and hearing nothing, was about to walk on when it came again, the clink of stone on steel. For the first time since he was a sixteen-year-old lad, Karel Moravec found himself afraid in his beloved cemetery. But as the noise came again, he had no doubt that what he was hearing was the sound of a shovel. The macabre image of a lone body snatcher at his grim work brought him up short. Gravediggers who let their imagination run away with them would soon find they could not bear to be alone after dark. Old Karel had seen it often.

He took a firm grip on himself. Drawing on his pipe he stepped quickly through the grove and followed the moss-covered gravel path into the center of the sprawling graveyard. The sounds increased. He could see a gleam of light ahead through the trees. He heard low voices and a man's laugh.

He knew where they were digging now. The German's grave. The one who was buried a few days ago: Manfred Erikson, Oberst, 1897–1941.

He began to move away. This German colonel had been assassinated by the resistance, and now somebody was digging up his body. It wasn't something Karel Moravec wanted to get mixed up with. Reaching the main gates by way of the cypress *Allee* that cut straight through the graveyard, Karel saw that a small black car was parked there. A man stood, hands deep in the pockets of his long coat. It needed no sixth sense to know he was Gestapo or SD.

The agent approached him. "Are you Moravec, the gravedigger?"

Karel nodded, although he would have preferred not to be known as the gravedigger. This year he had been appointed acting registrar.

"You see anything in the graveyard?" the man asked.

"Nothing untoward. Why?"

"Don't let it worry you. We're exhuming a body. Supposed to be the body of a Colonel Manfred Erikson. . . ."

"Buried last week. Victim of resistance terror." Moravec knew the phrases expected of him when he talked to the Gestapo.

"That's no doubt what it says on his headstone," the Gestapo man said. "It's even very possibly true. But the man in that oak box isn't Colonel Erikson."

"Who is he?"

"God knows," the agent said. "Let's have the keys."

Karel took out the keys. "My duty is to lock up every night."

The agent seized the bunch of keys from him. "Your duty is the same as any other Czech's duty—it's to do what he's told."

Karel took his bicycle from behind the stone gatepost and rode off toward his cottage at Lezaky. A few hundred meters from his house he stopped at the Dancing Bear Tavern and left his bicycle propped against the wall.

Inside a few old men sat playing skat. Karel crossed to the bar. "Can you get a message to František," Karel asked the man behind the bar.

"Urgent?"

"It could be. Tell him they're digging up that German colonel's body—4791B."

"What's that?"

"The number of the grave."

"So why should František be interested?"

Karel smiled, showing his big brown teeth. "If the story I heard is true, František put him there in the first place."

In the bitter wind gusting across London's Croydon Airport, Franklyn watched Greg Sefton's face crease in anguish as he slipped the photographs back into the brown envelope.

"Poor bastards," Sefton said softly. "Poor, poor bastards."

"You must have seen other evidence from other camps," Franklyn said.

"No photographs. Somehow statistics don't grab you by the throat in quite the same way."

They turned and walked toward the waiting staff car.

"What happens to this stuff now?" Franklyn asked.

"It joins all those statistics. It gets evaluated . . ."

"And filed?"

"Believe me, Jim, it won't be filed. Too many people, including you, have risked their lives to get us this information. But I tell you now there's no Pulitzer in it for you."

They got into the car. At the wheel Sefton glanced at Franklyn.

"You heard what I said, Jim; this stuff is way beyond the level of a newspaper story."

"Get the goddamn car started, Greg, before we freeze to death." Franklyn took out a pack of Chesterfields and tapped out two cigarettes.

Sefton shook his head. "I'm trying to give it up."

The engine started and the car began to move forward.

"I don't want to put you into deep shock," Franklyn said slowly, "but I don't give a damn about the Pulitzer, Greg. You're right about too many people risking their lives over there. I want those pictures to do what Christina Erikson and the others intended them to do."

Sefton raised his eyebrows. The car passed through the main gate. "You're on the road, Jim," he said.

For a few minutes they drove in silence, the faint headlight picking at the black tarmac ahead.

"Among the other evidence," Sefton said finally, "is an item from the Czech girl, František's daughter. She tells us that Heydrich has called a conference at Wannsee, in Berlin for just after Christmas. From the guest list we're pretty sure this is the beginning of the Final Solution proper. He's got administrators from the occupied countries coming, transportation specialists, camp commandants, the lot."

"Why are you telling me this, Greg?"

"I guess it's by way of assuring you that your pictures won't get lost in a government department file. But it's also probably the last time you and I are even going to mention this subject to each other."

The raid began as they drove through Battersea and crossed the Thames at Albert Bridge. Searchlights probed the banks of dark cloud vainly seeking an opening to the bombers above. From Battersea Park the 3.7 anti-aircraft guns opened up with their hollow, echoing reverberations.

Sefton grinned mirthlessly in the darkness of the car. "You'll find London," he said, "just like home. I mean Munich."

Chapter Nine

It was a raw morning. Almost an hour before sunrise four uniformed officers left the house of Karl von Brombach in the Berlin suburb of Dahlem and began to stow their luggage into the trunk of a staff car parked on the gravel drive.

The four men worked without speaking, their boots crunching softly on the gravel. When the cases were packed in the trunk, the four officers climbed into the car, closing the doors quietly behind them.

Karl von Brombach, at the wheel, rolled down the window and felt the cold, mist-laden air sting his nostrils. Starting the engine he drove forward slowly over the gravel. In the window mirror he could see that his wife Ulla had come to the door. Their small son, Kurt, in pajamas and bathrobe, stood next to her.

He reached the open gate between the tall yew hedges. A gray dawn was spreading slowly across Dahlem.

"You're off early this morning, Major." A voice spoke through the open window.

He braked the slowly moving car.

Herr Pfluger, the Brombachs' gardener, stood in the darkness beside the yew hedge.

"The army operates a twenty-four-hour clock; you know that, Pfluger, from the last war. Midmorning and midnight are all the same to the Wehrmacht. Incidentally," he added, "if you can cut out those brambles we shall be able to picnic by the stream again next summer."

"I'll do it today, sir."

"Karl"—one of the officers in the backseat leaned forward— "can't you leave your instructions until we get back? At this rate we won't make Nuremberg by nightfall."

Brombach waved good-bye to the gardener and turned the car into the narrow lane that led past the house.

"It wasn't just idle chatter, Jürgen." Brombach glanced at his friend's face in the mirror. "Old Pfluger is not just my gardener; he's also the Gestapo's local man."

"Christ, he's your blockwart?"

"Don't worry, he's seen me leave at every hour of the day or night. It won't even be worth a line in his daily report."

The car engine faded before the red rear lights disappeared at the end of the long lane. Pfluger took his hoe and hurried off in the opposite direction. A black VW was parked at the crossroads, its lights out.

Pfluger approached the car and tapped on the window. One of the sleeping men inside jerked awake.

"Herr Wirkner!" Pfluger bent as the window was rolled down. "Brombach and the other officers just left."

The driver switched on the engine.

"One of them said something about getting to Nuremberg before dark."

Wirkner nodded and let in the clutch.

"Don't forget to mention me in your report," Pfluger shouted after the car as it pulled away. "I'm not going to lose the best part of a night's sleep for nothing," the old man grumbled to himself as he trudged back toward the Brombachs' garden.

* * *

Christina switched on the bedside light. In the big farmhouse she felt for the first time totally alone, a nagging, recurrent loneliness that defeated sleep and made reading impossible.

Her worry about her brother and the other officers, now nearing the dangerous crossing of the Swiss border, was quite separate from the other ache. It was of course Manfred's death that had left this unfamiliar void. And yet she found constantly that her thoughts turned not toward her husband but toward the American.

It was almost six o'clock, still an hour or two before dawn. Yet she knew there was no point in trying to sleep. She got up and dressed. Going downstairs to the long, flagstoned kitchen, she lit the fire and put on the coffeepot. Switching on the radio, she tuned it to the BBC Overseas Service for the six o'clock news.

As the coffee bubbled on the stove, the BBC announced in flat, unemotional tones the sinking by Japanese naval air forces of two of the Royal Navy's most powerful capital ships, the *Repulse* and the *Prince of Wales*. The four-day-old Pacific war was going decisively in Japan's favor. Yet still, while their allies were embroiled in a life-and-death struggle against each other, Germany and the United States remained technically at peace.

"It had been announced by Berlin radio," the announcer continued with the second news item, "that Adolf Hitler will speak this afternoon from the Kroll Opera House Reichstag. At the same time the Italian leader will speak from the Palazzo Venezia."

She switched off the radio. She had no doubt that it meant a simultaneous declaration of war on America by Germany and Italy.

Heavy with loss of sleep, she poured coffee into a large breakfast cup. It was the usual acorn brew eked out with a few grains of Brazilian that a U-boat commander friend had given her husband almost six months ago. She sniffed it, hoping to separate the aroma of real coffee.

Somewhere on the Hochlingen road she could hear a motorcycle engine as it coughed and spluttered among the deep drifts which the night's fall of snow had brought. It was not an unusual sound, placed as they were between two Wehrmacht barracks on either side of the village, and when the noise died she carried her coffee to the plain deal kitchen table and sat down.

She sipped the hot coffee, grimacing at its bitterness. The old beamed kitchen, with its permanent faint aroma of woodsmoke and kerosene lamps, was warm now. The cat wove its slow, sinuous way between chair and table legs. The coffee gurgled in its pot on the stove. Yet amid all this familiarity, she was prey to a new feeling of loneliness.

A sound outside in the courtyard made her pause, the cup to her lips. She knew the noise of horses shifting in the stable, the dull clink of a hoof on the straw-covered flagstones. She listened. This was different—the crunch of a man's footsteps through the snow.

She got up quickly. The footsteps stopped outside the door. She crossed to the window and stood listening, but the heavy blackout curtain allowed only muffled sounds to penetrate.

"Who is it?" She called.

"Madame Countess?" The man's voice was familiar.

"Yes."

"This is Bahnhofmeister Frettner."

She pulled back the heavy bolts. A swirl of snow entered the kitchen.

"Come in, Herr Frettner." She slammed the door behind the old man. He stood there in a long overcoat, a gray woolen scarf wrapped around his head under his stationmaster's cap and knotted below his chin.

"Coffee, Herr Frettner?"

He shook his head. "Countess," he said formally, "I have some information which I believe you should have."

"Sit down, at least," she said.

He sat on the edge of a chair. "Countess, you are probably unaware that this is the only day of the week when the Berlin–Stuttgart express stops at Krevenden."

"No, I wasn't aware." She tried not to smile at his evident pride in the fact.

"Well, it was not for that reason that I was crossing the square to the station at something before five o'clock."

"To meet the train."

"To meet the train," he agreed. "So imagine my astonishment when I find myself caught in the headlights of an automobile which had just that moment turned onto the square."

"An army car," she said. "There aren't many others about these days."

"My own first thoughts," he said.

"But it wasn't an army car?"

"Two civilians. They were inquiring about the road to Hochlingen."

"Two civilians. Men, of course."

He nodded. "Men with a certain manner. Hitler's gentlemen."

"Gestapo."

The old man pursed his lips. "I informed them that as well as being Bahnhofmeister of Krevenden, I also occupied the position of mayor. I pointed out that Hochlingen came under the jurisdiction of Krevenden and that administrative courtesy required police forces to inform local authorities of their intentions."

"What did they say?"

"They care nothing for the proper ways of doing things," the old man said bitterly.

"They were coming here, to see me?"

"Yes. I sent them by the Beyerwald road. With the snow it will take them an hour at least." He stood up. "I must go now."

He turned for the door.

"Herr Frettner." He stopped with his hand on the latch. "You know that it's impossible to thank you," she said.

He stood for a moment, then shook his head. "Don't thank me, Countess. In these times we real Germans must stick together."

He opened the door and again the wind drove the snow across the flagstones until he slammed it closed.

She stood listening to the dull crunch of his receding footsteps, watching the fat snowflakes melt on the worn flags. When the sound of Herr Frettner's motorcycle died away on the forest road, she crossed to the stove and poured the ersatz down the drain. Then, using all the remaining Brazilian coffee, she made a new pot and sat down in its comforting aromas to await the men's arrival.

By early afternoon the green staff car was high in the mountains following the winding roads through the villages along the western edge of Lake Constance. The four men, now changed into civilian clothes, spoke little. In any circumstances a winter journey through this area of sudden snowfalls and treacherously enveloping mists was hazardous enough; but they all carried additional fears, not just for his own life if arrested, but for the lives of his family back in Berlin. The principle of *Siblinghaft*, guilt by family association, was an all-too-well-known element of the Nazi Peoples' Courts. None of them could ignore the appalling risk to which he was subjecting his family.

For the fifth or sixth time since midday, the clouds swirled down from the peaks, blanketing the road. Karl von Brombach slowed to a few kilometers an hour, leaning over the wheel as he peered out to where the headlights probed the wall of mist.

In the passenger seat Colonel Jürgen Delbruck was working from the map and odometer. He turned to Brombach. "You should see the frontier post lights any time now."

Brombach took a deep breath and nodded, his eyes never leaving the few meters of snow-covered road between car and mist.

In the backseat one of the officers opened his briefcase and again examined their visas.

The other officer took out a large cigar and lit it. "Well," he said defensively, "if we're supposed to be four staff officers who've fixed a silk stocking and brandy trip to Switzerland, we might as well look as if we enjoy the life."

"There it is," said Brombach.

The other three looked up. A row of what appeared to be fairy lights sparkled in the mist ahead. Brombach slowed the car to walking pace.

As they came closer they could make out clearly the two wooden huts on either side of the road linked by a red-and-white-banded pole. A string of bare electric bulbs swung between the buildings. Beneath the lights they could make out a frontier guard, his rifle slung, coming toward the car.

"Everything as it should be," Jürgen Delbruck said.

"Holy Mother of God." One of the officers in the back was staring out of the side window. "Look!"

Brombach braked. Six or eight men were sliding down the hillside toward them. On the other side of the road, a powerful fog light swept down on the car.

"Make a run for it, Karl!" Delbruck shouted.

Brombach thrust the gear into reverse and let the car hurtle blindly backward into the mist. The fog light followed and seconds later a fusillade of shots.

Delbruck switched off the car lights. "Pistol fire," he said. "We're out of range."

In the pale gray mist, Brombach swung the car to face back down the mountainside. Behind they could hear a powerful engine. The fog light seemed to race down the mountainside. As Brombach gunned the staff car forward, he guessed the vehicle behind was a half-track. With more engine power and more visibility it would be up beside them in a matter of moments.

He accelerated recklessly. The chains bit into the snow. "Get ready to jump for it!" he yelled at the others. He remembered that the road bent to the left. On the downward slope they were still just keeping ahead. Where the road turned left he swung the wheel to the right and the staff car skidded violently down the hillside, bouncing off young fir trees, being ripped and torn by snow-covered rocks until it slowed to a stop.

The four men leaped out, running in pairs into the mist. The fog light picked out two running figures, and a short burst of machine-gun fire brought them down. Then the powerful

181

engine roared, and with its light probing the mist, the half-track came fast down the hillside.

Karl von Brombach knew they had no chance at all. Jürgen Delbruck came to the same decision at the same instant. They slowed to a stop.

"I'm sorry, Jürgen," Brombach said as the half-track clattered toward them.

"Somebody else will try," Delbruck said. "It's too good a cause to let go now."

In the village of Kussel, the men had gathered in the Café Letterhaus, the only place with an aerial high enough to guarantee reasonable reception in midwinter.

About thirty men sat at the long wooden tables with mugs of beer in front of them. The Führer was to speak from the Kroll Opera House, which had been the official Reichstag building since the great fire. The radio played martial music, the old and beautiful marching songs of the Kaiser's army to which many of these men had belonged. Now they tapped out the tunes with their gnarled fingers or muttered the words almost under their breath. Nobody bothered to speculate on what the Führer's speech might contain. They were used to waiting, for the coming of spring, or new orders from Berlin. Lighting round-bowled pipes they puffed and tapped and hummed and waited.

When the door burst open every man in the village looked up in astonishment. Two tall civilians in expensive tweeds were brought in by a group of leather-coated men carrying pistols. Then the bodies of two more men, their tweed suits blood-stained and soaked with melting snow, were dragged by their heels.

The villagers watched in shocked silence. The martial music was coming to an end. The leader of the men in leather coats demanded the telephone and was shown the ancient wall instrument next to the bar. Beneath the last crash of cymbals they heard him ask for Gestapo, Prinz Albrechtstrasse, Berlin.

The president of the Reichstag was welcoming the Führer.

The villagers heard the phrases "honored by his presence . . . historic occasion . . ." and also heard the man in the leather coat's phrases ". . . if you promise that order is in writing on the desk in front of you."

The applause, the Sieg Heils died down. The Austrian's strange raw voice began. "We will always strike first, always . . . the criminal madness of Roosevelt and his government . . ."

They watched the Gestapo leader cross the room. "Outside," he said to Brombach and Delbruck. Then to two of his men, "Change of plan. New orders."

They followed him and the two prisoners outside.

"First Roosevelt incites war," the Austrian voice bellowed, "then falsifies the causes, then odiously wraps himself in a cloak of Christian hypocrisy . . ."

Outside, two pistols fired three, four times each.

". . . and slowly but surely leads mankind to war. . . ."

The door banged open and the Gestapo agent appeared. Behind him his men dragged the bodies of Jürgen Delbruck and Karl von Brombach.

"Shot trying to escape," the agent said to the watching villagers. They lowered their eyes to their mugs of beer.

". . . international Jewry . . . Bolshevik Russia . . . Roosevelt's regime . . ." the voice continued. Even the Gestapo agent was listening now.

"I have therefore arranged today that passports be handed to the American chargé d'affaires . . ."

In the Reichstag the rest was drowned by a bedlam of stomping and cheering. Germany and America were at war.

In the mountain Gasthaus the villagers sat silent, staring at the four bodies by the door.

Chapter Ten

In London it was one of those rare, clear winter days that seemed to mark the final end of November fogs and presage Christmas snow. The red buses rolled down an almost traffic-free Piccadilly. Conductors joked with old ladies and pretty Wrens, Polish officers caroused in the Polish club and Free Frenchmen in the St. James's Place French club. America was in the war.

To an embattled England and to a militarily defeated Europe, it was a deliverance. It was an assurance that whatever the setbacks ahead they were all now to be capped with final victory.

East End cockneys felt it, sifting through the dust and glass and splintered furniture of bombed homes. Winston Churchill felt it as he munched a Bath Oliver and drank his way through a celebratory bottle of 1898 Haut-Brion.

When Dr. Stanhope was shown into the first-floor sitting room at No. 10 Downing Street, the prime minister was already more than halfway through the bottle.

"Join me, Stanhope." He made the gesture of leaning over for the bell, knowing his visitor would refuse. "I'll get you a glass."

"I won't, thank you, sir. It's a little early for me."

Churchill grunted. "A man should develop the ability to drink fine claret at any time of the day. You drink wine, Stanhope?"

"In an amateurish kind of way," Stanhope conceded, "compared with yourself."

"Ah, the best wine has all the qualities of the best statesmen," Churchill purred. "Did you know that? No? The very best wine is, of course, mature . . . it can be no jackanapes of whatever pedigree. Mature with just that touch of acidity. Take this superb Graves." He lifted his glass to the light. "Like the very best in statesmen. Mature, clear-sighted, balanced, strong yet delicate." He paused. "An iron fist in a velvet glove."

Stanhope watched him, unable to decide, as many Americans before him, whether he was genius or poseur. Or perhaps something of each.

"I admire your president." Churchill took a mouthful of the wine and held it a moment before swallowing. "I enjoy his company, even over a distance of three thousand miles, because he, above anyone I know, appreciates this truth. You sure you won't try a glass?"

Stanhope shook his head. "No, thank you, sir. The ambassador has asked me to give you a report on the Erikson group."

The prime minister crunched a Bath Oliver. "Go on."

"I now have in my possession the documentary evidence that Colonel Erikson was trying to communicate to the Vatican."

"And . . ."

"Taken with other items from different sources, it leaves no doubt in the opinion of the Anglo-United States Committee that the Final Solution is a fact. And that Fall-Ost is scheduled to follow it."

"My instinct always told me that was so," Churchill said somberly. "I will instruct the British ambassador in the Vatican to renew our request to His Holiness to condemn this outrage in the strongest possible terms. Excommunication is called for."

"I believe this is the president's opinion too, sir."

"But we must not confuse issues, Stanhope. The purpose to which the Erikson group were putting this appalling information was, in the view of the president and myself, quite separate."

"I understand that, Prime Minister."

Churchill sat back in his chair. "Thus, what news from Switzerland?"

"Only a first report, sir. The Erikson group, led by his brother-in-law, Brombach, failed to cross the frontier to meet with our representative this afternoon. Initial reports suggest that they were arrested, possibly even shot, while attempting to enter Switzerland."

Churchill refilled his glass. "So, once again," he rumbled, "peace has been averted."

In his private apartments overlooking Vatican City, the pope consoled himself with the same thought.

The British ambassador and the American special representative had not so far renewed their request for a denunciation of Nazi Germany. It was as he thought: Churchill and Roosevelt were no more anxious for peace without victory (though for quite different reasons) than he was himself.

Furthermore, through the incomparable Vatican information channels which could call on the services of the most lowly country priest anywhere in Europe, he had already heard of the four German officers killed in an attempt to reach Switzerland. He considered for a moment how the secret police forces of the Reich might have known about the officers' intentions. And the thought crossed his mind that Bishop Hudal had provided them with information about the Erikson group.

He shook his head. He had specifically forbidden Hudal to mention the Erikson case.

And yet Hudal had so much to gain from the defeat of the general staff initiative. For a few moments Pius contemplated the idea of a bishop he had consecrated defying a pope. Then rejected the idea.

And yet the audience Hudal had asked for this morning was recorded in the Audience Book under the heading *Rebus iam dictis*, matters already previously discussed.

Pius XII had not been content with this meager notation. He had dispatched Father Dorsch to discover the precise object of the audience. The reply had been startling. From Bishop Hudal, who had rejected the idea of a peace initiative at the last audience, the reply had been that he had been contacted by highly placed German principals who wished to explore the possibilities of a settlement.

Pius XII walked through the library to the Audience Room at exactly ten o'clock. Father Dorsch and Bishop Hudal were waiting, a heavy silence between them.

Bishop Alois Hudal, rector of the Instituto Santa Maria dell' Anima, bent low over the long thin hand and kissed the bloodred papal ring. Raised to his feet, he struggled to contain his emotion before his friend and patron.

The lined, craggy head of Father Dorsch looked on, his expression blank as he watched the pope gesture the bishop to a chair.

The bishop stepped back, his dark eyes under heavy black eyebrows never leaving Pius. Clutched to his breast he held a dark green folder.

"You will know," the pope said gently, "that many groups of like-minded people in Germany, civilian and military, have already embarked on the difficult road to peace. We will not at this stage inquire about your principals, such we will call them in this audience, those Germans who have entrusted you with the search for such a road. When Father Dorsch told us of your request for an audience, we granted it immediately, with full trust in your judgment that these proposals you bring are of a unique nature. Speak to us freely, as a beloved son."

"Holy Father, I asked for this audience after meeting with those German principals you refer to. The meeting took place at our monastery at Aschen in Austria two days ago. The principals' first request is that Your Holiness should mediate in a peace between Great Britain and America on the one hand, and

Germany and Italy on the other. There is specifically no reference to the two other major belligerents, Soviet Russia and the Empire of Japan."

"With Your Holiness's permission," Father Dorsch said.

The pope inclined his head.

"Are there any proposals, even of a secondary nature, which include Russia and Japan?"

"None."

"In other words, Germany would continue to be at war with the Soviet Union, and Britain and America would continue to fight against Japan?"

"This is crucial to the proposal," Hudal confirmed. "It recognizes the real national interests of Germany, America and Britain."

"Continue," Pius said.

"The second item of the proposal is that Adolf Hitler should be removed as head of state."

"Removed?"

"That was the term used, Your Holiness."

"For which," Dorsch said dryly, "read assassinated."

"Or imprisoned and brought to trial?" Pius directed the question to the bishop.

"My German friends did not specify, Your Holiness. But they represent such powerful elements in the German state that neither alternative would be impossible from a practical point of view."

"The Holy See obviously cannot consent to or condone a murder for whatever far-reaching practical results. Tyrannicide is a mortal sin."

"This will be firmly communicated to my friends," Hudal promised.

Father Dorsch grimaced skeptically. "With great respect," he said, "how does this proposal differ from the many, all unsuccessful, requests from German opposition groups for the Holy See to mediate?"

"First," Hudal said, "in the very strength of my friends' position."

"Second . . . ?" Pius lifted the gold cross that hung around his neck.

"Second in the most important proposal of all."

"And that is?"

"That the Holy See should not present itself as mediator in this struggle. That the Holy See should first *endorse* the new German government and its justified war aims in the East, and then should call for an armistice conference of the belligerent powers here in Rome."

Pius stared down at the cross in his hands.

"The belligerent powers excluding Russia and Japan."

"Exactly."

"Your German officers are more naive than even I, as a German, believed," Dorsch said. "What they are saying is simply that they want to restructure the war. They're saying that Hitler got them into the wrong fight. So, get rid of Hitler, rearrange the belligerent powers in a more convenient manner and continue as before." He appealed to Pius: "The Vatican will lose all moral authority if it endorses this proposal. . ."

Pius lifted his hand. The old priest stopped, breathing heavily.

"Father Dorsch forgets perhaps that a further issue is involved—the program which we believe is called the Final Solution."

"As a German, Your Holiness," the priest said tensely, "I *never* forget that."

"Then consider." He turned to the bishop. "This outrage against humanity will be abandoned immediately by the post-Hitler government?"

"Immediately."

Pius turned to Father Dorsch. "Then we are bound, as Christians, to consider these proposals."

Dorsch remained silent.

"I have, Your Holiness"—Hudal took the green folder from under his arm—"a gift from my German friends. A token of their goodwill."

He crossed the flowered carpet to where the pope sat and extended the green folder.

The pope's hands took it and opened it slowly. Inside was a torn sheet of coffee-stained, lined paper. It was headed: "City of Munich District Police Report—January 22, 1922." Below, it contained a list of those present at a meeting at the Hofbrauhaus of the National Socialist German Workers' Party, Herr Adolf Hitler, Herr Anton Drexler and Herr Rudolf Hess speaking. The third name in the second column was recorded as His Eminence Cardinal E. Pacelli, Nuncio.

For a long time Pius sat with the green folder open in his hands. Then he passed it to Father Dorsch.

"My friends object in offering this token," Hudal said, "is, of course, to avoid the misunderstandings that might arise later if the Holy See decides to endorse the new regime."

In Dorsch's hands the folder closed with a snap. "Then I think, with His Holiness's agreement, that the time has come to know who precisely these friends are."

The bishop stiffened at the tone of the old priest's voice. He looked toward the pope, who nodded and said:

"You have mentioned powerful forces. For the fullest consideration of this proposal we wish to know now who would form the next German administration."

"Under these proposals," the bishop said, "the next Führer of the German Reich would be the Reichsprotektor of Bohemia, SS Obergruppenführer Reinhard Heydrich."

Jim Franklyn's taxi passed along Piccadilly and pulled up outside the Ritz Hotel. An ancient, liveried figure came forward and opened the door. Climbing out, Franklyn turned to the cabdriver. "How much is that?" he asked, a confusing collection of shillings, sixpences, half crowns and heavy copper pence in the palm of his hand.

"That's okay, sir," the cabby croaked. "You're an American, ain't you? 'Ave it on me since we're all in it together now."

Jim Franklyn had not been long enough in London to know

what a signal mark of approbation the cabby's gesture constituted.

The Ritz bar was crowded. Beneath the awning formed by a huge Stars and Stripes and Union Jack, girls in prewar silk dresses laughed and drank with men in every shade of khaki, air force or navy blue. Franklyn had never realized such a range of uniforms existed. But here, to celebrate the entry of the United States into the war, every Allied government seemed to be represented.

Among the civilians Franklyn saw Greg Sefton, and pushed his way through the crowd toward him.

"I see you've somehow got a uniform that fits," said Sefton, extending his hand.

Franklyn looked at Sefton's dark brown shirt straining across his huge gut and at the tan trousers bagging around the knees. "You ever thought losing some weight might help?"

"Listen," Sefton said, "I give up cigarettes and I put on pounds. My sadist of a doctor has even got his eye on my booze ration now."

They shouldered their way to the bar and Sefton ordered two large whiskies. "Did you see Stanhope?" he asked casually.

Franklyn's face tightened. "I was summoned last night. Plush office, big smile. Congratulations, Jim, you did a fine job, hints of a medal even."

"And?"

"I told him that if he'd been at Croydon Airport to meet me instead of you I would have strangled the bastard on the spot. It was a short interview."

"Listen," Sefton said, "The U.S. has been in the war for one whole week. Let's celebrate along with all these good people."

A pretty girl in a blue dress came up, glass in hand. "You're American," she said to Sefton.

"As apple pie."

She flung her arms around him and kissed him on the lips.

"I'm American too," Franklyn said.

"I can tell," the girl said, "you're so dreadfully forward." And smiling coolly she turned back to her friends.

"Here," Sefton said, "you have to learn the ropes. One hard tug and you end up on your ass. Either that or you just lack my charm."

"Okay, Greg," Franklyn said, "I'm in London and I'm in uniform. I don't plan to sit on my butt in that seedy Sloane Street hotel for the rest of the war."

"I'll let you into a little secret, Jim. Temporarily you're on my staff. And though it may come as a big surprise to you, that means *I* decide your next assignment, not you."

"Okay, Greg, I'm in the army now. But you don't have to blow reveille in my ear. I made a big civilian assumption. Now I'll put it another way—what happens next?"

Taking Franklyn by the arm Sefton led him to a corner of the room where the long windows overlooked the terrace with Green Park beyond.

"We're building up here in London," Sefton said. "The British were in ahead of us with clandestine forces. Their Special Operations Executive runs agents in most of the German-occupied territories. We want to work with them as equals. For that we're going to have to develop specialist staffs of our own, OSS staffs. I'm offering you a part in the operation."

"You're crazy. I'm not qualified to run agents."

"Right now no American is."

"Listen, Greg, to deal with these people you need a professional."

"We don't have one, Jim. That's why I'm asking you."

"Count me out, Greg."

Sefton nodded. "Okay, OSS is one area that has to be voluntary."

"Tell that to your friend Stanhope."

Sefton shrugged. "All the same you won't be going back to the States just yet. Tomorrow you'll start talking to every agency, British and American, that wants to talk to you."

"And after that?"

"After that we'll see."

"Okay."

The dark eyes in the heavy face looked up at him. "Jesus,"

Sefton said, "the noise here is something else. I've taken myself an apartment in Chelsea. Come back and we'll have a real drink."

Something from Franklyn's long years as a reporter triggered an alarm signal. "What is it, Greg? What is it you've got to tell me?"

Sefton hesitated, looking out toward the empty terrace. "I just saw the report on the Brombach story," he said. "All four officers were shot in a small village near the Swiss border. Our information is that they were probably shot deliberately after arrest, to prevent any sort of court-martial."

"And Christina?"

"Christina Erikson was arrested at her house sometime after she met you in Berlin," he said.

The news came to Franklyn like a kick in the groin. He opened the French window and walked out onto the terrace, trying to focus his attention on the black soggy leaves sticking to the broad flagstones.

Sefton joined him. "Jesus, Jim," he said gently, "you couldn't have known her that well. What was it, just three, four times you met her?"

"How did it happen, Greg?" Franklyn said slowly.

Sefton kept his eyes on Franklyn over the top of his raised glass. "Happen?"

"How did the Gestapo get onto them? They had nothing at the time I left."

"We've got no information on that," Sefton said. "The Gestapo's first move was to dig up the fake Erikson body in Prague."

"Why? Who put them onto it?"

"You could lose a lot of sleep trying to work that out," he said. "*I* have."

"Could the leak have come from someone in Prague?"

Sefton shook his head.

"Then how the hell did they find out about Erikson? What about leaks at the London end?"

Sefton shook his head silently.

"You're not saying it was her?" Franklyn swung around violently to face Sefton.

"I'm saying nothing."

"I'll bust your head in if your official report tries to push it onto her. I mean that, Greg."

Again Sefton was silent.

"Her own brother—you're saying she betrayed her own *brother*?"

"Christina Erikson's dead, Jim. She was released by the Gestapo two days after the operation aborted. She returned to Hochlingen and took her own life. That's all I'm saying," he said slowly. "Nothing official, nothing in any report, but I don't have to tell you the way that points."

"God in heaven," Franklyn said into the bleak emptiness of the park, "what did they put her through?"

They walked back across the terrace and entered the bar through the French windows.

"That offer you made me earlier," Franklyn said, "does it still stand?"

"Of course."

"Okay, then," Franklyn said, "if you think I'm the sort of guy you need. . . ."

"You're the sort of guy. Come back to my apartment—we'll have that drink."

Franklyn shook his head. "I like parties," he said. "I'll stay on and take my luck with the booze here."

Sefton pursed his lips. "If you feel like coming over later . . ."

"I'll call you tomorrow," Franklyn said. "Report for duty."

"Okay. But I'll be there if you change your mind."

Sefton lumbered toward the door; the girl in the blue dress glanced over her shoulder. For a moment she caught Franklyn's eye.

He crossed toward her. "I've lowered my sights," he said.

"Was it necessary?"

"I guess so. I'm no longer looking for a big kiss from the prettiest girl in the room. Right now I'd settle for a drink."

"We could try a little club I belong to around the corner, if you like."

"I'd like."

She frowned. "Quite sure? You're looking pretty miserable."

He shook his head. "Miserable? On a day like this?"

She hesitated, smiling at him quizzically.

"So about that club around the corner?"

"Okay, I'll get my coat," she said. "My name is Pam, Pam Denning," she flung over her shoulder before she disappeared into the throng.

Chapter Eleven

Notations from a Meeting at Wannsee.
January 25, 1942

PRESIDING: *Chief of SD Reinhard Heydrich*
PRESENT: *State secretaries of appropriate ministries*
NOTED BY: *SS Sturmbahnführer Adolf Eichmann, RSHA IV 4B*
SECURITY RATING: *Maximum secrecy*

Central State Security Bureau Chief Heydrich drew attention to the general aims set out in the Führer Protokol in connection with his decision to achieve a final solution to the Jewish problem as part of the Fall-Ost program.

Herr Heydrich indicated that some 11 million Jews were involved—131,800 remaining in the original Reich territory—5 million in the U.S.S.R.—3 million in the Ukraine—2¼ million in the Government General of Poland—¾ million in France and ⅓ million in England.

Outlining the method, General Heydrich said that the Jews now in the course of the Final Solution would be transported to the East for use as labor, in which task undoubtedly a great part would fall from natural diminution (S.S. Hauptamt has already calculated that in factory and quarry work a Jewish life expectancy of nine months is a reasonable basis on which to operate.)

Central State Security Bureau Chief Heydrich went on to say that the remnant able to survive the labor process—undoubtedly the part with the strongest resistance—must be treated accordingly since this was a case of accelerated natural selection and it would be unacceptable if this remnant were allowed to provide the germ cell of a new Jewish genetic development.

The State Secretary of Transport Industry begged leave to point out the extent of the problems involved in the transportation of West European Jews across the Reich territory to the East. This aspect of the question was noted by the conference.

State Secretary Dr. Josef Bühler, representing the Government General of Poland, begged leave to point out that there were no transportation problems in his own area since the Jews were already there. He concluded with the request that the Jewish problem in his territory should be solved as quickly as possible. This request was noted.

The Cistercian monastery of Aschen is built into the side of a mountain in the Austrian Alps somewhere between Innsbruck and the Brenner Pass. Facing due north and with the great mountain rising behind it, in summer it is almost completely bereft of sun and the gray stones seem never to relinquish their winter chill. By December it is lashed by snow squalls or blanketed with fog. Never chosen for the soft seductions of this world, the grim-walled building, with its almost Russian onion-domed church, rarely sees visitors throughout the winter months.

All the more surprising for the villagers of the scattered hamlet of Lower Aschen that on a single day in December two separate cars, an hour or two apart, followed the snow-covered road up to the monastery.

The second car had created even more stir than the first,

escorted as it was by four motorcycles, the troops muffled against the freezing wind.

In the cattle barns the big, raw-faced Austrian peasant women had put aside their wooden hayforks and hurried outside. Most had stayed watching while the motorcycles with their sidecars plumed snow behind them as they battled their way upward, and the women only returned to tend the cattle when the last tones of the monastery gate bell faded across the snow slopes.

In the biting wind Heydrich stood beside Hardenberg in the outer courtyard of the monastery, stamping his feet and rubbing his black-gloved hands together.

"Pull the thing again!" he shouted to Klein, his chauffeur, who stood next to a stone funnel from which a wet, rusting chain dangled.

As Klein reached up for the chain, however, they heard the sound of bolts being drawn and a half section of the arched door in front of them began to open.

The white-robed Cistercian bowed to the two officers and drew the door wider. The Germans stepped past him into an inner courtyard and waited while he rebolted the door. Then, still without a word, he led them across the cobbled courtyard to an arched doorway on the far side.

It was midafternoon and the clouds rampaged across a wild sky above them. But the high stone walls blocked the wind's bite, and the candlelit windows of the church that formed one side of the courtyard gave an impression of serenity and warmth. Within they could hear the rumble of the monks' voices at prayer.

The white-robed figure reached the arched doorway and stood aside to allow the officers to enter. Heydrich stepped forward and found himself in a covered cloister; iron basket braziers burned at intervals along the wall, throwing a red-and-yellow light across the flagstones and onto the carved figures of abbots long past. In wrought-iron holders clusters of fat-dripping candles illuminated the vaulting above their heads.

Hardenberg had joined Heydrich and both men stood listening to the footsteps approaching at the same moment that the door closed behind them.

"Is this where you met last time?" Heydrich hissed to Hardenberg.

"No, sir. Last time it was in the abbot's cell. Three meters by three meters. This is not only bigger—but believe it or not it's even warmer."

The small figure of Alois Hudal came into sight as he turned the corner at the end of the long cloister. He wore a black skullcap and a simple black soutane. Beside him walked the tall, craggy figure of Father Dorsch.

The officers stepped forward to meet them. The four men stopped beside a basket brazier.

Hardenberg clicked his heels. "Your Grace, may I present Reichsprotektor, SS Obergruppenführer Heydrich." And as Heydrich shook hands with the bishop, "His Grace the bishop of Aela."

"And this," Hudal said informally, "is Father Julius Dorsch." He offered no further explanation.

Hudal stretched his hands to warm them at the brazier. "I hope you approve my choice of a meeting place, General." He gestured. "Here we can pace the square of this beautiful cloister. We can be warm and quite certain that only we shall hear what we choose to say to each other."

Heydrich removed his gloves. "For the subject of our talks the setting is totally appropriate."

The bishop looked up at the tall figure from under his dark eyebrows. "Three days ago," he said, "I was granted an audience. I was able to present your gift to His Holiness and to describe your proposals at length. Father Dorsch was present and therefore knows my views."

"Since neither Brigadeführer von Hardenberg nor myself have met Father Dorsch before, it would be legitimate to inquire about *his* general views."

"I am a Catholic priest, General Heydrich," Dorsch said coldly. "My views are those of a Catholic priest. I recognize some of the pitfalls for the Church in these times—with God's help I hope to see others."

Heydrich smiled. "In other words His Holiness has sent you here as the devil's advocate," he said offensively.

"I do not always take the same view as Bishop Hudal. It is with this in mind, no doubt, that the Holy Father has sent me here," the old priest said firmly.

Heydrich turned back to Hudal.

"Very well. We know where we stand. What exactly is your brief?"

Hudal glanced up at Dorsch and then turned slowly from the brazier to face Heydrich.

His Holiness has asked me to explore, unofficially, your proposals, General. This is in no sense a commitment, you understand."

"I understand."

"First, I must make my own position clear," Hudal said briskly. "You are perhaps familiar with my book, *The Foundations of National Socialism.*"

"I am," Heydrich said. He glanced at Dorsch and saw his grimace.

"Five years ago I believed that National Socialist ideology and Christianity could and must live together. My book was an attempt to erect a Christian path to Nazism. I believed then that Germany's national ideology was vital for the salvation of Europe from *atheistic* Communism. I believe it still."

He turned and, with Heydrich on one side and Dorsch on the other, began to pace the cloister. "The change that has taken place," Hudal said, "is in my assessment of the Führer himself. I observe, from your proposals, that this parallels your own thoughts?"

"It does."

"In June this year when he opened Germany's struggle against Russia he had no more enthusiastic a supporter than myself. But this winter's setbacks have shown clearly that militarily it was a disastrous error. Not an error to have attacked Russia, but to have done so without first making peace with

Great Britain. Now he has committed the folly of voluntarily ranging the United States against him."

"The essence of my proposal," Heydrich said, "is that it is not too late. Peace with the Western Allies is still possible, but if National Socialism, without Hitler, is to remain the dominant ideology in Germany, then it will need the endorsement of the pope himself."

"In crude terms what advantage could His Holiness see in such an endorsement?"

"It is the only way to guarantee that the war will continue in the East until Soviet Communism is defeated."

"This was one of the questions to which His Holiness required an answer." Hudal nodded his satisfaction.

"As chancellor and Führer after Adolf Hitler's removal, I will guarantee the continuance of the Eastern war."

"How, precisely, do you believe you could seize power in the German state, General?"

"This is my own area of competence, Your Grace."

"Nevertheless the Holy See would have to be persuaded of the basic credibility of a change of government."

"Very well. If you can dispense with the euphemisms so can I. The first step must be the assassination of Adolf Hitler."

"You can't expect the Holy See to endorse such an act," Dorsch said forcibly.

Heydrich opened his coat and produced a pack of English cigarettes. Without asking Hudal's permission he took one out and lit it.

"Of course not. The technicalities of the political operation are not relevant to the Holy See's endorsement. Merely concurrent."

"Nevertheless," Dorsch insisted, "the Holy See could not recognize a regime which has achieved its position through a recent act of tyrannicide."

Heydrich drew angrily on his cigarette. Hudal could see, even in the light of the brazier, that his face was ashen white.

"I'm going to change the whole tenor of our conversation,

Your Grace," Heydrich said at length. "It seems to me that Pope Pius is not in a position to refuse my proposals. It seems to me that he ignores or perhaps does not understand that the papacy is facing a greater crisis than it has ever faced."

"The papacy has risen above the storms of history for almost two millennia," Dorsch said.

"At the end of our conversation today," Heydrich said contemptuously, "I will ask you to repeat that statement with the same confidence."

Dorsch looked at him. How he hated this arrogant German— as a churchman and as a German himself. But he said nothing.

His outburst had restored Heydrich's spirits. "I'm going to put my cards on the table. I'm going to put your cards on the table too, gentlemen. Then we'll all look hard to see who holds the black ace."

In the silence a bell tinkled in the shadows at the end of the cloister, and moments later a monk appeared carrying a tray with a stone jug and four rough stoneware wine cups. Without a word he poured wine and handed the cups to the men standing around the brazier.

Heydrich sipped the sweet, herb-flavored white wine and waited until the monk had withdrawn.

"Let us put ourselves first in the position of Winston Churchill. After two years of grim defensive fighting, Great Britain finds itself now, in 1942, with a Russian ally with infinite manpower resources and an American ally with infinite productive capacity. Why should he, even for a moment, consider a peace which will leave a National Socialist Germany in a commanding position in Europe?"

"Churchill no more favors a Soviet hegemony in Europe than does Berlin or the Vatican," Hudal said.

"True. But democracies operate in a world of apparent morality. Without a powerful *moral* inducement, Churchill and Roosevelt could not explain to their electorates the abandonment of their Russian ally."

"And you believe a papal endorsement of the new National Socialist state under your leadership will produce the necessary moral climate?"

"It is certain," Heydrich said, "because I will allow the papacy full credit for demanding that the new German leadership, that is to say myself, abandon anti-Semitism as the core of its ideology. I will publish current Hitlerite plans for the murder of ten million Jews. I will allow the pope to plead, and myself readily to agree, to save their lives. No American president, no British prime minister, can refuse peace if the salvation of ten million people is its corollary."

The four men stood silent around the brazier. Then Dorsch took Hudal's arm. "I must speak alone with the bishop," he said to Heydrich. "Please excuse us."

The two prelates walked quickly to the end of the cloister and were lost to Heydrich's and Hardenberg's sight.

"The man is a genius," Dorsch said, "an evil genius. He will destroy the Church."

"I can't agree." The excitement showed clearly on Hudal's face. "This is the statesman who will build on the work of Adolf Hitler, the innovator."

Dorsch was shaking, unsure himself whether from anger or fear. "He will drag the papacy back five hundred years. We must return to Rome immediately. I will plead with the Holy Father to have nothing to do with this foul exchange."

"Ten million lives saved? Is that a foul exchange?"

"Ten million lives which are menaced by the very ideology that man represents. Must we now be grateful to him for proposing to save them!"

"We have not completed the task required of us by the Holy Father," Hudal said stubbornly.

"I insist we return to Rome immediately," the priest said.

The two men faced each other.

"The Holy Father required us to satisfy ourselves on a number of other points. I will complete the task His Holiness has prescribed for us."

"It is an ill choice," Dorsch said. "An ill choice."

Standing by the brazier Heydrich offered Hardenberg a cigarette. "Priests, even bishops, " he said, when the younger man declined, "should not be treated with excessive respect." He laughed. "It's bad for them, Hardenberg. It reinforces their ludicrous idea that they have a direct line to God."

"You take enormous risks, General," Hardenberg said.

Heydrich drew nervously on his cigarette. "I do," he said, "but there isn't any other way."

From the darkness the long figure of Hudal appeared.

"The weaker spirits are already falling away," Heydrich said. "That is good. Finally we shall be left with the man in the Vatican himself. I plan to set him a moral conundrum that all his theology will fail to solve."

"Father Dorsch has decided that it is his duty to return immediately to Rome, General," Hudal said as he approached the brazier.

"I have the impression that Dorsch is somewhat shocked by this glimpse of the ways of the world, Your Grace. Or perhaps he doesn't see an atheist Bolshevism commanding a hundred and fifty million people as a particular menace to his and our Europe."

"Father Dorsch is a simple priest, General, but he commands the respect of the Holy Father."

"So he's left, hotfooting for Rome. But you've stayed, Your Grace."

"I have further questions to ask you."

"Go on."

"Let us be blunt, General, or rather let me be as blunt as you have been. If your proposals are to be accepted in Rome, it will be because of the advantages the Church will gain from their acceptance."

"Or the disadvantages the Church will avoid by their refusal."

"You've made that clear. Now for the positive side . . ."

"All right, Your Grace. First, the papacy will, as I've said, claim credit (with myself admittedly) for the salvation of European Jewry."

"Second, the defeat of Russian atheism," Hudal inter-jected.

"And third," Heydrich said, "an immensely favored position in Germany and in many territories still occupied by Germany after the peace treaty."

"An impressive list," Hudal conceded.

"But not because I believe I am negotiating from weakness."

"No, I see that." The bishop paused. "How long does the Holy Father have to decide?"

"Every day that passes makes the American voter more committed to this war; every defeat we sustain in Russia makes Churchill more confident." He paused. "As soon as possible, but even before that I will require a token that will indicate to me that this matter is being seriously considered."

"What sort of token?"

"In a few days President Roosevelt is meeting the South American governments in the Pan American Union. His stated intention is to bring them, or as many of them as possible, into the war against Germany."

"What are you asking, General?"

"If Pope Pius is serious in his consideration of my proposals, I expect him personally, and the Vatican diplomatically, to exert all the great influence he has in Catholic South America to frustrate Roosevelt's plans."

Hudal stepped back in shock. "It is an enormous request."

"*Expectation*, Your Grace." Heydrich's high voice was as thin as stamped tin. "By this I will judge the seriousness of the Vatican's intention."

The SS men, their gray scarves wrapped around the lower parts of their faces, climbed onto their Zündapp motorcycles. The wind, howling off the mountainside, swirled snow around the black Mercedes. In convoy they pulled away from the monastery and started down toward Lower Aschen.

In the back of the car Heydrich leaned forward and slid closed the glass panel in front of him. "Well, Hardenberg . . . ?" He took a flask of coffee from the built-in walnut cupboard.

"You'll forgive me, General, if I take the more mundane approach."

Heydrich poured coffee into a glass cup.

"Father Dorsch was not exactly sympathetic." Hardenberg took the hot cup. "What's to stop him sabotaging the whole operation?"

"How?" Heydrich said calmly.

"By making sure somebody knows about our meeting. The Reichsführer SS, for example. The Führer himself, even."

"You're frightened, Hardenberg."

"Frankly, yes."

"Listen carefully. When you return to Munich I want you to set up an investigation. It will be based on the fact that you have heard that Father Dorsch, forget Hudal, met certain German officers to discuss treasonable arrangements here at the monastery at Aschen. Gather reports from agents, people in the village who saw cars, whatever material you can get. Then extend your negotiations to Rome, if possible even to Dorsch's own friends in the Vatican. Write and file minutes of a meeting in which I specifically instructed you to conduct this investigation. The whole thing is directed against the army, successors of Erikson and Brombach. At my next meeting with the Führer, I will inform him of a new army-Vatican alliance which is being investigated. We shall create such a fog that no man will see through it."

The convoy sped on—through the mountain roads toward the old border villages near Füssen and then down into the Bavarian plain to pick up the main road to Munich.

Five floors up above the Bernini colonnades, Pius XII looked down on an empty, rain-swept square. No throngs of massed faithful lifted their arms toward him. No chants of *"Viva il Papa"* warmed his conviction or confirmed his prayers. Propelled by a west wind the rain kicked up water crowns and coronets on the flagstones far below.

His Holiness turned back into the room. Hudal stood in the center of the room. Father Dorsch seemed to merge into the obscurity beside the door.

They waited.

The man in the white robes looked from the bishop to the priest. "We shall pray for guidance," he said.

They came and fell on their knees and kissed his ring, but he knew neither man was satisfied.

"And on the South American question, Holy Father?" Hudal said as he rose to his feet.

"On that issue our path is in any case clear," Pius said. "We shall urge that the war should not be extended. It has always been the view of the Church."

In the shadows Dorsch bowed his head. That had not been the view of the Church in June 1941 when Germany, his own country, had attacked Russia. Then the extension of the war had been greeted with quiet satisfaction.

The rain continued in Rome all afternoon, its violence matching the pope's anguish. In his private chapel he spent four hours in prayer and meditation but rose a prey to the same doubts, magnified.

Even as a child he had kept his own counsel, listening to others and deciding alone. As a young priest, as nuncio in Germany, as secretary of state, he had cultivated a remote and solitary demeanor, but the responsibility had been heavy. It had been his practice during his time in Munich to walk in the deserted parts of the Englischer Garten, sometimes with a bag of cherries to throw to the birds as he spoke his problems aloud.

He walked into the library. The long shelves of books seemed to absorb the sounds of wind and rain outside. "They do not understand," he said aloud. "The pope is not only the head of the Church, he is its guardian. Nothing is as important as that the Church should survive the struggle. Father Dorsch sees this purely as a moral issue. He quotes me Spellman's letter from the United States that American Catholics are losing confidence in the pope's impartiality. He quotes me Archbishop Sapiena's letter from Poland, 'a life of terror, of camps from which few escape alive. . . .' Yet to condemn these oppressions must be to jeopardize the Church in Germany and in all the occupied territories."

He circled the long table. Sister Pasquelina, his housekeeper, had brought the canaries' cage into the library as she did every morning. The pope opened the delicate wire door and watched the two yellow birds hop nervously from perch to perch.

"In other vital ways too we are balanced between the opposing camps," he said. "Now that our income from the occupied countries has virtually dried up, we depend completely on the tithe which Hitler allows us from German Catholics and the contributions from Roosevelt's secret service funds disguised as donations from the American faithful. Neither source of income can we afford to lose."

The birds cocked their heads, watching as the pope stood in anguished silence. "How are we to survive? How are we to guarantee the continuing existence of the Church? One thing only we see clearly, that this is our overriding responsibility as pope." The canaries hopped to the door of the cage.

"But perhaps there is light at the end of this tunnel. A successful peace treaty arranged along the lines General Heydrich proposes will leave both America and the new Germany well disposed toward the Vatican."

One canary fluttered out into the room, circled and returned to the cage.

"At the same time," Pius said, "the crusade against the Soviets will go on and the appalling pogrom which Hitler plans will cease."

The pope walked back to the cage. "Yet will I ever persuade a priest like Dorsch that this course is necessary?" he muttered to himself. He stopped. "No. Will I ever persuade a priest like Dorsch that this course is *good*?"

His long, blue-veined fingers closed the cage door.

* * *

At 10:45 that same evening Sir D'Arcy Osborne performed an act uncharacteristic of his dignified image as His Britannic Majesty's representative to the Vatican. Opening the rear bedroom window of his apartment on the Via di Porta Angelica, he climbed onto the iron fire escape outside.

His valet handed him his hat and gloves through the open window. They both saw the humor of the situation.

"Damn ridiculous," the ambassador said, smiling.

"Yes, sir," said Jackson, "and take care, sir."

"I will," Sir D'Arcy assured him, and, with the cool dignity for which he was well known in the diplomatic service, he descended the rusting iron staircase to the overflowing garbage cans below.

Only in the Vatican City, he reflected, or just possibly in Gestapo-ridden Lisbon, could His Majesty's ambassador be picking his way through a rear courtyard at night on the way to an assignation. But in the Vatican the British ambassador's existence was conditioned by the fact that he was, in effect, a voluntary prisoner in this small area of nonbelligerent territory within the capital city of an enemy state. Constantly watched by members of the German legation, it was virtually impossible to make or receive a visit without being immediately reported for analysis in Berlin.

He had only a few hundred yards to go, past the Sala Stampa, the Vatican press office, and keeping almost parallel to the Via di Porta Angelica until he reached the gardens.

In these gardens he walked for half an hour every day, the only exercise that his confinement to Vatican City afforded him. And on most days he would maintain his practice of stepping out briskly with his eyes fixed on a distant bush or shrub, studiously ignoring any passing member of an Axis legation. But today it had been different, and when the priest had firmly placed himself in the ambassador's path, Sir D'Arcy had been forced to turn his deliberately Olympian gaze to the old man.

"Meet me," the priest had said, smiling as if passing the time of day, "eleven o'clock tonight. Here in the gardens. I know no way of telling you how urgent it is."

And he had again raised his hat and with a small bow passed on slowly, his head bent over the small leather-bound book in his hands.

All around him the Roman clocks were striking eleven as the ambassador reached the gardens. He took the north–south walk, keeping to the grass border. A few yards from where they had briefly greeted each other this morning, Father Julius Dorsch was waiting.

Chapter Twelve

"If you're going to be in London for a while, why don't you move in with me?" Pam Denning said. "At least you can be sure my old man's not going to pop back and surprise us in the act," she said.

"When was he taken prisoner?" Franklyn asked, pulling on his trousers, shivering in the unheated bedroom.

"Light-years ago," she said, reaching a naked arm from under the sheets for the pack of Craven A's on the bedside table. "God," she said, "it's cold. D'you think if I slept with the coalman he'd consider it worth an extra bag or two?"

"When was your husband taken prisoner, Pam?" Franklyn asked gently.

"For Christ's sake, why always go on about him?"

"Because you'll never talk about him, that's why. You'll pick Americans up at parties, you'll joke about sleeping with the coalman, but you'll never talk about your husband. What's his name?"

"Harry," she said sullenly, lighting her cigarette.

"And where *was* he taken prisoner?"

"Dunkirk, darling; that great British victory, you remember? We rang the church bells all over England. It's what I hate about this country," she said. "Where else would they celebrate a crushing defeat?"

"All of us handle the things that really hurt in our own way."

"Are you talking about the British?"

"Or you."

"Me?"

She sat up in bed, pulling the blankets up under her chin. "What about the German countess, Jim?"

"There's nothing left to say about her," he said.

"Who doesn't want to talk now?" she jeered gently. "It was the same with me, Jim," she said, "when Harry didn't come back. At first I would sooner have slit my throat than sleep with someone else. Just like you, the first night I brought you back here after that Ritz shindig. Too polite to say you didn't want to, weren't you?"

"Why are all women amateur psychologists?"

"Are you going to move in then? Keep me on the straight and narrow?"

"You mean sleeping with one man's better than the whole regiment?"

"Don't be too tough on me, Jim," she said. "This war may last another three years. Harry's already been a prisoner the best part of two."

"Well, once the Yanks come marching in . . ."

"God bless 'em," she said. "But if they come marching in before they're good and ready they'll all end up with Harry."

He sat on the bed. "I'd like to move in, Pam. One week, three weeks, six weeks, however long—but only if we both know the way things are."

"We do," she said firmly.

"Right, tonight I'll drag my box of Hershey bars from that crummy Sloane Street hotel and establish residence. As an officer, if not a gentleman, I also get a coal ration, so if I catch you with coal smudges on your bra, I'll know you are the upper-class whore I thought you were in the first place."

"Bliss," she said. "Now run off to the Foreign Office, or wherever important place you have to go. The milkman will be here in ten minutes."

"I get a milk ration too," he grinned.

"Spoil sport." She jumped out of bed and, naked, hugged him. "Is it only in wartime that a girl can have a real male friend?"

Franklyn hunched himself into his service topcoat as he walked across St. James's Park. From under the low gray cloud the drizzle was too fine even to pockmark the water of the lake. A few ducks sheltered in the reeds and an old man, his sandwich-board inscribed FEBRUARY 1942—SECOND FRONT NOW, parked beside a bench, threw scraps of bread onto the surface of the water. The ducks stayed where they were.

After six weeks in England, Jim Franklyn knew exactly why the British talked so much about the weather. It was winter. Yet some days were almost warm and clammy, others, bitterly cold with snow and sleet driving through his new uniform topcoat and seeming to reach his very bones. Occasionally, it was bright and clear and the optimists talked of an early spring. He himself had seen crocuses raising their heads in St. James's Park, only to be smitten the next day by a ferocious frost. Most Americans he knew in London were pretty sympathetic to the crocuses.

He was not sure whether he really liked the British. A lot of Americans felt that way. Two nations divided by a common language, Bernard Shaw had said. But that was only to take the heat off the Irish who were even odder.

Of course he knew from Pam Denning the "better late than never" attitude some Englishmen had toward the United States entry into the war, and in some ways he found it almost touching. This close identification with American democracy which made them baffled at the two-year delay. Japan for them was too far off to be a serious consideration, and somehow assumed to be a conflict that would be dispatched with ease once the real war was over.

Other things he found less touching, and other Englishmen far less agreeable. The Foreign Office official before him now was very much a case in point. It was Greg Sefton who had set up the meeting. After weeks of lecturing to RAF crews about escape possibilities if shot down over Germany, Franklyn had received a brief phone call from Sefton's office to be at the British Foreign Office in Whitehall that morning, Room 611 at 11:30 A.M. No explanations.

And he wasn't getting much in the way of explanations from this suave, old-school-tie Englishman who was asking the questions.

"So how many times in all did you see Heydrich?" the official asked him.

"Like I said, not many. Once in Munich. Three or four times in Prague when I stayed to do a story on the Protectorate."

"Three of four times, Mr. Franklyn," the Englishman said. "Which?"

"Which?"

"Yes, *three* or *four* times?"

"Jesus . . . four."

"But then you had a close friendship with one of Heydrich's senior subordinates."

"Hardenberg? I knew him. Drank with him in his office from time to time. I used him, he used me. No real friendship."

"He used you?" The voice was sharp. "How?"

"To feed me information he wanted passed on to the States, I guess."

"And you'd do that?"

"Yes," Franklyn said irritably, "if I had nothing else that week."

The Englishman suddenly smiled. "I'm sorry, Mr. Franklyn. I'm not really trying to put your back up."

"You're not doing a bad job, without even trying."

"All right. Back to Hardenberg. Did he talk a lot about his chief?"

"No. But Heydrich was everywhere. What I mean is every senior member of the Gestapo really had this feeling that someone was looking over their shoulder."

"Heydrich?"

"Sure. He had this ability at least to make them think he knew everything that was going on. Sometimes I guess he actually did. He got onto the Erikson officer group pretty quickly."

"Yes. How?"

"I don't know."

The Englishman glanced through the file on his desk. "What happened to Countess Erikson?"

"She's dead," Franklyn said shortly.

"But could she have been the weak link?"

"If you'd met her, you'd never in your life describe her as a weak link."

"I see. What about this other woman, the Czech girl, Dana?"

"Don't you like women?"

"I'm married to one."

"I mean what makes you assume the weak link was a woman?"

The Foreign Office man shrugged. "Nasty things they can do to women in those interrogation rooms."

"Pretty goddamn nasty things they can do to men too. I've seen them."

"Yes. You've read our biography of Heydrich. In it we try to detail everything, however trivial. Does it strike you as accurate?"

"It omits to mention that the guy has a whole bagful of charm."

"Really?"

"My impression is he can turn it on and off when he chooses—like almost every other reaction he has. You describe

217

him as a Nazi, for instance. I'm not sure he's any more Nazi than I am. I think he's some massive John D. Rockefeller opportunist with a willingness to slaughter ten million if the time seems right."

"Take the report with you and write a gloss for us, will you?"

"A gloss?"

"I'm sorry—the disadvantages of a classical education; it restricts communication."

"Jesus Christ," Franklyn exploded, "no wonder you spent the last two years without allies."

The Englishman smiled again and the warmth was curiously contagious. "My apologies," he said. "Genuinely meant."

He got up and took a bottle of gin from a cupboard behind him. "Let's have a drink. To Anglo-American friendship. If this fellow Heydrich gets the Vatican endorsement he's after, we're going to need all the Anglo-American friendship we can rustle up. Especially if the Soviet Union gets to hear of it."

"Okay." Franklyn succumbed to the man's curious charm. "I'll drink to that. But why should the Russians hear about it?"

He took a glass with two inches of gin in the bottom. As the tonic was being added, he said, "You know, I was never given your name."

"Philby," the Englishman said, raising his glass. "My friends call me Kim."

At Demiansk, in the Valdai Hills, on the evening of February 21, a strange quiet descended on units of the embattled German Sixteenth Army.

To the northwest, toward Leningrad, and to the south where the Volga River opens out into Lake Seliger, the flash and rumble of gunfire showed clearly that the Russians were maintaining their pressure on the salient. Yet here, along the line of the Demiansk railway, the quiet was absolute.

Men in straw-lined slit trenches, their faces bound with woollen scarves beneath their steel helmets, their hands and feet encased in wool and straw and leather against the incredible cold, shook their heads in apprehension. Did it mean that it was here, along the Demiansk railway line, that the Russians had decided to launch their next attack?

The early evening passed. To men like Medical Sergeant Franz Geller, in a dugout carved from the snow and earth of the railway embankment, there were no signs of an impending Russian attack. They had heard no clank and backfire of tanks being brought up into position, no singing as the Russian troops started on their generous issue of prebattle vodka. Most important of all, there was no extra issue of ammunition from their own German quartermasters.

For the tenth time in as many minutes Geller went to the observation slit and peered through the gap in the railroad ties. The cold air cut at his eyes, glazing his vision momentarily as the eyeball froze over. In forty-five degrees centigrade below freezing a man learned to blink quickly and keep blinking.

His vision cleared. Across the white slopes in front of him a pair of snow foxes plunged and wallowed in the deep drifts. It was part of the Sixteenth Army's mythology that an Arctic fox meant no Russian attack that night.

A voice called from outside and Geller dragged back the blankets that covered the dugout entrance. His friend Feldwebel Zeitz scrambled in, stamping his feet on the packed earth floor.

"Cigarette," he croaked. "And some of that medicinal vodka, for Christ's sake."

Geller poured him some diluted alcohol from the medical chest and lit his cigarette. "Well, what do you make of it at company headquarters? It's a mystery."

"I've got news for you," Zeitz said. "It's a cease-fire."

"What!"

"Temporary; don't get too excited. As from nine o'clock tonight, no weapons will be fired, no matter whatever apparent provocation."

"Until when?"

"Further orders."

219

Geller turned to the observation slit again. The tracks made by the snow foxes led back toward the Russian lines.

"What the hell is it, Fritz?"

"Prisoner exchange is my guess," the Feldwebel said. "We've probably negotiated an exchange of the badly wounded."

"There are enough of those," Geller said gloomily, "on both sides."

As the evening wore on, the German soldiers began to move about among their foxholes, warily at first, because the moonlight was bright on the snow, but gradually with more confidence, visiting friends, bargaining for tobacco and vodka. And across the slopes they began to see dark figures on the other side. Then small fires were lit and flickered and winked back and forth at each other across the half-kilometer of snow as the men on both sides began to enjoy their good fortune.

The arrival of the work party seemed to confirm the Feldwebel's guess about a prisoner exchange. From the dugout Geller and Zeitz watched the small group of Germans climb up onto the railway embankment and begin to examine the track. On the other side of the small railway bridge a group of Russians seemed to be doing the same thing.

Geller and Zeitz sat opposite each other at the rough table constructed, like almost everything else in the dugout, from railroad ties. As the oil lamp sputtered they cut slices of sausage which Zeitz had liberated from the quartermaster, and pushed the alcohol bottle back and forth between them.

"If war were always like this," Geller said, "I'd volunteer to be a soldier."

"If that's your Berlin sense of humor," Zeitz told him, "you can keep it. Anyway, what's a war without women? I thought that was a soldier's prerogative."

"If it's any Russian woman that I've seen so far, I'll pass. And in any case the only woman I'm really interested in is tucking up two small kids in my place in Berlin at the moment."

"As long as that's all she's tucking up."

Geller's head came up.

"Sorry, Franz," Zeitz said. "Soldiering up here in this godforsaken place makes you crude. I was a schoolteacher, you know. I used to believe I was doing well. Most of those I taught when I started out are probably up here too, half of 'em dead already. That's why you get crude; you can't believe in ordinary things anymore, like your wife I mean, in Berlin. I'm sorry I said that."

Geller passed the bottle over to Zeitz. They were both over forty, old men before their time. You couldn't hold a careless joke against a friend.

Zeitz took the bottle and lifted it to his lips, then paused. "What the hell's that?"

Geller could feel it now, the faint shuddering of the dugout. "It's a train," he said. He got to his feet and crossed to the observation slit. As Zeitz joined him, the shuddering increased and both men now could hear the snort and puff of a locomotive.

They saw the Russian one first. Where the track curved toward the stone bridge an ancient steam engine backed a single car toward them. In the moonlight they could see clearly the Red Cross signs on the sides of the blacked-out carriage. Then the German train passed over the dugout, and as it came into their line of vision, they saw that it too was a single darkened car, its side painted with red crosses, being shunted backward to join the now stationary Russian train.

With a clank of heavy couplings the two trains joined, and Russians and Germans in the two work parties leaped up and linked the two cars through a connecting door. The train stood high above the silent battle lines, watched by grateful Russian and German troops, a guarantee by its simple presence that the war was abandoned while it remained.

Inside the overheated Russian carriage, the tsarist crowned eagle still embroidered on the seat backs Vyacheslav Molotov, the Foreign Minister of the USSR, faced Joachim von Ribbentrop across the mahogany tabletop. The two men had met before, of course, when they had reversed history and signed the German-Soviet pact just over two years ago. If they failed to recognize in themselves their underlying mediocrity, they were

221

certainly each aware of the amoral opportunism with which they conducted their countries' foreign affairs.

An interpreter sat beside each of them in opposite corners of the carriage. Ribbentrop turned to Helmut Kleiber, his own interpreter, and nodded.

"Foreign Minister," Kleiber began the rehearsed opening speech, "Herr von Ribbentrop wishes to make clear that in acceding to this meeting at a time when our two countries are at war, he is not in any way admitting an equal interest in any settlement the Soviet Union might propose. The military situation is, in the opinion of the German general staff, so markedly favorable to Germany that it would be a dire mistake for Soviet Foreign Minister Molotov to interpret Foreign Minister Herr von Ribbentrop's presence here as an anxiety on the part of the Reich government to conclude a peaceful settlement. It was, after all, the Soviet foreign minister who requested this meeting in the most urgent terms. The Reich Foreign Ministry has done no more than comply with the request."

Molotov looked down at his small, fat hands. "I understand," he said slowly. "But then the purpose of my asking for this meeting was to explore a situation. Nothing more."

When the Russian translator had finished, Ribbentrop smiled loftily. "Perhaps to explore a situation that will arise in the spring and early summer when the Soviet armies will be reeling back to the Urals."

"We are neither of us generals," Molotov said placatingly. "Let us talk simply as politicians. That way we know where we stand."

Convinced he occupied a commanding position, Ribbentrop gestured for Molotov to continue.

"The position I wish to explore, Foreign Minister von Ribbentrop," Molotov said carefully, "is this. We know that there exist certain resistance forces in your country . . ."

"A handful of ex-Communists who should have been swept into a camp years ago."

"No, not just a handful of ex-Communists. Others. A group, for instance, representing officers on the general staff."

Ribbentrop stiffened. How had the Soviets discovered that? He had himself read Heydrich's confidential report to senior government and party members only last month.

"The leader was a certain Colonel Erikson, I understand." Molotov allowed a rare smile of triumph.

"Your information is good but out-of-date," Ribbentrop said. "The members of the Erikson clique have already been arrested, tried and put to death."

"All of them?"

"All of them."

"You can well imagine," Molotov said, "if that *is* the case, the Soviet Union could only draw satisfaction from their deaths."

Suddenly Ribbentrop believed that he knew what this meeting was about. His confidence came back. He lit a cigar and brushed nonexistent ash from the white lapels of his gray Foreign Office uniform. The Kremlin had obviously heard of the Erikson plot and was naturally terrified of the prospect of a Germany at peace with Britain and the United States and free to devote all its military might to the destruction of the Soviet Union.

"The exploration I wish to conduct," Molotov went on, "is along these lines. First, if a situation did develop in which an anti-Hitler group within Germany had reached some considerable area of agreement with Great Britain and America to negotiate a separate peace, the Soviet Union wishes the Reich government to know that it would be prepared to negotiate an instant armistice during which you might deal with your own internal problems."

"I see the logic of your position," Ribbentrop said. "It is, however, inconceivable that such a situation will arise. The Reich security forces have proved that they are more than capable of dealing with a handful of traitors."

For a long time Molotov stared down at his hands. From outside he could hear the shouts of drunken soldiers, but the heavy furnishings of the compartment made it impossible to know whether they were Russian or German.

"What sort of situation would arise, Foreign Minister, if it was the Reich Security Head Office *itself* which was prepared to negotiate a separate peace with the West?"

Ribbentrop dropped his cigar. Discreetly his interpreter trod on it.

"Your handful of traitors," Molotov pressed on, "is headed by SS General Heydrich. He is engaged at this moment in securing endorsement of the Vatican for a new National Socialist Reich headed by himself. I don't need to tell you what will happen to the present party leadership."

Ribbentrop heard the Russian interpreter through to the end, his face reddening. "This is a lie, an attempt to sow dissension." He rose to go.

"Please do not go, Foreign Minister. In this matter the interests of the Soviet Union and of Hitler's Germany are one, bizarre as that might sound while we are fighting a war to the death."

Ribbentrop subsided into his seat. "Where do you claim to have this information from?" he asked coldly.

"In London we have an agent, a senior member of the British Foreign Office. He has been briefed on these developments. I can provide you with all the ancillary information."

"Do you claim that Churchill and Roosevelt are in favor of this plan?"

"We do not yet know, but our agent will keep us fully informed. We in turn will inform you. But this is not a handful of officers. This is one of the most powerful figures in your state. And he is enlisting the support of the anti-Soviet Pope Pius. We need this plot destroyed as badly as you do; but if it has already gone too far, if you are incapable of stopping it dead, the Soviet Union is prepared to enter into immediate armistice discussions."

In the embankment dugout Geller and Feldwebel Zeitz were into their second bottle of watered alcohol.

"The first woman I ever had," Zeitz was saying. "Well, to tell the truth," he amended, "I suppose more she had me. So, the first woman who ever had me . . ." His voice slurred to a stop. Outside they had both heard the clank of an iron coupling.

Geller jumped up. "That bitch of a train," he shouted. "It's moving."

Zeitz stumbled drunkenly to join him at the observation slit. "Stay there," he pleaded, "just until tomorrow."

The two locomotives snorted steam. Very slowly they pulled apart.

Zeitz took the bottle of alcohol and blundered outside.

"Come back, you fool." Geller grabbed scarves and gloves and followed him out. "You'll get frostbite dressed like that."

Zeitz was standing on the embankment, waving to the darkened train as it clattered past. "At least those boys are going back home," he said. "What's left of them, that is."

Geller scrambled up the embankment and handed Zeitz his scarf and gloves. "Put those on quick."

Zeitz nodded and turned to look down at the cooking fires glowing next to the German foxholes. Across the snowscape the Russian fires seemed to be dying out, one after another. "Get those fires out," he yelled to the men crouched around them.

"You yell like that and your lungs'll freeze solid, you idiot. Go down and tell them."

On the Russian side the last fire died. The moon shone on empty snowfields and black clumps of trees. One or two of the nearest groups of German soldiers began to throw snow on their fires. Somewhere farther along the sector position, a machine gun stuttered briefly then stopped.

"I'll go down and tell them," Zeitz mumbled.

"No need," Geller said. "They knew it was too good to last forever." He pointed. All along the German line the fires were being extinguished.

From one side or the other, the machine gun fired again, a longer, more determined burst, and a clutch of mortar bombs exploded dully in the woods behind.

"Let's get back underground," Geller said, taking his friend's arm. "It's where we belong."

* * *

Six hundred miles southwest of the Demiansk front, at Adolf Hitler's East Prussian headquarters at Rastenburg, there were already the first signs of spring. Blondi, the Führer's German shepherd dog, scratched at wild daffodils and chased imaginary young rabbits through the pines.

Hitler, in peaked cap and long gray military overcoat, paced the woodland paths inside the headquarters compound, dreaming of victory on the Eastern front this coming summer. For the first time in his life the weather had importance for him. Each patch of melting snow gave him pleasure.

He looked around irritably, disturbed in his reverie, to see the SS guard commander approaching. The Obersturmführer stopped and saluted. "Herr von Ribbentrop presents his apologies for the disturbance, Führer, but he would like to speak to you on a matter of the greatest urgency."

"I'll finish my walk," said Hitler. "Tell him I'll see him at supper."

The young guard commander hesitated. "The foreign minister stressed the unusual importance he attaches to seeing you immediately."

The Führer smiled at the young officer's embarrassment. "All right, Ritter," he said, "I'll do it for you—wouldn't do it for anybody else. Tell the foreign minister to join me here in the woods. Do him good. . . ."

"Thank you, Führer." The young man saluted and hurried away.

Hitler returned to his slow pacing after Blondi. A plan had been forming in his mind all winter, that disastrous winter of defeat on the Russian front. What if the main thrust of this year's advance was to the south—toward the oil of the Caucasus?

He could hear Ribbentrop's footsteps crunching old pinecones and melting snow. He turned. "What is it, Ribbentrop?" he said without preamble.

Ribbentrop stood in front of him breathing heavily. He wore

his gray Foreign Office uniform with the white lapel facings, but there was a dark smudge down one arm where he had brushed against a pine tree. His normally pale face was flushed and his hair disheveled.

Hitler watched him fight to catch his breath. "Well, what did Molotov have to propose—a separate peace in the East? They fear this summer's campaign, Ribbentrop. They fear a blow into the industrial heart of Russia. . . ." He stopped. "What did Molotov want?"

"The Soviets have learned from an agent in London that a serious proposal exists for an armistice in the West, leaving Russia to fight Germany alone."

Hitler shook his head. "Peace between Germany and the West, never," he said. "Did I not propose this early in the struggle? But Churchill and myself are sworn enemies. To the death, Ribbentrop. And now Roosevelt too." He smiled. "Who does Foreign Minister Molotov put forward as the traitor on our own side?"

"It will come as a particular shock, Führer, a body blow. Obergruppenführer Heydrich is the traitor named."

Hitler's face was totally immobile, set in the same way Ribbentrop had so often seen him in the last few seconds before a Party Day speech.

Then to Ribbentrop's total discomfiture, he began to laugh.

Nobody in the Hitler circle enjoyed the Führer's laughter. Uncertain whether to laugh himself, Ribbentrop stood watching him. The dog Blondi came racing back through the trees, barking furiously, and started jumping excitedly around his master.

"Obergruppenführer Heydrich flew to Berlin two days ago," he said, wiping his eyes with the back of his hand. "He gave me information collected by the SD in neutral countries over the last month. Since the Hess fiasco last year and Heydrich's own defeat of the Erikson-Brombach treachery, there have been at least four strongly planted rumors of treasonable peace initiatives by senior figures in the Reich."

"Planted rumors? You mean you don't believe them to be true, Führer?"

Hitler reached down for a stick and threw it down the path. Blondi bounced after it barking. "Do I believe them?" He paused. "I think I'll leave you to make up your mind, Ribbentrop."

The foreign minister waited.

"The first rumor," Hitler said slowly, "concerned Reichsmarschall Göring."

Ribbentrop's eyes opened in alarm. "The Reichsmarschall?"

"Yes, supposedly he was negotiating with the Western Allies in Sweden."

Ribbentrop could hardly believe his luck. Göring was a serious rival to his own ambitions to rise even higher in the Reich.

"This is a serious allegation, Führer," he said weightily.

Hitler nodded agreement. "The second suggestion is that Himmler has current connections through Turkey."

"Himmler!"

"The third is the idea of a Moscow rapprochement developed by Goebbels."

Ribbentrop was speechless. His three major enemies in the party. "And the fourth initiative?" he asked.

"That one, Ribbentrop, is reported to have come from you."

Ribbentrop flushed with fear. Hitler cackled. The dog leaped and barked.

"And now," Hitler said, "you come trotting back from Demiansk with a little bit of gossip against Heydrich."

He was no longer smiling. "We are being subjected," he said, "to a crude attempt to sow mistrust among the senior party leadership." He thought for a moment. "The Soviets are behind it. They know that with the coming of spring the death blow is about to fall. We will strike for the Russian oil supplies with thousands of new tanks and guns. It is this fear that leads the Politburo to calumniate our leadership."

"Führer," Ribbentrop said anxiously, "I can assure you of my most intense feelings of loyalty."

Hitler held up his hand. "So can Obergruppenführer Heydrich. I am prepared to believe you both."

Chapter Thirteen

"Only Americans can afford to take a girl to the Café Royal these days," she said.

He looked around at the British officers lunching with their wives or girlfriends. "I'm probably the only American here."

"It'll be different soon," she said, "when America takes over the war. Although God knows when that will be. They've been in three months and I can't see it's made any appreciable difference. You're quite right, you're the only American here. And you're not going to the war—you're going home."

"I'm sorry, Pam," he said. "I wondered what all the sudden anti-Americanism was about. You're right, I've been given a sailing date."

She shrugged in an exaggerated fashion that emphasized rather than disguised the hurt. "Back home?"

"Greg Sefton seems to think I can be more useful lecturing the new boys in the States. So . . ."

She nodded. "Well, that was the deal. A week, two weeks . . . six . . ."

He looked across the table with no idea what to say.

231

"Sorry, Jim." She stretched out a hand and touched his. "I'm afraid it's just that in the last few weeks I've grown very fond of you. Very, very, very."

"As I have of you."

"No"—her eyes were brimming with tears—"not good enough, Jim. It's going to take more than Pam Denning to wipe that German countess from your mind."

"If you'd known her, I think you would have liked her."

"I suppose so," she said wearily. "I suppose after this damn war we're going to have to start to like them again. We're going to have to separate the sheep from the wolves, God knows how."

"You assume you'll win?"

"Of course," she said.

"No doubts."

"Don't be silly."

He was surprised to find he was thinking of old Herr Frett-ner, the mayor-*cum*-Bahnhofmeister at Krevenden. "You'll like the Germans," he said, "if you ever really get to know them."

"When do you leave?" she asked briskly.

"This afternoon."

"That works out fine," she said.

"It does?"

"The coalman calls tomorrow."

The two marine sergeants lifted the President of the United States from his bath and enveloped him in a huge white robe.

Lowering himself into his wheelchair Franklin D. Roosevelt took a hot towel and dabbed at his face. "That's better," he said. "Now I feel *clean* enough to make history."

At the end of the long corridor in the president's family quarters, John Winant paced anxiously, his eyes flickering constantly toward the wall clock. Few ambassadors, he concluded ruefully, had ever been asked to deal between two such willful eccentrics as the British prime minister and the American president,

Behind him the door opened and Franklin Roosevelt, his hair

disheveled, his face lobster red above the white bathrobe, wheeled himself into the room. "Give me a cigarette, John, will you?" he said without preamble. "Box over there."

Winant carried the cigarette box across to Roosevelt.

"This is a matter of the utmost urgency, Mr. President. Winston Churchill is pressing for an answer as soon as I get back to London."

Roosevelt lit his cigarette and settled back in his chair. "Political assassination has not, traditionally, been popular among Western statesmen. It's not an idea we much like to encourage. Can rebound, John."

"I see that, sir."

"Yet Winston is convinced there's no other way?"

"He believes the inducement held out to the Vatican by Heydrich is far too great for us to persuade Pope Pius against this course of action."

Roosevelt nodded. "Fortunately," he said, "Winston and I are in total agreement. Peace is the only way we can now lose this war, a premature peace. But it's ironic, John, that to win this war in the way we wish, the life of Adolf Hitler must be preserved from all would-be assassins." He paused. "Tell Winston that the direct course of action he favors has my full support."

Liverpool, Jim Franklyn decided, was hell. The weather was coming in from the west, driving over Birkenhead and Wallasey and across the Mersey in a stream of low, heavy, unrelenting clouds. The fine drizzle began to harden into steady rain and Franklyn quickened his step along the gray, deserted street. He turned a corner and hurried past the eighteenth-century town hall and on down Water Street. By the time he reached the docks, the rain was falling in an angled downpour and he was thankful the naval guard at the gate waved him through with no more than a cursory glance at his identification. It was the same at the entrance to the office building. He was becoming a familiar figure in and around Western Approaches Command.

In one of the long, dim corridors of the main administration block, he took off his coat. The rain had soaked through and dampened the shoulders and neck of his uniform. He cursed under his breath and hung the sodden coat and cap on a row of empty pegs beside a bulletin board. Between a couple of posters, a yellowing official directive caught his eye. It read, "No person shall ask or answer any question, or display or cause to be displayed any sign which furnishes any indication of the name of, or the situation or the direction of or the distance to, any place whatsoever." Jesus!

A civil servant sauntered by in pinstriped suit and stiff collar. He glanced down at the pool of water already forming on the floor under the coat and gave Franklyn a look of cold disdain.

Franklyn walked to the end of the corridor and tapped on a small glass window. It slid open and the well-scrubbed, suspicious face of a middle-aged Wren confronted him. "Yes?"

"I want to see the transport officer, Lieutenant Commander Perraton."

"What about?" she snapped.

Franklyn felt his temper rising but controlled it. "He's arranging a passage to the States . . ."

The Wren cut him short. "Name?"

"Franklyn, Captain James Franklyn. He knows me."

"That does not mean he'll see you. He's a very busy man. Wait here."

The glass partition snapped shut. Franklyn went to the window at the end of the corridor. It looked out over the docks. Through the sheets of rain he could see the lines of ships of every shape and size moored and anchored along the waterfront. Liverpool was, after London, the busiest port in the country. With practically all of Western Europe under German occupation, Great Britain was indeed an island fortress, but far from self-sufficient. It needed to import vast quantities of food and raw materials simply to survive. The oceans were its lifeline; at any one time there were over two thousand British merchant ships at sea, and on any one day more than a hundred vessels sailed from a British port, mostly half empty, to load with new supplies from the United States and Canada. So why was it so damned difficult to arrange a passage for one officer to New York?

"It's a question of priorities," explained Lieutenant Commander Perraton. He was a man of fifty-five with a square jawline and clear, blue sailor's eyes.

"Doesn't waiting around for days rate any priority?"

"I'm afraid not."

At their previous meeting, Franklyn had formed the impression that Perraton would much prefer to be out in the Atlantic hunting U-boats than sitting behind a desk shuffling paperwork. He had decided an appeal on that level might work.

"Commander, here I am doing nothing but eating food those ships bring over. All I want to do is to get back to the United States and get on with a real job."

The lieutenant commander leaned back in his chair, his face somber.

"Captain, I want to tell you something in utter confidence."

"You can rely on my discretion."

"When you first reported here I checked your papers and then submitted your name on the lists for two separate transatlantic convoys. Each time your name was crossed off."

"Crossed off? Who by?"

"The list goes upstairs for approval. We're a mixed bag here, naval personnel, civil servants from the Ministry of Shipping, couple of chaps from the Director of Trades Division. Could have been any one of several senior people."

"But I don't understand. Why me?"

"They don't give me reasons, I'm afraid. I thought you might have some idea yourself."

"Well, I haven't. I've got no idea."

Perraton leaned forward, lowering his voice. "If I had to guess, and it would be nothing more than that, you understand, I would imagine"—he pointed an accusing finger upwards—"someone received a memorandum, a phone call, some kind of directive to hold you here in Liverpool. And I'll say one more thing, it's not the navy."

"A civilian. By what authority?"

The commander stopped Franklyn with a raised hand. "Captain, I can't discuss this further; I've already said more than I should."

Franklyn could see he meant it. He stood up, ready to leave.

"What I am prepared to do," said Perraton, "is submit your name for the next convoy. It might slip through."

"I'm not sure I follow you."

"I'm suggesting that civil servants aren't infallible, and old directives get buried under more paperwork."

Franklyn smiled broadly. "Thank you, Commander."

"Good luck."

Outside, the rain had stopped. The sea breeze was gusting hard and the clouds scurried over much higher, their ranks broken by a few patches of blue sky. Franklyn strolled along the road running parallel to the river and the docks. The waters of the Mersey looked slow and unsure. The tide was on the turn; soon it would be surging in, raising the water level twenty feet and scouring the estuary, keeping it free of mud. Perraton had seemed to be on his side, but it still left the question of who was preventing him leaving Liverpool, and more importantly— why.

He stopped by an old man leaning on a rail overlooking one of the small, wooden jetties. A tender was landing wounded men. They lay on stretchers cocooned in thick red blankets as they were carefully carried ashore.

"They deserve medals, every one of them," the old man said.

"Who are they?"

The old man turned to him. His face was lined and hardened into a deep brown mask that only a lifetime at sea can produce, but his eyes were bright and sharp.

"Spent four days on a raft. Three survivors out of thirty."

The U-boat commanders called this the "happy time." The losses they inflicted were appalling. All British merchant ships were manned by volunteers, and out of a total of a hundred and fifty thousand, over thirty-two thousand would die at sea before the war was over.

The old man pointed down. "Tankers are the worst. That's what burning oil does."

The last man was being brought ashore. As he was loaded into the waiting ambulance, Franklyn glimpsed his face and upper body, a mass of hanging, blackened flesh.

"Deserve VCs, all of them," the old man said.

As Franklyn walked away, the old man still leaned on the rail, looking out over the water.

It was barely 6:00 A.M. The taxi driver worked on a hangnail on his left forefinger and wondered if any of the gas points would be open this early in the morning. He knew the unwieldy balloon of ordinary town gas on the roof of the Morris was less than half full and that would give him no more than fifteen miles of motoring. He hoped the punter he was waiting for did not want to be taken too far. This would be him now.

Franklyn hurried down the hotel steps, threw his two bags on the backseat and jumped in beside the driver.

"The docks, gate seven, d'you know it?"

"Do I know it? I was born down there, wack." The driver's voice had the thick Scouse accent of a native Liverpudlian.

"Fine, I'm in a hurry."

"Never knew a Yank who wasn't."

As the taxi drove away, Franklyn checked his watch. It had been a frantic rush to dress and pack but with luck he was going to make it.

Ten minutes ago he had been awakened with a start by an urgent banging on his hotel room door. It was the night porter. He had twenty minutes to get to the docks.

It was still dark as the taxi, with its blackout-regulation, single-hooded headlight, drove past the entrance to the Mersey tunnel and on down Victoria Street. The driver swung left along Strand Street and pulled up with a jolt. Franklyn collected his bags and paid him off.

The wind was coming off the estuary and Franklyn caught the tang of the open sea. He was on his way. His papers were checked and he joined a knot of passengers going aboard a tender. When his turn came, a naval rating glanced at his boarding pass and pointed off to the right.

"You're on 107. Down there."

"What?" said Franklyn.

"Tanker. She's moored at the next berth."

The *Rowena* had been built in 1912. Three hundred and fifty feet long with a fifty-foot beam, she was a three-island tanker. The name derived from the distinctive superstructures, a prominent forecastle, bridge and aft deck. At sea these would appear over the horizon first as three unconnected islands. The name *Rowena* had been painted out and the identification number 107 emblazoned in ten-foot-high figures on each side of the bow. The old ship had served her time bringing oil from the Americas to Europe; now she was a battered, salt-caked, rusting hulk smelling of rotting seaweed and diesel fuel.

A deckhand leaned over the rail and called down. "You the passenger?"

"Right," said Franklyn.

"Better come aboard. Captain's ready to sail."

Franklyn balanced his way over the single wooden plank that crossed the six feet of black, gurgling water between the quay and the peeling hull. One thing's for sure, he thought, this is definitely not the S.S. *Bremen*.

The deckhand took him to his cabin in the aft deckhouse. It was a cramped room with a bunk bed, a small wooden table and little else. As Franklyn surveyed his quarters, the ship began to vibrate with a deep rumble as the engines started to turn. He went back out onto the deck.

The lines were cast off and slowly 107 started to move out into the estuary. The first light of dawn was yellowing the eastern horizon, silhouetting the forest of derricks and cranes along the waterfront. The tanker gradually eased out into midstream. The breeze was fresh and cold as it came off the expanse of gray-black water, and Franklyn dug his hands into his pockets to keep them warm. Now he could make out the vague shapes of the other vessels in the convoy moving out toward the open sea.

The mate came back and told him the captain would like to meet him on the bridge. Franklyn followed the man forward and climbed up the central island. The captain was younger than he expected, in his mid-thirties, strong and well built. His large, open face sported the stub of an unlit cigar in the corner of the mouth.

"Frank Doyle," he introduced himself. The handshake was warm and firm. "Welcome to SC eighteen."

"SC eighteen?" asked Franklyn.

"Slow convoy eighteen. We average six knots, if we're lucky."

The bridge was as antiquated as the rest of the ship, but had a homey feel. A small toy teddy bear, faded and dirty with age, hung on a string above the head of the man at the wheel.

The red, burning edge of the sun was rising up, lighting the sky. Franklyn looked back; the coastline was fading away into the distance, its detail still in deep shadow. Ahead, the sea appeared an intense blue-black, with white streaks of foam threading its expanse like the irregular veins in marble. A large, camouflaged vessel steamed past, heading toward the estuary. It was packed with barrels and empty oil drums to give it extra buoyancy, and its decks bristled with antiaircraft guns.

"Barrage breaker. Don't see many of them in these waters," said the captain."

The special minesweeper went by on the starboard side.

"What a job," said the man at the helm. "The crew stand on trampolines so they don't bust any bones when a mine goes up."

The old tanker plowed steadily on, crossing the wide, swirling wake of the barrage breaker. The sun climbed higher and gained strength. Ahead, a gathering swell rose to meet the convoy. The sea was changing color to a deep bottle-green and the waves were flecked with long white manes as far as the eye could see. The ship began to move with the heaving water, the bow dipping and rising in time with the ocean, sending an increasing shower of spray hissing back along the foredeck.

Franklyn could clearly see the other ships in the convoy now, spread out in long, curving lines, freighters and tankers, large and small, but mostly old and slow like 107. The captain explained that fifty vessels would form into a large oblong and proceed sideways across the Atlantic. Ten columns, each column consisting of five ships in line ahead. This configuration would reduce the size of the target offered by the side of the convoy to the waiting U-boat packs. It was a formidable task to maintain station in such a formation, westbound against the prevailing winds, day and night whatever the weather conditions. Each ship was additionally required to steer a zigzag course in concert with all the others, and this involved altering course every few minutes. For a ship's master it meant curbing his natural instinct to go from A to B in the straightest line as fast as possible.

One of the Royal Navy escorts was coming up fast, plowing through the mounting sea, its bow cleaving a foaming path through the waves and leaving a huge, mile-long, frothing wake.

"Flashy git, must be doing thirty knots," commented the captain. Then he frowned.

The destroyer was slowing as it drew level off to port. Its whooping Klaxon began to blare out over the low howl of the wind.

"They're signaling, Skipper," said the mate.

The captain went over to the port window and looked out. A seaman worked the signal light, the intermittent flash blinking out bright against the gray paintwork of the destroyer's superstructure. "What do they want?" asked Franklyn.

240

The captain turned to face him.

"You, I'm afraid."

"Me?"

"They've got orders to take you back ashore."

The car speeded up as it left the outskirts of Liverpool. The main road now ran through open countryside and there was little traffic. The young, fresh-faced lieutenant at the wheel glanced at Franklyn, proffering a stick of chewing gum. He had only been in England a few weeks and the sun tan from his Kentucky training camp had still not completely faded.

"Gum, Captain."

"No, thanks."

Franklyn shook his head. "Where are we heading," he asked. "London?"

"Place called Knutsford. My orders are to take you to an inn there, the Royal George."

"What happens in Knutsford?"

The lieutenant glanced at him as they drove through the rolling Cheshire countryside. "I suppose you could say we have a school there."

"We?"

"The U.S. Army."

"A training school?"

"Yes, sir."

They drove in silence past the old town hall and turned into the cobbled courtyard of the Royal George.

"Don't worry about your bags, Captain, I'll deal with them later," the lieutenant said.

They crossed the cobbles worn smooth by centuries of iron-bound coach wheels and entered the timbered lobby of the inn.

"Pretty quaint, huh?" the lieutenant said, taking off his topcoat.

Franklyn nodded. Above the young lieutenant's breast pocket the light glinted on the metal wings of a paratrooper.

The lieutenant led the way up the gleaming oak staircase and along a wide corridor.

"The major got a kick out of this room," the lieutenant said, stopping at a door. "Seems some king used it way back."

He knocked and opened the door. Franklyn stepped inside and saw the shapeless bulk of Greg Sefton sitting behind a ludicrously small writing desk.

"For Christ's sake," Franklyn said, "what's all this cloak-and-dagger stuff about, Greg?"

Sefton got up and ambled across the room to a sideboard. "You're going to have to drink bourbon," he said.

"Well, the old country's at war."

"Take off your coat."

Franklyn took off his topcoat and sat down in the single leather armchair. "So . . . ?"

Sefton handed him the drink and turned to pour one for himself. "Seems we only just got to you in time. Can't see how that happened. I'd had a stop on your sailing clearance for the last five days."

"The transport officer at Liverpool figured somebody had. Why?"

Sefton turned from the sideboard. His heavy-lidded eyes seemed to pan the room before they rested on Franklyn.

"How long have we known each other, Jim? Ten, fifteen years."

"Something like that."

"Yeah," Sefton mused into his drink. "Known each other fifteen years. Never really been friends, would you say?"

"Jesus." Franklyn sat back, hurt. "Maybe I was wrong all this time."

"Maybe," Sefton nodded. He sipped the bourbon and grimaced at its sweetness. "Tell you the hard truth, Jim, I always thought there was something missing."

"What is this, an end-of-semester report?"

Sefton shook his fat jowls. "No, no . . . I just mean you started strong but around about age thirty, most of us could see you were already fading."

Franklyn shifted uncomfortably. "Okay, but you still offered me the Munich job."

"Because the nasty reality of this business is that someone in my job goes a lot further if he works on weakness than on strength. We wanted a boozy, skirt-chasing sleeper in Munich. We got just that. We wanted someone even the Gestapo would gradually lose their suspicions of. We got just that. We wanted someone we could force to pick up the ball and run the moment it came his way."

"And you got just that."

"I didn't enjoy doing it to you," Sefton said.

"And what are you doing now?"

"What I'm doing now is something different. Now I think I'm working on strength."

Sefton took the weight on his hands and lifted his heavy body to sit on the edge of the desk.

Franklyn registered the plaintive creak of the wood. "You didn't bring me here to tell me this."

"No."

"You've got some new orders for me?"

"Orders, no. . . ."

"Then what is it, for Christ's sake?"

"That conference I told you about, the one Heydrich called in Wannsee . . . our information is that it's set the whole Fall-Ost program in motion. Phase One is the final solution of the Jewish problem. That could cost up to ten million lives. Fall-Ost, in its entirety, envisages the complete clearance of Eastern Europe. Perhaps thirty million people."

"London and Washington are finally convinced."

"Yes."

"And what do they plan to do?"

"Churchill and Roosevelt will make an appeal to the pope to excommunicate every German Catholic who takes *any* part in the operation."

"Will it work?"

"If the papacy agrees. Certainly it would slow the whole pace of the killings."

"Anything else?"

"Yes." The round, sallow face looked down at him. A thick index finger scoured at his left ear. "We're going to kill Heydrich, Jim."

"Kill Heydrich!"

"Assassinate him. In Prague. Soon."

"Jesus. . . ." A wave of sick fear swept over him. "Why should you bring me back to London to tell me that?" he asked warily.

"You've guessed," Sefton nodded. "We want you to go out to Prague to take charge of the operation."

They stood in the long drive and watched a fat gray balloon with a wicker cage suspended below it rise on a steel cable over the elegant portico of Knutsford Manor.

After a few moments tiny figures began to leap from the cage, plummeting downward until the Khaki nylon parachutes billowed above them.

"The resistance situation in Prague is in ruins," Sefton said.

Franklyn frowned. "It didn't look that way when I was there."

"Gestapo rat hunts as they like to call them have been increasingly successful since Heydrich took over. We have some very demoralized teams over there."

"Not František's group?"

"No. One of the best. Probably *the* best."

Skirting the gardens they began to round the side of the great house.

"So even Fall-Ost apart, the Czech government-in-exile here in England is pressing for Heydrich to be killed?"

Sefton stopped on the gravel. "No, Jim, they're not. They're asking themselves, understandably, what the price could be in Czech civilian lives."

"And what could it be?"

"In reprisals for the Reichsprotektor? Ten thousand, twenty, who can guess?"

"Despite Heydrich's pressure, you're saying the resistance *isn't* in favor of killing him either?"

Sefton began to walk on. "They don't know about the idea."

"So how will it be handled?"

"We plan to use two groups. One active, one backup. The backup group has been trained in Britain for general assassination tasks. They have already been parachuted into Czechoslovakia."

"These you put on ice."

Sefton nodded. "Their code identification is Anthropoid. They know nothing more than that they will receive target orders from a coordinator who will be parachuted into Czechoslovakia at a later date."

"They're the backup. And the active group?"

"František. The coordinator's job is to brief the František group. They've got experience and most of all they've got the girl on Heydrich's staff. They're a natural choice."

"But they could refuse?"

"I guess that depends on how far they trust the coordinator."

"They could still refuse for the sake of twenty thousand Czechs."

"If they refuse, the coordinator activates the Anthropoid group. These are Czech members of the British army. They don't have the right to refuse. But they don't have the inside track that František has. And if they bungled it, it would be a year at least before Heydrich relaxed his defenses enough for anybody to take another crack at him."

"So you want me to persuade František that this is worth the lives of twenty thousand Czechs?"

"Tell him what you believe the Final Solution will mean to millions of Jews. Tell him we are desperate to buy time even at the cost of Czech lives."

"And you think he'll believe me?"

"I don't know, Jim. But he's sure as hell not going to believe any other American we can put into the field right now."

Franklyn exhaled slowly.

"Well . . . ?" Sefton watched him, heavy-lidded.

"Just one question," Franklyn said. "How do I get there?"

Sefton pointed up to the small figures parachuting from the balloon. "You guessed right. This is Number One OSS Training School, European Theater. Normally, parachute training takes a period of six weeks. Day and night jumps from ballon and aircraft. But don't worry, Jim, you don't have that sort of time. You're going to have to do it all in five days."

Chapter Fourteen

A group of rooks cawed raucously high in the branches of a line of elm trees as the sound of the train receded into the distance.

"Captain Franklyn?"

Franklyn turned to the uniformed corporal behind him. "Yes."

"I was told to meet you here, sir. Car's over there."

Franklyn followed him across the station forecourt to a drab khaki Humber saloon with RAF plates.

"Staying with us long, sir?" the corporal probed.

"I doubt it," Franklyn said.

"First time we've had an American on the base."

"It won't be the last," Franklyn said tonelessly.

The corporal got the point. "No, sir, I don't expect it will be," he said and concentrated on the driving.

It was late afternoon when the Humber turned into a wide entrance in a high yew hedge flanked by stone columns. The wrought-iron gates they had once supported had been removed and melted down for scrap, along with railings, garden fences and disused streetcar lines from all over the country. Amberly was one of a series of new airfields dotted across the flat, open fenland of East Anglia. Mostly they sprawled over the dark, rich farmland, but Amberly had once been a country house and estate. The main runway passed an ornamental lake in the extensive grounds, and the buildings were a collection of Nissen huts and corrugated iron hangars and workshops around a crumbling, three-story mansion that must have been imposing in its day.

A sergeant sat at a trestle desk in the center of the high-vaulted hall, looking completely out of place against the dark oak paneling and decorative stone floor. Franklyn identified himself and was taken up a wide staircase to the intelligence officer on the second floor. The sergeant knocked and opened the door, standing aside for Franklyn to enter. The room was small and cosy; an ancient gas fire glowed in one corner, giving the air a dry, claustrophobic edge. The intelligence officer was a dapper man with a fast, almost jerky manner. His handshake was one quick downward movement.

"You're going out with a bombing wing, middle group," he announced.

"A raid?" Franklyn said. He had seen the flak over Berlin and flaming bombers falling from the sky.

"That's right," the IO said matter-of-factly. "The target's Mannheim. You'll skirt around it of course and fly on to your destination west of Prague."

"Any particular reason for mixing me in with the bombers?"

"It's safer—marginally. Two ways of looking at it really. One aircraft might fly straight through without Jerry ever realizing it was there. On the other hand, if you *were* spotted you'd be the center of attention—chances of survival, minimal. Anyway it wasn't my decision."

Nor mine, thought Franklyn.

An airman took Franklyn over to one of the crewrooms and introduced him to the pilot he would be flying with, a tall, rangy

New Zealander named Leggat with a DFC ribbon on his blouse. Franklyn felt an instant liking for the man.

They had exchanged no more than a few words when the flight commander bustled in, checked the roster, announced the crews for that night and read a new air firing regulation which Franklyn didn't fully understand. After a few moments of small talk with the men, the flight commander started to leave but paused by Franklyn and Leggat at the doorway.

"You're on Special Ops, I hear," he said to Leggat.

"Makes a change," said Leggat with a toothy grin.

The FC glanced at Franklyn curiously, but decided not to ask what it was all about.

"Well, keep out of trouble. Good luck."

The crews began to drift away.

"You want to ask about anything?" asked Leggat. "Any special worries?"

"You're kidding," Franklyn said dryly.

"Did they get around to aircrew emergency drill during your training?"

Franklyn decided it would be better not to go into too much detail concerning his training. A crash course in parachuting might not exactly impress.

"Not too much."

They went outside to a Wellington bomber, the first in a line of twenty or so stretching away toward the edge of the lake. The spring air was clear and turning cold. A ground crew was still working on the plane, cleaning the Perspex windows, testing the gun turret hydraulics, checking their way down a routine list. Leggat had a brief word with the NCO in charge, then clambered up into the belly of the aircraft. Franklyn followed. He felt awkward in the suprisingly cramped interior, scrambling after Leggat through the maze of wires, cross struts, cables and pipework. Leggat showed him the liferaft and explained the procedure if they came down in the sea, then demonstrated the position he should take up for a crash landing.

"If it comes to bailing out, you're the expert; we'll follow you."

Franklyn managed a smile. Leggat grinned back and then went forward to the cockpit to exchange a few words of friendly abuse with one of the ground crew who was perched outside checking the windshield wipers.

Alone for a moment, Franklyn contemplated what would soon be happening. In a few short hours he would be jumping out of this bird's nest of steel and wire into a black void somewhere over Czechoslovakia. The events of the last few days, since he had told Sefton he would do it, had that patchy, half-remembered quality of a hangover. Now he found himself unable to judge whether volunteering had been a conscious decision or a reaction to the news of Christina Erikson's death. What did it matter? This aircraft with its confusion of colored wires, its mass of aluminum struts, racks, trays and clips, this was the stark reality.

As they dropped down from the hatch the armorers had arrived and were standing by to bomb up. They sat astride the long caterpillar trailers carrying the two-hundred-pounders.

"We'll be carrying bombs?" asked Franklyn, a little surprised.

"This isn't our crate. You're a VIP, you get a modified aircraft. Special drop hole cut in the bottom. Want some tea?"

The mess was full of noise, the clatter of knives and forks and a stream of animated conversation. Tea consisted of two fried eggs on a thick slice of buttered toast cut from a national wheatmeal loaf which had a grayish, dirty look. The rumor was it had aphrodisiac qualities, a rumor almost certainly put about by the Ministry of Food's information service.

"How are the Yanks reacting to the war—I mean the ordinary people?" asked Leggat over the top of a steaming mug of strong sweet tea.

"I haven't spent a lot of time in the States in the last couple of years."

"Probably hasn't fully hit them yet."

"Could be."

"And you?"

"Me it's hit, you can believe that."

Leggat checked his watch. It was almost six. Two and a half hours to takeoff. Somewhere in the corridor outside a bell rang.

"Briefing bell," Leggat said. "See you later."

In the intelligence officer's room, Greg Sefton was crouched down by the gas fire warming the palms of his hands. He was wearing a huge sheepskin coat, which made him look fatter than ever, and a knitted woolen hat.

"It's turning goddamn cold," he said moving forward and holding out a hand to Franklyn. "How you doing, Jim?"

"Ask me tomorrow." Franklyn's voice was flat.

"This is Middleton from SOE." Sefton indicated a tall man with a thin, classically featured face standing near the window. "British Special Operations Executive."

"How d'you do?" The voice was clipped and very English.

Sefton undid his coat; the room was now quite warm. "Let's get straight down to it."

Middleton nodded. Picking up a suitcase from under the window, he opened it on the desk.

"You'll wear these. Made here in England but indistinguishable from the genuine article."

He handed Franklyn a coarse gray woolen suit, blue shirt, white cotton underpants and a dark blue peaked cap.

"No necktie?" Franklyn meant it as a joke.

"You'll look more authentic without. Wear the shirt done right up to the neck. Now, footwear."

He tore the brown paper wrapping off a pair of well-worn heavy black boots with a thick gray sock tucked in the top of each.

"These *are* the real thing," he said with some pride, but he held them by the tabs at the back as if not particularly anxious to have any contact with anything as unseemly as secondhand boots.

The action confirmed a growing suspicion in Franklyn that he didn't like the man. He glanced over at Sefton who shrugged back.

"Now cover." Middleton took a wallet and some papers from his inside pocket. "You are Josef Kadlec, professional photographer, but now working in a factory. Your identity card, travel permit, ration documents, some letters, one from your mother, with photograph, a couple from a friend in Prague."

"A girl?"

"Male. Wrote them myself. Very chummy."

Franklyn glanced at Sefton again but this time he wasn't looking.

"Some money."

"How much?"

"Five hundred crowns."

"What's that in American?"

"Approximately fifteen dollars."

"Fifteen dollars!"

"The resistance has substantial funds. It's wiser not to carry too much personally."

Franklyn flicked through the papers and money on the desk top with the tip of one finger. Middleton stood back, crossing his arms on his chest.

"Is that it?" asked Franklyn.

"Yes."

"No secret pockets in the suit? No compass under one of the buttons?"

Middletown allowed himself a smile. "I think the service has outgrown that sort of amateur theatrical."

"So I'm Josef Kadlec, a Czech?"

"Naturally. You *are* being dropped into Czechoslovakia."

"Then it may interest you to know, I don't speak the language. Not one goddamn word."

"I see." Middletown appeared genuinely horrified.

"So you can take this rubbish . . ."

"Hold it." Sefton stepped quickly forward between them,

252

then turned to Middleton. "Why don't you wait for me downstairs? Couple of things I'd like to say to Franklyn."

Middleton hesitated for a moment but then left the room, closing the door with an almost inaudible click of the catch.

"Where the hell did you find that guy? Josef Kadlec, the Czech who can't speak his own language!"

"They had two days for something that usually takes a month. I'm sorry, Jim, it didn't occur to them you wouldn't speak Czech."

Sefton went over and sat down behind the desk. "Let's look at it square on. The problem is you getting caught, maybe the moment you hit the ground. That's what we're worried about."

"I find that reassuring."

"The papers might just help," Sefton said doubtfully.

"And if they don't?"

Sefton slid his hand forward across the desk top, then lifted it to reveal a single, cellophane-covered capsule. Franklyn stared down at it.

"You think of everything," Franklyn said.

Sefton leaned back in the chair, embarrassed. "It slips behind the pocket of your new jacket."

"I said you think of everything."

"We're doing our best, Jim."

"There's still something you seem to have missed."

"What's that?" Sefton asked uneasily.

"So far all I've heard is about getting there."

"Yes."

"So what are the traveling arrangements for the return journey?"

"We're working on those now," Sefton said.

"You're what!"

"Listen, Jim, there are problems."

"I don't want to hear about your problems, Greg. I want to hear in detail, convincing goddamn detail, how I'm going to get back. I won't have the Gestapo to work as travel agent for me this time."

253

"Czechoslovakia's a long way, Jim. The British pickup plane for agents is a single-engine little beauty called the Lysander, but it was designed for France and the Low Countries."

"You mean it can't *reach* Prague?" Franklyn said incredulously.

"We're flying in a Liberator bomber from the States."

"You mean it's not here in England yet?"

"It'll make it, Jim."

"Did it enter anybody's head to delay this operation until it got here?"

Sefton was silent.

"You bastard, Greg."

The crewroom was in an uproar. Nobody seemed to notice Franklyn in his Czech factory worker's outfit. The men rushed around in a kind of high-spirited frenzy, shouting at the top of their voices. Packs, navigation bags, harnesses, flying suits and helmets lay scattered about the floor and tables. Rations lay everywhere; the men filled their zipped pockets with what they wanted, mostly chewing gum and chocolate. Franklyn saw Quinn, the navigator on Leggat's crew, and worked his way over to him through the jostle and noise. He was stowing navigational equipment into his satchel, along with maps, rulers, compass, pencils, code book, astro tables, a watch, a sextant. A youth with blond curly hair was helping.

Quinn looked up. "Hello there."

"Is it always like this?"

"Course not. Sometimes it gets bloody noisy." The boy had a strong Cockney accent and a cheeky grin.

Quinn introduced him. "This is Sonny. He's our rear gunner."

Franklyn wasn't sure what to think; he looked fourteen years old. Leggat came in, towering over most of the others, and gave Franklyn a flying jacket, helmet, gloves and scarf. Then the two of them went along to the comparative quiet of the parachute store. The parachutes were laid out in neat rows on long trestle tables. The WAAF girls who packed them tied on labels with their names. Some had added a telephone number or a message to the unknown recipient of their work. "Come back safe." "Be lucky." "Give Adolf one from me."

"Take your pick," said Leggat.

"Does it matter?"

"Probably not, but you're the only one of us who knows for sure he'll be using a chute tonight."

Franklyn took the first one in the line. It had no message, just the packer's name, Ellen Trimm, and underneath the impersonal rubber stamp of the inspection checker. Nothing frivolous about Ellen Trimm.

Outside, the sun had just set behind the tall banks of rhododendrons on the far side of the lake. The crews were drifting out and climbing up into the waiting trucks. As each one filled, it drove slowly away toward the long line of waiting bombers. As they bumped along Franklyn watched the faces of the men. The euphoria of the crewroom had gone. They were subdued, thoughtful. The truck stopped with a jolt and the driver yelled back from the cab, "Q for *Queenie*. Anyone for Q?"

Leggat nudged Franklyn's arm. "That's us."

They jumped down onto the tarmac. Two of the crew were already waiting—McAndrews, the second pilot, and Lennox, the radio operator—standing under the wing of the Wellington. The starter battery was in position and connected and the ground crew standing by. Fifty yards away the truck stopped again at the next bomber and a crew piled out.

Franklyn checked his watch. It showed twenty minutes to takeoff. One of the armorer's empty trolleys trundled by, heading back toward the hangars.

"You okay?" It was Leggat.

"Sure."

"You looked miles away."

"Maybe. How many airfields like this around here?"

"I don't know—dozens, I suppose."

"And at each one—men waiting—over eight hundred aircraft; that's a lot of bombs."

Leggat pulled on a cigarette. "What's your point?"

"I don't know, but I've been on the receiving end."

"Where was that?"

Franklyn shrugged.

"You don't mean in Germany?"

Franklyn nodded. "Berlin has taken quite a hammering."

Leggat thought for a moment. "So has London."

It was a simple answer, but Franklyn knew that, for him at least, it would never be that simple.

Quinn and Sonny arrived in the next truck, and after Sonny had gone by to spit on all the wheels for luck, Leggat led the way aboard. Inside the aircraft, Franklyn could see little difference from the other standard Wellingtons, except for the addition of a passenger seat. He made himself as comfortable as possible by wedging himself in with a couple of packs. He was immediately behind the cockpit near the navigator's position. The crew loaded the guns, stowed all the equipment away and settled down. Quinn showed him how to use the oxygen mask and plug his headset into the intercom.

The port engine turned over twice then belched a cloud of thick black smoke and roared into life. Leggat raised his right thumb and the starboard engine was started. The preflight checks began, gas cocks, magnetos, propeller pitch control and the boost. The engines were opened up to check the revs and test the magnetos again. The flaps were tried and the compass and gyro set.

Four mintues to takeoff. Other Wellingtons taxied slowly by, then the chocks were waved away and Leggat moved smoothly out to join the line. The light was failing fast now as the slow procession made its way to the downwind side of the airfield. Franklyn shifted uncomfortably in his seat. His main feeling now was one of tension, as he sensed the way it was beginning to take hold of the others.

The leaders were in the air now. Leggat's voice came over the intercom: "Stand by for takeoff."

The okays came back from the crew.

Leggat turned *Queenie* into the wind. "Here we go."

He removed two front upper false teeth and put them in his

pocket. He had lost his own teeth in a crippled Whitley, crash-landing on the Yorkshire moors. The throttles were opened and the plane lumbered forward gathering speed, then lifting, smoothly airborne.

They circled the airfield, gaining height. Quinn called out the first course, Leggat checked it back and set it on the compass, and the noise of the two fifteen-hundred-horsepower Bristol Hercules engines settled down to a steady drone. A few minutes later Quinn announced they had crossed the coast; they were now over the North Sea. A hundred miles ahead lay the Dutch coastline and the waiting shore batteries.

Sefton and Middleton sat in a corner of the empty mess. An orderly was wiping down the tables. He gave them a glance of bored indifference as he wrung the cloth out into a galvanized bucket.

"You going back to town tonight? There's a train at ten."

"What?" Sefton looked up.

"Back to London."

"No, I think I'm going to hang around here. We should know something by morning."

Sefton stirred his untouched coffee for the third time, then realized it was stone-cold and pushed the cup away.

"How well do you know Franklyn?" Middleton asked.

"Pretty well."

"It's only an opinion, of course, a personal opinion, but I'm not convinced he's entirely suitable."

Sefton felt a surge of anger. "Not entirely suitable! Who the hell is?"

"We offered an SOE agent as you know. Czech speaker, very experienced man."

"Jesus!" Sefton said angrily.

"I can understand you wanting an American in on this operation, but—" He pursed his lips deprecatingly.

"Franklyn's the man I wanted," Sefton said, "British or American."

"That's all right, then," Middleton smiled.

257

He stood up to leave, carefully replacing his chair neatly under the table.

"A word of advice. Sitting up into the small hours won't help Franklyn or anyone else, British or American. Get a good night's sleep, old chap."

"ETA Dutch coast eight minutes," announced Quinn.

"I can see it. Looks busy," said Leggat.

Franklyn craned his neck to look forward through the cockpit window. All he could see was an occasional pinprick of light, gone in a moment. They were climbing hard, wearing oxygen masks. Franklyn edged back a few inches to look out of the beam window. He could see the searchlights now, dozens of them, scanning in wide, probing arcs. And the tracers at five hundred rounds a minute—red, yellow, green and orange— weaving and crossing in all directions, sweeping up into the blackness to eight thousand feet and then exploding. He was surprised to see how slowly they seemed to rise from the ground.

Sonny suddenly yelled out: "Somebody's in trouble, skip. Eight o'clock."

It was a Wellington, a thousand feet below them, trapped at the apex of a cone of searchlights. The pilot was weaving his aircraft desperately, trying to shake loose, but the searchlights hung on.

"Get out of there," yelled Leggat.

Almost as he spoke, a shell blew off half the weaving aircraft's starboard wing. The bomber seemed to hang in the air almost motionless, then it plunged down out of the lights and was lost in the darkness.

"Jesus!" Sonny's voice was cut short as a deep-throated roar rocked their own aircraft, viciously throwing it up and over on its side. Pieces of shrapnel ripped through the fuselage. Franklyn was hurled back from the window, momentarily blinded by the bright, exploding light of the shell as it detonated somewhere below. Everybody was shouting at once along the intercom. Leggat fought frantically with the controls to regain equilibrium.

"For Chrissake shut up." Leggat had to yell it three times before the intercom was silent.

"Everybody okay?"

The replies came back from the crew.

"You okay, Jim?"

It took a moment for Franklin to realize Leggat meant him. "I'm okay." He glanced down at his hands and found they were shaking.

Q for *Queenie* leveled out at ten thousand feet. The met. officer had been right about the temperature: it was very cold. But he had been wrong about the cloud cover. Suddenly it enveloped them. As ice began to form on the wings, Leggat decided to try to climb above it.

At twelve thousand feet, the gauge showed twenty-eight degrees centigrade below freezing and the cloud still persisted. The icing increased. It was flying off the props and beating against the side of the fuselage, and the wings were covered in a thin glaze. At thirteen thousand five hundred feet the temperature registered at minus thirty-six and the Perspex of the windows was frosted with a thick crystal rime, but at last they were out of the cloud.

On a dead reckoning Mannheim lay forty miles ahead. They had covered about three hundred and fifty miles in a little over two hours. Quinn gave a change of course, and the Wellington banked around onto the new bearing to circumvent the raid. They flew past twenty miles north of the city and Franklyn could clearly see the dull, semicircular glow of blazing fires, and occasional bright specks of light that seemed to hang in the air.

He watched the faint lights in the distance. They seemed remote, unconnected with death and destruction, but he could imagine down in the streets of the town, the explosion of bombs, the roaring fires and the cries and screams of ordinary people.

* * *

Sefton waved aside the proffered whisky bottle. "No more, thanks."

The intelligence officer shrugged and poured a little into his own empty glass. The gas fire in the corner spluttered spasmodically; there was something wrong with the pressure. Sefton paced across the room and stared at the blackout curtain covering the window, then wiped the palm of his hand back over his balding head.

"What time d'you have?" he asked.

"Eleven forty-seven."

"Where d'you figure they are?"

The intelligence officer took a drink, smacking his lips. "Difficult to say. Depends on the strength and direction of the wind, how high they fly, how the engines perform . . ."

"Yeah, I understand."

"Whether they run into any trouble—night fighters—could lose a lot of time. Could get lost completely—never find the drop zone."

"Lost?" said Sefton in amazement.

"Easily done. One degree off course—after an hour—you can be thirty miles from where you think you are."

Sefton tapped his pockets, looking for a pack of cigarettes, but then remembered he had given them up.

"On the other hand, your man's with a good crew—best in the wing. If anyone can get him there they will."

"I think I will have that drink."

A gathering breeze rustled the thorny branches of a clump of bushes. Crouched on his haunches beside them, Stefan looked up as he sensed as much as saw something fly quickly overhead, a bat perhaps, or a small owl. It was very dark, with no moon, and a wind was beginning to gust across the scrubland. A crunch somewhere behind him made the young Czech stand and whip around to the sound, snapping off the safety of his rifle and leveling it at the hip. The shape of a man loomed out of the deep shadows. It was František.

"Everything all right?" he asked.

Stefan lowered the rifle, clicking back the catch. "Quiet as a tomb."

They lit cigarettes, hand-rolled from coarse black tobacco, cupping their hands over the glowing ends.

"I hate this time," said Stefan. "Waiting is always the worst part."

He took a piece of rag from his pocket and started slowly to polish the butt of the rifle.

"Don't you ever stop playing with that toy?"

"Toy." Stefan glared, but then smiled as he realized František was only teasing him. Everyone knew the rifle was his prized possession. It was a standard Soviet semiautomatic Tokarev, firing a ten-round clip. Stefan had managed to steal it from a batch of captured arms coming back from the Russian front, and in fact it was more effective than anything the Germans had in its class. František ground his half-finished cigarette under his heel. "I smoke too much."

"Listen," hissed Stefan.

"What?"

"Listen."

"I hear it. An aircraft."

Now it was unmistakable, the deep drone of distant plane engines, growing stronger every moment.

"Flash the light," ordered František.

"It's too high."

"Do as I say."

Stefan switched on the powerful light masked with a piece of green celluloid and angled it skyward. František ran back, crashing through the undergrowth toward the other light positions.

The Wellington was at three thousand feet, and the airspeed indicator nudged a hundred and eighty-five miles an hour.

"What the—" Leggat suddenly bent forward in his seat, staring ahead. Then he was sure. "Lights—green—dead ahead."

"I see them. One, two and there's the third." McAndrews confirmed the sighting.

Franklyn gulped in apprehension. A short time before, Quinn had announced an ETA at the rendezvous of twenty minutes.

The navigator's brow lined into a frown. "I don't understand."

"Well, is it, or isn't it?" Leggat demanded. "What the hell's happening, Quinny?"

"I'm not sure, skip." Quinn's eyes raced over the charts. "Maybe that wasn't the Loupy, another river. . . ."

Leggat turned in his seat. "Forget the bloody maps. We're overflying bloody green lights right now. I need an answer."

The navigator worked frantically on his calculations, muttering to himself. "A tail wind; we must have picked up a strong tail wind."

The words rang in Franklyn's head; he knew a strong wind was the secret dread of all airborne troops. The sergeant instructor at Knutsford had glossed over the possibility. "We've only got time to teach you one thing, Captain," he had said: "how to land without breaking your goddamn neck."

But he had added later, after watching Franklyn's first attempts to jump and land properly off an eight-foot wall, "If that's the best you can do, you'd better pray there isn't a wind, Captain."

The Wellington was banking in a tight, left-hand circuit to get back into position for another run. Leggat straightened out and brought the bomber down to an altitude of eight hundred feet, dropping the airspeed to a hundred and twenty miles an hour.

Franklyn clambered back to the drop hatch. He could feel his pulse pounding in his temples. He carefully positioned himself on the edge of the opening, facing forward, then gingerly lowered his legs out and down into the slipstream.

McAndrews went forward to use the bombsights to center on the lights. "Left . . . left. Hold it there." They were now directly ahead. The Wellington was now on line, three miles from the target.

Franklyn tried to collect his thoughts, remember the points the instructor had stressed. He looked down and noticed a sheen on the toe caps of his boots dangling down in the rushing air. They were catching and reflecting the light from the bulb over Quinn's navigation table. Beyond the boots an impenetrable blackness, beyond the blackness the unseen ground. Head up and arms by your side. Straighten the legs and fall out into the night. They must be close now. The opening suddenly seemed very small. What if the metal edge caught him a vicious blow under the chin as he dropped? He would be knocked senseless, stunned. . . .

The gray, open-topped Adler Six with the markings of the 1st Reconnaissance Group, 18th Cavalry Regiment, stopped on a signal from Lieutenant Gunther Voight in the front seat. The driver and the six steel-helmeted soldiers behind him listened intently.

Beside the Adler the patrol dispatch rider switched off his engine. For a few moments they could hear nothing but the rustle of the hedgerow and soughing wind in the tall trees.

Voight stood in the passenger seat, leaning forward on the square glass visor, his head turned toward the west. He had heard an aircraft passing low a moment ago, but now the engine noise was no longer receding. In fact he realized with excitement that the plane was banking to come around again.

"Load the gun."

The men snapped the two circular ammunition drums into place, one each side of the breach of the MG 34.

Across the hill slopes Voight saw the black shape, flying low. He lifted his Zeiss binoculars. The night was very dark; a positive identification would not be easy. He managed to center on the plane and focus the field glasses. Then for a brief moment the outline was silhouetted against a marginally lighter background, a cloud perhaps, but it was long enough. It was a Wellington bomber; he was certain of that.

"That's fine," McAndrews said from the bombardier's position. "Keep her steady. About one mile, dead ahead." He had the line of green lights centered in the bombsight.

Leggat held the bomber level at eight hundred feet.

"Ready this time?"

"He's ready," said Quinn, crouching down by Franklyn's side. He shivered and glanced up at the navigator. His legs had been out so long in the slipstream they felt frozen to the bone.

Sonny was the first to see the tracers from the MG 34, streaming up behind them in a brilliant yellow trail. He yelled a warning but they were wide by a long way.

Franklyn braced himself. Behind him Quinn rechecked the static line.

"Over first light," McAndrews said.

Franklyn closed his eyes.

"Second light . . . now!"

"Jump!" yelled Quinn and slapped Franklyn's shoulder.

Franklyn pushed himself forward and dropped out into the darkness.

The parachute spewed out and up over his head. Then it opened with a smack and the harness jerked up under his arms as his headlong fall was slowed. Franklyn gulped in cold air. The bomber was already out of sight. He floated down through the silent darkness.

"Parachute, Herr Leutnant!"

Voight signaled the dispatch rider. "Get back to the village. Tell the adjutant we need more men. Parachutist in the Hluboka area."

As the motorcyclist roared away, the Adler turned off the road and bounced through the thin scrub.

Standing in the passenger seat, gripping the windshield frame, Voight watched the parachute and tried to estimate its landing point. The Hluboka quarry lay less than a thousand meters ahead. If the parachutist were landing on the far side, they would get around the area of waterlogged quarry pits before he got away. On the other hand, if the parachutist were landing between them and the quarry, he would stand no chance.

"Headlights," he shouted to the driver, and bent to pick up his machine pistol from the rack.

He knew he was drifting badly now and his attempts to correct seemed to be having little effect. Below him, what had seemed an uninviting moonscape he now saw to be a menacing area of craters, the light from the night sky gleaming leaden on the water which filled them.

He hauled down desperately on the webbing guidelines, aware of the danger of spilling too much air from the canopy. Then, as he was about to brace himself for the impact, the ground seemed to tilt violently as he swung outward to crash among a clump of bushes.

His eyes opened to see the canopy keeling over above his head, its shape collapsing. Then a gust of wind took it, horizontally now, and he was lifted from the bushes, helpless to control the billowing silk as it raced like a giant kite toward the quarry.

Five times he thumped down across the broken ground, helpless, half-staggering to his feet only to be dragged forward, sometimes facedown across the gorse and broken stone at the quarry's edge. Only half-conscious, he saw the rim of the quarry seconds before he was engulfed in icy water. As he was dragged under, he saw the canopy deflate slowly on the surface of the water.

Painless, pale, womblike. . . . He slid downward, bumping gently on rock and submerged tree trunks, turning slowly in the coils of the string and webbing.

Waist-deep in water, František grabbed at the sinking canopy. Dragging it behind him, he stumbled to the quarry edge, hauling the sodden fabric after him. A young boy fed fistfuls of nylon string through his hands.

The black shape broke the surface. František and the boy hauled it onto the rocky rim of the pit.

Vomiting water, Franklyn was only dimly aware of the great weight pressing rhythmically on his back.

"He's breathing," he heard a voice say. "He'll live, Mirek. Get him to the truck."

Hands rolled him over and he saw he was looking into the face of František.

"So, my friend," František laughed, "we meet again, as they say." He slapped Jim's cheek with his huge hand. "On your feet now. There's a German patrol close by."

Helped by František and the boy, Franklyn clambered to his feet. The sudden sensation of cold brought on an orgasmic shudder.

"There," František grinned. "You're alive again."

Behind them two figures came running through the gorse bushes. One of them, Stefan, carried a rifle at the trail.

"An Adler patrol," he said breathlessly. "They're searching the bottom of the slope."

František reached forward and took the rifle from him. "You and Karel"—he nodded toward the other man—"get Mr. Franklyn away from here. You too, Mirek," he included the boy. "I'll see what I can do to bring them down into the quarry."

Stefan stepped forward and took Franklyn's arm, dragging it across his shoulders. Karel moved around to the other side, and between them they half ran, half dragged Franklyn along.

In silence, František stopped at the foot of the quarry and raised the rifle in the air. He pressed the trigger and the shot echoed and reechoed around the rough-cut walls of stone. Up on the rim he could see four or five soldiers silhouetted against the pale sky.

He fired again into the air, twice, and saw the dark shapes scurry like rabbits for cover. Then he moved off among the rocks, climbing now toward the far side of the quarry.

Franklyn sat propped up in the back of the truck, watched anxiously by the young boy, Mirek. His clothes still dripped water and from time to time his whole body gave way to a spasm of uncontrollable shivering.

"You want my coat?' The boy spoke in German.

Franklyn shook his head. "But if you've got a cigarette . . ."

"Of course." Mirek eagerly pulled a pack of Julis cigarettes from his pocket and handed it to Franklyn.

The truck bumped and lurched along country tracks, stopping every few minutes. Franklyn took advantage of one of the stops to take a light from Mirek.

"Why do we stop so often?" He handed the cigarettes back to the boy.

"In the front they're listening."

"Listening, what for?"

"Out here in the country the Germans use mounted patrols. Very dangerous to us," the boy said ingenuously. "They wrap the horses' hooves in cloth and tie down the bridles. This way they move silently along the country lanes. Only sometimes can you hear the thudding of the hooves at night."

Franklyn nodded, drawing on the coarse black tobacco. "How far have we got to go?"

"Another few kilometers. We're going to my father's farm," the boy said proudly. "My father is a farmer but he is also a great collector."

"A collector?"

"Of Czech coins. Before the Germans arrived professors would come from the university in Prague to speak to him. It was said in the village that Ata Spinza knew more about our old coins than the professors themselves."

On the far edge of the quarry, František turned and looked back. He thought he could just make out the Adler, stationary among the gorse bushes, its headlights now extinguished. The soldiers would be somewhere down at the bottom of the great pit searching the rocks, nervously prodding the gorse that grew straight out from the rock face.

He nodded to himself. It would take them until daylight. He

swung the rifle onto his shoulder and set off on the long walk to the crossroads where Stefan and Karel would pick him up.

Away from the quarry the track led through a pine plantation, so thick in parts that it was almost impossible to penetrate it. Before the war it had been well husbanded and thinned by woodsmen who believed in the value of their work. But in the last years, no Czech worker felt like that any longer. The saplings had been left to grow unweeded, the bushes twined between them; and the pines stretched hungrily for light, thin and useless as timber.

František moved quickly along the track. He was not entirely sure what made him stop, perhaps something atavistic and premonitory. But once stopped he could hear. A dull, rhythmic thudding was borne toward him on the wind.

He ran wildly off the track, but was thrown back by the thick undergrowth. A horse neighed and the thudding rose like a heartbeat. He was lifting his rifle to the huge, greatcoated mounted figure when the hooves struck him. As he recoiled from the impact, the second rider trailed his saber across the spinning figure.

Around and above him František could see the mounted patrol reining their Hanoverian grays. The blood was pumping through his fingers as he clasped his neck. Already it had formed a small puddle on the stony track.

The batlike figure, leaning over him in great cape and steel helmet, straightened up.

"Is he dead, Herr Major?" a voice asked.

Major Knetzen, commanding the 4th Anti-Partisan Mounted Company, knelt down and pushed František's hand from his neck. The blood pulsed strongly, bloodying the major's gloves. "He will be," he said, "by the time we get him back."

The first light was already appearing across the eastern hills as the truck pulled to a halt.

"We are here," Mirek said, opening the back door.

Franklyn clambered forward and eased himself down from

the truck. His legs and arms ached as he stretched, sharp pains shot across his chest and shoulders, and a bout of dizziness made him grasp at the door for support.

As his vision cleared, he could see the dark outlines of a cluster of farm buildings arranged to form a rough courtyard in the middle. Cattle lowed in the barns and three long-necked geese inquisitively circled a mound of dung to inspect the new arrivals.

The farm door opened, spilling a soft light. In the moment before it closed behind her, Franklyn saw Dana emerge into the courtyard.

She was wearing a heavy sweater and the cord trousers and boots of a rider. Crossing the mud of the courtyard pockmarked by cattle hooves, she stopped in front of Franklyn, peered in the half-light and burst out laughing.

"What's so goddamn funny?" He was still holding onto the van door for support.

"Poor Mr. Franklyn. . . ." She controlled her laughter and looked around as Stefan and Karel got down from the cab.

"Where's my father?" She was no longer smiling.

"We had some trouble with a German patrol," Stefan said. "František took off through the quarries to lead them away from us."

"What sort of patrol?" she asked anxiously.

"Not night riders. A truck. They'll probably end up in six meters of water."

"Good," she said fiercely. "How is my father to get here?"

"We arranged to pick him up at the Zdib crossroads at daybreak. By then we can use the truck openly."

"Let's go in." She turned and led the way back to the farmhouse, and Franklyn was struck with the authority she seemed to assume over the group in František's absence.

The farmhouse seemed to comprise one great, stone-floored living room on the ground floor with bedrooms above. In the light of the oil lamps he could see a black kitchen range against the far wall and an enormous stone sink with an iron pump above it. Somewhere in the darkness at the end of the room, he could hear the shuffle of farm animals in straw.

Ata Spinza, Mirek's father, was a small man wizened by weather. His sleeveless jacket was a patchwork of rough darns and his rubber boots were capped with caked mud, but his German was fluent and even courtly. For a few minutes he fussed around Franklyn, insisting he put on a dry shirt and evil-smelling sweater and placing him closest to the warmth of the kitchen range. Then when they were all seated around the table and Mirek had been dispatched outside to listen for horsemen, he brought a breakfast of bread, soup and boiled eggs. Washed down with a mug of hot beer and honey, it seemed to Franklyn one of the most welcome meals he had ever eaten in his life.

"Now at last," Dana said, "I begin to recognize the debonair Mr. Franklyn again."

Franklyn scowled at her across the table, then was forced to laugh at the sheer, provocative liveliness of her smile. "Goddamn it," he said, "you don't realize I nearly drowned in that quarry."

"Ah!" Ata Spinza's wizened head came forward into the lamplight. "Nearly drowned? An excellent omen. Did you know that there is an old Czech legend about Boleslav the Second? One day it seems he fell while hunting and rolled into a quarry. Only with difficulty was he hauled out by his attendants. And to reward them and commemorate his narrow escape he struck a coin. It was of course the denar of Boleslav the Second."

Franklyn looked at Dana but she had no explanations to offer. "The denar of Boleslav the Second?"

"On the obverse, the Czech royal crown. On the reverse, the lion. Perfect workmanship. It became the best known of all Czech coins, current all over Europe. In those days you see"— his voice dropped—"the whole world acknowledged the worth of the Czechs." He smiled. "And this escape of Mr. Franklyn's I see as a similar omen."

Dana cocked her head. "Ata Spinza," she said smiling, "I

think you could be right. But now Stefan and Karel must go. It will be daylight soon and my father will be waiting at the crossroads. And if you will excuse us, Ata Spinza, I have to talk to Mr. Franklyn before he takes some rest after his night's escapades."

The group of men around the table got up in response to the girl's words. Again Franklyn was struck by her natural assumption of command.

"Don't think I'm making fun of you, Mr. Franklyn," she said when the others had left, "but you did look a very sorry sight when you first arrived. Are you very tired?"

"I find there are two things that tire me out more than anything. One is a prolonged period of sheer, unrelieved fear."

She smiled. "And the other?"

He shrugged.

"Then your age is telling," she said briskly. "Now what instructions from London?"

"My orders are to speak directly to František."

"I'm his daughter."

"Sure. But I'll still wait till he gets back."

"Very well." She got up and turned out the lights. A faint gray light seeped under the doors and filtered through straw dust from somewhere above the cattle stall. Dana went from window to window, opening the shutters, and a cool, sunless light filled the room.

"How big is your group?" Franklyn asked her.

"Shouldn't you be putting your questions to my father?" she asked archly.

"How many active members?" He ignored her reaction.

"Nine," she said. "With a backup of people like Ata Spinza, about twenty."

"All farmers?"

"No. Farmers, workers, one or two professional families who are prepared to offer safe houses for a few nights."

"Are you in touch with other groups?"

271

"In theory, no. Each resistance group tries to work as a cell. This way one Gestapo success does not inevitably lead to another."

Outside they heard footsteps squelching through the mud of the yard. The door opened and they could see from Ata Spinza's face that something was wrong.

Dana dropped both hands flat on the table. "What is it, Ata?"

The old man hesitated. "Mirek just talked to some people from the village. An hour ago the Germans brought František down from the woods." The old man stopped again, staring at the girl whose whole frame had gone rigid. "They brought František's body down," he said quietly.

Franklyn and the old man watched her as she straightened up slowly. Spinza motioned to Franklyn and he crossed the room and followed the farmer into the yard.

"My prize possession," the old man said, closing the door after them, "is not my farm, Mr. Franklyn, or my livestock. It is a gold piece of King John of Luxemburg, the first Czech king to strike gold coins. I would give it now," he said.

Mirek came across the yard and stood beside his father, already taller than the old man.

"Was František an old friend?" Franklyn asked.

"No," Spinza said. "Not an old friend but a good friend. And in this country today something even more important than that. Among all our doubts and uncertainties, our feelings of being betrayed by the rest of the civilized world, František always knew what to do next."

The old man looked up at Franklyn then toward his son. He lifted a grimy finger. "In life, Mirek," he said, and Franklyn was made to wonder what opportunity the old man felt he'd missed, "in life, nothing is more important. Now I think Dana will always know what to do next."

Behind them the door opened and Dana called to Franklyn across the yard. From where he stood, Franklyn could see that her face had momentarily lost its youthfulness. She looked haggard and red-eyed, but icily composed.

He passed through the door she had left ajar and closed it after him. She was sitting at the table.

"People need to say these things," he said. "I'm sorry about your father. I didn't know him well but I liked very much what I knew."

She nodded.

He sat down opposite her. "Why don't you just burst into tears, curse the German army or whatever you feel like doing? You're only eighteen years old, for Christ's sake."

"I know what I'm going to do, Mr. Franklyn. . . ."

"The old guy said you would."

"I'm taking charge of the group František. We will keep the name in memory of my father."

"Will Stefan and the others agree?"

"If they don't they must go off and form their own groups. Your orders from London are to deal with František. From now on that means me."

"You are one hell of a tough young woman."

"What else would you expect from the times we live in? Let me have the message from London, then you must sleep and I must return to Prague. Today I am on duty."

"With Heydrich?"

"General duties. Heydrich is in Berlin and doesn't return until tonight."

He wanted to ask her when her duties ended, but found he couldn't form the question. The silence lay heavily between them.

"The London instructions," she said finally. "We know already that it is a special operation. We have assembled explosives and recruited a new technical adviser for sabotage operations. We feel, as a group, that we are well prepared."

"This is not a sabotage operation," Franklyn said slowly. "And before we get into it, I'm going to have to outline to you my role. I am not simply the messenger boy."

"I assumed you were sent because of some specialist knowledge you have."

"I was sent to take charge of the operation."

273

"That's impossible." Her chair flew back as she stood up, her body taut and angry.

"Sit down, Dana," he said.

She pushed her chair forward and sat down.

"You have a very simple problem," Franklyn said gently. "You have to decide whether you can accept any leadership other than your father's. If you can't, tell me now."

She stared at him, a hardness approaching malevolence in her incredible blue eyes. "I accept your role for this operation only," she whispered.

"Okay. Since I'm not looking for a life appointment, we've got a deal. You take my orders. But I work through you as far as the group is concerned."

She nodded sharply.

"Look," Franklyn said, "I've had a tough night. Does old Spinza have any hard liquor around the place?"

She got up and went to a shelf in the corner of the room. Taking a bottle she unscrewed it and poured some colorless liquid into Franklyn's empty glass.

He sniffed it cautiously. "What's this, horse rub?"

A smile touched her face. "Potato vodka. You'll like it."

Franklyn drank some, grimacing. "You have a cigarette too?"

She took a small leather satchel that had been hanging over the back of a chair and brought out a red pack of Craven A's.

"English cigarettes? Where the hell do you get English cigarettes?"

"You know where," she said briefly.

He took one and rolled the cork tip in his fingers. He lit the Craven A, watching her across the exhalation of blue smoke.

"A special operation," she said. "But not sabotage."

He shook his head. "No. An assassination."

"I could give you a list of candidates as long as my arm."

"No need," he said. "It's Heydrich. London wants him dead."

She sat for a long moment without speaking. "Do you know,

274

Mr. Franklyn, what happens here in Czechoslovakia if a German soldier is killed?"

"No."

"Let's say Private Schmidt goes to a bar, say Zdenda's in Unter-Habern. He meets a girl and after a drink or two she suggests a walk. Private Schmidt could think of nothing better. He knows lots of quiet lanes around Unter-Habern. But then so does the girl, and, in one of them, members of a resistance group are waiting. Next day the body of Private Schmidt is found floating in a ditch. What happens?"

"Go on."

"The SS move into Unter-Habern. Nobody admits that it was Anna Morisova who took Private Schmidt for his last walk, but all the same fifty people are taken as hostages. Not Anna Morisova; she is already hiding out somewhere on a farm in the hills. And in a week or perhaps a month, the fifty hostages are shot or transported to God knows where. All for Private Schmidt who kept the great war machine running by his indispensable activities as the battalion barber."

"What's the point of the story—that assassination is a waste of time?"

"No," she said fiercely. "The point of the story is that if they take fifty hostages for Private Schmidt, how many will they take for Obergruppenführer Heydrich. A hundred?" She shook her head. "A thousand? Ten thousand? Has London any idea of what they're asking?"

"You mean have they counted the cost?"

"The cost in Czech lives?"

"I think they have," he said slowly.

"Yes," she said, "the way they did before, when Chamberlain and Hitler met at Munich. 'Peace in our time,' the old fool said. 'Slavery in our time' is what he meant. Jesus Maria, what does London know about the cost!"

Franklyn stood up. "Let's take a walk," he said.

"Very well." She got to her feet and took her bag from the back of the chair. "I could show you the sights of Krivoklat. We have a castle over the hill and a fine cemetery in the church-yard. A little full at the moment. But that's because a German Gefreiter, a corporal, was ambushed on the forest road on New Year's Eve. They only shot ten men for that—although, on second thought, they could hardly have shot more. There were only ten adult men in the village."

They walked through the farmyard and down the steep hill-side toward the stream. Ata Spinza had already finished the milking and he and Mirek were driving the small herd into the meadow.

"Czechoslovak people probably seem very remote and strange to you," Dana said as they reached the fast-running stream and sat in the dawn sunlight on a medieval stone pack-bridge. "But think that two of the hostages might be Ata Spinza and his son. They are people. People you know. That's what hostages are if you are a Czech. Not numbers to be quoted in London with long faces."

"You know why London wants him dead?"

"Because of the Jews."

"Because he is in charge of the plan to destroy them, yes."

She stood on the low parapet of the packbridge and looked down into the racing water. "We believe this war is a fight for survival."

"Lots of people believe that."

"We don't necessarily believe it's a fight for someone else's survival."

"For Christ's sake, what difference is there?"

She turned angrily, balancing on the parapet. "Don't dare ask that question of a Czechoslovak!" she said savagely.

"You're saying you want no part of this operation. Is that right?"

She jumped down and began to pace the bridge. He sat watching her full figure moving with each angry step.

She stopped abruptly. "You talk about London giving these orders. Do you mean London?"

"Sure."

The British government or the Czech government-in-exile?"

"On a project like this there's going to be no difference."

"In September last year, Mr. Franklyn, there was a proposal to assassinate the newly arrived Reichsprotektor. London, that's to say Dr. Beneš's government in London, turned it down. The cost was believed to be too high. What's happened now?"

"How do you mean, what's happened?" Franklyn was aware he was well out of his depth.

"I mean how has the assassination of Heydrich suddenly come to make sense?"

Franklyn pushed himself up off the stone wall. The rising sun was warming him now, but at the same time inducing sleep. "I've got another question for you, Dana—like the one I asked you back in the farmhouse."

"What is it?"

"Are you prepared to accept London's orders? Because if you aren't there are those who will."

"Czechs, here in Prague? No, Mr. Franklyn, you'll find most resistance groups think as I do."

"Most," he said, "not all. I have been given a contact with a Czech army group, London-trained. They're soldiers. They'll obey orders."

She nodded slowly. "The Anthropoid group."

"You know them?"

"We know of them. Their contact is Kostal, a coin dealer in Zamecka Street. A friend of Ata Spinza. They have remained inactive since they parachuted in. Now I understand their role."

"Dana," Franklyn said slowly, "you must see that it would be infinitely better if the Anthropoid group were not used on this operation. Of course they'd provoke reprisals."

She looked at him without speaking.

"It's possible, just possible," he said, "that we could get away with a completely different scenario."

"I don't understand you."

"Listen carefully. Heydrich *is* going to be killed—whoever does it. But if we can make it look like a jealous mistress, there is just a chance that there'll be no reprisals at all."

"London wants *me* to kill him?"

"The next time you spend the night with him."

She drew a deep, slow breath. "It will be a pleasure. And it may even work."

He looked at her grim young face. "You'll do it?"

"I told you, Mr. Franklyn. It'll be a pleasure."

The hands of the clock on the bedside table stood at six. Franklyn dragged himself up onto one elbow, the coarse white sheets scratching his bare shoulder. For some seconds he felt at a complete loss. Daylight broke through the crack in the curtains. The room was small, bare and low-beamed. Almost instinctively he turned, expecting a girl to be lying beside him in the bed. That had happened often enough. Then last night came back with a rush. He had finally got to bed sometime before midday. Six o'clock must be six o'clock in the late afternoon.

He got up and drew the curtain. The farm was at the head of a valley. Two or three kilometers away, across the slopes of woodland and young wheat, stone village houses clustered around an onion-domed white church.

He stood for a moment looking across the rolling countryside. The sun was already falling in the west, throwing long black shadows from trees in startling green leaf. A pair of crows flapped ragged black wings toward a wood of high elms. Their croaking penetrated the quiet of the bedroom.

"The country people in these parts hate crows," Dana's voice said behind him. "In the old days they believed three crows together signified an unwanted pregnancy in the family."

He turned, self-conscious in his nakedness. He got back quickly into bed. "Have you no shame, young lady?"

"Very little." She smiled. "For an oldish man you're not even very fat."

"Thanks."

A knock at the half-open door brought Ata Spinza into the room. "Coffee," he announced. He carried a large stoneware jug and a chipped brown cup. "This coffee," he said, "may smell like cow dung, but I promise you it is brewed purely from the best acorns to be had."

He placed the cup on the table beside the bed and poured the dark liquid from the jug. "In a few minutes," he said, "a German truck will arrive. Do not be alarmed. The quartermaster Feldwebel at Hlinsko down in the valley sends men up every evening to buy milk."

"You want me to hide down by the stream?"

"No need," Spinza said. "We have an old Czech proverb which says the darkest spot is under the light. Just stay in the house. My son Mirek will give any warning necessary."

Franklyn reached for the cup and sipped the bitter brown brew. "Acorn or not," he said, "it tastes pretty good."

The old man lifted his eyebrows in disbelief. "Now I will leave you. Mirek and I must get on with the milking or Feldwebel Dartmann will not be at all pleased with us."

Dana sat on the side of the bed. "Would you like a cigarette?" She brought the red-and-white pack of Craven A's from her bag.

He took one and she lit it for him.

"I'm preparing the ground," she said. "This afternoon I burst into tears during an interpreters' conference. Afterward the German Hauptmann in charge of interpreters invited me into his office and asked me if I had problems at home. Problems at home!" she laughed bitterly.

"What did you tell him?"

"I burst into tears again."

"You can do that at will?"

"More or less. A lot of women can, Mr. Franklyn. Haven't you learned that over the years?"

He shrugged. "So what happened?"

"I just let the kind, fat Hauptmann see that I couldn't take any more."

"Any more of what?"

"All these stories of the Reichsprotektor's girlfriends."

"What did he say?"

"What could he say? Everybody knows Heydrich has women in Berlin, in Munich, Poland . . . everybody except his wife."

"So you left the captain in no doubt."

"In no doubt. The Reichsprotektor's Czech mistress is jealous . . . overwrought. Your scenario just might be played through, Mr. Franklyn."

"When?"

"He returns tonight," she said evenly.

Raising himself on one elbow he reached out and took her hand. "Our orders are to strike as soon as possible."

Her hand was cold and motionless in his. Outside he could hear Mirek's whoops as the boy drove the cows back into the meadow.

She stood up. "We can discuss the details downstairs," she said.

He got up and dressed and moments later followed her downstairs. She was sitting at the table, staring blankly at the stove.

"Stay away from the windows," she said. "The Germans have come for the milk."

Franklyn eyed the door anxiously and crossed to sit opposite her at the table. "You know it means you will have to come back to London with me," he said, taking one of her cigarettes.

She nodded.

"A Liberator bomber is standing by in England. A radio message from the Lezaky transmitter could have it here within a few hours."

From out in the farmyard cheerful German voices called to Ata Spinza and milk churns clanked as they were loaded on the back of the truck.

Franklyn looked at the grave-faced girl opposite him. "When shall I tell London we need the plane?"

In the silence between them they heard the engine of the

German truck cough alive and the mud and cow dung swish under the wheels as it made a half circle across the yard and headed back toward the village.

"Tonight," she said. "Tell London we'll need it tonight."

Chapter Fifteen

They sat before the wood fire in the Führer's favorite room at the Berghof. The red curtains were drawn across the great window which in daylight overlooked the valley to the spectacular mass of the Untersberg. The room, its walls pine-paneled, dominated by a huge brick chimney-breast, smelled of wood smoke and coffee. In the deep, chintz-covered armchair Hitler lolled, his head back, eyes half closed. Opposite him sat Heydrich, a file of papers on his knee.

"My struggle in the Protectorate, Führer," Heydrich said, "is as much against the German companies who now own the Czech arms industry as against anyone else."

Hitler nodded, his head still resting on the back of the chair. It crossed Heydrich's mind that he was falling asleep.

"The Ruhr industrial barons, Führer. They are interested only in the profits of their Czechoslovak subsidiaries, not the vast increase in production I could achieve if I could offer higher wages."

Adolf Hitler grunted. He could rarely be roused now by

anything but an apocalyptic vision, or a drama in which he played a central role.

"Average wages in the Skoda works, for instance, are thirty percent below those of Ruhr workers doing precisely the same job. Production equally is thirty percent below the Ruhr factories."

"I see," the sleepy voice said.

"I have done everything possible, Führer," Heydrich persisted. "I have arranged a distribution of two hundred thousand pairs of shoes to the families of Czech armament workers, I have requisitioned hotels to give holidays to the most productive workers and their wives. I have organized a system of social insurance comparable with that in the Reich. But unless I can pay more, production will continue to drag."

Hitler's head came forward. He reached for his coffee cup on the low table between them and selected a cake.

Heydrich seized the moment of complete wakefulness. "If you would come to Prague, Führer, if you yourself would announce to our Czech Germans a wage parity with the Reich . . ."

Hitler was awake now. He already saw the outline of the speech he could make. Coinciding with the announcement of new crushing victories over the Soviets in the great summer drive toward the Caucasus, he could use the wage parity as a counterpoint to military success. The impression of the Reich's inexorable expansion would be overwhelming.

"I'll come to Prague," he said, "the first day of June."

Reinhard Heydrich felt physically sick. To Klaus von Hardenberg meeting him at Munich airport, he looked white-faced and drawn; but since he was an experienced pilot it was unlikely to be the effect of a bad flight.

"I'm going back to Prague," Heydrich announced, as they stood together on the oil-stained apron.

"Is everything well, General?" Hardenberg asked anxiously.

Heydrich ignored him, "Go back now to the Marienplatz," he

said. "Clear your desk immediately. I want you in Prague tonight. Contact me as soon as you arrive."

"In Prague, sir?"

"I am appointing you principal RSHA commander of all Prague police forces as from midnight tonight."

Hardenberg was shaking. He knew what the appointment meant.

"Yes." Heydrich took a deep breath. "The Führer has agreed to visit Prague."

He poured champagne for her and it bubbled over the lip of the glass and ran down her wrist. Watching him as he filled his own glass, again spilling the champagne, Dana tried to decide whether he was drunk. If so he would certainly want her to spend the night with him.

And yet there was some other element in his behavior that she found difficult to identify, a sort of excited preoccupation. Alone with her, Heydrich's concerns were normally limited to the prospect of sex. Some champagne, a few compliments and he would be bundling her toward the bedroom. Yet tonight he was different. Was it possible that he would send her home after all?

She pressed her knees together and felt the cold metal of the knife strapped to the inside of her thigh. Somehow she must break his mood, make him more aware of her.

She stood up. "You didn't say whether you liked the dress."

He looked briefly at her and grunted approval.

"It's one of those you had sent from Paris for me."

He ignored her, sitting on the arm of the sofa, one booted leg crossed over the other. She noted, as soon as he had come in, that he was wearing his black dress SS uniform. Normally he would wear the silver-gray service uniform of an SS general. From the change she guessed that he had seen the Führer while he was in Berlin. She would include it in her weekly radio report to London on Heydrich's movements.

285

"I hope you'll give me a chance to say thank you." She smoothed the dress over her hips.

He gulped down his champagne and poured himself some more. He was looking at her now. "Drink your champagne," he said, laughing, "I'm a busy man."

She finished her glass, put it down on the table and moved toward the bedroom. He followed her, taking off his black jacket and dropping it on a chair.

"I want you to take a holiday, Dana," he said, sitting on the edge of the white-silk-covered bed.

"A holiday?"

"Yes. Take some leave and go to Paris or Berlin. Buy yourself some clothes."

She stood behind him on the far side of the bed. "But you've just bought me some clothes."

Heydrich hauled off a boot and tossed it across the room. "I want you out of Prague for a week or two. I have a visitor coming. Understand?"

"A woman?"

He turned, still sitting on the bed. "Not a woman," he smiled, "no."

She watched him hesitate. Then he turned back to deal with the other boot. "I'm going to have a busy time ahead of me, Dana, official arrangements to be made. My adjutant will arrange your trip. Do as I say."

She bent and reached under her skirt, fumbling as if she were taking off a stocking. Her right hand took the handle of the knife. She glanced up at the broad, white-shirted back bent over a recalcitrant boot. And at that moment the bedside phone rang.

As Heydrich stood up she let her dress fall as she straightened. He lifted the receiver, turning toward her.

"Hardenberg," he said, "you made good time. Where are you?"

He listened, his eyes never leaving Dana. "Of course you're disturbing me," he said at length, "but for once I'm ready to be disturbed. Come straight up."

He put the phone down and, rounding the bed, placed his arms on Dana's shoulders. Even in his stockinged feet he was still a head taller than she was. "I regret," he said.

He turned away and she followed him into the apartment drawing room. Already, she noticed, he had reverted to his strangely preoccupied manner.

At the door he paused. His eyes moved slowly over her body. "You could have an impressive future before you, young woman," he smiled. "You know how to please me as few do. Now off you go to Paris. I'll send for you when I want you back."

Franklyn completed the encoding in the light of the oil lamp on the kitchen table and handed the slip of paper to Ata Spinza. "You're sure it's safe for Mirek to take it to Lezaky?" he asked anxiously.

"Safer than for you or even me to try. He is fit and young, he knows deep ditches to travel partway in." He looked at his son. "Last winter, Mr. Franklyn, I discovered he was making the journey every night to Lezaky."

The boy flushed.

"At the invitation of a young widow there!" The old man's eyes twinkled. "At fifteen years of age!"

He was about to hand Mirek the paper when all three heard the sound of a car approaching from the Hlinsko road. Mirek ran quickly to the door, opening it a crack while his father turned down the oil lamp.

Franklyn, rooted to the spot, watched the boy's face relax into a smile. "It's Dana," he said.

Ata Spinza turned up the lamp as the car drove into the courtyard. Franklyn pushed back his chair and walked quickly to the door. It was barely midnight. If Heydrich was already dead there was ample time for the Germans to raise the alarm before the Liberator could get here. And once the alarm was raised there was no chance of an aircraft landing in the heavily patrolled countryside. The girl had acted too quickly. Nervous anger made him wrench the door open. Dana, approaching across the yard, stepped inside and turned to face him.

"Well?" he demanded, his face tense.

She looked past him to where Ata Spinza and Mirek stood beside the table. "Has Mirek taken the message?"

"He was just about to leave."

"Good." She nodded and crossed to the table. From her bag she drew a pack of cigarettes, took one and threw the rest on the table for anyone else to take.

Franklyn watched her light the cigarette and draw deeply. "Is he dead?"

"No. . . ." Cigarette smoke tumbled from her mouth. She turned to Ata Spinza and his son. "We'll still need Mirek to go to Lezaky. But the message will be different."

The old man nodded and with a finger laid on his son's sleeve indicated they should withdraw. "We will let you talk together," he said. "Call when you are ready."

She crossed to the cupboard and brought the potato vodka and two mugs back to the table. Pouring the vodka she pushed a mug toward him. His anger had evaporated. He could see in her face the fatigue that only tension brings. "What happened?" he asked quietly.

"Somebody arrived at the last moment." She laughed grimly. "At the second before the last moment."

"Drink your vodka," he said. "There'll be other opportunities."

She shook her head. "Not for a week or so. He wants me out of the way. I've been told to make a trip to Paris or Berlin. Anywhere but Prague."

Franklyn frowned.

"He told me he's expecting some sort of official visit. I think it even could be a visit from Adolf Hitler."

Franklyn pursed his lips. "Okay. So we radio London. The Heydrich operation can't take place until after Hitler leaves Prague for the simple reason you won't even be here."

She nodded thoughtfully and sipped the fierce spirit. "I nearly killed him tonight," she whispered. "So nearly."

Franklyn got up and rounded the table. Taking her hand he drew her to her feet. "Get some sleep," he said. "I'll encode the message for Mirek. I'll wake you when he gets back with London's answer."

She stretched and kissed him lightly on the mouth, "You know I like you, Franklyn," she smiled, "but don't tell my lover. He can become horribly jealous."

He watched her cross the kitchen floor and pause at the foot of the staircase. For a moment he thought, hoped, that she was going to turn toward him. But after a second's hesitation she continued on up the stairs.

At four that morning, as the first streaks of light touched the hills behind Prague, an SS guard on the battlement walk of Hradčany heard voices. He motioned to his companion and they moved silently forward, their machine pistols at the ready. As they listened they heard a voice rise almost to a shout, then a burst of laughter. Perplexed now, more than alarmed, they moved past stone buttresses and peered along the section of battlement looking down on the Vltava and the Charles Bridge far below. Two officers, champagne bottles in their hands, were standing in the medieval walkway. One of them, jacketless, almost seemed, in the dawn light, to be without his boots.

The two guards stopped in the deep shadow of a buttress. Almost simultaneously they had recognized the high-pitched voice of the Reichsprotektor himself.

In shadowy silhouette they saw the jacketless figure raise his bottle and drink from the neck. "Master of Prague, Hardenberg, Reichsprotektor of Czechoslovakia, that's what I have in mind for you."

The two guards retreated as silently as they had come.

"All yours, Hardenberg," the tinny voice went on. "And afterward some juicy fief in Poland or Russia. All yours."

Both guards took a quick, involuntary glance over their shoulders as they began to round the last buttress. Both saw the champagne bottle rise from the Reichsprotektor's hand and sail over the battlement to shatter a few seconds later on the huddled roofs below.

* * *

Daybreak of May 25 was a full, early-summer dawn. The sun rising through the stands of fir trees behind the farmhouse drove the mist from everywhere but the deepest valleys. Cattle lowed, their bells tinkling as unseen farmers drove them across the hills to their milking sheds. In the hedgerows small birds chattered, and above the farmhouse a flock of pigeons circled and swooped with a rush of beating wings. But still Mirek had not returned.

While Franklyn stood anxiously watching the Lezaky road, Ata Spinza continued with the dawn routines of a Czech hill farmer. From time to time he passed Franklyn, muttering at each pass a variant of his hopes. "It's that strumpet widow woman, I tell you. She got her hands on him again. Please God."

At seven o'clock Dana joined Franklyn in the courtyard, her face smudged with sleep. Glancing quickly toward Ata Spinza working alone in the cowshed, she had no need to be told that Mirek had not yet returned.

It was almost another hour before the boy was spotted jogging resolutely up the lane toward them. The old man, called from the cowshed, muttered fiercely to himself to disguise his relief. As his son stumbled into the courtyard, Spinza moved toward him menacingly. "Well, boy, the widow woman, was it?"

Breathless, Mirek stopped before his father, shaking his hands violently. "At Lezaky," he said fighting for his breath, "the baker asked me to wait." He looked toward Franklyn and Dana. "London asked me to wait," he said proudly.

"London asked *you* to wait," Ata Spinza said. "What nonsense is this, boy?"

"It's true," Mirek insisted. "It happened like this. After the message was passed to London, I was unable to leave immediately. A horse patrol had stopped in the square; they do sometimes at night to water their horses. . . ."

"You should know," his father growled.

"I stayed perhaps an hour. They gave me soup and honey

beer while I waited. Then suddenly a message arrived on the radio. It asked if I, the messenger, was still there. And when London was told yes, I was ordered to stand by for a reply, urgent."

Franklyn put his hand on the boy's shoulder. "You did well, Mirek. Your father must be proud of you."

Ata Spinza shuffled grumpily and finally nodded. "You did well, Mirek. Now give the gentleman his message and come and help me clean out this shed."

Franklyn took the message and, with Dana by his side, hurried into the farmhouse. Quickly he took the code book from where he had hidden it under the stove and flattened the slip of paper on the kitchen table. She lit a cigarette for him while he worked.

After a minute or two he pushed aside the code book. "I don't understand." He looked down at the decoded message. "They say a week's delay is out of the question. The operation must go ahead immediately."

She stared down at him angrily. "Then your friends in London have no conception of what they're asking. A rushed street-corner attempt could easily fail. Almost certainly those involved would be killed or captured. All for a matter of a day or two!"

Franklyn looked down at the message and up at the girl's face. "They understand," he said slowly. "The order is repeated. 'Operation before May twenty-eighth, at whatever cost.'"

She swung angrily away from the table and walked toward the window, her high heels ringing on the flagstones. "You realize this brings the whole question of reprisals back into the picture," she said, swinging back to him.

"Yes," Franklyn carried the message to the stove and opened the lid. "I know it," he said quietly, "and London knows it. A street-corner job means reprisals. Nevertheless our orders are to go ahead. President Beneš endorses those orders." He held out the slip of paper to her.

Crossing the room quickly she took it from him and read.

Then she let the paper fall into the stove. Together they watched the edges blacken and burst into flames. Then he replaced the lid.

"I'll make contact with the coin dealer, Kostal, this morning," he said. "The Anthropoid group must be alerted."

Tears were streaming down her cheeks.

"We can't avoid it, Franklyn. Tomorrow we become responsible for tens of thousands of innocent lives."

He knew it was true. Stanhope, the planners, the faceless men in London, were in every sense too far away. He and Dana would face a different, more immediate responsibility.

"Can you take that?" she said. She was no longer speaking to him as the man from London.

"I won't know," he said, "until the reprisals begin. But I know we're going to have to, you and me."

She nodded slowly, then taking two quick steps toward him she flung her arms around him and clung hard.

The coin shop on Zamecka Street was ancient and bowfronted, its black paint cracking and split. A neglected sign beside the door said that Peter Parler, the architect of the Charles Bridge, had lived here while working on his drawings, but Ata Spinza cheerfully dismissed the idea as pure fabrication. They had entered the dark interior and were waiting for a response to the bell.

"This building," Spinza said to Franklyn, tapping the support beams, "is no more than early seventeenth century; by then poor Peter Parler had been dead three centuries."

An old man shuffled out of the back of the shop and glared at Spinza.

"Why do you perpetuate these historical untruths, Kostal?" Spinza spoke in German. "Is the rubbish you sell here as coins described with any greater accuracy? For myself, I doubt it."

The old man looked at him with friendly malice. "Then go and buy your Saint George silver crown somewhere else, Ata Spinza," he said, flattening his hands on the scratched glass of the counter top.

"You've a Saint George crown, Kostal?"

"*You* wouldn't say so. *You*'d say it was a modern fake because of the almost complete lack of wear."

"It's in good condition?" Spinza asked anxiously.

Franklyn smiled at the success of old Kostal's technique.

"Let me see," Spinza said, trying too late to revert to casualness. "It's probably as you say a modern fake. The forger Mandek stamped a few dozen in the 1880s. They're good but to the expert eye the seams show. Let me give you my opinion."

Kostal smiled and disappeared into the back of the shop.

Spinza turned to Franklyn. "Patience, my friend," he said, "this is *life*."

When Kostal returned he laid on the glass counter a dark blue velvet pouch. Lifting open the flap he revealed a single silver coin about the size of a half-dollar. An elaborate mounted figure was deeply etched on its face.

From the pocket of his old sleeveless jacket Spinza took a black eyeglass and screwed it firmly into his eye. Resting both hands on the counter he bent forward.

Outside in Zamecka Street groups of people strolled by, the men shirt-sleeved in the warm spring sunshine.

After a few moments, Spinza used the edge of the velvet pouch to turn the coin. Franklyn glanced at Kostal. The competitive banter had stopped. He was waiting anxiously for Spinza's verdict.

After a few moments Spinza straightened up and removed the eyeglass. The rim had left a deep mark around his eye socket. "You must be a very proud man, Kostal."

Kostal smiled, showing teeth that were brown and chipped. "You would agree to sign a paper saying Ata Spinza believes this coin to be genuine?"

"I would."

"Thank you, my old friend."

"On the other hand I would be most happy to make you an offer for it."

Kostal carefully slid the coin into the pouch and closed the flap. "The denar of Boleslav the Second," he said. "I would take that in exchange."

"Only if you include the Ferdinand tolar from the Jarchymor mint."

Kostal nodded slowly. "It is a bargain, Ata Spinza."

"I will come to Prague next Tuesday," Spinza said. "We will make the exchange then. Now," he said, turning to Franklyn, "I have here a friend from another country. He wishes to be put in touch with certain people."

"In London I was given your name," Franklyn said to Kostal. "They told me to ask the whereabouts of Gabcik and Kubis. The group Anthropoid."

Kostal nodded slowly.

"I will vouch for this man as I would a gold piece," Spinza said.

"Nevertheless," Kostal said, "information can be more dangerous to possess than guns or dynamite. Hitler's gentlemen know well how to extract it from the most reluctant mind." He paused. "I will arrange a meeting place. Do you know the Dutch Mill?"

"A café," Spinza said. "I know it well. Is it a good place to meet?"

Kostal nodded vigorously. "It is much frequented by German soldiers."

Franklyn smiled. "The darkest spot is under the light."

"Ha!" Kostal said delightedly. "You know our Czech proverbs, I see. This Dutch Mill will be good. Be there at midday. I will close the shop now and go to make the arrangements. I will bring Gabcik and Kubis to you."

The strains of chamber music seeped through the night mists which enveloped the great white mansion at Panenske-Brezany. In pairs the SS guards patrolled the neat lawns below the chandelier-lit windows. On the gate the four armed soldiers were the only visible part of a twenty-man perimeter guard. In the village itself, the houses had been cleared of Czech civilians since the Reichsprotektor had chosen it for his home, and an SS barracks had been built to house over two hundred men.

The white mansion at Panenske-Brezany had been chosen as the Heydrichs' home early in the previous November. To Lina Heydrich it was the first home they had had on a scale fitting her husband's eminence in the RSHA, and the first time, as she was prepared to tell anybody who cared to listen, that they were not actively short of money. Given her reputation nobody took Lina Heydrich's protests seriously.

For her husband the house was ideally situated. Sixteen kilometers was just far enough away for Lina not to feel free to visit him at his Hradčany offices and close enough to make a pleasant morning drive on those occasions when he had stayed the night at home.

More than that, Panenske-Brezany was a vice-regal palace, and to it Heydrich summoned members of the Czech government as peremptorily as he would his own most junior subordinates.

But tonight was a German evening, a dinner of RSHA-Protectorate leaders and Gauleiters in honor of Hardenberg's promotion to Prague. And the music, the most important part of the evening to Heydrich, was to be his own father's works played in the great music room.

Listening to music was the only time Heydrich could lose himself. But even tonight when his father's compositions were being played, he found his absorption was not total. The realization of the immensity of the stakes he was now playing for never left him, not even in the most intense moments of sensation—in music or sex.

The last piece came to an end and the guests applauded politely. Philistines; there wasn't one of them except perhaps Hardenberg who had the least real appreciation of his father's music. As the applause died to a murmur of conversation, he let himself think for a moment about tomorrow. The flight to the Berghof would get him there in time for lunch. Immediately afterward he would present his plans for the Führer's visit to

Prague. If all went well Adolf Hitler would be standing on the podium before Hradčany Castle on the morning of June 1, vulnerable to a fixed line machine gun fired from among the chimney stacks of the roofs opposite.

He walked to the platform and stood just in front of the musicians. His guests waited, their expressions politely composed.

"In the small and perhaps slightly self-important town of Halle where I was born, my father was director of the music conservatory and my mother's father, Professor Dr. Eugen Krantz, was director of the royal conservatory at Dresden. Music, therefore, is in my blood, although in times like these it must be reserved for few and very special evenings. This is one such—a concert of my father's chamber music performed by a quartet made up of his most distinguished old pupils from the Halle Conservatory."

He half turned toward the musicians. "Gentlemen, I thank you for playing for us this evening. Ladies and gentlemen, it would be expecting too much for you to have been moved as I was—" The guests shuffled uncomfortably. "After all," he added, "these were my father's own compositions, deeply familiar to me, deeply loved. I hope you enjoyed them as much as you were able."

Hardenberg moved on the uncomfortably small gold chair. That undercurrent of insult and hostility was never far from the surface after a bottle or two of champagne, and Heydrich had certainly had that much tonight. "Herr Reichsprotektor," he called from the back of the room, "to complete our evening— will *you* play for us?"

Heydrich hesitated, gauging the nature of the request. He stretched his fingers automatically as he thought of the violin.

"You must, Reinhard," his wife said. "I'm sure most of our guests have never heard you play."

He nodded slowly to himself, then looked across to his adjutant standing by the door. Correctly interpreting the glance, the adjutant left to fetch Heydrich's violin.

The guests were silent. Violin tucked beneath his chin, the Reichsprotektor of Czechoslovakia began to play, a solo of his father's own composition which recalled a vivid childhood past, but he played with a savagery and attack that reflected nothing but the violence of the present.

The walls were lined with glass cabinets containing rows of ancient Czech coins set in a bed of musty dark blue velvet. With each movement of one of the figures hunched around the oil lamp in the middle of the table, the yellow light gleamed on the copper or silver profiles of John of Luxemburg or Boleslav or even the great Charles himself. From time to time a gold piece glinted dully in the barred case opposite Franklyn.

Dana sat next to him pressed tight against him around Kostal's small table. The three Czech sergeants who made up the Anthropoid cell faced them.

In turn they studied the rough map Franklyn had drawn up, before silently passing it back across the table.

Franklyn looked down at the torn page of the exercise book with the streets drawn in red crayon, and thought how inadequate a document it was on which to ask men to risk their lives. Lifting his eyes to Josef Gabcik he broke the silence. "Well . . . ?"

Gabcik spoke as the leader of the group. "If London wants the operation carried out immediately," he said in his deep, slow voice, "It's as good a plan as any. But it leaves little chance of us all getting clear."

Franklyn glanced quickly at Dana then back at Gabcik. "Can you suggest a better place?"

"No," Gabcik said, "Kirchmayer Boulevard is good. It fits perfectly with what Dana has told us about the Hangman's movements. But she must know how the German cordon system works when any incident occurs. It's quick and efficient."

Franklyn nodded. "Which is why each of us will have a bicycle on hand. The moment he's dead you jump on it and ride like hell. Far enough away to escape the net."

Gabcik looked at the two men beside him and interpreted

their barely perceptible nods of agreement. "It might work. In any case there's obviously no time to establish any escape route. We already have a safe house in the crypt of the church in Resslova Street. We have room for two more."

Franklyn shook his head. "My orders are to return to London immediately after the operation."

"And Dana?" Gabcik looked toward the girl.

"If I get clear of the cordon there's no need for me to go into hiding. If I don't . . ." She shrugged.

Gabcik and his two companions stood up, their bodies casting huge shadows across the coin cabinets.

"No questions?" Franklyn said.

Gabcik smiled grimly. "We could go over the plan a hundred times, Captain," he said, "but it still wouldn't change the essentials. When the Hangman's car appears around that bend, we throw everything we can at it and run. What questions can be left?"

Franklyn shook hands with each in turn, Gabcik; the stolid, blond-haired Kubis; and the youngest member of the group, Valcik.

Old Kostal had heard the movement of chairs in the back room and came in from the shop to show the sergeants out. Bustling, tears welling in his eyes, he clasped each young man in turn. Then, silencing the bell with his hand, he opened the shop door and let them out into the darkness of Zamecka Street.

For a few moments he listened, holding the door ajar. The sergeants' footsteps receded in the direction of the cathedral steps and he closed the door and returned to the back room.

"I'll sleep in the shop," he said briskly, collecting a rug and cushion from the chair beside the fire. "You two'll need a good night's sleep before the morning." He looked at Dana, his eyebrows raised. "There's only one bed."

She smiled as if she hadn't heard. "Good night, Kostal," she said, closing the parlor door behind him.

"I could sleep down here in the chair," Franklyn said when they were alone.

"What good would that do?"

"It might help to give you an uninterrupted night's sleep," he said.

She turned and climbed the bare wooden staircase to the small bedroom above. Following her, Franklyn saw that virtually the whole floor space was occupied by an enormous brass bed.

She walked to the far side of the bed and began to take her clothes off. "I suppose," she said matter-of-factly, "that for most girls of my age their introduction to sex is with someone they love. Or at least think they love."

He nodded. "I guess so."

She slid into bed. "Are you coming?"

He quickly pulled off his clothes and got in next to her. In the huge bed they lay without their bodies touching.

"For me, Franklyn," she turned toward him, "it was different."

He was facing her, propped on one elbow. "Yes, it was different all right."

She smiled. "I don't love you, Franklyn," she said, "but I do like you. That's good enough. Show me what it's like, will you? With someone you don't hate."

Chapter Sixteen

The morning of May 27, 1942, dawned bright and clear with shreds of spring mist hanging low over the Vltava River. In the gardens of the mansions at Panenske-Brezany, the Heydrich children, Klaus and Heide and their younger sister Zilke, were already at play when their father came down to say good-bye.

Lina Heydrich was with the gardener, swishing her riding crop at the long grass around the ash trees when her husband crossed the lawn toward her.

"These trees," she said, pointing the crop, "let's have them down."

"What for?" Heydrich felt in his silver-gray uniform pocket, then decided to wait for the first cigarette of the day.

"They are useless," she said. "We could plant apple trees instead."

He shrugged. He had not confided to his wife that he did not expect to be occupying Panenske-Brezany for more than a few days longer.

"In any case we could sell the timber at a good profit," she insisted.

"Marvelous, my dear," he said, "and throughout Prague it will be said that the Reichsprotektor is married to the only female timber merchant in Czechoslovakia."

The children came running up and he went to kiss them one by one.

"It's possible," he said to Lina as they walked toward the big dark green open Mercedes, "that I won't be Reichsprotektor for very much longer."

"That damn Himmler," she flared. She blamed Himmler for anything since he had tried to force Heydrich to divorce her as unsuitable.

"No, Himmler's not responsible." He paused at the car. "This would be a promotion."

"Promotion?" She lowered her voice.

He leaned forward and kissed her perfunctorily on the cheek. "Forget your apple trees, my dear. And your new career as a woodcutter. I'm having flown from Paris a selection of coats and dresses from their spring collections. I am ordering you to buy at least ten complete outfits."

"Reinhard, money does not grow on trees."

"You've made a joke, my dear," he said, getting into the passenger seat beside Klein. "I'll be back tomorrow evening."

He pointed ahead and Klein put the huge car into gear, pulling away from the woman and the gamboling children through the gates and toward the long Kirchmayer Boulevard which would bring them in ten miles to the edge of the city at the suburb of Prague-Kobilisy.

At exactly nine that morning Jim Franklyn propped a bicycle against the wall of a house in Na Kalinske, one of the small lanes off the Kirchmayer Boulevard. At the window the curtain parted briefly and a woman's head appeared. She smiled quickly and nodded. It was Franklyn's assurance that when he needed the ancient ladies' model bicycle in a hurry it would be there waiting for him.

He took the brown briefcase from the handlebars and walked slowly toward the corner of the lane. Jan Kubis stood there, stocky, fresh-faced, somewhat ridiculous in his wide-brimmed black hat. He too carried a cheap brown briefcase. Keeping about twenty paces between them, Franklyn followed Kubis until he turned the corner at Kirchmayer Boulevard. There Josef Gabcik, wearing a light raincoat and carrying a briefcase, walked out of the Three Trees Café.

From the opposite direction, Dana approached the hairpin bend on her bicycle. She and Franklyn had agreed on the sharp corner together. It had the obvious advantage that Heydrich's SS driver would have to slow down to make the sixty-degree turn across the streetcar rails. In addition, the maze of small lanes off Kirchmayer Boulevard favored a getaway. Beyond that they had no plans other than to use the guns and grenades they carried in the briefcases.

Leaving her ancient ladies' model bicycle in Na Kalinski close to where Franklyn had left his own, Dana ignored Gabcik and Kubis as they took up their positions on the far side of the boulevard and walked along the pavement to where Franklyn had stopped.

"Valcik is in position." She nodded in the direction of the sharp bend. "At the speed Klein drives, Valcik's signal will give us less than six seconds' warning."

"It's enough. As long as there is no escort."

"I've driven with Heydrich a hundred times," she said. "He's armed. Klein's armed. But an escort isn't Heydrich's style."

They watched Gabcik and Kubis positioned on the other side of the boulevard. It was 9:05 A.M. There was little traffic. The stream of workers' bicycles had long dwindled to an occasional housewife off to the country on an egg search. A few delivery trucks passed and from time to time a green Wehrmacht *Kübelwagen* or Adler Six. But even the chance of a passing army vehicle was not as worrying to Franklyn as the possibility of a crowded streetcar climbing the hill where the road descended to the river at just the moment Heydrich approached. Then they would either find themselves blocked off from the target or risk injury to Czech civilians if they pressed the attack.

They stood together, staring toward the bend in the road. So

far she said nothing about last night. When old Kostal had
awakened them at dawn they had got up quickly, washed and
dressed and hurried downstairs where the Czech sergeants were
waiting. Since that moment this was the first time they had
been alone together.

In the distance a train whistled and they both stiffened
momentarily.

"Franklyn," she said, her eyes still on the bend, "I want to
tell you. It *was* different last night."

He nodded, glancing at her quickly. "It was different for me
too," he said.

She was laughing. "The only problem now," she said, "is to
decide whether it was different because I like you—or because I
love you."

She touched his hand quickly and walked on twenty yards,
stopping at the baker's shop on the corner of Na Kalinske. It
brought her twenty yards closer to the point where Heydrich's
car would appear.

Ten minutes passed slowly. From time to time a woman
would appear at a window or in the front garden of the houses
that lined the street and glance curiously at one or other of the
waiting men. And now as traffic and passersby reached some
midmorning low, Franklyn saw that the four of them were
dangerously exposed. He crossed the road and reached Gabcik.
"We'll give it five more minutes," he said.

Gabcik nodded. "He must have decided to spend the day at
Panenske."

Franklyn glanced toward the houses. "If he comes now, there
are at least half a dozen women who could give a detailed
description of any one of us."

"To the Gestapo? Never."

"You can't trust everyone, Josef, not even every Czech."

Gabcik shrugged. "Perhaps."

As he spoke they both heard the long blast on the
whistle.

"Valcik's seen him." Franklyn turned and ran across the

road, glancing instinctively to his left. A streetcar was struggling up the hill from the river. It was what he had feared.

Reaching the other side of the road he pulled open the flap of the briefcase. Thrusting his hand inside, his fingers closed around the segmented surface of a British 36 hand grenade. He waited.

The streetcar reached the top of the hill and began to rumble toward him. He could see that it was crowded. At that moment the green open Mercedes rounded the bend. The streetcar was fifty yards away.

"Now," he yelled and saw the Czech sergeant drop his raincoat to reveal a Sten gun. Lifting it to his shoulder Gabcik crouched and pressed the trigger. And again.

The screaming tires of the braking Mercedes and the clank and rumble of the streetcar were obliterated from Franklyn's mind. In that second all he registered was the appalling silence of a jammed gun.

From his left Franklyn heard the stutter of an automatic. Dana, crouched by a streetlamp, raked the big Mercedes, bursting the front near-side tire.

Klein, the driver, hit the brakes hard. The heavy Mercedes skidded wildly across the shining worn metal of the streetcar rails. As the car flashed past Kubis, Heydrich was standing in the passenger seat pulling his pistol from its holster.

Franklyn and Kubis hurled their grenades at the same moment. They struck the back of the skidding car with a violent double explosion. Screaming past Franklyn's head, the baseplate of one of the grenades crashed into something metallic behind him. Then while the badly damaged Mercedes bumped to a halt, the streetcar rumbled slowly between Heydrich's car and Franklyn's position on the other side of the road.

When it had passed, both Heydrich and Klein had already jumped from the open car. Women ran from the houses and threw themselves to the ground screaming as shots from Heydrich's pistol passed over their heads.

Franklyn could see no sign of Kubis. As Heydrich came

running across the road, the American pulled out his pistol and fired at the Reichsprotektor at twenty yards' range. The gray-uniformed figure, in his long greatcoat, went down sprawling like a spavined horse.

Turning, Franklyn ran for the alley where he had left his bicycle. A middle-aged blond woman screamed in his face and lashed at him with her shopping bag as he passed her.

Dana was kneeling in the alley beside her bicycle. The base-plate of the grenade had torn through the spokes of the back wheel. Grabbing her by the arm Franklyn hurtled her forward to where his own bicycle stood. As she got on it and began to pedal away he ran left into the narrow alleys of Na Kalinske.

The road was a scene of complete confusion. The streetcar had now stopped and people streamed from it. Frightened women climbed to their feet and ran forward to join the circle around the figure of the Protektor. Some were crying, others laughing hysterically, as the enormous Klein, himself limping from a wound in the leg, hurled them aside to get to Heydrich.

The Reichsprotektor pushed himself up onto one knee and stood up. He was hatless and a streak of blood painted his cheek. Many women said afterward that they would never forget the look on his face as his contemptuous eyes raked the crowd. Others said they could only remember the great red patch on the back of the silver-gray greatcoat spreading before their eyes.

Then they saw him take a step forward, and they pressed back away from him as he reeled like a drunk, his face ashen, his breath being sucked between his teeth.

Like a wild animal he glared around him. His hands now were on the great blood patch, pressing hard on his kidneys. Nobody moved to help him. Another step forward and again he reeled, the crowd recoiling from him.

Then the figure of Klein burst through the crowd and caught the Reichsprotektor as he pitched forward into the SS man's arms.

There was no time to call an ambulance. Supporting his

master to an open-backed grocery provisions truck, he helped him over the tailgate and dragged open the driver's door. With one hand he hauled the man out and left him sprawling on the road. Then climbing behind the wheel he drove off, the Reichs-protektor of Czechoslovakia rolling in agony in the back among the cooking oil and bloodstained bags of flour.

Chapter Seventeen

Abandoning the bicycle at the base of the Zamecka Steps, Dana walked quickly toward Kostal's shop. She pushed open the black door and the brass bell rang over her head.

"So," he said, "It's done?"

She nodded.

"And Kubis and Gabcik?"

"As far as I know both got clear. Valcik too. The only doubt is the American, Franklyn. The militia cordoned off the area almost immediately. On foot I'm not sure he was clear in time."

"Were you seen at the crossroads?"

"We waited almost half an hour on the spot."

Kostal nodded. "Then the Gestapo will find someone to give them a description. Willingly or otherwise."

The old man crossed to the corner of the room and switched on a large wooden-faced radio.

"*Tristan*," Kostal identified the thunderous music with a smile. Reinhard Tristan Heydrich had been named after the Wagner opera. He turned the radio low. "Ata Spinza is waiting in the yard."

On the radio the music stopped. "Prague Station News," the announcer said in Czech. There followed a bald announcement of the attack on the Reichsprotektor's life and an appeal for witnesses.

They passed through the back door into a small courtyard.
Ata Spinza's wizened face appeared in the cab window of an old
truck.

"Yes or no?" he asked.

"Yes," Dana answered.

"Jesus Maria," Spinza said jubilantly. "Praise to God."

"I want you to go without me," the girl said quietly, "I'm
staying here. Franklyn hasn't returned."

Under the eyes of a section of militia gendarmes, the line of men
straggled untidily down Korcek Street, shuffling forward slowly
to the police barrier at the corner. There an SS detachment
examined papers and roughly estimated the height of each man
before allowing him through. At hurriedly constructed barriers
in a crude circle around the Kirchmayer Boulevard crossing,
similar checks were taking place, the police and SS having at
this stage only one fact to go on—a report that one of the
attackers was unusually tall.

Ten or fifteen paces from the barrier all Franklyn could see
taking place was a brief examination of each man's papers and
his name and identity number noted before he was passed
through. There was no sign of anyone being detained, but his
heart seemed to develop a heavy irregular beat as he shuffled
forward. Three men to go . . . he could see the shaved temples
of the SS trooper under his gray steel helmet . . . two men to
go . . . the second trooper seemed to be paying him some
attention . . . The man in front of Franklyn was passed
through.

"Papieren."

Franklyn handed forward his papers. Beside him the second
SS soldier stepped forward. For a moment Franklyn had the
curious notion that the SS man was measuring his height
against him.

Uneasily Franklyn stretched out his hand for his papers but
with a sudden movement the first SS trooper tossed them into a
box on the pavement.

"Into the truck." The SS man beside him jerked him by the

sleeve of his coat. Franklyn stumbled forward. Clambering into the back of the truck, he joined five or six frightened figures peering anxiously at the newcomer. Neither then nor later did he register that they were all taller than average men.

At the Bulovka Hospital, SS men were dragging Czech patients from the wards and driving groups of sick people wrapped in hospital blankets out into the street. Hardenberg had decided on total security. A battalion of Waffen SS was already cordoning off the hospital. Within fifteen minutes the Bulovka would have one single patient.

In the operating theater the Prague specialist Professor Hohlbaum examined his distinguished patient with trembling hands. He knew he had to control himself, but as he cut away the bloodstained cloth of Heydrich's overcoat he was aware of the SS doctor watching every movement. If this patient died on the operating table, Professor Hohlbaum knew that he himself would not live long afterward.

Yet the first indications were bad. Pieces, small and large, of leather, horsehair, and steel spring from the Mercedes upholstery had been driven through the layers of uniform cloth and were imbedded in the area around the base of the spine. It was difficult to avoid the conclusion that some of the foreign matter had penetrated deep enough to imbed itself in the spleen.

Outside the Bulovka a mixture of hard news and rumor spread across the city. Within an hour the first of ten thousand hostages had been arrested, and orders were telephoned from Himmler in Berlin to shoot the first hundred immediately.

Klaus von Hardenberg, outside the Bulovka operating theater, knew that Heydrich was fighting for his life; he was certain too that the moment Heydrich died his own life would be in danger. Once the Protektor's armored safe was pried open, who knew what secrets would crawl out?

Karl Hermann Frank, as state secretary, Heydrich's official deputy, unleashed his own sadistic hatred of the Czechs. A state of emergency was declared, the curfew extended, and by that evening the one-eyed secretary had authorized the shooting of

311

hundreds of hostages, dragged terror-stricken off the SS trucks. At the same time individual Gestapo officers like Kriminalkommissar Trautmann were conducting their own savage investigations, beating statements from possible witnesses in the vaults of the once staid Petschek Bank, and SD cars prowled the streets, ready to believe that any curfew breaker must be connected with the assassination attempt. It was a night, many Czechs would recall afterward, of anarchic terror.

Yet in the midst of the confusion and fear, Heydrich's established system had begun to operate. A reward of one million Czech crowns was announced, and the sinister black-on-red notices were posted all over the city inviting informants to contact Gestapo headquarters, 20 Bredovska, Telephone 200–1, extension 156.

More important, certain information was already coming in. By late the same evening Hardenberg was able to issue, with the authority of State Secretary Karl Hermann Frank, the first description of the event. The reward, it was now decided, would be raised even higher:

ATTEMPT UPON THE REICHSPROTEKTOR'S LIFE

Ten million crowns reward for all information leading to the arrest of the guilty men. At about 1000 hours on 27 May 1942 an attempt on the life of the Reichsprotektor, SS Obergruppenführer Heydrich, was committed. The Reichsprotektor was trav-

eling from Panenske-Brezany by Kirchmayer Boulevard and his car was turning to the right in Holesovickach Street, Prague-Liben, in order to reach the center of the town. At this point a man stood in the road and endeavored to open fire on the occupants of the car with a submachine gun. At the same time another man threw a bomb that exploded on touching the car. After the attack, one of the men ran away along Kirchmayer Boulevard, Na Kolinske and Na Zapalci; there he entered Brauner's butcher's shop at number 22. He fired several shots from the shop and then continued his flight along Na Zapalci and Holesovickach, probably toward the center of the town. The other man made off on a bicycle toward Stara Liben. Reports have been received of a third man whose escape route is not established.

The second man, of average height, slim, and dressed in a dark brown or black suit, wore a black hat.

The first, the man who fled by way of Kirchmayer Boulevard and Na Kolinske, answers to the following description: height 5 foot 3 inches to 5 foot 4 inches, broad shoulders, strongly built, round sunburned face, thick lips, dark brushed-back hair, age 30–35. This man was wearing a brown or dark brown suit with light stripes and brown shoes. He was bareheaded.

No description is available for the third man, except that he was well above average height.

One of the criminals left behind him a pale beige, waterproof-silk coat with light buttons. Each man had a dark brown brief-case. These were found at the place of the outrage. One of the briefcases contained a dirty beige velour beret with the label of the White Swan stores. One of the criminals who fled on foot left a damaged woman's bicycle near the spot: it has the mark Moto-Velo J. Kromar, Teplice, and the manufacturer's number 40,363. The wheels have black rims with ⅜" red stripes, the handgrips black, the saddle (in good condition) red-brown, the tool-bag brown, the chain guard black. The bicycle has a nickel-plated pump with a footrest; the tube is 10" long. One of the briefcases found at the place of the crime was hung on the handlebars of this bicycle.

The criminals must certainly have been waiting for the Reichsprotektor at the place of the outrage a considerable time, perhaps for several hours.

James Barwick

With reference to the promised reward of ten million crowns for information leading to the arrest of the guilty men, which will be paid in full, it may be pointed out that the following questions arise:

1. Who can give information on the criminals?
2. Who noticed their presence at the place of the crime?
3. Who are the owners of the objects described? And above all, who has lost the women's bicycle, the coat, the beret, and the briefcase described above?

These objects may be seen from 0900 hours today onward in the window of the Bata shoe shop at 6 Wenceslas Square, Prague 11.

Whoever is capable of providing the information called for and who does not come forward voluntarily to the police will be shot together with his family, according to the terms of the ordinance of 27 May 1942 on the proclamation of the state of siege.

All may be assured that their information will be treated as strictly confidential.

Furthermore, from 28 May 1942 onward, it is the duty of all owners of houses, flats, hotels, etc., to declare to the police the names of all persons in the whole protectorate whose stay has not yet been registered at the police station. Disobedience to this regulation will be punished by death.

Information is received by the secret state police at the chief office in Prague (Staatspolizeileitstelle Prag) at 20 Bredovska, Prague 11, telephone 200 41, or at any German or Protectorate police station; and this information may be given by word of mouth or by telephone.

Prague, 28 May 1942

SS Obergruppenführer and Chief of
Police attached to the Reichsprotektor
in Bohemia and Moravia
K. H. Frank

At his forward headquarters in the Ukraine, Adolf Hitler sprawled in an armchair alone in the long wooden briefing room. Outside he could hear the sounds of the Ukrainian forest, the creaking of the tall pine trees, the shriek of unseen night birds that the German soldiers hated for their scavenging of the battlefield dead.

For an hour Hitler had sat like this. He knew Himmler and a whole bevy of party officers, headed by Bormann, were waiting outside the door. But before he let them in, before he decided exactly what steps were to be taken in his Protectorate of Czechoslovakia, Adolf Hitler had another, much more important question to resolve. Why the attempt on Heydrich's life? Given the totally predictable consequences in terms of reprisals, what arguments had been used by the Western Allies to persuade the Czech government-in-exile that it was a necessary act?

He stared at the situation map covering the end wall. A double line of red and black flags marched north to south across two thousand miles of front. The winter defeats had given way to a spring stalemate, but soon he would be launching his new attack toward Stalingrad and the Caucasus.

He dragged his mind back to Heydrich. There had been in two and a half years of war no other single assassination attempt on a member of the Nazi leadership. Why Heydrich now?

He could not escape the memory of Ribbentrop the day, now nearly two months ago, when he had announced his secret call to a conference with Molotov and his shocked face when he had told him that Heydrich was plotting a peace initiative in the West. Could it have possibly been true after all? Had Heydrich's smokescreen successfully convinced him that there was no plot, when in fact it was already advanced enough to terrify Churchill and Roosevelt?

The mind of Adolf Hitler worked most efficiently on a low level of intrigue. His success in maintaining his position in the early days of the struggle was based on a certain wily appreciation of the working of ambition and power lust. Yet he had thought by his very promises to Heydrich that he had sealed off, capped, at least temporarily, the dangerous drive he saw in the man.

But had he? London and Washington wanted him dead. Was it because they could not refuse a papal-endorsed peace intitiative which would leave Germany supreme in Europe?

He got to his feet and pulled down his rumpled uniform jacket. Crossing to the conference table he pressed the bell push beside his seat.

Outside, Himmler and Bormann exchanged a quick glance. Leaning forward, Bormann opened the door and together they went in.

The Führer was leaning against the conference table, his back to them. He turned as their footsteps sounded across the wooden floor. "What's your latest report on Heydrich?" he asked Himmler.

"Preliminary surgery has confirmed the presence of steel spring and horsehair fibers lodged in the spleen. The Czech surgeon has succeeded in removing some of the foreign matter. A further operation will be necessary. Meanwhile the Reichsprotektor is gallantly fighting for his life."

Hitler's slow nods punctuated the report. The Reichsführer SS had not been told of Molotov's accusations. "Gallantly fighting for his life," the Führer repeated approvingly.

"As you might expect, Führer," Himmler confirmed.

"These Czech surgeons," Hitler said, "I want them removed from the case immediately."

"I have already dispatched by air a team of senior RSHA surgeons, led by SS Surgeon General Stumpf."

"You can trust him, this Stumpf?"

"Absolutely, Führer."

"Good. Then listen carefully. He will examine Heydrich. His decision will be that no further operation is possible. SS Obergruppenführer Heydrich is to be allowed to die."

The steel-rimmed spectacles fell on Himmler's nose.

"Bormann," the Austrian said, "I want you to begin preparations immediately for a state funeral in Berlin. I will personally give the address at the catafalque."

* * *

At the Bulovka Hospital a complete stalemate existed. The team of German specialists demanded immediate surgery to remove the remaining foreign matter from the patient's spleen. Professor Dr. Stumpf refused. Later some doctors would accuse him of culpable negligence.

On the night of May 27 the Reichsprotektor's temperature had passed a hundred and two degrees. Stumpf's report recorded it as a hundred degrees and falling. The wound, he claimed, was discharging freely. From that night on the German civilian specialists were refused permission to examine the patient.

But it was evident now, even to the most junior nurse, that the crisis was approaching. Those who saw the barely conscious figure in the iron frame bed, struggling to rise above the delirium that possessed him, knew that the next twenty-four hours would decide. Professor Dr. Stumpf knew it too. Every hour, on the hour, he telephoned Heinrich Himmler in Berlin, using a scrambler telephone installed in his sleeping quarters next to Heydrich's room.

In the confusion of overlapping police authorities the hundred or more men arrested at the cordon thrown around Kirchmayer Boulevard were left throughout the day of the twenty-seventh and the following night under guard on the parade ground of SS7 barracks at Panenske. Phone calls throughout the day by the guard commander to Gestapo headquarters at the castle had produced no one prepared to authorize the detainees' interrogation. Nobody informed the guard commander that though technically this was a suburban Prague incident normally dealt with by Gestapo district headquarters, the principal investigating officers were operating from Prague city headquarters.

The night passed. With every hour Franklyn's hopes rose. He had been present at enough identification parades as a reporter to know that very little time was necessary for an eyewitness to become confused and uncertain. He was sure the blond woman who had screamed at him on the Kirchmayer Boulevard was too frightened or outraged to be able to make a positive identification twenty-four hours later. But then there were others—women who had watched them from behind lace curtains as they waited for Valcik's signal. Would they volunteer? Could they be forced?

Sometime during the morning of the second day, the detainees were formed up and marched from the barracks. A line of SS trucks awaited them. Their guards, almost as weary as the prisoners themselves, divided them into groups, twenty-five men to a truck.

In Prague that early morning at the end of May, the atmosphere was electric. Throughout the whole Protectorate the Czech nation waited fearfully for news from the Bulovka Hospital. No one could guess the extent of the Nazi reaction if Heydrich died; no one could conceive living under the Reichsprotektor's vengeance if he lived.

Both the German authorities and the Czechs waited tensely, the Germans for a full-scale uprising, the Czechs for a backlash of indiscriminate terror.

In the crypt of the Orthodox church on Resslova Street, the Anthropoid team, sealed in by the priest, were among the few on either side who knew that no general rising was planned. Their orders from London were at least straightforward. After the attack on Heydrich they were to go into hiding with their backup group and wait out any period of reprisals. On further orders from London they were to emerge and establish separate resistance groups of their own.

Among the German forces all leaves were canceled. In the towns SS troopers patrolled the streets, and in the countryside motorized and cavalry patrols scoured the fields and lanes for weapons caches and groups of armed men. At regional RSHA headquarters, Gestapo executive agents received conflicting orders from the murder commission appointed that morning under Kriminalkommissar Dr. Gerhard Wehner, from State Secretary Karl Hermann Frank, or from the Berlin-appointed policeman Daluge, known even among Gestapo men as Dummy Daluge. In this confusion witnesses were shot before interrogation, or false leads followed with a time-consuming mindlessness.

Then in the quiet of the vortex a minor clerk at the Bredovska Street Gestapo office, checking lists of registered bicycle numbers from arms factories and state organizations, came upon the records of a disbanded Hlinsko Hitler youth squad.

Against the name of Mirek Spinza (germanized to Max Spinzer), aged 13, was bicycle number 40,363 Kromar, Teplice, woman's model.

Alone in the cold dark room, Mirek Spinza fought back the tears. All he had seen when they had pushed him inside was a low basement room with some sort of bench on the far wall. When the door had crashed shut he found himself in total blackness. Outside he could hear the bellowing of the guards in the corridors and the cries of pain of the prisoners.

Perhaps they left him alone an hour. Perhaps longer. He had felt his way across the room and found the wooden bench. Sitting on it he had begun to cry. He was just sixteen years old.

When the door opened the tears had dried. The light flooding from the doorway revealed a boy, shivering with cold, his hands pushed down between his legs, his knees pressed tight together.

"Now what are you doing sitting in the dark like that?" Hardenberg leaned outside and snapped on the light.

Mirek stood up nervously. The tall German in a gray flannel suit crossed toward him and put his arm on his shoulder. "Come upstairs with me, Mirek," he said easily. "It's warmer in my office. And if we're lucky we'll get them to find us a cup of cocoa."

He guided Mirek across the room and out into the corridor. The man at the desk looked at him with a face of stone but the tall German ignored him.

"My name's Hardenberg" he said. "I can't imagine why they brought you down here in the first place. It's only a couple of questions we want to ask about a bicycle."

"My father's here too," Mirek said, emboldened by the kindliness he felt coming from Hardenberg. "Can he come up with us to your office?"

"Of course." They were on the ground level now. "But let's just get our little bit of business over first."

He opened a door and Mirek walked into a large, comfortably furnished office. He looked around, intrigued with the shining wood and the carpet that covered the floor from one wall to the other.

"Now sit down, Mirek." Hardenberg pointed to a deep armchair. Taking from the desk a sheaf of papers stapled together, he sat on the arm of the chair opposite the boy.

"Well, Mirek, I see here it says you were once enlisted in the Hitler Youth. And dismissed a week later for anti-German statements."

Mirek was silent.

"Well, Hitler Youth certainly doesn't suit everybody. But you took a bicycle along—a lady's model."

"It was my mother's," Mirek said defensively.

"And have you still got it?"

"I lost it."

"When was that?"

"Before Christmas."

Hardenberg nodded slowly to himself. "That's a shame, Mirek," he said. "I thought we could be friends, you and I, but the first thing I ask about you start lying. You see I know you had that bicycle after Christmas." He tapped the papers in his hand. "It says so here."

Hardenberg looked at the boy, his expression registering his disappointment.

"It could have been after Christmas," Mirek said.

"Or it could have been last week, but it wasn't, Mirek. You never lost the bicycle at all, did you?"

"I lost it while I was shopping in Lezaky one day."

"Shall I tell you what I think happened?" Hardenberg said. "I think one day last week some of these terrorists came up to the farm. I think they forced you and your father to give them the bicycle. And if that's what happened I just don't see how you can be accused of doing anything wrong."

In the brightly lit comfortable office Mirek Spinza felt his courage returning. He knew what Hardenberg wanted him to say—but he was not going to cooperate.

"I lost the bicycle," he said. "When I went shopping in Lezaky, somebody took it from outside the baker's shop."

"You're lying," Hardenberg said shortly. He glanced quickly at his watch. There was no more time. He regretted what he had to do. As a senior member of the RSHA he had never indulged in Stone Room beatings. Mostly he found it wasn't necessary.

Keeping his eyes on the bright-eyed boy in front of him, he lifted the phone. "Get Spinza up here," he said.

He refused to see his wife. He had declined three urgent requests from Hardenberg for the key to his private safe. Flushed with the ever-increasing infection he struggled to sit upright and demanded champagne. It was a gesture. When they brought it to him he wretched over the glass.

The SS nurses watched him in silence. But he still refused to believe he was going to die.

The boy was screaming in terror but powerless to struggle out of the SS Scharführer's arms locked around him. On the floor his father Ata Spinza was vomiting blood on the carpet. Hardenberg looked on with fascination and disgust.

Hardenberg drew heavily on his cigarette. "Again," he said, and the second Scharführer's boot thudded against the old man's ribcage.

"Enough! Take him downstairs." Hardenberg walked around and sat at his desk. The stench of vomit was sticking in his throat. "If I don't call you within ten minutes, take him out and shoot him."

The Scharführer bent down and grabbed the old man's collar.

With a powerful jerk he brought him to his feet and dragged him out of the room.

Hardenberg took off his watch and placed it on the table. "Ten minutes," he said to Mirek. "If I'm not satisfied by what you tell me, I'll take you down to see him shot."

He nodded to the Scharführer, who released the boy. Mirek stood sobbing in the center of the room.

"Let's start with the bicycle. It wasn't stolen, was it?"

Mirek shook his head.

"So . . . what happened?"

"An American, a parachutist came to the farm."

"Not alone."

"No. There were others. No one we knew."

"You're lying again, boy. I'll get the truth from you. But first this American. He borrowed the bicycle?"

"Yes."

"Where is he now?"

"An airplane was coming from London."

Hardenberg grunted doubtfully. "There were three, perhaps four men involved in the attack on the Reichsprotektor—were they the ones who came to the farm with the American?"

"No."

"So you know who murdered the Reichsprotektor."

"No. Please telephone," he said, "about my father."

The boy was trembling in front of him. Hardenberg got up. "Another five minutes." He glanced down at his watch. "Who were they, the others?"

"They were parachutists too."

"Americans?"

"No, Czechs."

"And they're still here? Hiding out in Prague?"

Mirek began to sob quietly. "Please call about my father. They'll take him outside."

"Not if you answer my next question. These Czech parachutists, where are they hiding?"

Mirek stood swaying in the center of the room.

322

"Please . . ." he said.

"Where are they?" Hardenberg lifted the watch from the table. "Two minutes to tell me. Where are they hiding?"

"The church," Mirek gasped. "The church at Resslova Street."

He had lost count of the hours they had stood, perhaps a hundred or a hundred and fifty men crammed together in a warehouse. No facilities had been provided by their SS guards and the acrid tang of urine was mixed with the sweat of frightened men. To Jim Franklyn the nightmare prospect of a Stone Room interrogation had taken a giant's step closer.

He knew that they could not all be serious suspects. But even in a random roundup as he imagined this was, it was certain that his inability to speak Czech would be quickly discovered.

Shuffling men whispered fearfully among themselves. Cigarettes, lit at waist-level out of sight of the SS guards, were passed furtively. It was dark, perhaps even after midnight, before they heard trucks outside and shouted orders to get the detainees aboard.

Nothing presses on the political prisoner as fearsomely as ignorance. In this condition man needs information about his fate more desperately than bread and water. As the prisoners were bundled onto the trucks, they begged their guards for a scrap of information. Were they hostages? Were they to be sent to a camp in random retaliation? Pushing them into the trucks the guards remained silent. Perhaps they knew no more than the prisoners.

From his position near the tailgate of the truck, Franklyn could see that the convoy was keeping to the city center. Watching the street names at every corner, his impression was that they were somewhere west of Hradčany Castle. Ahead, the leading trucks had slowed to turn off, and immediately a word passed from man to man in the crowded truck. To Franklyn, "Bredovska" meant nothing more than the street name he could see in the lamplight until the trucks stopped outside an imposing building where all the lights were shining and men in leather overcoats were arriving and leaving with that air that only the Gestapo had.

Hardenberg impatiently drummed his fingers on the window-pane. If he could be seen to be personally responsible for the detection and capture of Heydrich's attackers, there was a chance that he would come out of this mess with his head still attached to his shoulders. When the SS signal sergeant handed him the phone, he took it quietly. "Colonel, this is Brigadeführer von Hardenberg, Bredovska Gestapo. I want a battalion of infantry to surround the Orthodox church in Resslova Street. No one is to be allowed to enter or leave the area. Alert your men that we believe the Reichsprotektor's attackers are sheltering in the church. Take no other action until I arrive."

He handed the receiver to the signals sergeant and continued for a moment to look down into the courtyard below. A great file of men was passing a table set up on the cobbles where a frowsy blonde was sitting like a hanging judge examining each prisoner as he stood before her.

Hardenberg shrugged contemptuously. They would get nothing from her. In any case now, they needed nothing. He was about to turn away from the window when he saw what seemed to be a familiar figure enter the pool of light around the blond woman's desk. Franklyn? For a moment Hardenberg's mind failed to make any intelligible connection between the American journalist in Munich and his presence in the courtyard below. He leaned forward, doubting the evidence of his own eyes even when Franklyn stepped full into the light. Then something of the horrendous possibilities struck him. It *was* Franklyn, the man he, Hardenberg, had sponsored with his friendship in Munich. The American that Mirek Spinza had just described as one of the Reichsprotektor's assailants!

They faced each other unbelievingly.

"Let's not waste time with lies," Hardenberg said slowly.

"You planned the attack. The Spinza boy, Mirek, told me it was an American. It was you."

"Yes." To Franklyn there seemed nothing else to say.

Hardenberg crossed toward him and gave him a cigarette. "Why?"

"Why?" Franklyn took a light and dragged down the cigarette smoke. "You can't be so crazy you'd ask why!"

"I'm asking you why, of all the leadership of the Reich, your masters decided to assassinate Reinhard Heydrich?"

"The Final Solution is in his hands. Do you need another reason?"

"I don't," Hardenberg said evenly, "but you might."

"There is no other reason."

"You fool, Franklyn. Your government has told you nothing. Nothing of Heydrich's peace initiatives. Nothing of his request for papal mediation. They appointed you the hit man—and they didn't even tell you why."

"I don't see why you're telling me this." Franklyn fought back waves of nausea. If what Hardenberg said was true, he understood now who had betrayed Christina and her brother to the Gestapo. If what Hardenberg was saying was true, it could have been no one else but Stanhope and the faceless figures around him.

Hardenberg turned toward his desk. "I'm telling you this because I know now that whether Heydrich lives or dies makes no difference. Churchill and Roosevelt will never negotiate the sort of peace he was proposing. Which in turn means for me that unless I can dissociate myself from Reinhard Heydrich's treasonable activities I am a dead man."

"And me?"

"You, Franklyn, are a dead man already."

Casually, as if taking a box of cigars from his desk, Hardenberg reached into a drawer and lifted out a long-barreled Mauser. "Open the door," he said to Franklyn. "Walk down the stairs."

* * *

Outside 20 Bredovska, a crowd of women had gathered at first light, the wives and daughters of the detainees. They stood silently waiting, like miners' women at a pit disaster, facing the sentries at the open courtyard gate. Among them Dana stood, her hands deep in the pockets of her belted coat. Through holes cut in the cloth, she held, low across her stomach, a Sten gun.

She had no coherent plan. She was not even certain that Franklyn was among the detainees, although from the accounts of the cordon around Kirchmayer Boulevard, it seemed likely. All she knew for certain was that she would not let him die alone.

Through the open gateway she could see into the courtyard where the blond woman was examining the last of the line of detainees. Those already past her were lined up under SS guard along the facing wall.

As the gray dawn light broke across the rooftops, the smudge of faces sharpened. The women, pressing forward cautiously, strained their eyes for the husband or father they hoped to see. Dana moved with them, stopping as they did when the SS bayonets were lowered toward them.

The blond woman had finished and the table was being carried away when a door opened in the side of the building and two men descended the short flight of stone steps into the courtyard. The two men walked rapidly, one four or five paces in front of the other.

She knew immediately it was Franklyn and a moment later recognized Hardenberg from his frequent visits to Heydrich in Hradčany. She pushed her way fiercely to the front of the group of women, her eyes never leaving Franklyn's face. He was walking toward the open gates, head down, his hands in his jacket pockets. For only a second she thought he was being freed. Then as he passed the sentries, she saw the pistol in Hardenberg's hand.

Under her coat she cocked the Sten gun as Hardenberg fired. Four shots tore into Franklyn's back.

The women surged forward, carrying Dana with them. She heard, above the women's screams, Hardenberg's voice calling for the guard commander. Elbowing her way forward she saw Hardenberg and the guard officer. "Enter in your report—shot trying to escape." Hardenberg touched Franklyn's body with the toe of his shoe. "And get this Czech rubbish cleared away."

The women from the back of the crowd pressed forward, praying they would not recognize the dead man's face. Before Dana could get a clear field of fire, Hardenberg had regained the stone steps and had disappeared inside the building.

Kneeling next to Franklyn's body, she took his hand. She told herself, without really believing it then, that Franklyn had seen her just for a second before he died. Later as the memories coalesced she began to believe it more. She was with him, she said, when he died.

Chapter Eighteen

At dawn the next morning Professor Dr. Stumpf was dressed and waiting when the orderly arrived with the quarter bottle of champagne and jug of orange juice that he habitually took for breakfast.

"Open the bottle, Kordler," he said casually, and was about to help himself to orange juice when he noticed the man's face. "What is it, Kordler, something wrong?"

The man was close to tears. "As I came along the corridor, Herr Professor, one of the nurses came from the Reichsprotektor's room . . ."

The phone rang and Stumpf lifted the receiver. "I see," he said after a moment. Replacing the receiver he walked quickly from the room. At the end of the corridor he could see a small group of nurses gathered outside Heydrich's room.

They drew aside as he made for the door. Opening it he saw a cluster of his supporting doctors around the bed. They stepped back without a word. Professor Stumpf approached his patient's bed and looked down at the narrow white face, the nose strangely protruding in death. The pale blond hair still stuck to his forehead from the night's sweating. Stumpf examined him almost cursorily. He had seen too many dead men to be in doubt. Then he returned quickly to his office and telephoned Heinrich Himmler on the scrambler. "Herr Reichsführer," he reported. "Obergruppenführer Reinhard Heydrich is dead."

In Prague the SS had been cheated of their revenge. On the pavement outside the Resslova Street Orthodox church, five bodies were lined up. An army photographer was placing roughly cut squares of white cardboard on their chests before photographing each one. He had already finished the first three, whose cards read: Gabcik, Josef, suicide; Kubis, Jan, suicide; Valcik, Miroslav, suicide.

They had fought bitterly for hours. Every attempt by the SS battalion surrounding the church had been repulsed by the men in the crypt. When the fire companies had been ordered to drown them out, they had hurled back the hoses as they had countless stick grenades throughout the afternoon.

Despite the desperate urging of senior officers, attack after attack had failed. Only when no sound had come from the crypt for over half an hour was an SS trooper lowered in by rope. He found the bodies floating facedown in three feet of water. They had saved their last bullets for themselves.

Klaus von Hardenberg was afraid. Standing in Heydrich's Hradčany office he stared at the blackened edges of the safe. The door, burned and twisted by an oxyacetylene torch lay on the carpet. The safe, of course, was empty.

He turned and left the room. Among the many calculations he had made in his decision to allow himself to be involved in Heydrich's plans, he had never once considered the possibility of the Reichsprotektor's assassination. Now he was alone. And the document originally designed to cover for him and which now might equally incriminate him was in the hands, almost certainly, of Heinrich Himmler.

As he walked out into the Matthias Courtyard, a secretary came running after him. "Herr Kriminalkommissar . . ."

He turned frowning. She was waving a piece of yellow paper in her hand. His heart began to pound. Yellow was the color of priority signals.

"Herr Kriminalkommissar, we've been looking for you everywhere. The main gate assured us you were somewhere in the palace . . ."

"Get on with it," he snapped.

"A message from Berlin." The girl swallowed hard, trying to catch her breath. "From the Reichsführer SS. You are to fly there immediately. An aircraft is standing by for you now."

He took the yellow paper from the girl's hand. The telegram ended: "With affection, Heinrich Himmler."

Affection. What did that mean in the Third Reich in June 1942?

Chapter Nineteen

In Rome it was a serene night. No cloud marred the brightness of the moon. Within Vatican City the stone facades were brought into a sharp relief that belied the wear of centuries. Saints prayed and Virgins grieved with a Gothic intensity unknown to the daylight hours.

It was a moon which threw long shadows, of fountains, fluted columns and the occasional nightwalker on his way home. Its long fingers probed the crevices between buildings and brushed the domes and turrets of St. Peter's.

In the pope's private chapel Pius XII raised himself from prayer. The moonlight, penetrating the west window, threw strange patterns on the polished woodwork. Perhaps no pope for a thousand years had borne burdens such as his. Destruction, famine, strife, this had always been Europe's way, but the very existence of the Church had not really been in doubt. If any phantom plagued his dreams it was himself as the last pope. Of course he knew prelates who dismissed it as pure fantasy, but for himself he did not. How could the idea be dismissed when Europe's future was either Nazi or Soviet? He had no doubts about a Soviet future, the bishop of Rome a peripatetic, shorn of ancient position and power.

The Nazi future was much more in the balance. Hudal would say that it was *the* future, that all the difficulties of the present would dissolve with victory. Pius doubted things would be that easy. But then he also refused to accept the view of Dorsch, that these men who controlled his country were so irredeemably evil that mere association with them brought inevitable moral corruption.

It was necessary, Pius felt, to see things in perspective, not *sub specie aeternitatis*, but from the viewpoint of the century. He had no real sympathy with or understanding of the democracies. He was himself the last of the absolute monarchs. Democracy was perhaps not dead, but for Europe it was, in the twentieth century, irrelevant. The task of the Church, he believed, was to deal with Nazism or Communism. From prayer and meditation Pius had received the same answer. He had no choice. There was no deal to be made with Soviet atheism, but now Heydrich was dead, and he, Pius, was forced again to look toward the power of the Austrian in Berlin.

He left the chapel and passed through his private apartment to the library. There Sister Pasquelina was awaiting him. "Holy Father," she said, "these late nights do you no good."

"I have an audience." He spoke in German to his housekeeper.

"At this hour? It's after midnight."

"I know," he said placatingly, "but Bishop Hudal requested the audience. He has with him at this moment at the Dell'Anima a special emissary from Adolf Hitler."

"That man," she said.

The pope smiled. "Yes," he said, "*that* man."

He sat at his desk. "Get me Father Dorsch, will you, on the telephone?"

"He does nothing but upset you," Pasquelina said stubbornly, not moving toward the telephone. "I've seen it time and again."

"Perhaps that's because he has become the keeper of the pope's conscience."

She didn't like the Holy Father in this vein. She had seen it too often of late, this streak of self-pity. He was a great pope, the greatest for over two centuries, and his greatness came from his careful weighing of impossible decisions. She was a tough, practical woman. She knew self-pity only blurred the issues when decisions had to be made.

"It's my belief, Holy Father, that you should see the bishop and this emissary alone," she said firmly.

Many aspirants to high office in the Church, viewed with alarm this old German nun with the scrubbed face and determined manner. After a lifetime of service to Pius, as cardinal and pope, she had reached a position of undoubted influence over him—such in fact that she was referred to, never openly, as "*la papessa.*" Yet her actual concern was for the pope's well-being only, and the intrigue of which she was constantly accused was only on the most minor scale, directed entirely to reducing his burdens and maintaining the even flow of those minute areas of his private life which he allowed himself.

The pope shook his head. "Please telephone to Father Dorsch," he said.

She lifted the phone on the long oak desk and dialed 4–2 for Father Dorsch's cell. The Pope reached forward to take the receiver from her as Dorsch answered.

In his bare cell Father Dorsch had been reading the book he hated most in the world. When the phone rang he got up from his desk, laying aside the copy of *Mein Kampf,* and lifted the receiver. Hearing the Holy Father's voice he struggled down onto his knees, feeling, as he always did, slightly stupid kneeling in front of a disembodied telephone voice, but doing it, as he always did, out of loyalty to the pope's expressed wish.

Receiving the summons to the pope's study, he replaced the telephone and got to his feet. He was sixty-nine last month and the pope's own doctor had examined him and found him fit as a young man. But Dorsch remembered when he was a young man, when he had believed in a Germany whose culture and civilization were the envy of Europe. He glanced at the book bedecked with the hooked cross of Nazism. As a German and a priest, he knew that his one remaining task was to prevent the pope from compromising with the anti-Christ.

The three men sat informally opposite Pius at his desk, the young German in civilian clothes flanked by Hudal and Dorsch.

"It is late, my son," the pope said. "You have a communication for me from Adolf Hitler."

"I have," Hardenberg said, "but first I must put it into perspective."

"Perspective, yes." The pope nodded to himself.

"The Führer is aware of the treasonable projects of the late Obergruppenführer Heydrich. He is also aware of the support the Vatican was prepared to give these projects."

The pope's face was pale. He crossed his long thin hands in front of him on the desk. He considered a statement that the Holy See was bound to view favorably any proposal for peace but decided against it. In any case wasn't this the very same young man who had opened the discussions on behalf of Heydrich? He remained silent.

"The Führer," Hardenberg said, "is willing to consider the matter closed."

The pope bowed his head slowly. "With the death of General Heydrich, the Holy See also considers that the question no longer arises."

"Yet there is one issue," Hardenberg said, "which became an element in the late negotiations in which the Führer has expressed an intense interest."

"And that is?" Pius asked.

"During the negotiations General Heydrich treacherously betrayed certain German state secrets. Or at the very least confirmed Reich intentions which had already been betrayed by the Erikson officer group."

"What are you referring to?"

"I am referring to the so-called Final Solution and Fall-Ost projects."

The pope lifted his eyes to Dorsch for a brief moment.

"As German state secrets," Hardenberg continued.

"With Your Holiness's permission." Dorsch pulled his chair slightly forward and leaned toward Hardenberg. "What Herr von Hardenberg is implying is not in fact the case. The details of the Final Solution and Fall-Ost were indeed recently revealed to the Holy See. But the preparations for this *res terribilis*, this policy of unique ghastliness, have been well known to us for some time, through our brothers in Poland. I cannot therefore see that the German Führer has any grounds for asking the Holy See's silence on this matter. Nor could I conceive the possibility of remaining silent," he added defiantly.

Hardenberg knew that he was fighting for his life. At Tegel airport Himmler had made it perfectly clear that only a totally successful mission to Rome could save him. "Is the view expressed by Father Dorsch also the Holy Father's view?" he asked, insolent in his desperation.

"The facts yes, not necessarily the conclusion drawn from the facts," Pius said.

"Your Holiness," Hardenberg said angrily, "the Führer expects a solemn promise. Nothing less."

Nobody spoke.

"A solemn promise," the pope said at length, "a solemn promise of this nature can be no part of the diplomacy of the Holy See."

"A solemn promise of silence," Hardenberg said tensely. "The Führer requires no less."

"Requires?" Dorsch said.

"Herr von Hardenberg means . . ." Hudal began.

"We all know what requires means, Your Grace, Dorsch said. "And we know too that it implies a sanction to back it up."

"In the Führer's view," Hardenberg said, speaking directly to Dorsch now, "the Vatican has been involved in negotiations with an internal enemy. To reveal publicly or comment upon any element of those negotiations will be construed by the Reich as an unfriendly act." He paused. "I am authorized to go further—as a belligerent act."

"We will not be threatened in this manner," the pope said icily. "I have no doubt that Adolf Hitler has the military power to occupy the Vatican but it will not profit him. Thirty million German Catholics would protest in horror."

"The Führer has no intention of occupying the Vatican," Hardenberg said. He was aware he was about to play Hitler's trump card. "An occupation would not be necessary," he said.

"Of course it's out of the question," Hudal said hurriedly; "National Socialism and Christianity have too much in common."

"May I suggest, Your Holiness, that we ask Herr von Hardenberg exactly what sanctions will be brought to bear?" Dorsch said.

Pius turned to Hardenberg.

"First," the German said, "I am authorized to describe the position of the Church in Germany from the Reich's viewpoint. The German state has been immensely generous in its dealings with the German Catholic Church. It has declined to react against the constant provocations of Count von Galen, the bishop of Münster. This despite the fact that on innumerable occasions he has preached sedition from his cathedral pulpit."

"The bishop has described evils in the state. Morally he was obliged to preach against them," Dorsch said.

"The investigations of the RSHA, of which I am a senior officer," Hardenberg replied oddly, "suggest that Bishop Count von Galen has merely succeeded in distressing many loyal Catholics."

"I'm not surprised," Dorsch said.

"You misunderstand me, Father—deliberately, I suspect. Catholic Germans have described to the RSHA a deep sense of distress that the bishop should be so openly disloyal to the Führer and the party—to Germany itself."

"We understand you," Pius said placatingly. "Please go on."

"I was discussing the generosity of the Reich treatment of the German Church," Hardenberg said. "I will not need to remind you of the vast financial support which flows from the Reich coffers—which was indeed increased as recently as last year."

"Your point is?" the pope asked.

"My point is this. W:thout Germany and the Catholic countries it controls, the Vatican is entirely dependent on financial aid from the United States. We are aware that this is already being given clandestinely by President Roosevelt. He will not be able to increase these funds without exposure in the American press and without massive protest from Protestant and Jewish Americans."

"Adolf Hitler's sanction therefore," Dorsch said, "is the threat to cut off the German tithe?"

"No." It was time for the trump card. "I said the Führer requires a solemn promise of silence on the Jewish question and Fall-Ost. Unless this promise is forthcoming he is prepared to reform the Catholic Church in Europe."

"Reform?" Pius said coldly.

"The Führer is prepared to act on the strong feelings aroused among German Catholics by the statements of such as the bishop of Münster. He is prepared to dismiss all antiparty bishops."

"He has no power," Pius said.

"He has the power and the will. New bishops will be appointed throughout Europe—in Germany, France, Belgium, Poland, Slovakia, and Croatia. These bishops will be called to conclave."

"To elect a pope?" Hudal whispered, aghast.

"To elect a new pope," Hardenberg said.

Pius rocked forward in his chair. A schismatic pope. The disaster of the great Western schism repeated—of a pope in Avignon and a pope in Rome—a disaster, almost as complete as his own fantasy of being the last pope. And the price of avoiding this disaster for the Christian world was silence. Silence on what Dorsch and many others would consider the greatest moral issue facing the Church in this century. It was as Dorsch had once said—the future of the Church as an institution was in jeopardy, but direct and brutal jeopardy from a man with the power to carry out the threat of schism.

Against this concrete threat of disaster, the confusion of the faithful, against the duplication of the voice of Rome, against the destruction of the unique moral authority that Dorsch was so desperate to preserve, what was being asked of him?

First, that he ignore the pressure Churchill and Roosevelt were bringing to bear to excommunicate and condemn.

And could it possibly help the sufferers if he did? The answer to that question was of course a matter of political judgment—not, in the strictest sense of the term, a moral issue at all.

Thus what was opposed was one political judgment against another.

"We will discuss these matters no further," Pius said. "Tell the Führer that he has my solemn promise."

The Junkers 52 landing at Berlin's Tegel airport carried only one passenger. As the plane taxied off the runway and across the maintenance apron, Hardenberg shook himself awake. Wiping the condensation from the square window with the edge of his palm, he looked out. Dim blue slit-lights marked the administration huts and concrete air-raid bunkers. Luftwaffe ground crews in black overalls and forage caps, crisscrossed the apron, hauling fuel lines and wheeling air pumps. In the center of the activity below stood a long black Mercedes, its uniformed driver standing motionless with one hand on the rear door handle.

The aircraft came to a stop and an aluminum ladder was placed in position. Hardenberg took his briefcase and soft brown hat from the seat next to him. Thanking the pilots he descended the steps and walked quickly across the concrete apron to the black Mercedes. The driver saluted and jerked open the back door. Hardenberg climbed inside next to Heinrich Himmler.

The standing joke among Berliners was that Himmler always wore a uniform because he'd be mistaken for an Albanian forced laborer if he didn't. Tonight, unusually, he was wearing a dinner jacket and, even with medals, managed only to look like a waiter from the Adlon coffee terrace.

"You must be exhausted," he said to the younger man. "However, the Führer is anxious to know the result of your audience."

"It was entirely successful, Herr Reichsführer. His Holiness has agreed to give a solemn promise to remain silent as to central issues of the Final Solution and Fall-Ost."

Himmler frowned. "The central issues."

"Yes. The pope reserved the right to speak if necessary on the question of the treatment of Jewish converts to Catholicism."

Himmler nodded slowly. "Yes, I think we can accept that. You have a document which sets out this undertaking?"

"I have. It is signed by Pius and myself as acting minister plenipotentiary." He took the document from his briefcase and gave it to Himmler.

The Reichsführer leaned over and pressed the light switch. Half turned toward the light he studied the paper, with Hardenberg reading over his shoulder. "You should give up smoking, Hardenberg," he said grimacing. "I can smell it on your breath."

He folded the paper and put it in his inside pocket. "Good. The Führer will be satisfied. Now I must get some sleep. There is a car waiting behind to take you to your hotel."

Hardenberg got out of the Mercedes and closed the rear door. As the big black limousine pulled away, he allowed himself a cautious optimism. It was not impossible to pull yourself back from the brink even in the Third Reich.

An Opel sedan drew forward from the blue-tinged shadows beside the administration building.

"Brigadeführer Count von Hardenberg. Take me to the Adlon Hotel," he said to the driver.

The man leaned forward and opened the back door, and in that second Hardenberg knew he was doomed. With a gleam of blue light on chromium he had seen the free pendulum swing of the useless window handle. The Opel was a Gestapo arrest auto.

He got into the back seat and registered with no further interest that the inside door handles had been removed. When the driver on the other side of the toughened glass screen took the road not for the center of Berlin and the Adlon, but for the woods and lakes to the northeast, he knew there was no point in protesting.

As they entered the wire gateway of Oranienburg Camp half an hour later, the first streak of dawn colored the eastern forest skyline. By noon, Brigadeführer Count Klaus Baldur von Hardenberg's name had been entered in the camp diary: shot, trying to escape.

In Prague the roundup continued day and night. Every district came to know the hammering on the door and the desperate screams of distraught women. At SS depots and at the main rail station columns of men were assembled and transported to oblivion. No record was ever kept of their numbers.

Yet it fell to a small village just outside Prague to be chosen for the single most savage reprisal. Among the six hundred inhabitants of the village of Lidice, the news of the arrival of German civilian film crews circulated rapidly. The children came out to see them set up their equipment, the women watched curiously from the shadow of their doorways. In the surrounding fields the men glanced up from time to time wondering what could be of interest to the German filmmakers in the unremarkable life of the village. There was no sense of alarm.

It was still early when the first SS troops arrived and the men were driven from the fields and assembled in the town square. Not even small children could escape the fear now.

On the order of the film director the cameras began to roll. Women and children were gathered on the outskirts of the village. Under their eyes their husbands and fathers were arranged in two small, neat lines. The machine-gunning of the male inhabitants of Lidice was quick and efficient. As was the dynamiting of every single structure in the village. When the women and children had been driven off to captivity, the cameramen packed their equipment and left.

Only one child would survive the reprisal at Lidice.

At 3:00 P.M. word arrived that the Führer had left his private cinema. In the darkened Mosaic Room of the Reich Chancellery in Berlin, the four SS officers at each corner of the catafalque came to attention on a discreetly given word of command. Among the Nazi leadership assembled to honor Reinhard Heydrich for the last time, the shuffling ceased.

When the great bronze door opened, Hitler's footsteps could be heard approaching, his heels ringing on the marble floors.

Entering the Mosaic Room he lifted his arm in salute. The Nazi leaders, Himmler, Goebbels, Ribbentrop, Frisch and Rosenberg among them, watched the Führer as he stood staring at the ornate metal coffin. The four great candles cast flickering shadows in the darkened room and the yellow light gleamed on the metallic sides of the coffin.

In the darkness at the end of the room the Berlin Philharmonic Orchestra waited.

"I will devote but a few words to the dead," the Austrian rasped. "He was one of the finest of all National Socialists. He was one of the bitterest foes of all enemies of the Reich. With his own blood he has given us a pledge for the preservation and security of the Reich."

To the astonishment of the Nazi leaders, accustomed to three-hour orations on any subject, however trivial, these brief sentences were totally stunning. And what exactly had that last sentence meant? How was Heydrich's blood a pledge for the preservation of the Reich?

The orchestra under Professor Heger played the Funeral March from Wagner's *Götterdämmerung*.

Leaving the Mosaic Room, Hitler returned to his office. Calling for Martin Bormann, he watched from the Chancellery window while the funeral procession made its slow way to the Invaliden Cemetery, where Heydrich was to be buried with full military honors.

When Bormann appeared, Hitler was sitting at his desk. "I want you to circulate a message, maximum secrecy, to all party leaders down to and including Gauleiters. There is to be no discussion of the recent event in Czechoslovakia," the Austrian ordered, "neither in public nor in private."

In the conviction that anything less than complete
victory would endanger the principles we fight for
and our very existence as a nation, the United
States of America will prosecute this war until the
Axis collapses. We shall not allow ourselves to be
imperiled from behind while we are talking peace with criminal aggressors . . . what they won through
treacherous war they will not be allowed to retain
by a treacherous peace. We consider the Axis-
inspired proposals of "peace" would be nothing less
than a blow aimed at us. In the present position of the belligerents, we can readily understand how
strong a pressure the Axis Powers may bring to bear
on the Vatican. We therefore feel it a duty to
support the Holy See in resisting any
undue pressure from this source.

> Personal Message from President
> Franklin D. Roosevelt to His Holi-
> ness, Pope Pius XII (Actes et docu-
> ments du Saint Siège, vol. V)